Soundbyte

Cat Connor

Editor: Jayne Southern
Formatting: 9mm Press
Publisher: 9mm Press, New Zealand
Publication date: 2013
Country of first publication: South Africa
Current country of publication: New Zealand.

ISBN: D2D paperback: 978-1-0670072-1-8
ISBN: 9780615797847
ISBN: 9781301487417

For Mum.

A mother is not a person to lean on but a person to make leaning unnecessary –

Dorothy C. Fisher.

Chapter One
Memory Motel

A massive thump vibrated through the wall.

I grabbed my Glock from the nightstand. Welcome to Wednesday night in a crappy motel. Noel rolled off his bed, Sig in hand. He shoved his feet into his boots and crept to the window of our motel room. A long day hunting a fugitive named Oswald Randall and the attendant adrenaline made sleep an elusive wisp of an idea. My brain tried to carry on working and my body attempted to relax. It was a fail on both counts. The search would start again in the morning, sleep or no sleep.

I slid off my bed and dragged on my cowboy boots.

"Psst," I hissed.

"What?" Noel whispered from the edge of the front window overlooking the first floor walkway. He tweaked the cruddy curtain and peered out the small gap.

"Who is it?"

"Can see a back. Staggering. Looks drunk."

I had two seconds to wonder what a drunken back looked like.

Crash. Glass smashed and sliced the curtains as it fell into the room from the window on the far left of the door.

"Another male," Noel said, still watching. "Don't know where he came from but he threw the first guy at our window."

"We're not ground floor so there shouldn't be any through traffic. This could be guests going to their rooms."

I was glad I'd put my boots on as more glass fell.

"Could be. The fight probably started somewhere else and travelled."

We'd both seen that before. One drunk who just can't let things go and follows along looking for an opportunity to taunt the other person some more.

There was another loud crash as an arm broke through jagged glass in the window. Blood sprayed. Both men were yelling at each other. An undertone in one of their voices sounded familiar. I picked him as a Virginian.

Noel flung open the door. "Federal Agents," he hollered. I moved up on his left, with my weapon in a two-handed grip.

One man was holding his dripping arm. The other punched him in the face then rocked back.

"Stop," I said and aimed at the puncher's head.

The bleeding man stepped farther away.

The punchy male lunged at the bleeder. He overreached which nudged him off balance and brought him closer to Noel.

Noel smacked the guy on the side of the head with his elbow. He dropped like a wet sack of manure. With the attacker on the ground and Noel cuffing him, I turned my attention to the bloodied victim. His face was somewhat obscured by his hood.

"Elevate your arm and put pressure on that. I have a

first aid kit in the room," I told him.

Noel used his cell phone and called police and an ambulance while I grabbed the first aid kit. I took a bunch of wound pads, opened them, and then told the man to hold them on his arm. I rolled a small towel into a tight wad and put it inside his elbow, then bent his arm over it. He looked shaky.

"Sit down," I said, holding his other elbow and helping him to slide down the wall. "Bend your knee up, so you can rest your elbow and still keep your arm up, and folded over that towel." I figured his arm would get tired. I remembered how tired mine got when I'd needed to do something similar a long time ago.

He nodded. His dark hair inched forward from inside the hood and fell over his face. The way his hair fell sent pangs shooting through my heart.

"Do I know you?" I couldn't get a clear look at him. He was keeping his face out of the light and head down.

He shook his head.

"You don't talk?"

He shook his head again.

"That's funny. Pretty sure I heard you both shouting at each other earlier."

He didn't reply.

Noel was watching. He'd been talking to the man he'd cuffed and now held face down on the verandah.

"El, this gentleman told me his name is Nicky. And Nicky thinks your bleeder is a cop."

"Local?"

"No."

The guy face down on the verandah spoke, "He's a pig."

"And you know this, with no room for confusion?" I said.

"Yeah." Nicky spat. Spitting face down is never smart.

"Awesome. Assaulting a law enforcement officer will earn you no end of favors."

A police car pulled into the lot.

"Noel, can you take your man down to the car? I'll wait here for the ambulance and have a chat with our bleeder."

I waited until Noel dragged him to his feet and took him away. With them out of earshot, I spoke to the man. The flow of blood had reduced with the pressure on the wound but he was still bleeding.

"He's gone. Do you have ID?"

He shook his head. Without a free hand, he couldn't stop his hood from slipping partway off his head and revealing more of his face. Hazel eyes met mine. I knew those eyes.

I was looking at a ghost.

He dropped the wound pads, pulled his hood over his head, and scrambled to his feet. The bloodied towel fell. Blood ran down his hand and dripped off his fingers. I picked up the towel and rolled it back into a tight wad.

"Fold your arm back on this," I said pressing the towel into the inside of his elbow. "The plan is for the combination of the towel and your bent arm to apply pressure and stop the bleeding." I grabbed more wound pads and pressed them to his wrist. It was almost impossible to process what I thought I'd seen.

"I'll be okay," he said with a hint of a slow drawl in his voice. I'd heard it a million times before.

I wanted to shake him and demand to know who he really was. His face, eyes, voice, all told me he was Mac.

Impossible.

Was I was face to face with his doppelgänger? My body screamed in agony as I fought to control the urge to throw myself into his arms. Nothing made sense. I wanted to slap him and hug him. Shake him and melt into the arms I used to know. I took a breath and focused my energy on reality.

Breathe.

Think.

I plunged my hand into my pocket and pulled out a small vial. Unscrewing the top, I took a deep breath of the healing aroma. I knew the Synergy would ward off a migraine and I expected one to charge through my brain at any minute. I took another deep breath, inhaling the soothing vapor deep into my lungs. With care, I screwed the top back on the small bottle and shoved it into my pocket.

"What's that stuff?"

As soon as he spoke, I knew what he was doing. He was using a technique I'd used myself hundreds of times to engage a person and help them focus on now.

"Synergy," I replied. "Aromatherapy for migraines."

"Does it work?"

"Yes."

"Where do you get it?"

"New Zealand." Angry noise from the parking lot below intruded. "I have it sent over."

I stepped closer to the railing and looked down. It was dark and difficult to see.

"Who makes it?"

I glanced at him then back to the noises below.

"Le'Esscience," I replied and shifted my concentration to what was happening in the dark. Shuffling. Skin on skin. Hard contact. Grunts. Men tumbled into a pool of light. One of them was Noel. Instinct took over. I aimed at the male fighting with Noel.

"Stop!" I hollered.

"Shoot, bitch!" he yelled back.

The man with me spoke, "What's happening?"

"The guy with you is causing a problem for my partner."

"Nicky's an asshole."

Nicky, yes, that was his name.

Noel threw Nicky on his ass. He struggled back up. Noel punched him. Reeling from Noel's blow, he staggered into a pool of light. I got a clear look at his bloodied face and confirmed it was Nicky. Nicky wasn't wearing handcuffs anymore. Noel drew his weapon. More scuffling. I heard the gun hit the blacktop.

This was not going well.

"You okay, Noel?" I asked, training my weapon on

Nicky.

"Sure," he puffed without looking up. "I'm getting too old for this shit."

"I can finish this anytime," I called back.

"I got it," Noel said as he scrabbled across the ground for his weapon. His fingers missing it as Nicky kicked the gun. Noel hauled himself to his feet and took a swing at the guy. His fist connected with jawbone. Nicky's head jerked.

I saw two police officers approach - neither drew their weapons. Noel made another lunge for his gun. Nicky ran and dove for a cop: In one movement, he'd snatched the gun from the officer's holster and spun around to face Noel. The gun in his hand aimed at Noel's chest.

I fired. My bullet punched a hole right in the middle of Nicky's forehead.

"Goodnight, loser," I whispered.

Nicky dropped to the ground with a dull thud. The gun smacked into the blacktop and bounced out of his hand.

"Thanks, El," Noel said as he kicked the weapon away from the man's lifeless body. "Nice shot."

"I'm allergic to fucktards. They make my trigger finger itchy."

And I'm a little worried about the possibility of zombies, so a head shot is the only shot that counts.

Noel nodded.

"Is this our scene or local police?" I asked. I had no desire to have the rest of my night consumed with paperwork and statements.

"I'll figure it out," Noel said.

I turned my attention back to the man I was supposed to be helping.

His voice held the promise of a smile as he said, "You're a hard ass."

I shrugged. Oh, the joy of the questions to come. How did the loser get free of the cuffs? How did he disarm Noel? How did he take a gun off a police officer? But not right now.

"Who do I contact?" I said.

"My handler. Tierney. Jonathon Tierney."

Well, ain't that just peachy?

"Jonathon Tierney. You're CIA?"

I moved back to the railing and yelled down to Noel, "This is ours, this is federal."

"Got ya," Noel replied. I could hear his voice as he explained to police how they could help us as I moved back to the bleeding man.

"I'm working a joint task force," he said.

A joint task force was a familiar story. He moved his arm again. I was ready for the movement this time. I had a thick wad of gauze in my hand, just in case.

"I am trying to help you," I said wrapping my hand around the gaping wound and pushing the gauze hard over the gash. "You need to keep still and keep your arm bent over the towel." I pressed his arm back on itself, with the towel in the crook of his elbow. "If you don't, I will strap your arm back. Got it?"

"Yes, I've got it," he said wincing.

9

"This is West Virginia, a small town at that. Not the sort of place I'd associate with a joint operational task force. What are you really doing here?"

"Work," he replied. "I can't tell you much more than that. You know how it goes."

"You can't tell me *much* more than that? So you can tell me something?"

"It's a drug operation. Offshore investors setting up drug labs all over the eastern sea board."

"You have a name?" Calling him Mac would be ludicrous.

"Chad." His eyes smiled. "You?"

I heard an ambulance approaching.

"You really don't know?"

"No, I don't."

It was hard to bite back the urge to yell at him that he did know my name and this game he was playing had to stop.

An instant of clarity prevented my outburst. Mac is dead. I *know* that. I took a breath, counted to five, and said, "Gabrielle Conway. Ellie."

Flashing red lights drew my attention. I waved at the paramedics as they disembarked from their truck.

"Ellie Conway, *the* Ellie Conway?"

"I don't know what that means."

"I've heard of you. You're on Tierney's list."

Shitlist, I presumed.

"List?"

"Safe list. You're someone people like me can approach

for help. He trusts you."

How fortuitous for Chad that he staggered into our motel wall.

"I'll call Tierney. What do I tell him?"

His fingers closed around mine. "Tell him ... Socrates ..."

Footsteps pounded on the stairs.

"Did you say Socrates?"

Paramedics hurried toward us.

Chad nodded. "Socrates needs extraction."

A solid block of ice formed where my stomach used to be. I hadn't heard that name since Mac's death. Mac used two screen names in our chat room, Galileo and Socrates. Our chat room no longer existed. Galileo no longer existed. Socrates no longer existed.

Someone was messing with me. Tierney was messing with me. But why? To what end. If I'm on his safe list, why let a Mac clone loose where I could stumble upon him? But he didn't, he couldn't have known where I would end up while chasing our fugitive.

"We'll take it from here, Agent," a paramedic said and unwound my hand from the dressings. "Good job."

I could feel my blood draining from my head as they moved his hood and shone a flashlight at Chad's face. He was the spitting image of Mac.

"Pull his other sleeve up," I said.

Chad shot me a confused glance. The paramedic did as I asked, despite the vocal protests from Chad. Each word he said spiraled through my ear canals, and felt just like they did when Mac spoke them. I recognized a scar on his arm. Everything I'd felt over the last few years, all the pain and the loneliness, churned and coiled inside me. He was turning the key and tightening the spring. The potential for this to end in a bloody mess was high.

"Mac."

His eyes met mine, and his head shook. My heart broke all over again.

"We'll take him, ma'am."

Noel ran up the stairs. Chad pulled his hood back on and sank into a dark pool.

Was there something more to the man who looked and sounded like my dead husband? I could see sanity drifting away. Cerebrally entertaining or mentally hilarious, my ass! I was heading down the slippery slope to full-blown nuts.

"El?"

I shook my head and watched the paramedics wrap Chad's arm and help him away.

"Where are you taking him?" I said.

"City Hospital, Martinsburg. We're eighteen minutes out," a paramedic replied.

Chad looked back at me with his familiar warm eyes. "Call Tierney."

"I will."

Noel touched my arm. "You need to clean up."

I looked at my hands.

Blood.

Blood?

"Cotton swabs," I muttered and searched the first aid kit. Pawing through it, I contaminated everything I touched without care. I found a pack of cotton swabs and a paper envelope. I swabbed the blood on my hand and sealed the swab into the envelope. On the outside, I wrote my name and the date. For safekeeping, I stashed the envelope in the first aid kit. My intention was to take it to the lab as soon as we were back in Washington.

"What's that for?"

"DNA."

"Is he someone?"

I shook my head. This was too nuts even for Noel.

"El?"

"Let's just get out of here."

Far, far away from the ghost and the mess.

I walked back into the room, stepping over glass as I did so. I threw my stuff into my backpack. We needed a new room or, my preference, a different motel.

"You and I need to stop winding up in motels in West Virginia. It never goes well, does it?" Noel said, packing.

I smiled. "No, it never does. At least this time nothing exploded."

"You're two for two."

"And both times you were with me ... it's you. You're bad luck." I stopped what I was doing and looked at him for a moment. "What happened out there?"

"That moron had a universal handcuff key in his back pocket," Noel said, inspecting his torn and bruised knuckles.

That explained how he escaped the cuffs. Handcuff keys are small and concealable. I didn't remember Noel patting him down but then I was more concerned with Chad and the wound on his arm.

"How'd he get your gun off you?"

"I'm getting too old for this shit, El. That's how."

NCIS Special Agent Noel Gerrard was human after all. Imagine that?

Noel's phone rang. A few moments later, his conversational tone changed. He sounded pissed. I pulled on my jacket. My mind wouldn't shut up. Every inch of me thought I'd come face to face with my dead husband. It didn't matter that I knew he was dead. Nor did it matter that I saw his cold dead body lying in the coffin. It was of no consequence to my screwed brain.

My eyes *saw* Mac. It must be true. I talked to him on MSN. I'd seen him step out of the shower in a room at the Marriott. It must be true. I heard his voice right there in front of me. I saw the scar on his arm. It must be true.

And the kicker? Tierney was involved. CIA. Anything was possible. The mere thought of Tierney catapulted me back in time. I knew him well: I worked for him once. Deep dark secrets never stay deep dark secrets. They have a habit of creeping back to the light at the worst possible moment.

Noel was still talking. I think he called my name a few times before I heard him.

"El?" When I looked up Noel was right in front of me.

"What's up?"

"Car accident. Randall is on his way to hospital, in critical condition."

"Convenient."

"Very."

"What happened?"

"One of the police cars sent here went to pick up the coroner. On his way back, he attempted to stop an erratic driver. The driver took off, there was a short pursuit." He smacked his hands together. "Car hits tree."

"He did what? He pursued with a civilian in the car?" Incredulousness invaded my voice before I could check it. "Where in hell are we?"

Dark humor filled Noel's reply, "At the very edge of civilization."

I shook my head in astonishment. "Where are we headed now?"

"Hospital. I'll make the arrest if shit-for-brains makes it."

"It's that bad?"

"Wasn't wearing a seat belt."

"Oh."

Might have been handy having a coroner in the police car.

Noel was on the phone again. This time I recognized the tone and the instruction, "Grab your gear."

His team would be there in a few hours, just in case our guy required transport.

As we walked down to our car, I broached the subject of Chad and Tierney. "The other guy, the bleeder. He is one of us. I have to call someone for him."

"So the ass-hat was right about him being a cop. Do what you have to do."

He climbed into the car. I pulled out my phone and made the call from the parking lot.

It was a number I knew by heart. Memorized in another chapter of my life. The wait was almost unbearable. Finally, a woman's voice answered.

"Shangri La Special Services."

"I have a bird problem."

"Can you be more specific?" she replied.

"I keep chickens."

There was a click and then silence. Two breaths, and then another voice.

"Agent Conway, you have another problem?"

My words felt sticky in my throat. "No, but you do."

"Do I?"

"I have a message for you. Socrates needs extraction. He is injured."

Without hesitation Jonathon replied, "Can you help him?"

"I already have."

There was a pause. "Thank you. We will take care of Socrates. Where is he?"

"City Hospital, Martinsburg, West Virginia."

"I'll take care of it." I imagined his beady bird eyes darting across the screen I knew was in front of him, deploying a team to bring in Chad. "How compromised is he?"

"I don't know for sure."

"Loose ends?"

"I took care of one, his name was Nicky." It was inadvertent but he didn't need to know that. "I don't know if there are any more."

"Thank you. Are you well, Agent Conway?"

"I am well," I replied and hung up. As well as can be expected considering whom I thought I saw.

I slid into the passenger seat and closed the door. My mind was busy pondering the irony that meant Chad turned up outside our motel room.

Noel started the car. "Everything all right?"

"Yeah." Why the hell wouldn't it be? "Let's go see Randall."

I hoped he wasn't pulp because justice needed to be served. A part of me considered that if he was pulp, it had been served. Maybe.

Mac's voice resounded in my head, "Maybe's ass."

How can his dead voice be in my head and be identical to the voice I'd heard from Chad or Socrates or whoever the hell he was? I knew enough to know it wasn't either name he'd given me.

Fifteen minutes later, we found the hospital and were standing in the emergency room. Noel waited to hear back from a doctor regarding Randall's status. I saw the paramedics who picked up Chad.

I stopped one and asked after their patient.

"He's in surgery."

"Any idea how long that will take?"

The paramedic shook his head. His partner mumbled and they both headed off into the night. I looked around for a nurse and found one.

With a flash of my badge, I asked about the patient, describing him but not using his name. I had no clue what name he'd told the paramedics or hospital.

"Let me check for you, ma'am." She tapped a few computer keys. "That patient is John Smith."

I guess that's a step up from John Doe. I jotted his name down in the notebook in my hand but didn't believe for one second it was his real name.

"Got a birthdate there? We need it for our records."

"September 26, 1970."

The pen fell from my hand, clattered onto the floor and rolled away. I watched. It rolled to Noel's booted foot. He picked it up and brought it back to me.

With a grin he said, "Butter fingers."

I tried to smile back but my face didn't move.

"El?"

The nurse looked at me. "Ma'am, are you all right?"

Come on voice. "Of course. Thanks."

Noel grabbed my arm just above the elbow and steered me to a quiet corner.

"What?"

I went for broke on the insanity plea and voiced the crazy thoughts, "The guy with the cut wrist. He's using the name John Smith and his birth date is the same as Mac's."

"A lot of people share birthdates, El."

18

"Not too many have the exact same scar on their forearm, the same eyes, the same face, the same voice, the same height." Despite trying to control my internal panic, I could hear it in my voice.

Noel and I made our way out of the hospital, away from anyone who could overhear the conversation. We stopped not far from the emergency entrance. There was a small raised garden. The solid edge was just high enough for me to sit on.

"El, Mac is dead."

"Then who the hell is John Smith?" I whispered.

"Didn't you call someone? Can they tell you?"

"I'm confessing to you that I have clearly lost the plot. Let's spread it around."

He smiled. "You got blood." His smile faded. "You really think DNA will come back as Mac?"

"I don't know who he is. All I know is that John Smith looks remarkably like my dead husband."

"All right. We'll get the sample to the lab. Meanwhile, go see what else the hospital has on him and let's get a picture and prints."

"Am I insane?"

"No more than usual, El. No more than usual."

"Good to know."

"I only met Mac that one time." His eyes bore traces of disappointment. "I'm no help here at all."

That one time he met Mac was part of a scenario that would be stuck in my mind for eternity. No matter how much good we did or how many kids we saved. That memory to me would always be the night my husband died.

Noel leaned against the wall opposite me. It was still dark and cool. I couldn't imagine how he thought I was sane after the things I'd told him. It surprised the hell out of me that he hadn't called my boss, SAC Caine Grafton, and suggested an immediate psychiatric evaluation. At that point, it occurred to me that he may have. I wouldn't know until the men in white coats showed up.

And with that, I shuffled sideways into a *Men in Black* scene. The theme song filled me to the point I was singing along. We all know I can't sing. It wasn't going to go well for anyone who valued his or her hearing.

"El, *Men In Black*?" Noel blew out a long sigh. "Really?"

"Sorry."

"You sure you're okay?"

"Never better. My dead husband is having surgery on his wrist and I thought his ashes were buried in Fairfax."

"They are. There is no way that guy is Mac. Think someone might have noticed if he'd come back to life?"

"I'd like to think so. Doctors, nurses, someone in the morgue."

"We'll find out what's going on here, that much I can promise you."

I nodded. "It's the uncanny resemblance that's screwing up my head here."

"They say we all have doppelgangers."

"I know." I should know. It wasn't that long ago that

Lee thought I was lying strangled in a parking lot in DC. The woman not only looked just like me but her driver's license identified her as Gabrielle Conway. Discovering her body caused all manner of shit to spray forth and meant I needed to contact Tierney for help.

I stopped and stared up at the stars. A helicopter circled the building then disappeared from sight. By the noise, I'd say it landed on the roof. Someone's night ended badly and required an airlift to hospital.

I was exhausted and empty. I consoled myself with the thought that my life was so *normal* it should be a season of *Days of Our Lives*. There was way too much going on for it to be a single episode.

I was sure I should be clutching the back of a chaise longue, dramatically looking into space, while wearing four-inch heels and a designer gown. Any minute the camera would pan out then fade to another scene, with a handsome man looking desperately worried and staring into the flames in a fireplace of some alpine ski lodge.

Sometimes it sucked to have my imagination. This was one of those times. Noel was watching me with curiosity. For a second I could've believed he'd never seen *Days of Our Lives*. But he looked too much like the guy in front of the fire.

A nurse emerged from within the hospital. She looked over at us and beckoned.

"We have an update on Randall," she said, holding the door open for us. I read her name badge. Tamsin.

"Thank you, Tamsin," I said.

She smiled. "The doctor is waiting for you – down the hall, second on your left."

Noel nodded.

Moments later, we learned Randall died from his injuries.

Closure of sorts. For my case, there was a certain amount of relief. The victims would no longer be required to go through the third degree in a courtroom. His DNA was on file. We knew he committed the rapes, but it remained "alleged" until proven guilty in a court of law. As far as I was concerned, he was a dead serial rapist. Seemed to me it was the best possible outcome.

Down the hallway, the dark night waited. From the darkness, I heard the whine of the engines and the unmistakable *thump* of helicopter rotors.

Tamsin waved us down as we headed to the door.

"Ma'am, I have some news regarding the other man you were asking about. John Smith?"

"That's him."

"He was airlifted to another hospital."

"I didn't know his arm injury was that severe?"

"Special circumstances, ma'am. They've transferred him to another hospital."

"Do you know where?"

"No, ma'am, only the pilot would know that." She dropped her voice to a whisper, "All his records were taken as well, and his treatment paid for in cash."

I nodded.

Gone.

Once our lab processed the blood sample, I would know more. It seemed so simple: Take the blood to the lab. Reality was different. It could be months before I got an answer. Being nosy isn't a priority. A blood sample with no case number meant I would have to wait until there was nothing else in the queue even with the favors various people owe me. What was I going to do? Push out someone's time-sensitive blood work and run the risk of letting a rapist or murderer go free for longer? I couldn't do that.

The voice in my head muttered, "Good luck ever getting an answer from the blood."

There was no point hanging around. Randall was dead and Smith was gone.

"Home," I said as Noel held the door open.

"Yeah, I'll send my team back – they should be halfway here by now." He pulled out his cell phone and made a call.

We swung back to the motel, my idea. Our short stay at the miserable motel was over but I couldn't just leave the motel owner out of pocket. I paid for the broken window. It just seemed easier than the owner trying to squeeze cash out of the estate of the dead man or a man who didn't exist.

Dawn broke with slow deliberation.

In silence, we headed into the daylight.

Chapter Two
Angels Came Down

"It's late. We've got this organized, Joe?" I asked as I spun my chair back to face my desk and stretched. It'd been a long Thursday and I wanted to go home. Noel dropped me off at the Hoover Building around ten in the morning. I hadn't slept for forty-eight hours. That doubtless explained a lot of things, in particular the surprise I'd just arranged for Carla and Rowan. Funny how someone else's cool can be another person's hell. In this case, I'm the one who is going to hell.

The face looking at me from my computer screen frowned and seemed to consider my words. "Yes. I am all set at this end."

I nodded. "We'll see you tomorrow night."

His crooked smile pixelated on the screen. "See you then. You might even enjoy it."

"Goodnight, Joe," I said with a small wave, then shut down Skype.

I'd pulled one helluva last-minute favor to get tomorrow night organized, but I didn't imagine I would enjoy it.

I stood up, closed my laptop, pulled on my jacket, and walked out the office. The clock on the wall said it was coming up to ten p.m. The day disappeared in a fog of reports and case files. Carla would be in bed. Dad would've waited for her to fall asleep then set the alarm and headed home, it was his poker night.

There was no one on the floor. Delta was morgue-like and just as creepy.

I checked the Glock on my hip. It was still there. The edgy jittery feeling I felt walking down the corridor made sense in a sleep-deprived way.

A shadow lingered on the off-white walls as I walked. I glanced up to see a shimmer of orange. At the elevator, I waited. The stairwell doors were closed. Through the small glass panels of the doors, I saw nothing but darkness. I didn't feel like running down all those dark stairs to the parking garage. Tonight I would take my chances with the square steel coffin everyone else called the elevator. The shadows took form on the walls. Butterflies. Orange and silver flittered across the silent creamy canvas.

The elevator doors opened. With one last look down the empty hall, I slipped inside and waited for the doors to close. Wisps of gossamer skimmed past the closing door. A shiver went up my spine.

Maybe it was time to move to a new office or call a priest. I smiled. A priest. That'll work. Kurt suggested a priest a few months earlier while I was staying at the Marriott. He could've been joking. Not.

The drive home was uneventful as I expected. I didn't always get uneventful, but I always expected it. Forever hopeful – the most unlikely Pollyanna in town.

Random sentences from a previous conversation rattled in my head.

Rowan had expended a lot of effort to try to persuade me to attend a concert. I pulled into my driveway and waited as the electronic gate began to open.

I wasn't convinced I wanted to do it even though this time it was my idea. Sure, there is nothing to suggest it would go badly, likewise, there is nothing to suggest it would go well. The events that unfolded in Christchurch still haunted me and put a serious dent in my ability to even think of attending a rock concert. My enjoyment is irrelevant.

The gate stood fully open. I checked behind me before pulling in, and waited for the gate to shut before continuing up the driveway. The garage door opened as if by magic, as I approached. It closed behind me once I cut the engine.

Or at least that's how it always seemed. In reality, my security system recognized authorized vehicles via small sensors placed under certain cars. It amused me to imagine my garage door and gate were enchanted.

The hall light was off. Enough silvery moonlight shone through the windows at the top of the staircase that I didn't need lights to climb the stairs. I checked on Carla. She was asleep. But she'd left me a note on her nightstand.

Goodnight, Mom, I love you.

I kissed her head, pulled up the covers and turned out her bedside lamp.

"I love you too, Carla."

Shrek lifted his furry grey head and looked at me as I

left the room.

My bedroom phone was ringing. I could hear it as I walked to my room. I didn't hurry. If it were that important, whoever it was would've called my cell. The phone stopped by the time I entered my bedroom. The message light flashed. I ignored it and dropped my jacket onto my bed. I walked into the bathroom and turned on the shower, with thoughts of killers in the closet and murderers under the bed high in my mind.

The boogieman is real.

My instant paranoia threw me into a B-grade horror movie complete with fog. No amount of trying to convince myself I was being stupid helped. No amount of telling myself it was steam from the shower and not fog worked. I left the shower running, pulled the Glock from my hip, and checked my bedroom. Satisfied it was clear, I closed the bedroom door as I moved on and repeated the exercise. Four bedrooms, including Carla's and the small room I used as my upstairs office space.

The stupidity factor was almost intoxicating. Who the hell could get in without triggering the alarm system and an armed response? Wasn't that the whole point of building a brand new house with a state-of-the-art security system? How many houses have to explode before I consider this kind of security?

Two. The answer is two.

The shower was still running. I holstered my gun and went back to my room. The hairs on the back of my neck prickled. Something wasn't right. I turned off the shower

27

and walked back along the hallway. All the doors remained closed.

Slipping down the backstairs, with my gun drawn, seemed a little foolish until I thought about Carla. Nothing about security is foolish with a kid in the house. Nothing. It didn't matter how many times I said it, there was a little voice in my head that told me I was being irrational, and it sounded very like my mom.

"Pots and kettles, Mom, pots and kettles," I whispered to the ghostly voice in my head.

A shadow crossed the hallway ahead of me. My mind said it was nothing more than a branch moving outside, a shadow cast from moonlight.

Moving how? It was a still night. No breeze.

Breathe.

Light flickered, and then shone from the living room.

The moon can't turn on lights.

Breathe.

My heart pounded. With my left hand, I reached for my cell phone, and came up empty. It was in my jacket. My jacket was lying where I'd dropped it, on my bed.

Crap.

Think.

Control panel. At each end of the downstairs hall were control panels. I hurried through the hallway to the one nearest me, which was just beyond the kitchen. Pressing two buttons turned on all the audio surveillance within the ground floor. There were no cameras inside the house, with the exception of my office. I pressed another button sequence, which sent a silent signal to the security company which monitored my home.

Light streamed from the open living room door across the darkened hallway.

Maybe Carla left the light on. Maybe Dad left the light on for me. But I knew that it wasn't on when I arrived home.

And it wasn't on when I first came downstairs. I paused over the idea of a faulty light switch. Clutching at straws seemed a good way to go.

A long shadow appeared in the pool of light on the carpet.

Crap.

Crap.

Crap.

I edged toward the doorway with my back against the wall. Every nerve in my body screamed for action. Every brain cell in my skull ran through possible scenarios and came up blank.

Think, dammit.

No one could get into the house without the security company knowing about it.

State of the art security systems. State of the fucking art.

I leaned against the wall, chewed my lip, and was not in the least comforted by knowing how good my security was.

Shutting out the noise from my heart pounding in my ears, I concentrated on my surroundings. The quiet clunk of a glass on the coffee table. A glass?

Screw this.

I adjusted my hold. Two-handed grip on my Glock, I took a breath, and stepped into the doorway. An arm reached for the glass again.

I stopped, right foot back, left foot forward, ready to fire.

Controlling the surging adrenaline was not easy. My right hand shook as I let my left hand fall away from the gun and lowered the weapon. I took another deep breath.

A dead man with a death wish.

Asking how he got in my house seemed ridiculous. As absurd as Mac sitting on my sofa drinking. Yet there he was, taking a sip of the yellowish tinted liquid in the glass.

"This must be what it's like to disassociate," I said, and sat on the two-seater opposite him. I slid my gun on the coffee table between us and tried to calm my racing heart.

"Babe, it's pretty close."

Intense fascination filled me as I watched him lift the glass to his lips. He took a mouthful of liquid and swallowed.

That shouldn't be possible. Dead men don't drink and a live man could not have got through security without setting off the alarms.

I had no clue how any of it was happening.

My eyes roamed the room. Everything else was as it should be. The only anomaly was Mac.

What else did I need? A neon flashing sign that

screamed "mental patient" in fifteen-foot letters?

Yeah, maybe I did. Maybe that would remove all doubt.

He looked up. His hazel eyes met mine; his dark brown hair slipped forward brushing his top eyelashes.

"How's your arm?"

"There's nothing wrong with my arm."

"You're sure? You didn't put one through a window in the early hours of this morning, in West Virginia?"

He shook his head. "No."

Good to know. Not sure that I want to deal with a dead man who isn't.

"What do you want?" Under the surface, I felt the bubbling and fizzing of rage. It threw me a little bit. I'd thought I was moving on until the incident at the motel, and now this.

Damn.

"To see you."

"Haven't you done that before? You know, with Messenger windows and appearing in the bathroom of the Marriott?"

"We were interrupted. I needed to see you without interruption."

In less than two minutes, the cavalry will storm the house. That will be an interruption.

"I'm sure there have been many opportunities. I'm not buying it." I was counting in my head, trying to keep my wrath in check.

The glass clinked against the tabletop when he set it

down. As he leaned back, the cushions dented around him as if he was real and sitting on my couch. My breath caught in my throat, then rose and tangled around my uvula.

"Is Carla still seeing her therapist?"

"You tell me, you're the dead guy with all the answers."

"Carla needs help. Something is going on and she's unwilling to talk about it."

As far as I could tell, Carla was all right. Sometimes temperamental and often surly but she's a full-blown teenager, that's to be expected.

"If you know so much then tell me what it is that's going on."

"Joey is involved."

I heaved a sigh. "You know what. Forget it."

He frowned. "What?"

"You heard. Time you left me alone."

My patience waned as my annoyance waxed.

"I can help," he said.

Resentment seethed through me.

"You don't get to do this, not now."

Yet he continued. "There's something wrong, and you know it."

"What's wrong is you're dead." I was trying so hard to keep a lid on my anger. "Carla and I are none of your damn business!"

A small smile played along his lips. I remembered all the times that smile became a laugh. All the times that smile meant everything was okay. Well, it wasn't okay.

"There's something wrong with Carla."

"And you know this? You, the hero, you know this?" It didn't matter to me that he heard the anger in my voice. He deserved to hear it. He'd earned it. I needed him to hear how I felt and what I hid from the world. How much I wished things were different. How I disliked him for what he did but at the same time loved him more *because* of what he did.

Incongruous.

Oh, I was just getting started.

"Babe ..."

"No!"

"Ellie, let me help."

Dead people need to keep out of my business.

"You are dead! A dead hero. What fucking use is a dead hero?"

"Dead but not blind."

"Dead, it doesn't get any worse than that!"

His interfering was going nowhere.

"You left me." I pointed my finger at him. "You. Left. Me." I was on my feet, the anger I'd kept so close for so long spilled all over the room. Running down the walls like blood.

Splashing onto the new carpet. A wave of foaming red rolled over the coffee table, swallowing the glass, lapping at the sofa. Mac was knee deep in frothy blood. "*You* took off your vest. *You* left me."

"I did my job. I saved her."

"Where was it written that you had to sacrifice *us* to do

33

that?"

"I did my job."

A moment of calm engulfed me. "And this is my life. I'll take it from here."

Somewhere outside a car stopped. Doors opened and closed.

"Buckle up," Mac replied.

"What the fuck is that supposed to mean?"

"Buckle up, it's going to get rough."

Sudden anger coursed unchecked. He started to stand up; as he did, my hand wrapped around the grip of my Glock. I lifted my arm. His face registered surprise. "Ellie, don't." His words hung in the air.

"It's. My. life."

I fired twice. My bullets tore through his forehead. Blood sprayed across the back of the couch. The gun fell from my hand, dropping onto the coffee table and sliding across the surface to tumble off the edge onto the silent carpet. I watched Mac fall in slow motion. He crumpled to the floor, just missing the coffee table. His words fell letter by letter and melted on the table surface.

A voice from the front door called out. "Conway?"

"Living room," I replied and sat back in the chair. I could see Mac's blood all over the couch. I could see the bullet hole in the wall.

I was going to need hydrogen peroxide and a lot of cold water to clean the blood off the couch and rug.

Booted feet ran through the hallway from both directions.

I saw the gun before I saw the man holding it. Sean stepped into the room, looking lethal and dressed head to toe in black.

"You all right?"

"Sure."

He wasn't looking at the couch or the floor. His steel-grey eyes were on the right side of the room. Another man came in behind him and moved to the left. There were more feet out in the hall, going room by room.

"Clear," they both said together.

Clear? Dead body.

Hello. Blood all over the room.

"Did you do that?" Sean said, tilting his head toward the wall.

I nodded. "I shot him."

"Who?" He motioned to the man with him. "Could be a wounded person somewhere."

"I killed Mac. Double tap to the head."

Sean frowned. "Where is he?"

Oh, come on. Open your eyes.

"Right there," I said pointing to Mac's body between the table and the couch. I didn't want to get any closer than I already was, just in case it wasn't Mac but Whoopi Goldberg. My head was jumping about, flashing between the present, my past, and the movie *Ghost*. I didn't want to have shot Whoopi. She was one of my favorite actors.

Sean turned to the other man and said, "Stand down."

I leaned back in the chair until my head touched the leather. Carla's voice yelled out from upstairs. I jumped to my feet only to have Sean push me back down. He spoke to the other man again. "Stay with her."

Then Sean was gone.

The smell of blood made me feel sick. Its cloying stench permeated the room. I doubt I will ever get used to that smell. "Can I get a drink of water?" I asked the armed man in black.

He pointed to the glass on the table.

I shook my head. "I don't think that's water."

Sean reappeared. He picked up my gun from the floor and shoved it in his waistband.

"Carla is fine. She heard the gunshots and thought you were watching a movie."

"She's not coming down here?" I don't want her seeing the blood everywhere. The mess.

"No, she's settled and going back to sleep."

"Didn't she wonder about you?"

"Yes, said I was visiting on my way home from a call-out."

Clever.

"What now?"

"Now, we make this go away."

I killed Mac. That doesn't just go away. Or does it? The bloodstains on the couch started to shrink. I pointed at the shrinking pools of blood and dissolving splatter. "What the hell?"

"What?" Sean asked. His line of sight followed my finger.

"The blood, it's disappearing."

36

"Everything is fine," Sean said. I recognized his tone. I used it on Carla often enough, when she was upset or panicked over something. "Just breathe."

"I'm okay. You don't have to talk to me like I'm special."

Okay. Yep, I felt okay. I just put two bullets in my dead husband's head and I felt okay. There were so many things wrong with that, I couldn't begin to comprehend them all.

The blood vanished. The smell evaporated. I stood up and peered over the coffee table. Mac was gone. The only thing left was the hole in my wall. "I'm okay."

Uh huh. Never better.

I sat back down.

"Shall we listen to the audio?" Sean offered. To his credit, he managed to keep his expression neutral despite how insane the situation was.

My head nodded without my bidding. Audio. Captured by the computer system that protected the house. Sound bites were stored on the secure servers in Sean's office building. I just hoped I was going to hear two voices and not just mine. Doubt kicked in and escalated.

He set up his laptop on the coffee table and connected to the company servers. After pressing a bunch of numbers and keying in what I expected to be an elaborate password, a file with today's date and my initials appeared on the screen. Sean sat next to me and adjusted the speaker volume. He double clicked the file. We listened. I heard my voice. I was talking to someone.

Crackling, hissing, and another voice replied. Me talking again. The same crackling and hissing then another reply. It was a male voice replying, there was no doubt. We listened to the whole thing. My yelling, his barely audible replies. What to believe?

"Can you hear it?" I asked Sean.

"Yes."

"Not just me?"

"No, I can hear a male voice responding to you."

The voice stopped with the gunshots.

"He was here," I said. "I shot Mac."

Sean nodded. "I heard him."

"I don't know how to process what happened here tonight." Honesty tumbled from my lips. "I don't know how to make sense of this."

"Sit tight. I don't know either, but I'm going to figure it out. We'll start by cleaning this recording to make it easier to hear that other voice." He rubbed my shoulder. "Once it's cleaned, I'll have it compared to sound bites we have on file."

"You have Mac on file?"

He smiled. "No, but I'll bet he's in one of the FBI databases."

"Good bet. We all are."

A chicken walked across the coffee table and paused at the laptop before moving on. My first thought was one of finality. My brain was overcooked and I was done. The very familiar chicken stopped, turned, and looked at me with beady black eyes. Her rusty brown feathers shone in the light. Her name rolled around my mind, stirring up memories of her before the Son of Shakespeare nailed her upside down to the door of my home in Mauryville. Abigail pecked at the pale table surface, pausing at the glass. She stuck her beak in and tasted the liquid. It didn't agree with her. With a violent shake of her head, she disappeared.

Great. First, I shoot my dead husband and now, my pet chicken, which I also shot but for different reasons, comes back from the grave.

I curled my legs up underneath me. I needed a drink and I didn't want water. I wanted to know what was in the glass on the table. Something chickens don't like.

"What's in that glass?" I said.

Sean leaned over and sniffed it. "Tequila. You weren't drinking?"

"No, Mac was." And then Abigail tasted it and was most unimpressed. Best to leave that out.

He turned to the other man and said, "Don't touch this glass."

"Sean, will you call Kurt, please."

He smiled. "Sure, you feel okay?"

I shook my head then stopped. "I clearly have no concept of what okay is. Just get him here."

I stole a furtive glance around the room, hoping there were no more ghosts lurking.

"Done."

The man with Sean went away. I heard him and other men talking. They left the house.

Sean rose, walked over to the hole in the wall, and stood next to it but facing me,

"Ellie, how tall was Mac?"

"Six foot one."

"And you double-tapped him?" He pressed his index finger into the middle of his forehead. I looked from Sean to the hole. The hole was level with the middle of Sean's forehead. That put it above Mac's head. Sean is six feet seven inches tall.

"I didn't shoot him?"

"Not unless he grew in death."

"But ... I ..."

"Imagined shooting him but aimed high."

"I didn't shoot a ghost."

"No doubt you wanted to and you thought you shot him."

"So is this good or bad?

"Good question. Audio confirms a male in the room."

"Great. Still insane then."

Sean and I went through to the kitchen. He made coffee while I sat on a bar stool at the counter and tried to figure out what happened.

A priest was starting to look like a good idea.

As loathe as I was to admit it, perhaps a psychiatrist as well.

Nah. No need to hit that particular slippery slope.

Soft footsteps in the passage way caused Sean to look over my head at the man walking up behind me. I knew the footsteps. No need to turn around.

"Sean."

"Kurt."

"Conway."

"Kurt."

Yeah, I was smiling a little. 'Who's on First?' popped into my head. Abbot and Costello were winning. Who's on first? What's on second?

I needed help. Sean was talking and I was lost in an ancient comedy sketch. If I were to be honest, I wasn't listening because I didn't want to hear.

When I did start to pay attention it was as Sean said, "If you've got this, we'll get going."

"I got it," Kurt replied. "Thank you."

They shook hands.

Sean came around to me. He shook my hand, and then gave me a fast hug. "I'll find out what that was. I'll take the glass that is on the coffee table with me."

"Thanks."

I watched as he walked away. The front door closed. Car engines fired. Then silence. It was not a nice silence. Not a comfortable silence. It was thick with unasked questions.

"Let's go upstairs," Kurt said.

"Coffee?"

"Not a good idea. I'll make you a hot chocolate."

"You'll make me hot chocolate?"

He smiled. "I'm multitalented." With that, he warmed milk in a pot and found a block of chocolate in the pantry. Real hot chocolate. I watched as Kurt dropped four squares of chocolate into a mug then poured hot milk over it while stirring.

"That's not enough, put more chocolate in."

"You're lucky your migraines are not triggered by chocolate," he said, adding another three squares and stirring the hot milk with vigor.

"Yeah, lucky."

A warm mug of hot chocolate.

"Come on, upstairs."

Kurt carried the mug. I could see how that was a good idea. I saw my gun in his waistband. Sean must've given it to him. As I walked behind him up the stairs and along the hallway, I realized I was being rather obliging. That's so not right.

Kurt stopped at my bedroom door, his hand rested on the door handle. "Is it okay if I come in?"

I nodded like an idiot. He turned the handle and swung open the door. My jacket was still on the bed.

"I want to check on Carla," I said as Kurt went into my room.

"Good idea. I'll come."

Oh, now I got it. I'm not to be alone. "I'll be right back, stay here," I said.

"I'll ..."

"No, wait for me here."

That felt better. More normal. Less shell-shocked.

Kurt set the mug on my nightstand and picked up my jacket. I hurried to Carla's room. She was asleep.

Satisfied I went back to my room to see what Kurt was

doing. He was sitting on the sofa in my room.

"When did you last sleep?" he asked, pointing to where he'd put the hot chocolate.

"A while ago, two days, maybe a little longer. You know what it's like when we're after someone."

He nodded. "You need to sleep."

A loud crash came from downstairs. Kurt and I looked at each other for a split second. He jumped to his feet and threw me my gun.

"Where was it?" he said.

"Sounded central, living room." I was already out the door. "You go to the front stairs I'll take the back."

There was no other noise. I watched Kurt as he stepped out into the downstairs passageway. He paused to check the front door and alarm panel. His hand signaled two areas illuminated. I waved him forward. We stood either side of the living room door. All lights were out.

"On three," Kurt whispered.

I counted. I went through the door first, and secured the right side of the room. Kurt was behind me, looking left. There was no one there. In the moonlight, I could see the couch where Mac sat was upended.

"What the hell ..." I muttered. It took both of us to right the couch. Yet something that heavy just tipped itself over?

"Spooky," he said.

"No kidding." I smiled. "You still think this is some sleep deprived psychosis?"

Kurt's hand was flat on the small of my back guiding me back upstairs. "I don't know what it is. The alarm is on. Everything is working. Let's get you to bed."

A small chuckle popped out. "Bed?"

"Yeah, I wish." His whisper was just audible.

"Excuse me?"

"Climb those stairs, Conway," Kurt said louder.

Biting back a smile, I replied, "That's not what you said."

"You're awful smart-mouthed for someone who tried to kill a ghost and shot a wall."

Chapter Three
Thorn in My Side

It wasn't quite five on Friday morning when my cell phone buzzed off the nightstand, hit my boot, and bounced onto the rug beside my bed. My hand followed it. It took a few seconds before I could grasp the phone. My fingers were half-asleep and uncooperative.

Nothing unusual there.

My eyes were also half-asleep and uncooperative.

I answered the call. "SSA Conway."

As soon as I heard his voice, I knew I would rue the day I answered the stupid phone.

"Ellie, its Eddie, I saw Mac."

I hung up. He called right back. I let it go to voice mail. Eddie's the inherited ex-brother-in-law from hell. I have fun little daydreams involving Eddie's demise at my hand. Most often it's the knife in my hand that facilitates the demising.

I fought the tiredness in my brain so I could take counter measures to protect myself against his insanity before I listened to the voice mail he'd left. There should be an Eddie inoculation. Like measles, he had the potential to cause brain damage. He rambled on, his fat lips smacking together as he spoke. Eddie saw Mac in Manassas and wanted me to investigate the sighting. I doubted he'd seen the same guy I'd seen. My guy was in a hospital somewhere with a nasty arm wound.

I deleted the message before hearing the whole thing and dropped my cell phone on my quilt. Eddie had salad greens for brains and bourbon for blood; I doubted the person he saw even resembled Mac.

And Mac is dead.

Rolling over I saw that the telephone on the nightstand was flashing its red message light. Guess I was too tired to notice it the night before. My fingers found the message button. The robotic female voice from the message service said, "You have sixteen new messages. First message received two p.m. Thursday."

I pressed one to hurry it up. The first message was from an unknown number and the female voice told me I was playing with fire.

Good. I like fire. It's pretty.

The next twelve messages all sounded like the same woman. I got the impression she didn't like me very much.

Friday was shaping up to be vaguely threatening message day.

Two messages from Rowan followed. He liked me. He said he was going to be in town for a gig and was hoping we could spend the weekend together. Yeah, me too.

Then the last message was from the woman again. She didn't leave her name and sounded a little cross.

"Leave Rowan alone. He doesn't need someone like you. You are no good for him."

So her messages went from warning me I was playing with fire to telling me to leave Rowan alone.

I curled up in my bed with a smile on my face.

Women everywhere hate me and now one of them has my phone number.

Great.

It's not as if my phone numbers are a secret. Plenty of people I've come across have my business cards. I smiled some more. If she had my card then I'd come across her in a professional setting. I must have interviewed several Grange fans in the course of my career and not known it.

Chapter Four
Wuthering Heights

When Friday started properly, I spent two hours with Sean, listening to how he established the presence of Mac's fingerprints on the glass and that there was no blood on either round. Good confirmation that I hadn't shot anyone. They did however find minute traces of an unknown substance on one round. More testing was required. He had the sound bites analyzed by his experts. They cleaned up the recording and ran it through the latest voice comparison software. When nothing came back as a match, he opened the search to deceased federal employees. Snap. It came back as Mac.

This horrible feeling of relief that I wasn't nuts melded with the very real fear that I couldn't control the situation. Mac turning up as he did in our home called into question my ability to protect Carla. I always thought ghosts were incorporeal beings, left over energy. But he was interacting, capable of lifting a glass. That just wasn't right.

Poltergeist?

Time for a priest.

Music weaseled its way into my head. *The Ghost Busters* theme song took over. If that wasn't just a movie I'd be on the phone already.

"Okay, so is he a ghost, or is he alive?"

I regretted those words as soon as they left my lips.

"Alive? You think that's possible?" Sean said, pouring me more coffee.

Coffee is my crack.

As I tried to shake my head, it nodded. What the hell? My body is betraying me now?

"I don't know what to think."

"That's obvious."

It sounded just a little wacky. But Sean wasn't in West Virginia with me and Noel. He didn't see the guy who was the living image of Mac.

"I have a blood sample from someone I spoke to, who looked just like Mac," I said. "Don't look at me like that."

"You never mentioned it ... who knows about this?"

"Yeah, well, it just happened and it's not something I'm going to rock up to everyone and say, 'hey, guess who I saw in West Virginia the other day?'"

He smiled. "Fair enough, but who knows?"

"Noel Gerrard."

"I think you better tell me what happened."

Funny, I believed the same thing.

"I wish you could just see into my brain."

Sean chuckled. I gave him a run down on the motel happenings.

"Ellie, who do you think it was that night?" he asked.

I shrugged. "Not Mac, but beyond that I don't know. I took the sample to the lab when we got back from West Virginia, but it isn't urgent and didn't have a case number attached to it." Even if it was urgent and did have a case number, it would be months before the lab could process

49

it. Everything they get is urgent.

"You want to pull it from the queue and let my lab test it?"

No. Maybe I don't really want to know whose blood it is.

"All right, if you want to run it."

He smiled. "We don't require a case number to process possible evidence, and it's not evidence from a crime scene so we're not risking interfering with an actual case. You know it makes sense to let me do this."

"Yeah, it makes sense."

"Then let's get it, and get it tested."

"Meanwhile ... know a priest who can do something about my home?"

"I don't think that'll help. It's you he's attached to."

Great.

"Exorcism then?"

"He's not possessing you, is he?"

"No." Not yet.

I thanked Sean for confirming that I'm not as wacky as Mac makes me feel.

"Keep in touch," Sean said. "Courier that sample direct from your lab to me. I'll deal with it. We'll have an answer in the next few days."

"Sean?" I chewed my lip.

"Yup, spit it out."

"Tierney was involved with the guy in West Virginia. When he's involved, anything is possible."

Tierney is a magician. He's all smoke and illusions.

"Even he cannot resurrect the dead, Ellie."

"You sure about that?" I smiled. "Standing in front of you is a dead woman, remember?"

"That wasn't the same sort of situation. I'm damn sure Tierney can't resurrect the actual dead, and I will prove it."

But wait there's more.

"My ex-brother-in-law called me at five this morning. He swore he saw Mac in Manassas last night."

"Do you consider him to be a reliable witness?"

"No. He's a fucktard. Just making you aware of another sighting is all."

Amusement danced in Sean's grey eyes. "He could have seen someone who looked like Mac. Keep in touch."

"I will."

It was a relief to be back in the office.

Waiting for me were the tickets for the special surprise. I crammed all thoughts of ghosts and blood as far down in my mind as I could and sat a big heavy cinder block on the whole lot.

Chapter Five
All Out of Love

I busied myself in my office while Delta A helped another team with an arrest. Eddie's call twisted my craziness. I wanted a photo of the bleeder from West Virginia. Security cameras.

I called the motel we'd stayed in and asked if there were cameras and if they kept security footage. They did. I requested a copy of all the footage for the last week and list of who checked in, how many people were staying in each unit, and which cars belonged to which rooms. I knew the owner would have a taken note of the cars tags associated with guests.

With a bit of convincing I managed to get the motel owner to courier me a DVD copy of the security footage, along with photocopies of guest information going back eight days. I was hoping he'd scanned driver's licenses and Chad's would be one of them.

My theory was if I could locate a decent photo then I could run it through our fancy biometric facial recognition program. The program would tell me if it was Mac or just someone who looked a bit like him.

It's not like I believed it was Mac. But Chad looked too much like him and knew Tierney. All kinds of twinges and twangs were happening in my gut. Something funky was going on.

I needed coffee. Hot, strong, black coffee.

Coffee.

I headed out of the building. Fresh air would work wonders. On the way over to The Firehook coffee shop, I dodged a horde of schoolchildren coming up out of the Metro. I leaned against a wall and waited until the teachers and parents did a head count and organized the children to walk to wherever they were going. When they were out of my way, I ducked into The Firehook and ordered a quad espresso in a tall cup. I topped my cup up with cold water so I didn't scald myself, left off the takeout lid to facilitate cooling and I was set to enjoy my coffee.

I walked up 13th to F Street on my way back to the office on 10th and Pennsylvania. It was a beautiful clear spring day. I love spring: Cherry blossoms, tulips, the smell of fresh mulch in the gardens, and the bright green new growth on what had been barren trees all winter. Washington in the spring was a sight to behold.

I walked and enjoyed the sights and smells of spring. As I took a sip from my cup, something knocked my left arm. My coffee sloshed but didn't spill. No harm, no foul. I spun around to apologize to whomever I'd bumped into but no one was there.

Weird.

The nearest person was across the street and walking the other direction, a male who seemed to be in a hurry.

I carried on walking. It wasn't until I lifted my cup to my mouth for another sip of precious black liquid that my arm felt a little sore and reluctant. I switched my coffee to the other hand; no need to run the risk of spilling it.

My arm complained. It wasn't a loud boisterous complaint, more of a localized stinging sensation. The voice in my head said, "That's not right."

I kept walking and told myself that a rampant bee stung me. No matter how ridiculous it seemed. But there was another voice, louder, that told me I'd been shot. That couldn't be right. Why would someone shoot me in the open like that?

All sorts of notions piled up in the front of my brain. The last one to arrive curled around my tongue. No sense being a drama queen in the middle of the sidewalk, I kept moving and closed my mouth tight to prevent the escape of any loud expressions of horror. I expected to feel a bullet slam into my back at any second.

It was a relief when I saw the intersection ahead and knew for sure I wasn't far from the office. I hurried around the corner and down 10th, passed Ford's theater and kept going, while a dilemma brewed. I needed to make a phone call but I couldn't hold my coffee and make a phone call at the same time. Left-handed phone user and right-handed shooter.

One more road to cross and I would be safe. As I approached The Hard Rock Café, I could see two uniformed FBI police talking beside a marked van blocking the FBI underground car park exit on E Street. I crossed the street toward them.

Instead of attracting their attention, I walked past them and set my cup on one of the large concrete bollards out front of the chained-off stairs on 10th; the bollards are feebly disguised as planters. I pulled my phone off my belt and looked at it for a few seconds, deciding whether to call Kurt or just go on in and surprise him. I didn't think this was the sort of surprise he'd appreciate. Also I didn't want to drip on the floors. Blood is slippery on hard floors. Someone could get hurt.

I glanced down the street toward Pennsylvania Avenue. The employee entrance seemed a long way away.

Outside the building, standing near the road were another group of FBI police. They weren't taking any notice of me, what with a constant stream of people walking past and mine being a familiar face.

I leaned on the bollard garden and called Kurt. A pretty red substance dripped off my fingertips. Two possibilities surfaced, it was blood or a random invisible stranger had poured seedless raspberry compôte down my arm.

It was time to acknowledge the voice that told me I'd been shot. Shot in the middle of the city while drinking coffee. That was quite some feat. I wondered who was pissed at me this time.

Kurt answered his phone on the second ring. "Conway, how can I help?"

"I'm outside the building, by the stairs on 10th, and I have a little problem," I said.

He went quiet. There was nothing there.

Moments later, Kurt flew out down the stairs carrying a red backpack with a white cross on it and vaulted over the yellow chain. His eyes scanned the area in front of him. I waved. Blood flew from my hand and cast drippy patterns on the ground. He looked right and hollered at two men in uniform who'd been leaning on the wall by the guardhouse, "Are your eyes painted on?"

One man jumped, the other's back stiffened.

"Sir?" they said in unison.

"You have an injured agent out here," Kurt growled. He dropped a backpack on the ground by my feet.

"Hey, Kurt," I said with a smile. "How'd you know you'd need the first aid kit?"

Kurt gave me a look. "Seriously?"

"Never mind."

"What happened?" Kurt asked, looking at my arm for a moment before opening the backpack and taking out scissors.

"I'm not sure," I replied. "I thought someone bumped into me, but there was no one around."

"No one at all?"

"There was a person walking away on the other side of the street but no one near me." I was looking at my upper arm as Kurt poked about. He'd cut away my sleeve.

"It's not serious," Kurt muttered. "Looks like you were shot at. You didn't hear anything?"

"No. I didn't hear anything."

Good to have confirmation that I was indeed shot.

"The bullet grazed your upper arm instead of going through."

"Looks like a deep graze ..." I replied.

"More like a gouge." He beckoned to the uniforms. They hurried over. "Conway, where were you when this happened?"

"Near the intersection of F and 10th."

He looked at my coffee cup and spoke to the uniformed officers.

"Agent Conway was en route by foot from the Firehook Bakery on 13th heading up F to 10th. You're looking for shell casings and maybe a 9mm round. Count the traffic cams, and check how many stores have video surveillance at street level."

"You want us to talk to the stores and procure the footage?" one man asked.

Kurt read his nametag. "Please, Jeff. That would be helpful."

The other man stepped forward. "Time frame for the footage?"

I saw his nametag. "The last forty minutes, John. Both sides of the street, I saw someone on the opposite side of the street from me. He was walking fast and away from me."

They hurried off talking into their radios.

Kurt delved back into his backpack and took out everything he needed to clean and bandage my arm.

"No stitches?" I asked, watching him.

"Oh, you're getting stitches, just not out here. I'll do it in the sick bay inside."

Damn.

He wrapped my arm. We went inside and up to our

floor where Kurt escorted me to the sick bay. He stitched the cut then stuck a waterproof dressing over it while mumbling something about my body starting to look like a road map.

He wasn't wrong. My body bore quite the collection of scars from various escapades and lucky escapes.

"Mom used to say life should not be a journey to the grave with the intention of arriving safe and sound in an attractive and well-preserved body, but rather to skid in sideways, thoroughly used up, worn out and screaming, 'Woo hoo, What a Ride!'" I looked at my arm. "And again, I need a new shirt so I can carry on with the day."

Kurt laughed. "You're welcome."

"Thanks," I said with a smile. "Should we go help Jeff and John?"

"We should," he replied.

"I'll just grab a shirt from my office then we can get going."

Ten minutes later, we were re-tracing my steps.

Jeff saw us before we saw him and waved to get our attention.

"No one has anything usable on tape. We have a clear picture of a man's back though. Looks like he's picking something up off the ground." Jeff thrust a print out of the picture into my outstretched hand. Kurt and I gave it due consideration.

"And no other cameras or witnesses could add anything?" Kurt asked.

"No, sir."

This is Washington, DC. There is security everywhere. There are cameras everywhere. The only way to avoid being captured on surveillance is to know where all the cameras are. Whoever shot at me was no idiot.

"He's policing his brass," I muttered. "He's picking up his empty cartridge cases. He knows where all the cameras are and which stores have armed security guards and he just grazes my arm with a bullet?" I looked around but saw nothing out of place. "Grazing my arm like that and doing no other damage takes talent."

Kurt's eyebrows rose. "Something doesn't add up."

Maybe if I hadn't come across something that didn't add up in West Virginia, I wouldn't have been so suspicious, but I had, and I hated the cloak and dagger bullshit that seemed to be prevalent in my life all of a sudden.

"I'm going back to the office," I grumbled. "He didn't want me dead. He wanted my attention but didn't leave any crumbs for me to follow. This shit will do my head in."

Kurt handed out orders to Jeff and his partner. They were to stay and see if they could find anyone who saw the mystery man's face. I smiled when I heard him tell them he wanted a report on his desk by that evening.

Fine by me.

I had evening plans with Carla and Lee. A little bit of Joey-free mother/daughter time, with Lee along for security.

Chapter Six
Shout

Our Friday evening destination was FedEx Field. Joe, Grange's tour manager, was waiting for us at the gate.

"Follow me. I'll take you to your seats. I've had some of the crew sitting in them."

We followed close behind him, even so the band and crowd were so loud it was difficult to hear him as he spoke. "Having three empty seats with reserved plastered on them would've made Rowan curious."

A thousand booted feet danced in my stomach, whipping my dinner into a foamy frenzy. It took a lot of control to follow Joe when all I wanted to do was grab Carla and get the hell away from the seething mass surrounding us. Visions of the last Grange concert I attended swam in front of my eyes complete with explosive blood splatter. It was so fresh that the metallic odor hurt my nose.

Lee took Carla's arm as the crowd closed in. He used his body to cut a path behind Joe for Carla and me. It was like parting a brain-dead sea.

We made the switch while Rowan was changing instruments. He turned to face the crowd holding a six-string acoustic guitar and Tony belted out the opening bars of a very familiar song.

By the time, Rowan hit the first chorus he was grinning at me. The crowd was going nuts. At the second chorus, he beckoned. I looked around expecting to see someone famous right behind me. When I looked back he changed the next line to, "Ellie, you and Carla get on up here."

Carla screamed with joy. Lee poked me in the ribs. "I think you're wanted." I felt the color drain from my face. Rowan smiled from the stage and the big screen above the stage. He was everywhere. The crowd responded with raptures and screams. Rowan looked down at me, knelt on one knee at the edge of the stage, and held out his hand. Women in the first row squealed and grabbed at his hand. He smiled and focused on me.

"You can't leave him hanging there. They'll pull him off the stage," Lee said, his voice rumbling below the screams into my ear.

Rowan's security team was moving in. He'd be fine.

Lee parted the two rows in front of us, leaving me no choice, and delivered us to the front of the stage. Rowan's hand grabbed mine, and there I stood on the stage, trying not to look out at the seething crowd below, and trying harder still not to puke. Lee boosted Carla up. She joined me, grinning from ear to ear. "They'll just die. The girls at school will die."

Cameras flashed.

"I'm glad their deaths bring you such joy, kiddo," I said, struggling with my terror.

The guitar was gone, a stool materialized; Rowan motioned to me to sit then gave Carla a hug. I perched on the stool with Carla leaning against me while he sang the rest of the song.

Nausea surged in relentless waves. For the first time ever I wished for a debilitating migraine, just so I had an excuse to leave. My body didn't oblige.

During the out-of-control shouting that erupted at the end of the song, he pulled me to my feet and wrapped an arm around my shoulders. No microphone, just forty-eight thousand high-pitched fans, and us.

"Thank you for coming," he whispered.

His eyes flashed. "I want you to stay up here."

"I can't leave Lee."

He kissed me, the screaming echoed through my head louder than ever. "Go back to your seat, but you all have to come back up for the last song."

Rowan walked us to the edge of the stage. Carla turned for one last wave at the band, still pumping out music. Martin blew her a kiss and she exploded into the biggest smile I'd ever seen. A security guard motioned for her to sit on the edge of the stage. He then lifted her to the ground. I jumped into a clear space Lee created for me. Rowan bent down. "The last song Lee, the three of you should be up here."

Lee nodded.

A voice whispered through a gap in the screaming women next to me. I looked over and saw a dark-haired woman with eyes full of tears. I smiled. The same whisper flowed again. This time the words took form. "You don't deserve him." Her voice sounded familiar. She could've been the same woman who left so many loving messages on my phone.

The woman blended back into the crowd. I shrugged. Fans are possessive creatures. I get that. I don't like it. But I get it.

We went back to our seats amidst jealous comments and sniping remarks. If looks could kill, my blood would've flowed and flowed. I'd be nothing but an empty husk.

I'd noticed a definite escalation in nastiness over the last few months, ever since photos of Rowan and Carla were plastered all over the television and gossip magazines. Cameras flashed, phones flashed, a lot of it seemed directed at me. Knowing I was armed was of no comfort. The constant media attention and cameras in my face was not something I adjusted well to or wanted to adjust to.

It was three quarters of an hour before Rowan called us up again. The crazy women around us stopped with the snarky comments.

Lee and Carla were whisked backstage to watch from the wings and I was back on the stool – when the song ended, Rowan introduced me. I sat terrified, clutching the edge of the seat lest I should fall on my face. He said, "On our new album I was lucky enough to work with Special Agent Ellie Conway – we co-wrote five of the thirteen tracks and that was one of them."

The crowd went wild. I felt dizzy. This was not a good way to conquer my terror of large crowds, concerts, and public speaking. My mouth opened, no words surfaced.

After a few seconds of my best goldfish impression I spluttered, "Thank you."

I scrambled off the stool and tried to escape and almost succeeded in falling flat on my face. Rowan's arm encircled my waist. The band thanked the audience for coming and for supporting the Butterfly Foundation, and then disappeared off stage taking me with them. The screaming was deafening, yet all I heard was laughter from Lee as he stepped up next to me.

"Shut up!"

Rowan lowered himself into a chair and downed half a bottle of water then grinned at me. His hair was damp, and sweat trickled down the sides of his face. He smelt incredible. How could anyone expend that amount of energy and still smell so damn good? Amidst a flurry of backstage activity centered around the band members and involving towels, hair dryers, and bottled water, Rowan took something out from his ear, it hung over his collar

I could still hear the screaming. Earplugs sounded like a great idea but I was pretty sure that's not what Rowan was wearing. Curiosity got the better of me. I think I was deflecting, trying not to think about where I was.

"What's that?" I said, pointing to the molded object hanging by a wire.

"An IEM."

My brain stalled. I heard IED. Damn concert bringing back too many unpleasant memories.

"Say again?"

Rowan looked up at me. "An I.E.M. In-Ear Monitor."

"And it does?"

"Enables me to hear the band, my own voice, and still interact with the crowd. The ones I wear are called Sensaphonic 3D Active Ambient In-Ear Monitor system."

Now that was a mouthful.

"It doesn't explode?"

"It doesn't explode."

"You all wear them?"

"Yep – not always the same type but we all wear them."

"Does it protect your hearing too?"

"Yes. Man, you have a lot of questions," Rowan said with a grin, which told me the subject was about to change. "I thought you were gonna hurl out there." His hand gestured to the stage.

"Thanks," I contrived a glower and directed it at him. "Thanks a whole fuc'n lot."

He hooted with amusement. "Come on, we've got an encore, join us for four songs?"

"Hell, no!" I stepped back semi-concealing myself behind Lee.

"Come on, Ellie," Tony said. "We'd love it if you would."

"You should do it, Mom," Carla added. "Then I get bragging rights."

"I can't leave you on your own," I said.

"She'll be with me," Lee replied, wrapping an arm around Carla's shoulders. "Nice and safe."

My middle finger took on a life of its own and flew at Lee. Who captured it in his hand with neat precision and folded it back into the flock.

Deafened by earsplitting screams from fans and a desire to escape, I slunk back into the shadows.

"We're up," Rowan said, grinning. "Come on – the first one's for you." He took my hand. Next thing I knew I was on the stage.

Rowan whispered, "I'll let you go, I promise … after this song."

There was no stool.

"Where's the fuc'n stool?" I whispered back.

Rowan's breath tickled my neck as he leaned into my ear and said, "You can do this, follow my lead."

The band launched into their newest hit 'Another Night.'

His warm hands took mine; he lifted one to his shoulder, slipped an arm around my waist, and held my other hand close against his chest. Then he pulled back a little and looked into my eyes.

"Is that a Glock on your hip?"

"If I was that pleased to see you I think we'd have some major issues."

His eyes shone as his smile widened, and he pulled me close and whispered, "You came armed …" His smile gave nothing away; no one but me knew he was upset.

"You picked a great time to have an issue with that."

"There's a time and place for weapons … this isn't one." He was dancing me around the stage, a smile stuck on his face so none of the cameras flashing would catch what was going on.

Through my smile I replied, "Babe, I'm a Fed and that by definition means I am armed. It's not a job, it's a vocation."

His smile became real again. "Touché." Rowan danced me around the stage until we were by Lee and Carla on the wings, with a quick hug I slipped off to watch the rest of the encore with them. It was an odd feeling, watching the performance from the side as we were.

I saw more of Rowan's back than I did anything else. He bounced around the stage like the energizer bunny

"He's into you big-time," Lee commented, nudging me just as Rowan turned his back on the audience for a brief moment and flashed a fabulous smile in my direction.

Beyond his left foot, I saw the dark-haired woman from earlier dissolve into hysterical tears. She stood out because I'd heard her comment. No doubt the rest of them thought or even said similar things. Why hers was the one I heard with such clarity I did not know but I'd hazard a guess it was because I'd heard her voice before in my messages.

From the corner of my eye, I saw Tony beckon to Carla.

"Can I, Mom?"

"Sure, go!"

She shot across the stage to Tony, who kissed her on top of the head and handed her a tambourine. I hoped he knew what he was doing.

My kid looked so happy. "Lee, she's okay isn't she?"

"I think so," Lee said. "She's been acting like a teenager but I think she's okay."

I looked at him. So he'd noticed it too.

"If there was something wrong, something she was worried about. She'd talk to one of us, right?"

"She always has. Although she's older now and teens tend to talk to each other more than mom and grandpa." Lee nudged me and pointed at Carla and Tony. "Right there, that's a happy kid."

I willed my brain to take a snapshot of the moment. I'd need to remember this moment when teenage Carla reappeared with demands and boys and parties.

"Are we taking the night off, or do you wanna get some work done?" Lee asked.

I grinned. "I have other plans, Mr. Jacked-Up-On-Adrenaline out there ..." I tilted my head toward Rowan on stage. "... for one."

As long as the gun thing doesn't come up again and ruin those plans.

I nudged Lee, "Gracey just smiled at you."

"Really?" He smiled then frowned. "You think she likes me?"

"Would that be a problem?"

"Yeah, no, musicians aren't really my thing. I have a fondness for LEOs."

"You don't say." Like that was news. Lee wasn't the best at covering his tracks and Delta is a close team. We all knew who he was seeing, but let him believe it was a secret. If he wanted to keep it quiet, or if it was more exciting that way, it wasn't our business.

The smile locked. "Yeah."

I pressed the car keys into his hand. "Take the car, I'll be okay."

"You want me to drop it off at your place?"

"Nope, not tonight."

"What about Carla?"

"Rowan and I will drop her off at Dad's." For the weekend.

"Call me." He made a phone with his fingers.

"You'll hear from me sometime."

Lee started to walk away then turned back. "Tomorrow morning?"

"Unless something major comes up, I'm not planning on calling you until at least Sunday."

He left with a grin and backward wave.

Rowan bounced toward me across the stage. His every move followed by thousands of eyes. He took my hand.

"Come on," he whispered in my ear. "Dance with me, baby."

The heat from his body drew me in.

Chapter Seven
Under My Umbrella

Breathless.

Not the ideal way to start a Monday.

With my hands on my hips, I bent at the waist and breathed hard. I sucked in air trying to fill my lungs. Thick humid air clogged my throat, choking me. Washington in the spring can be a special type of muggy hell. Pounding feet from across the street came to an abrupt stop. I looked over. Lee was standing on the street corner. One hand resting on a rain splattered building as he too attempted to draw in vast quantities of air. I caught his eye and shook my head.

A song erupted from somewhere close, I looked into the windows next to me, expecting it be a café or hair salon which might account for the music. No such luck. Kevin Costner and Modern West sang 'Maria Nay.' My private concert and it made no sense. I wasn't chasing a woman. Or was I? Maybe my mind didn't know any songs about chasing an Unsub in a spring rainstorm.

Another set of pounding feet came up fast behind me.

"You all right?" Kurt said, stopping at my side. We sheltered under a sagging awning.

"Yep, just catching my breath. It's too fuc'n wet and hot for foot pursuit." I scouted around, no sign of police. "What the hell happened to police support?"

A sharp ripping sound above me caught my attention.

A small tear appeared in the awning. With a sudden splash, a bucketload of water landed on Kurt's head and poured over his face. Kurt's cool, calm, Kevin-Costner-in-a-suit-look poured onto the pavement and mingled with the runoff from more normal people. Laughter erupted. Kurt shot me a silencing glare. It didn't help. I turned away and tried to contain myself.

"I don't know. Maybe they're still at the crime scene," Kurt growled, moving away from the cascading water.

The song continued. Could be I was hearing it because Kurt was with me. It made me smile just thinking about it, I'd made the association between him and Costner some time ago and it stuck so tight, it's all I can think about when he's around. Thank God no one can see inside my head.

I needed to shake it off before I did something thoughtless. Another smile crept across my face as I watched Kurt straighten his suit jacket and flick beads of water from his shoulders. I'm sure it helped.

"What are you grinning at?" Kurt muttered, looking left then right. "We lost him!" "Unrelated," I replied. I couldn't wipe the smile from my face.

Time to focus.

Kurt brushed more water from his suit. How he could wear a suit and tie in this heat was beyond me. I bit my lip but the smile kept coming. In a last ditch effort to cover the smile I covered my mouth with my hand and pretended to yawn.

"Are we keeping you up, Conway?"

"Yeah," I replied and concentrated on the situation at hand. "It was a man we saw running away from the scene, yeah?"

"I think so," Kurt said.

"The murdering thief went inside somewhere."

"Into one of the buildings?" Kurt said, staring back down the street.

"There's nowhere else."

"That's a lot of doorways and buildings, and even more offices once you're inside."

Lee ambled across the road and joined us.

"He's gone, I dunno how, but he disappeared," Lee said. "Freaking Houdini."

"He must've gone into one of the buildings," I restated my theory. We weren't anywhere near a metro stop that I could see, so I doubted he disappeared via train. Doubting it and ruling it out were two different things. "Where's the nearest metro?"

"Which line?" Kurt replied.

I shrugged. "Any."

"13th Street."

Of course. Silly me. We were between Metro Center on 13th and Federal Triangle on 12th. I scanned the area again, hoping he'd pop up somewhere and wave a white flag. A laugh deep in my mind echoed the folly of my thoughts. Our Unsub isn't popping up. He's running.

"You think the Unsub took the Metro?" Kurt said.

"I hope not."

Orange, blue, and red lines passed through the Metro

Center, orange and blue through Federal Triangle. The Unsub could be gone for good. From the metro system, he could get out of DC and into either Virginia or Maryland. He could get to the yellow and green lines. He could take the yellow or blue line and go to Ronald Regan airport. He could take any line and connect with buses or pick up a car. If he chose the Metro, he could already be mist on the wind.

In my mind, it was a fine red mist as a speeding train hit him.

"Me too, but just in case I'll get Transit Police to go over the surveillance video." He pulled his phone from his pocket and made a call. I could hear Kurt talking to Transit but I wasn't listening. I did hear him say he'd forward a photograph as soon as we received one.

We hung around for a few minutes, watching the street for any sign of someone who looked like our man emerging from a building. Umbrellas in every direction. What a great way to hide, under a sea of umbrellas. The more mean-spirited part of me hoped for a gust of wind. Broken umbrellas upended in garbage bins along the streets always tickled me. My mind paused expecting to hear Rihanna singing 'Under My Umbrella.' It didn't happen. I thanked the music gods for sparing me that horror.

"Screw this, I need a coffee," I said, trying in vain to hide the snarly mood that had crept up on me.

"Strong black coffee," Kurt elaborated while wiping moisture from his brow. He ran his hands through his sandy blond hair – water flew in all directions.

"Good call, we'll stop in at the Firehook on Columbia Square on our way back." I bit my tongue before I asked if he could sing. The crazy was taking over. The dark masses were gathering. I hoped no one would shoot at me today.

I walked in silence to the Firehook, ever hoping to see our Unsub ducking out of Metro Center. No such luck. Armed with a double espresso the silence continued back to the office. A mute me seemed safest. The rain stopped. I took the lid off my coffee cup to let the precious black liquid cool. The men talked. They went over and over the escape of the alleged thief-murderer. I sort of listened. My brain was trying to understand how he disappeared as he did. He was right in front of me, running hard, arms pumping. He dodged a group of people on the sidewalk; by the time I reached them, he was gone. Vanished.

Maybe he slipped on a metro grating in the sidewalk and skidded down a storm drain? My mind went nuts with the storm drain thought. A balloon squeezed out of a drain opening in the gutter and floated away. A terrifying voice followed, "Want a balloon?"

Pennywise.

"Beep-beep, Ellie. They all float down here."

I tried to look away but everywhere I looked, I saw his hideous face and balloons. "Take your pick, E-E-E-Ellie."

Stop it, Ellie! Focus for God's sake. I shook my head. Pennywise tumbled to the brink of the storm drain. I shook again. He slithered over the edge and was gone.

Balloons drifted skyward. I was pretty sure our Unsub didn't slide down a storm drain. Pretty sure a freaky clown didn't pull him down one either.

A balloon inflated and popped. I jumped. Coffee sloshed in my cup threatening to splash over the rim. A quick look over my shoulder told me Kurt noticed.

"Everything okay?"

"Yeah," I replied. "A balloon popped."

The expression in his eyes changed from humor to confusion. "There was no balloon," Kurt said.

"Good," I replied. "Must've been in my head." I closed the conversation with a matter-of-fact tone and left it at that. Twice now someone has disappeared on the streets of Washington. My shooter vanished. Our Unsub vanished. I'm not a fan of coincidence. I tucked both thoughts away for safekeeping; something told me they were related in some way.

The disappearing Unsub caused several real scenarios to come into play, other than the Metro one. He could've stashed a disguise somewhere. We were looking for someone his approximate height, weight, and gender. Would we have noticed a woman leaving any of the buildings in the vicinity? Depending on how cocky he felt, he could've sauntered right by us dressed as a woman.

It entertained me that I imagined him as a woman. Not just a change of clothes, oh no, he changed gender. Atta girl! At least he didn't become a clown.

He couldn't have just grabbed an umbrella and strolled away in the crowd?

Another thought was that he never left the area. I fought the images of Pennywise pushing into my consciousness. He never left either. Fuck off, Pennywise, you don't exist!

Another balloon popped.

My mind scrambled to gather the thoughts released by the balloon.

The Unsub could have gone into one of the buildings and stayed there. Maybe an appointment. Who would think of committing a murder, robbing a jewelers, and then trotting off to keep an appointment with say, his accountant? If he arrived breathless, he could say he was running late. Or maybe he had time to chill in a stairwell and catch his breath for ten minutes prior to the appointment.

Then there was a new scenario involving Pennywise the clown and me losing my mind. I shut it down fast. Took a long sip of my coffee and let something other than clown-based-terror free. What if he worked in one of the buildings? I wanted the jewelry store's CCTV footage. If we had a picture we could ask around, see if anyone recognized him.

Chapter Eight
Bad Moon Rising

It was a relief to be back in our building. I scanned the foyer, no clowns. Once out of the elevator, I hurried to my office, leaving Kurt and Lee to fill Sam in.

I kicked my door shut. Before I could set my cup on my desk, my phone was ringing. Carla.

"Hey, honey, shouldn't you be in school?"

"I am, just wanted to see if you were coming home for dinner."

"At this stage I will be. What's up?"

"Nothing," she replied in usual teenage fashion. I'm supposed to use my motherly intuition and know what it is. Then she continued, "I want to have dinner – us, you know, family."

"Sounds good to me. You sure you're okay?"

"I'm fine, Mom." Her words were almost swallowed by an impatient sigh.

"Grandpa will be waiting for you after school. I'll be home as soon as I can. You sure everything's all right?"

"I said I was fine!" she snapped into my ear. "It's not me that gets shot going for coffee."

Ah, crap! I had nothing to say to that. She adjusted her tone before I could reprimand her. "I just want you to come home for dinner."

"Okay. I'll do my best." I'm not keen on making promises that I may not be able to keep.

"Please, Mom ... dinner tonight."

Her plea tugged at my heart.

"I'll do my best. Now I gotta change, I'm soaked. Be good." I hung up and placed my phone and coffee on my desk.

Fine?

Not.

Something was going on with her. How the hell did she hear about that shooting incident? As my child, Carla had every right to request my presence at dinner. We got used to being together while I was on leave for three months, then I went back to work and life went crazy. I felt I was failing her as a parent. She saw more of Rowan than she of did me, and he was a touring rock star. For a minute or two, I let images of Rowan float in front of my eyes. His smile. The way he flicked hair out of his eyes. The way he looked at me.

I studied the image in my mind. That wasn't Rowan. It started as Rowan but it wasn't. The blue eyes looking back at me were Kurt's. Oh, man. I batted the image away. With a sigh, I carried on.

From the cupboard, I took dry clothes and changed. My wet clothes hung in the corner of my office, steaming, with my boots under them. The silence in the office deafened me for a beat before the whir of the fans from the computer kicked in and added a dull background hum. Anything was preferable to the constant replaying of 'Maria Nay' in my head. Don't get me wrong, I have Modern West on my iPod. I'm a fan. Just not keen on hearing the same song over and over, to the exclusion of logical thought.

How did Carla hear about the shooting on Friday? Time to ask the all-knowing Google. I found a story on a gossip site. The headline was sensational, Rowan Grange's girlfriend shot on DC streets. Someone from one of the stores in the vicinity gave an interview about how I was shot. There were few details and it didn't sound like an eyewitness report. I suspected the person used information from one of the uniformed agents. I looked at how many times the story was shared over the various social media sites. Three hundred and fifty shares. There is no way Carla could have avoided it. Once again, Rowan being Rowan made life harder for me. Great.

Sipping my coffee, I pulled up satellite images of the area and traced my route from the jewelry store to where we lost sight of the suspect, six blocks west. I leaned back in the chair and thought about the chase.

Ten minutes later my email alert sounded. Sam forwarded me the CCTV recording from the jewelry store. As I watched the footage, I found a partial face. I cut the face and copied it to another program. I hoped to be able to run it through a few databases and maybe get an ID. I also sent a copy of the picture to Transit Police. It would help the Transit cops when they sat down and checked through the footage from the Metro Center. If they found him, they could track him through the Metro system. All was not lost if the Unsub took the Metro.

I repeated that to myself and did my best to believe it. You'd think the number and variety of cops within DC would prohibit this kind of crime in broad daylight. Running through the streets draws attention. Chasing someone draws more attention, yet no one reacted except to get out of our way, and our guy disappeared. It was perplexing.

Have people become that indifferent to their fellow man?

No, it was raining, unseasonably warm, and more crowded than a usual day in DC. The week before spring break meant large groups of schoolchildren on supervised outings, plus the usual volume of tourists and people who work in DC, all coming together on various sidewalks throughout the city.

Tourists, balloons, scary freaking clowns.

I watched the footage five times but could not tell if he stole anything or not. The Unsub and the jeweler discussed something. There was much arm waving from Bleich, the jeweler. A heated discussion by the look of the body language. But it ended. The Unsub turned away first and took two steps toward the door. Bleich turned his back as if he were walking away. Bleich never made it to the other side of the counter. He was dead within a minute. Every time I reached the part where the suspect killed the storeowner, I cringed. It was one thing seeing the aftermath but quite another watching the life snatched from someone.

Some sick part of me found that moment when life

evaporated fascinating. Snap. It was quick. I slowed down the images, frame-by-frame, watching what the Unsub did. Did he come unprepared? No. Did he think the jeweler would hand over his jewels? I doubt it. Did he want us to think this was opportunistic? Maybe. Did he always intend to subdue the jeweler but it went wrong? No.

I watched it again. This time without cringing, without closing my eyes. He'd been trained. Was he there to kill the jeweler? I considered the possibility that it was a hit. He'd killed like that before. It was fast and professional. Yet I had the feeling they knew each other. Why turn your back and walk away after what looked like a heated debate unless you didn't consider the person a threat?

It was time to run a quick background check on the jeweler. A few key strokes and quite a bit of information surfaced.

The jeweler was a man named Sigmund Bleich. He was fifty-four years old. Married to Marika, with three grown children. Sigmund Bleich, as far as I could tell with a cursory background check wasn't a known associate of anyone in the criminal world. He wasn't just a jeweler. He was a diamond cutter. A smile crossed my lips as I read more and learned something. I'd always thought all people who carved, cut, engraved, gem stones were lapidaries. But not so, diamond cutters are diamond cutters. No fancy name for them despite the special skills they need. So, Sigmund cut diamonds. I imagined he also was a man with nerves of steel and a very steady hand.

Without thinking, I found myself admiring the princess-cut diamond I still wore on my finger. Maybe it was time to take it off and put it away. Reflected light cast tiny butterflies across my desk. Not yet.

How did a man like Bleich come across a cold-blooded killer?

Using the mouse I scrolled through the pages churned up by Googling his name. In 1999 he cut a huge diamond. The Heathcote Diamond was reported as having an initial weight of four hundred and thirty-five carats before cutting which became four forty-five-carat diamonds, and a fifth diamond that weighed forty-eight carats after the cut. They were collectively called The Heathcote Diamonds. I struggled with that. It didn't matter how many times I looked at the one- carat diamond on my finger I could not imagine something forty-five or forty-eight carats. Tallying up the total diamond weight I discovered there was a lot lost in the cutting process. As far as I could tell, the diamonds were never sold. They remained in the possession of Sigmund Bleich. There was a display in 2002 soon after the cut was complete and again at a prestigious jewelry-cum-fundraising event in Washington about two weeks ago.

I picked up the phone receiver from its cradle and pressed three numbers.

Sandra answered within seconds.

"Has anyone spoken to Bleich's family?"

"Police have visited the family home but there was no one there."

"Let Metro police know we will handle it. There is something fishy about this whole case. I'll take a drive out to the house. Do you have an address?"

Sandra read out the address. I scrawled it on my desk blotter.

"Thank you." I hung up. I did some more searching and came up with both younger sons. "Ephram and Jonah," I mumbled, looking at pictures of them on their Facebook pages. Identical twins. Neither of them was involved in the family business. Both boys were in college; Ephram was completing a doctorate in mathematics and Jonah was at med school. They were twenty-five years old. The older brother, Zachary, worked with his father, but was in London on a buying trip. That was a pretty good alibi. Where was Mrs. Bleich? I wondered.

A photo of her came up in a search. Marika Bleich was an attractive dark-haired woman. She was involved in a fair amount of charity work; nice that she gave back to the community. I compared the photographs of her and her twin sons. It would be fair to say they favored their mother in looks.

Marika was similar to Maria. I waited to see if the song would reappear. But no.

Where was she? I surfed the net some more and discovered she was a lawyer who offered free legal counsel twice a week at an Anacostia community center. That's where she was. It said on the website that she was available from eight in the morning until five in the afternoon on Mondays and Thursdays. That saved a trip out to her home. I checked the time. It was almost midday.

I grabbed my jacket and called Sam. "Field trip."

"Meet you at the elevator," he replied.

I filled him in on the way down to the parking garage. The community center was twenty minutes away. We were blessed by the traffic gods, and nothing untoward happened on our journey. I've known it to take forty minutes to get to that side of town.

Chapter Nine
I Believe

We found the community center without any trouble, it was a pleasant building without too much graffiti, in an area Sam and I knew quite well. Most people would think long and hard about venturing across the river to Anacostia and then run in the other direction. Not us. We're all kinds of stupid. A smile flickered on my lips. It wasn't stupid – we'd done some good things in Anacostia and made a few friends in the process.

I looked around as I got out of the car, and wondered if I'd see any familiar faces. None was obvious on the street. I knew enough to know that our presence registered. The car alone would've sent whispers of Five-Oh through the streets. I just bet not one of the kids whispering five-oh had ever seen or heard of the original *Hawaii Five-o* police procedural drama series. I'd heard that the series was named in honor of Hawaii being the fiftieth state but I had no idea how five-oh came to mean police.

Sam opened the door to the building. Inside kids played basketball; on the far right was a doorway. Outside the door, several people sat on a bench seat. They didn't look like they were waiting for a game.

Sam indicated the bench. I nodded. We walked over, doing our best not to panic anyone. Not easy. It was a jumpy part of town. One guy scrambled to his feet and took off at a sprint. Sam hollered after him, "We're not here for anyone. Chill."

He slammed out the door. A second later his head popped back in.

"For reals?"

"For real. Chill man," Sam replied.

The young man put on his swagger and sauntered back to the seat. "Yo, Five-oh not here for us," he drawled.

I smiled then said, "You know Caps or Tats?"

The kid looked at me with open suspicion and with a shake of his head he refused to answer.

"I'm Agent Ellie – do you know Caps or Tats?" I dropped my voice which forced him to listen.

A light went on deep in his eyes. "Yo, Agent Ellie – why didn't you say so? Everyone round here knows you."

Sam knocked on the door. No one answered, yet we could hear muffled voices from within the room.

Sam knocked again.

Still nothing.

"Hey, what's your name?" he said to the kid.

"Jermaine."

"Jermaine – is the lawyer in?"

"I hope so, man." He looked disturbed by the question. "I been waiting all day, y'all."

The other two people on the bench nodded in agreement.

"All day?" Sam affirmed checking his watch. "It's half twelve."

"Yo, all morning, all day." He shrugged. "I be waiting a long time. She's real good – otherwise I'd go somewhere else."

I got the feeling there wasn't much choice and somewhere else would cost a lot more than the kid had.

"All of you been waiting a while?" Sam said to the others.

They nodded.

My heart sank. Sam and I looked at each other for a beat, his eyes saying what I thought. There was nothing good behind the door. I took latex gloves from my pocket and put them on. Sam did the same.

I pulled my Glock and motioned for everyone to move away from the door. Sam's gun was in his hand. The basketball game stopped. An ominous silence fell.

I knocked on the door and called out. No answer.

I tried the handle.

Locked.

I looked at Jermaine. "You can run, right? Go get Caps." Caps would know if any strangers had been around, he'd also help us keep everyone calm. We were going to need some calm.

"Yes, ma'am." He took off as though his ass was on fire.

"Want me to do that, Chicky?" Sam whispered indicating to the door.

"Nah, I got it."

He shrugged. "I can kick in a door."

"Humor me. You can do the next one."

Sam stepped aside.

I took a breath, braced myself on the doorframe, and

kicked the wood by the door handle and the lock. Wood splintered. The lock groaned. I kicked again. The door scraped the frame as it opened.

I staggered a little getting my balance and almost fell through the doorway. Sam grabbed my arm to steady me.

"You okay?"

"Yep," I replied. My eyes fell on the desk by the far wall. A woman was slumped in a pool of blood. The metallic smell hit me hard and took me back to every crime scene I'd ever visited.

Someone gasped behind me. I took a quick look over my shoulder. It was one of the basketball players. Color faded fast from his face and neck. "Sit on the floor. Put your head between your knees. You'll be okay," I said. "Just breathe."

Meanwhile, I tried not to breathe. The cloying, metallic smell of blood crawled into my nose and throat; its foul tendrils grabbed at my tonsils and threatened to choke me. I coughed. I smothered the desire to pull up my shirt to cover my nose and mouth to filter the smell out; I fought it with every fiber in my being. Unprofessional conduct.

My eyes were drawn to something on the floor. It was the origin of the voices: a CD player. That was just clever enough to keep everyone from suspecting what was going on behind the closed door.

My breathing was shallow and controlled. Viewing the room in increments seemed safer than letting the scene pummel me with its horror. I steeled myself for the inevitable. Not without effort, I mentally stepped back from the scene and looked around. Forcing myself to see the entire room and deal with what was in front of me wasn't easy.

My focus changed with each slow breath until I could approach the task with objectivity. There was nowhere for anyone to hide. The window was half-open, but barred. The door had been locked from the inside. I moved her hair and placed two fingers on her carotid artery. No pulse, not that I expected one. A lot of blood had spilled from the desk onto the floor. I inspected Marika's wounds. Someone had beaten her about the head and face with something solid.

She was more hamburger than human. I could see bits of skull and hair on the walls. Splatter. Maybe the weapon was a baseball bat or chair leg.

I considered it possible that she died before her husband but the killer did not want her discovered until much later. Which made sense – if she were found too early, it would ruin his plan to kill the husband. Why would someone want to kill them both?

I ripped the soiled latex gloves off my hands, balled them up and handed them to Sam. He dropped them into an open evidence bag he'd placed by the door for our trash.

My hand slipped onto my phone. "Sandra – we need to locate the Bleich boys. Find them and set up protection – I want them in a safe house." It was possible they were behind the deaths; it wouldn't be the first time children killed their parents. Working on the adage innocent until proven guilty, their safety was a priority.

"I've got the address." Her fingers tapped at the keys on her keyboard. "I will send Lee and Kurt."

"Thanks, and send uniforms with them." I paused. "Call me when the kids are safe." I wanted at least one of the boys to do the formal identifications; it would cut down on the requirement for DNA and there was the possibility that viewing the bodies would trigger something, a smidge of visible guilt, a confession, or a memory.

"Absolutely," she said and hung up.

I slid my phone back into my pocket, pulled out a fresh pair of latex gloves, and used one to turn off the CD player. There was a CD jewel case on the floor. I looked at the cover where it lay. An audio book. I checked the CD player settings. It was on repeat. The damn thing had been playing for hours.

Sam disappeared from view. His head bobbed up from the other side of the desk. "Look at this," he said.

I joined him, dodging congealing blood puddles. Sam pointed to something long and wooden, hair and blood stuck to it like a macabre artwork. I bent down a little and peered under the desk.

"Is that a wooden baseball bat?"

"I'd say so," Sam replied. "Could be our murder weapon."

"Yep."

We left everything where it was so the crime scene unit

could photograph the room and gather evidence when they arrived.

A babble of voices and commotion outside interested me. I went to investigate. Caps stood in the middle of the basketball court slinging orders. He stopped and nodded at me. "Setting up a perimeter, Agent Ellie, until you can get your crime scene people here."

No surprise. If it weren't for a string of convictions and some decent jail time, he'd make a damn good Fed. His leadership and people skills were enviable. I know I envied them, because me slapping anyone upside the head was frowned upon.

"Thanks, Caps. You and I need to talk, but gimme a few, yeah?"

"Yeah." He carried on doing a fine impersonation of a drill sergeant.

I hustled back to Sam. He was calling in the murder and requesting a Crime Scene Unit.

The woman at the desk stared at me with lifeless cloudy eyes. A couple of times I thought her eyes followed me. Creepy.

Thoughts about the dead husband and wife revolved in my head. It could be over a diamond but it sure didn't feel like it. 'Maria Nay' started up again. And again, it made no sense. The song interfered with my thought processes. I let the words wash over me hoping one or two would flag something useful. Nothing grabbed me.

It took a lot of effort to ignore the performance in my mind and concentrate on the now. I looked at the lock. It wasn't the most secure of locks, one of the older types within the door handle. You push the button to lock the door. I knew from the bathroom at home when we were kids that you could lock it then shut the door. My brother used to think it was funny to leave the bathroom with the door locked. It also taught me how easy it was to pick that type of lock using a knife. I checked the outside, no marks on the lock. It seemed feasible that Marika let the person in. The visitor then clubbed her to death, locking the door as he or she left.

Vicious. Would've been noisy too.

I went back out into the hall and said, "Who was here first this morning?"

They all looked at each other and shrugged. Caps rocked up in front of me. He took a step back and stood next to me. "Yo yo, y'all, don't be trippin', the lady has a question."

He got their attention.

"Who was here first and what time did you arrive?" I said.

A young man about twenty years old came forward. "I gots here at eight-thirty."

"Thank you. Anyone earlier?" Everyone shook their heads. "So you and Jermaine were here the earliest? What's your name?"

"Mikey," he said.

"Was anyone else here, someone who looked out of place?" I swept my arm around the hall. "Or in there with Mrs. Bleich?"

He looked at Caps. There was an almost imperceptible nod from Caps. I knew that nod and that look.

"Mikey, you need to tell me."

"Ms. Marika she was talking to someone, talking loud when I arrived."

"Loud like shouting? Or loud excited talking."

"Like shouting but not angry, controlled and loud."

"Did you hear anyone else?"

He shook his head. "But I did record Ms. Marika."

I smiled. "You recorded her?"

"Was playing with my mp3 player. It records shit. So I tried it out. No harm."

"None at all, can I hear it?"

He handed the small black device to me. "Keep it."

That was my intention. "I'll get it back to you once we've downloaded the recording."

He nodded. "I never saw no one leave."

"Were you here the whole time?"

"Yeah, I wanted to see Ms. Marika today. Ya know if you leave, someone takes your spot." He glanced toward Jermaine. Little bit of rivalry perhaps.

"Did you hear anything else?"

"No. I recorded some of the talking then listened to music."

Music. I didn't imagine for one second he was listening to anything I classified as music. I checked the volume on his mp3 player. Volume set to stun. He sure wouldn't have heard anything external. A bomb could've gone off and it wouldn't have interrupted him.

"Thank you."

He stepped aside. I called out to Jermaine, "Jermaine do you have one of these too?" The mp3 player was in my hand, I held it up for him to see.

"Yes, ma'am."

"Show me."

Jermaine ambled over. He took his mp3 player from his pocket and handed it to me. I checked the volume. Also set to stun, as I expected.

"Why'd you do that?" he said as I handed it back with a smile.

"Were you listening to that this morning?"

"Yeah. Can't sit here with no tunes." He shrugged.

As I thought. You'd be hard pushed to find anyone under thirty who didn't wear headphones or a smaller equivalent. They may as well live in a fuc'n bubble. No wonder this generation will suffer from hearing loss by age twenty-five.

"Thank you, Jermaine." I turned to Caps. "I'll be back there with Sam."

"I'll be here. You need anything, you holler." A frown creased his brow. "Is it true what they said … you were shot on F?"

I shrugged. "It was nothing, a flesh wound."

Caps frown flipped and became a full-blown grin. "Watch your back out there," he said. "I ask around …"

"I appreciate it."

Armed with the recording I went back to Sam.

"We have a recording of Marika to listen to." It bugged

94

me that someone was here but no one saw anyone leaving. I handed Sam the mp3 player and looked around the room. We knew there was one door and a barred window, but how else could someone leave? It dawned on me as I looked up. "Sam, a trapdoor, right above the desk."

He looked up. We both looked at the surface of the desk. A sizable blood pool. Marika's head. Paper work and the desk surface splattered in blood and brain matter. Not much by way of a clear space. No footprint, but the pooled blood right under the trap door was displaced toward one edge. We looked at each other; I'm guessing my frown mimicked his.

"Unless he's Houdini I don't see how he got up there without leaving some kind of trace," I said looking from the desk to the ceiling. "And tall, or at least six foot. On second thoughts, I would take off my shoes and throw them up first, then climb up. Socks leave less impression than soles of shoes. See this?" I pointed to the displaced area. "No footprint as such but the edge of the pool is different from the rest of the blood. I'd say he was wearing socks not shoes. It would be easier to dodge the bulk of the bloody goop in socks."

"And again, you are scary."

I smiled. "I would make an excellent criminal – you're only scared because you know no one could catch me."

He lit the room with his brilliant smile. "I'd catch you. Let's find out where it goes," Sam said. He pocketed the mp3 player and headed out the door. "Yo, Caps. Trapdoor in the ceiling in Marika's office – is there another one?"

"My brutha, Agent Sam." Their right hands met in midair, which was followed by a fast but solid man hug. "There is another trapdoor in the kitchen." He pointed to the other end of the hall.

We ran over and looked. The trapdoor was open. It opened upward. There was a brownish smudge on the floor underneath. I inspected the smudge and followed a short mucky trail to the window above the sink. "There's blood here, potential transfer from clothing." I saw smears on the edge of the counter and across a cupboard. "The killer went out the window then pushed it almost shut from the outside." I leaned over the countertop and peered out the window, it was a long drop to the ground below. "We might get lucky with prints on the outside of the frame."

"This wasn't an opportunistic thing – or a death after a heated argument," Sam said.

"Nope, this was planned. The Unsub already knew how to get out. We're looking for someone who has been here before."

I stuck my head out the kitchen door and called Caps over. "Seen anyone new around in the last few weeks?"

"Not myself."

"Someone has?"

"Yeah. There was talk of someone hanging around the hall wanting to talk to Mrs. Bleich. A couple of the boys ran him off. She comes here to help our community, not suits who can afford to hire her."

A suit.

"How many times did the boys run this person off?"

"Two, maybe."

And for the first time since I'd shot him, I heard Mac's voice loud and clear, "Maybe's ass." Guess he hadn't gone after all.

I raised an eyebrow. "Two?"

"Could be three, no more than four."

"Persistent. Can you find someone who saw him or spoke to him?"

"Sure." He beckoned a young man over. He wasn't more than sixteen. "Bring me Carmine and Samuel."

Five minutes later two young men appeared in front of Caps. He told them to answer all our questions. They shuffled from foot to foot and kept their eyes lowered. I asked them about the stranger. They didn't know his name. Sam called the office and asked for a few pictures of the family and one of the Unsub sent to his phone. First he showed them a picture of Mr. Bleich, just in case it was her husband visiting. Then all three of the Bleich boys. None of them was recognized. He showed them a photograph of the Unsub pulled from the surveillance footage of the jewelry store.

"That looks like him," Carmine said, then peered closer.

"You're sure?"

"Suits all kinda look the same," Carmine said with a lazy shrug.

I showed the picture to Samuel again. "This guy?"

"Maybe. I dunno. They all look the same."

"So a definite maybe?"

Both nodded.

I looked at Caps. I'd seen dogs make better witnesses. Come to think of it I've seen goldfish make better witnesses. He dismissed them saying they weren't to talk to anyone about this and to be ready to answer more questions later.

Movement by the door caught my eye. Uniformed officers entered the hall. I waved. Behind them, I saw the familiar dark jackets of the FBI Crime Scene Unit. Then I saw Cheryl Harris, our Medical Examiner. I waved. She waved back and joined us.

"Cheryl," I said, shaking her hand. "A time of death would be helpful."

"Are you staying?"

I shook my head. "No, call me."

"Will do."

We didn't do a lot of small talk. Cheryl followed the Crime Scene team into the office.

"Let's get out of here," I said to Sam. "We need to talk to the sons and ID the Unsub. Back to the bat cave."

On our way to the car, Sam handed me the Mp3 player he'd dropped into his pocket earlier.

"Have a feeling you'll want to listen to this," he said.

"You'd be right." I shoved it into my pocket for later.

Chapter Ten
Complicated

I left Sam trying to get an update from Lee and Kurt while I disappeared into my office and took a virtual look at the area around the jewelry store. We were dealing with someone who planned details. We had witnesses saying our Unsub may have been seen at the community center, asking to see Marika Bleich. Really, all we knew was that a man in a suit went looking for her a few times. I scanned the route the Unsub took from the jewelry store hoping to find an answer as to his whereabouts.

He could have used any one of a variety of possible escape routes. It appeared logical to me that the Unsub went into a building. I put myself in his shoes. Nothing about the crime felt opportunistic – it might have been to start with, when all we had was a tip-off about a robbery in progress and then a foot pursuit of a possible robbery gone wrong. Everything changed when we found Marika's body. He'd planned every aspect with meticulous care, every aspect. We came in with the jeweler's death, but that wasn't where this all started.

I listened to the recording of the call I received tipping us off to the jewelry robbery. A woman's voice. She didn't give a name. Sandra traced the call to a public phone at a Metro station. Uniforms found nothing. Public phones are lousy with fingerprints, hence of little use to our investigation.

I played the phone call again. Kevin Costner started back up. I shut off the recording. The song stopped. When I turned it on again, Kevin was back singing 'Maria Nay.' I wrote across my desk blotter, "The woman who tipped us off was Maria." The song stopped. I still needed to rule out Marika Bleich as the tipster, even though my gut told me she'd been long dead and it was someone called Maria.

Maybe I should start referring to my gut as Kevin? Talk about a slippery slope.

From my pocket I fished out the mp3 player I'd borrowed from one of the young men at the community center. I plugged it into a USB port on my computer and found the file he'd recorded earlier, copied the file to the computer and disconnected the mp3 player. I didn't want to risk corrupting the original file in any way. The recording of Marika and her possible assailant wasn't as clear as I'd hoped. I listened twice then the third time I wrote key words. The clearest voice was hers. The words that stood out were, "no", "stop", "Sigmund." Then a clear sentence, "The boys don't know anything."

If someone wearing a suit hadn't been hanging around the community center I'd be wondering if Sigmund murdered his wife. In all fairness, he still could have.

It was possible that Sigmund murdered his wife and was then himself a victim of an attempted robbery gone bad. Possible maybe.

I made a call to the Forensic Audio, Video, and Image Analysis Unit in Quantico. "It's SSA Conway. I have a recording I need analyzed. Can you give this priority and run both voices against all known databases, please."

"Yes, ma'am. Special requests?"

It's as if he could read my mind.

"I need to confirm the identity of both parties on this recording. One party may be Sigmund Bleich. I doubt he'll be in any of our criminal databases but he was interviewed by the media in 2002 about a large diamond. On second thoughts, make sure you do run both voices through all our databases even if you get a media match."

People aren't always who they seem to be. Sigmund Bleich didn't show up in my background check but that didn't mean he didn't operate under an alias. Something hinky was going on. My gut was insistent that this was not a simple case of husband kills wife and then is the random victim of a killer himself. Way to go, Kevin.

"Yes, ma'am. I'll send someone to collect the recording."

"Thank you."

It would've been quicker to email him the recording but the mp3 player was the vessel that contained the evidence and the vessel in this case could hold secrets a downloaded file might not, it also could add its own noise to a recording. So best to send the whole thing and let the experts deal with it.

I filled in the back of an evidence envelope with my name, the case number, time and date then dropped the mp3 player into it.

For a minute I let myself think about Mac and the

whole shooting his ghost incident. I gave Sean a call.

"It's Ellie – any progress on the blood?"

"Not yet. I'll let you know as soon as I do."

"Thanks."

"Ellie, don't worry. I'll figure it out."

I hung up and pressed the worrisome thoughts deep in my mind. I needed more than one cinder block to hold them in place. I added a couple more and anchored the craziness but for how long I didn't know.

My mind flipped back to wondering how the Unsub left the city without touching the puddle-filled streets and without risking capture. I thought the Unsub was a planner; that meant he knew about the CCTV in the store. Time to accept that he knows we know what he looks like and assume he knows we are coming after him. How does that help him? I doubt it helped him in any way, except fueling his adrenaline and upping the stakes. If that's the case, then catching the sick son-of-a-bitch might be real fun and even interesting.

Another thought popped up and I found myself staring at the ceiling.

Helicopter. But private operators were not allowed to fly within Washington DC airspace, not without special clearance, unless it's a life flight or air ambulance, because they already have clearance. The alternative would be military or police use – but that's not private, that's government.

Government would put a whole new spin on things. I pulled back from that.

How could someone order a life flight for a specific time? Well, a person could, if the pilot was in on the crime.

I checked the online street map up of the area again and looked for buildings with helipads. There was one in the vicinity. A disused heliport on top of the Washington Post building. Time to make a call. I called the Delta SAC, Caine Grafton. If anyone would know the protocol for bringing a helicopter into the city, he would.

"Caine, I have a question?"

"This about the police case?"

"Um, it's not police, it's mine," I replied. It's interesting, police aren't getting this case. "Can a private helicopter land on any heliport within Washington?"

"You're talking about a Flight Restricted Zone."

"So, no?"

"Not necessarily no, there is a restriction to government, some scheduled commercial, and limited waivered flights."

"Thanks, would a life flight be waivered?"

"You should check that. 'Limited waivered flights' is what I have in front of me and that would make sense for medevac."

I imagined his twitch becoming extreme. "Since when did government *anything* have to make sense?"

"Exactly. Check."

I hung up and called Ronald Reagan Airport and asked if any helicopters lodged flight plans for the DC area, and which companies were allowed to fly within DC. They had nothing unusual to report.

STAT Medevac was based at Children's National Medical Center on Michigan Avenue N.W, DC. I pulled up their primary coverage area. They fitted. MedSTAR were at Washington Hospital Center on Irving. As much as they sounded like they were miles apart they were in fact very close.

I put in calls to both.

Neither sent helicopters to anywhere helpful to our Unsub. MedSTAR received a call to a multi-vehicle crash in Maryland but that was it except for some patient transfer work. STAT Medevac had two patient transfers. I checked hospitals in the surrounding areas, just in case. Nothing flying into, or out of, DC within two hours of our disappearing Unsub.

So, if it wasn't a helicopter that got him out, where did he go?

An accomplice.

I went back to my original thought. Was there a connection to one of the buildings? My digging continued. Five minutes later, my desk phone rang. Kurt's name flashed on the display.

"Kurt?" I said as I answered the call.

"We're in Georgetown, sending you pictures now."

My cell phone buzzed on my desk. I picked it up. Sure enough there were pictures.

"Are they both dead?"

"Yes. Found them in the apartment."

"Guess they didn't kill mom and dad then. I'm on my

way."

"We'll wait."

While I had my phone in my hand, I called Cheryl hoping she could tell me something.

"It's Ellie. Do you have a time of death for Mrs. Bleich for me?"

"Liver temp at the crime scene suggested between eight and ten this morning," Cheryl replied.

"Okay, thank you. You heard from SSA Henderson?"

"Yes, a double murder in Georgetown," she replied. "Busy day."

"Very ..."

I pocketed my cell phone and called out to Sam. "Another crime scene. Let's go."

He was already outside my door. I saw him put his phone in his jacket pocket. "I know, got the update."

Chapter Eleven
Blood on Blood

Sam was talking to uniformed officers standing a few feet away from the apartment door. I paused and tugged disposable bootees over my boots and put on latex gloves.

The inside of the apartment was decorated with more taste than I'd expect to find in a student's abode. There were no take-out containers strewn about, or empty beer cans. The muted brown tones of the furnishings felt warm, inviting and a little like a woman pulled it all together rather than two young men. Lee moved across a doorway, then stepped back and smiled at me.

"In here, Ellie."

"Whose room is this?" I said.

"Ephram's," Lee said. He took a step back opening up my view of the bed.

A man wearing pajamas lay sprawled face down across the bed, his head hanging over the far side. That didn't look comfortable. Crouching for a closer inspection, I saw the telltale petechial hemorrhaging in his eyes.

Parts of my training ran through my head: "The presence of petechiae often indicates a death by manual strangulation, hanging, or smothering. The hemorrhages occur when blood leaks from the tiny capillaries in the eyes, which can rupture due to increased pressure on the veins in the head when the airways are obstructed." Nice.

I looked for signs of strangulation. There was no

bruising or marking of the neck. I thought back to the video footage from the jewelry store then ran through a probable scenario again. A sleeper hold or, if you prefer, a carotid restraint hold, can be used to strangle someone, because the arm is used to apply pressure to the neck and not just the fingers, often leaving no bruising or marking.

"He's on top of the bed, not in it," I said. "Anything to indicate he fought back?"

Lee shook his head. "His clothing isn't skewed at all either. He may have been asleep on the bed not in it when he was attacked."

That was a possibility. Or he could have gone to the bathroom and been taken by surprise. I lifted his pajama top. There was bruising on his back. To me it looked as though someone knelt on him. I imagined a scene where Ephram came back from the bathroom. The Unsub approached from behind, knocking him onto the bed, planting one knee firmly in the middle of his back and applied a sleeper hold.

Goodnight Ephram.

"Where's the other one?" I said.

"Next door," Lee said. "Come on."

The next room was just as well put together as the first but in different colors, more greens than earthy browns. Jonah's body was on the floor on the far side of the bed. Another asphyxiation. Why was he on the floor? I looked at how his body lay. Crumpled. He was strangled from behind and then slumped to the floor. Or lowered by the Unsub so he didn't drop and wake his brother with the thud. For all we knew he may have been first.

"I don't get it. The mother was beaten with a horrific amount of force and the father's neck broken. By the look of these two they were strangled by someone who knew what they were doing. Their deaths are very controlled. Three very controlled deaths and one displaying extreme violence that does not fit." I considered the Unsub was a person capable of cold, quick death; I'd seen him break Sigmund's neck. But why beat the mother? So much anger in that death.

Anger was out of place. If he were an independent contractor, he wouldn't be killing out of anger.

"It's a conundrum," Lee said.

"Been reading the dictionary again?"

He smiled. "Doing crosswords."

"We're going to need full autopsies on the entire family." And that would take way too long but I needed to know if anything else was going on. I had to be sure of the cause and manner of death. "Do you think anything is missing here?"

"Look how tidy this place is? If anyone turned it over they did so with great care and put everything back," Lee replied.

"Or they knew where whatever they wanted was kept ..." I said, looking around the room. "Did you find a safe?"

Lee shook his head. "You think there is one?"

"Yep."

Kurt strode over. "Medical Examiner is here. You ready for Cheryl to come in?"

"Yes. See if we can get a time of death. Kurt, have you found a safe?"

He shook his head. "I'll take the ME into Ephram first."

I nodded and pulled my phone from my pocket. "Sandra, we need to track down the remaining brother in London. Misha is in London - can you ask if he would locate Zachary Bleich and escort him back to Washington. Get Scotland Yard involved too. Make sure everyone understands Zachary could be in danger."

Lee oozed patience as he waited. Four members of one family dead. Monday was not going well for the Bleich family at all. Lee and I began hunting for a safe. There didn't need to be one, it just felt like there was something more to the deaths. Maybe I wanted there to be more.

I waited, but Mac's voice didn't ring out in the cavernous space in my head.

"Hey, what's up?" Lee said. He was standing in front of me.

"Nothing," I replied. "Nothing at all." Then it hit me, as intrusive and insane as it was hearing Mac all the time, I missed his voice in my head. A sadness I couldn't explain threatened to swamp me.

"Doesn't look like nothing, Chicky." Concern laced his words together, matching the gathering frown on his brow.

"I'm okay." I shook off the feeling. "If I were a safe where would I be?"

Lee smiled. "In the floor, under the carpet in a closet."

"How about in the bottom of the pantry in the kitchen?"

We smiled at each other and hurried to the kitchen. The room was immaculate. So much so, I figured they had a housekeeper. I called Sandra back. "Can you find out if the Bleich boys had a housekeeper and if the parents did as well, please?"

"Sure."

"I know the list is getting pretty long over there, but any luck with Misha?"

"I've spoken to him. He's looking for Zachary."

"Police?"

"Them too."

"You rock."

"I know," she replied and hung up.

Lee opened the pantry doors and crouched down. He pulled out a vegetable bin from the bottom of the cupboard and looked behind it, shining his flashlight into the very back. "In anyone else's house I'd say there would be dust to let us know whether something had been moved recently or not. But there isn't even a crumb on the floor here."

"Is there anything there?"

"Yep, there is." He dragged out the vegetable bin. "Have a look." Lee lit the floor within the pantry with his flashlight beam.

"Looks like a safe to me," I said. I could see the combination lock. It was set just below floor level. "Get someone in here to look for latent prints before we try opening it."

Lee summoned a crime scene tech who wasn't busy like the other three.

We stood out of the way and talked while the tech lifted prints.

"Do you think the Unsub knew about the safe?" There was some pure speculation required on Lee's part if he was going to attempt an answer.

Cheryl appeared in the kitchen. "Ellie, I'm estimating time of death for both boys at between three and six this morning. They are the children of the earlier female victim, yes?"

"Yes."

"This is where the killing started," she replied. "The mother was killed between eight and ten."

I nodded. "Thank you."

"I'll get the autopsy reports to you as soon as possible."

Cheryl disappeared leaving Lee and I staring at the safe.

"You think this has something to do with what is or isn't in that?" Lee said, pointing at the safe.

"I have no idea." For once, I was clueless. No songs. No possible motive for the twins' deaths, or why it all started with them.

Lee rocked back on his heels. "If our Unsub wanted something – the twin's health and wellbeing would be leverage?"

"You asking me, or telling me?"

"Both."

"They could well have been leverage, maybe it didn't work; maybe the mother was tougher than the Unsub thought? Something pissed off our guy – if indeed it was our guy who killed the mother. The violence of the attack was too much. Her death doesn't fit."

He nodded. "What do we know for sure?" Lee said watching the crime scene techs moving around the apartment. "The boys were killed first – their deaths were quick and clean. The mother beaten to death a few hours later. Someone wearing a suit was seen at the community center a few times asking for her."

I interrupted Lee. "She clearly said her husband's name while in the room with an Unsub. She also said, 'No', 'stop', and 'the boys don't know anything.'" I stood in the middle of the room and shoved my hands in my pockets. "The boys don't know anything."

"We need to know what the boys didn't know," Lee muttered, joining me. "Was there a time stamp on the CCTV footage of the father's death?"

I nodded. "He was killed at ten-thirty-two a.m."

"Precise," Lee said.

"I watched it a few times."

We stared at each other. My mind calculating the distance covered by the Unsub and the timing. It could have been one guy. Could. But if it was, he had some kind of personal connection to Marika Bleich.

Chapter Twelve
Bullet

There was no sense waiting at Ephram and Jonah's apartment for the locksmith. We left the crime scene unit to do the scene examination, intending to go back with the locksmith once the scene was cleared.

Everyone was working as I strolled through the bullpen on my way back to my office with a fresh coffee. I glanced up at the clock on the wall. Four deaths and it wasn't even late afternoon.

Even so, I could see dinner with Carla slipping away. I was going to have a sulky teenager on my hands. Sulky teenagers are not my favorite things and it doesn't matter that I *know* it's all about them. I was struggling with this new phase of Carla's; until the last week or so she'd always been a sweet, accommodating, loving kid. It was hard to see her with sharp pointy horns. It was little consolation that I knew teenagers were not the most altruistic of creatures and that mine was better than most.

The noises of the office surrounded me. All of Delta A and Delta C, and a couple of Delta B agents were in the office. Tapping of keys on computer key boards, low voices, phones ringing. No one looked up. I paused as my foot connected with something on the floor, half under a desk. With a shake of my head I called out, "Wanna tell me whose Beretta this is?" I looked around and was met with amused stares. "I'm not joking, people. Someone is missing an M9."

I couldn't even think who used an M9 in Delta. Everyone I could think of used either a Sig or a Glock. M9 was old school military. I thought a moment longer. SAC Caine Grafton used an M9 as his backup weapon. His gun would not be on our floor.

I scanned the room waiting for an answer.

Perplexed heads shook.

That was less than helpful.

"The things I find on the floor in here defy reason." I leaned down and straightened back up, leaving the gun where it was. Why would a gun be on the floor? For no *good* reason. My stomach sank. Time to get everyone out. I took a few steps away from the new-looking black gun and cleared my throat. Everyone looked up.

"I want you all to leave the building, now." Chairs rolled on the carpet as everyone stood up. Kurt appeared next to me, I sensed him without seeing him and said, "Send out an alert, evacuate this section and put the rest of the building on alert." He pulled his cell phone from his pocket and made the call while shepherding agents from the area. A warning siren sounded. I glanced at Kurt; he nodded his head and carried on.

Somewhere deep inside a sense of urgency bonded with a desire to run. I quelled it with a hefty lump of responsibility.

I lifted the receiver of the phone closest to me and called the bomb squad. "It's SSA Ellie Conway, Hoover building. We have a suspicious handgun in the Delta Bullpen."

"And you call us?"

A smile crept over my face. "Tony, you're a shit. I'm not having my team touch dodgy ordinance."

"Be right there, Conway. You evacuating your section?"

"Absofuckinglutely."

I hung up.

"Let's go," Kurt said, wrapping his fingers around my upper arm and steering me to the nearest exit. Within seconds, we were filing down the stairs with the occupants of the other rooms in our area of the building. A gentle buzz gathered by the walls, I recognized the buzz as left over words from owners who'd moved on. A small silver butterfly darted from shadows high on the wall, spiraled downward, then soared up and out of sight.

A gun in the bullpen. An Unsub who disappeared right in front of us. A family all but annihilated. Today was fun.

My phone rang, filling the gap at the bottom of the stairwell with Grange. I didn't need to look to know who was calling me. I answered as Kurt escorted me across the foyer and down the steps.

"Carla?"

"Mom, can Joey come for dinner?"

What happened to a family dinner? At least she sounded somewhat happier.

"Sure, tell Grandpa I said it was okay." I checked my watch and girded my loins before continuing. "Honey, I might be late."

She sucked in air. "How late?"

"Don't know yet, we have a situation developing here."

Carla sighed. She hung up; no goodbye, just dead air. It was her usual reaction when things didn't go her way.

Once outside I called her back. "I will do my best to be home for dinner."

"I know, Mom, you *always* do your *best* to be *home* for dinner," she muttered, her anger power-punching little holes in her words.

Kurt was watching me with interest. He mouthed the words, "Everything all right at home?"

I shrugged and mouthed back, "Don't think so."

"Carla, what's wrong with you today?"

"Nothing." Her tone lacked the conviction of her words.

"Try again."

"I just want you to come home for dinner, please."

"I said I'd do my best." I sensed an escalation in tension but was powerless to stop it.

"You're *never* home! Anything could happen!"

It felt like she'd slapped me. I forced calm into my voice, "What could happen, Carla?"

She paused a little too long before snapping, "Didn't you hear about New Zealand, and the earthquakes?"

Earthquakes? She's worried about earthquakes in Virginia? I remember one about eight years ago; it sounded like a train and was over in an instant. I doubt it was even as high as a four on the Richter scale.

"Another one?" I said, hoping she'd tell me what was wrong.

"Yes, they had another big one! Thought your cop friend would have told you." Carla's tone bordered on accusation. "Did you check your email?"

"Honey, I've been working." I heard her huff with annoyance. It was time to lay it out for her. "Right now, there is a possible bomb outside my office door and I'm investigating the deaths of an entire family. I haven't been at my desk much today to check my email."

"Dead people don't count, Mom." Her voice rose to an uncomfortable squeal. I held the phone away to protect my hearing. "Do they care if you don't come home for dinner or if an earthquake makes the house fall over or if someone shoots you on the street?"

I took a breath. I could feel steam pouring out my ears as I fought to contain myself before I boiled over.

Calm. Think calm. Soothing blue. Think facts. I decided to ignore the shooting comment. There was nothing I could do about that.

"Carla, the house is not going to fall over. We live in Virginia, not New Zealand, or even California. Here in Virginia we are in the middle of a tectonic plate, not on the edge like California, New Zealand, or Japan. Virginia hasn't had a big earthquake since eighteen ninety-seven and even then it was a five point eight, nowhere near as big or devastating as the earthquakes overseas in recent months."

With hindsight, mentioning Japan wasn't smart.

"But we could, Mom. We could and you wouldn't be here." She took a breath. "There could be a tsunami."

"It's doubtful. You'll be okay. If something happened, I would get to you." I crossed my fingers. Never promise something you can't deliver. "We have an earthquake plan, yes?" I knew we did and she knew we did. We also had a zombie survival plan. It's how I roll.

She said yes, but it was reluctant. When the 'but' began to emerge I said, "Do you know how much I love you, Carla?"

A smile lifted her voice as she spoke, "More than all the stars in the sky. I love you too, Mom."

It wasn't easy to hang up. There was something wrong and it had nothing to do with earthquakes in New Zealand or tsunamis in Japan. It had something to do with me working long hours though. I did know I'd be taking five minutes to check in with Faye down in New Zealand to see what they needed from us by way of support. If there was anything the FBI could do, I knew we'd do it. Another mental note was scrawled across the whiteboard in my mind, in big red letters. Call Faye.

Kurt and I stood together in silence. Sam, Lee, and Sandra were about four feet away. I saw Caine talking with Director O'Hare across the road. Agents milled about. Waiting. The waiting was the worst. It never occurred to me that the gun might have an innocent explanation. Last week it might have, but not today. Not after my random shooting on F Street. Not after a phone call tipping us off to a 'robbery'. Not after four people in one family were murdered. I didn't for one moment feel guilty about disrupting the afternoon of a bunch of agents. A long time ago I learned not to second guess my gut.

It told me something was wrong in Carla's world and that the Beretta M9 in our bullpen was a sinister twist to an already difficult day.

My phone rang and vibrated in my pocket. I answered it to find Tony on the other end.

"Good call, Conway. The barrel on that berretta was packed with a plastic explosive compound."

"And?"

"You should come see this."

"On my way." I tapped Kurt's shoulder as he talked to someone, and then called out to Lee and Sam. "Bomb Squad wants us to see something."

The four of us hustled back inside and up to our floor. I saw Tony in the main reception area of our floor. Two other bomb squad members stood close by, all wearing heavy bombproof gear.

"Hey, what did you want to show me?"

Tony waved. "This," he said stepping back and allowing me room to see.

"It's safe to be here without gear on?" I said, taking note of the heavy bomb-resistant gear he and his team were wearing.

"It is now," he replied.

On a sheet on the floor, I saw the gun. Tony had removed the magazine and taken it apart. I saw a circuit board and wires.

"Ah, crapdoodle, they shouldn't be there."

"Nope, they shouldn't. Someone placed an IED in your bullpen." Tony's eyes met mine. Improvised Explosive Device. "You've got a problem, Conway."

Add it to the list.

"Placed." I thought about where the gun was. Under edge of the nearest desk to my office. Coincidence? "Not good."

Almost everyone was in the pen. *Almost* everyone.

Lee cleared his throat. "You're saying that someone walked into the Hoover Building, carrying a Beretta packed with explosives, and no one challenged them?"

Tony raised his eyebrows in agreement.

"Then we all have a problem," Lee added. He looked at me and I nodded. "Have you got the dogs doing a complete sweep of the building?"

A knot twisted in my stomach.

Tony nodded and replied, "Yes, two teams started at the top and two at the bottom."

"Can you get anything useful off the gun by way of prints or ID?" I said. The knot of fear in my stomach was now the size of a tennis ball.

"We'll try," he replied.

I knew I wasn't going to make it home for dinner.

I could hear voices over Tony's radio. Teams reporting in. They'd found nothing else. There was a collective sigh of relief.

"Can I use my office?" I said.

"Go ahead," Tony replied. "We're almost done here. I'll run another sweep through the building just in case, then give the all clear."

"Thanks, Tony."

"Good call, Conway."

I sat behind my desk and took a breath. I'd left the door open. We needed to find out who the intended target was. Could've been anyone from the three teams but I was the one shot at on the street and I didn't like where that thought was heading.

Part of me hoped my gut had an answer. Come on tell me who it was. No music. Maybe there wasn't a song about IED's.

With a touch of disappointment, I called Caine.

"It's me. IED in our bullpen. I need access to the visitor log and surveillance cameras."

"I'll authorize that now."

"Everyone has to sign in, yeah? If they're not FBI, they sign in ... even police?"

"Yes, everyone," he said. "Unless they're a guest of an Assistant Director or above."

My mind tallied up the possibility of the weapon being placed by a guest of one of our assistant directors; now that was a potential shit storm I didn't relish being caught in. I could just imagine how much fun it would be to ask Assistant Director Owen about her guests. I'd managed to keep out of her way since my outburst a few years ago. I was powerless to stop my mouth moving, "I need a list of all guests brought into the building today."

"I'll get it."

Within seconds of hanging up, I was transported back to the day I lost it with Owen.

Memories I could've done without surfaced and enveloped me. There she was, Executive Director Owen talking on her phone while I watched on a monitor. Innocuous? You'd think. But no. My brother sat in a chair in front of her. Then she did it, the unthinkable, she asked him where he was when our mother was killed. Aidan was horrified. He did not know mom was dead. That was the precursor to my outburst at Owen.

I stormed into the room, throwing words like daggers. The exact phrase on entering the fray was 'fuck you and the horse you rode in on'. She didn't even blink. The bitch just sat there and threatened to have the incident written into my permanent record.

Aidan looked stunned, as if someone smacked him with a sledgehammer. Our mother was murdered and *that* was how he found out.

And I just kept going. I told Owen exactly what I thought of her. It has seemed smart to keep out of her way since then.

Everything came back into focus. I blinked the memory away and wished it gone forever.

While Caine worked on getting me the list of guests and visitors, I turned my attention to playing "Name that Unsub." I rocked forward in my chair, planted my elbows on the desk, and dropped my head into my palms.

I hated that even thinking about Owen bought out the

worst in me. The thought of having to deal with her caused memories to suffocate me. It wasn't easy pushing my feelings aside and focusing on the Unsub.

Chapter Thirteen
Brutal Planet

The row of clocks above my door – Los Angeles, Moscow, London, Sydney, and Auckland – indicated it was tomorrow morning in New Zealand. Faye would be at work. I put a call through to her extension and sure enough, she answered.

"I hear it is rocking down there again?"

"Good to hear from you, Ellie. Christchurch *was* hit again by another quake, it's becoming far too commonplace. Suppose you saw the news?"

"Carla told me. I've been crazy busy all day. Do you need anything? Is there anything we can do to help?" My fingernails tapped on my desk, not with impatience; I was thinking.

"Think we'll be okay. It wasn't as bad as the February quake."

"Let me know if you need anything at all. We have resources we can send if you need a hand with policing."

"Thanks, I appreciate it. We still have some American port-a-loos here from the last quake, still in use too. Sewerage system is still munted according to the mayor of Christchurch."

"Munted?"

"Broken, fucked, screwed," Faye replied.

"You Kiwi's sure have some strange words."

"Yeah, but at least we spell things properly," Faye said

with a laugh.

"Ha!" An intact sense of humor was a good thing. "What's the crime like down in Christchurch?"

"Lower than usual, bigger police presence on the ground though. We have brought in officers from all over the country. We're doing reassurance patrols, and mucking in, helping the public out where and when we can."

"Have you been down?"

"Yes. All the places you saw while you were there, with the exception of Riccarton racetrack, are unrecognizable now."

"I saw pictures after February ... a friend of mine lived in Christchurch then ... looked like a war zone."

"That's right, Sean O'Hare your Director's brother? Is he still there?"

"That's him. No, he and his wife left last month."

"Smart."

"I gotta get back to work. Let me know if you need anything, anything at all. Even if it's a place to stay that doesn't shake for a few weeks."

"Thanks, Ellie, I might take you up on that."

"Say the word, I'll pick you up at Dulles. We have more than enough room."

We hung up. I had no idea how anyone was still living in Christchurch; the universe seemed to have it in for the city. Upon reflection though, I realized I wouldn't leave Fairfax without a fight. Sometimes you just have to ride it out.

I spent half an hour chasing possibilities with the case in front of me then called Kurt into my office. He'd been working on the disappearance of the Unsub while I was working on a name. My investigation crossed his, wove webs through it, and then tied it all into fragile silvery bows. I'm pretty sure gossamer wings were involved; maybe they were diamond bedazzled gossamer wings.

Kurt shared his theories. "He could have stayed in one of the buildings. Or he could've hidden under an umbrella and made his way out of the area that way. Could've had a car nearby and driven away. Haven't heard anything from Transit."

"He may have done one of those. What if we're barking up the wrong tree and he had an accomplice?"

He tapped his foot on the edge of the desk. "Tell me ..."

Smiling, I said. "What if fairies sprinkled sparkly diamond dust on his fuc'n head and he flew?"

"Do you have anything or not?"

Impatient.

He wasn't enjoying my playful insights. Some people have no sense of humor. Kurt did, maybe he was having an off day. Perhaps he didn't appreciate having a soaking wet suit and an IED in the office? That was when I realized he was wearing a different suit, black with a white shirt and silver tie. A little too dressy for work. Glad I didn't notice it at the crime scene, it made him look even more like Costner, if that was possible.

I flipped through images in an internal photo album until I found Rowan in a tuxedo. I needed to get hold of

Rowan. I wanted to see Rowan. If I told myself that often enough it would be true and everything else my mind tried to conjure regarding Costner would fade away forever.

"Conway?"

He was still waiting for an answer. I cleared my throat. "Actually I do." I slid a piece of paper across the desk to him. He spun it with his finger and glanced at it for a few seconds.

It was fun watching the words he read sink in.

A moment later, he picked the paper up and stared at it.

"Not fairy dust, but he flew," I said pressing the visions of balloons to the outer limits of my mind. They floated back into focus. An evil laugh filled one of the balloons until it popped, spilling the laughter all over me. Under the cackle, I heard a hissing, "E-E-E-Ellie."

Leave me alone, you fucktarded clown!

"Chartered helicopter. And we're sure that's him, this Quinn Sutherland?"

I shook my head. "Not at all, but that's who chartered a helicopter that took off with one male passenger fifty minutes after the robbery from a private heliport in Vienna, not from DC as I'd first considered."

I'd already sent the helicopter company a picture from the CCTV in the jewelers. They said it was possible that the man in the store was the man who hired the helicopter. It was possible but I suspected unlikely.

"How did he get there?" Kurt looked at me and smiled.

"From the middle of the CBD in DC to Vienna – how?"

The easiest way would be via the Metro but I didn't think for one second, he'd taken the train. There were too many cameras involved in Metro travel. My gut was adamant.

"Company car or his car," I replied. I considered my next words. "When we lost him in the middle of the city, he must have had access to a car."

"Underground car parking ... then why would he need a helicopter?" Kurt said playing his role as devil's advocate well.

Theories manifested. "He could have known about the CCTV, and that we would see his face, or whoever he was meeting may not be in the DC area."

"Whatever his reason, to have a helicopter standing by makes this very well planned."

"I think we know it wasn't opportunistic – you don't kill an entire family in one morning on the off-chance." I watched Kurt digest the information. "I've run his name. I have an address – if you're interested." It came back with nothing except an address and a driver's license. There wasn't so much as a parking fine attached to his name. That would make him almost the perfect patsy. No priors, no reason for his fingerprints to be in any databases, except that it was DC and almost everyone had some connection to government and therefore their fingerprints existed within databases. "I'm pretty sure it's not him but the driver's license picture is similar to our Unsub." Similar as in about twenty percent of white males holding drivers' licenses in the State of Virginia could bear some resemblance to him. Similar in a generic white male kind of way.

I'd sent his name to the crime lab. They would run prints from all the scenes and see if he popped up. My gut told me not to hold my breath. Good advice.

Kurt planted both feet on the ground and stood.

"Let's go find out."

"I'll get Lee and Sam. If it's something, we might need the back up. If it's nothing, then we've had a nice field trip."

I whistled. Sam and Lee appeared.

"You summoned us, O Genie of the Bullpen," Lee said, with a theatrical swirl of his hand and a feigned bow.

A smile broke free and beamed from Sam's face.

Kurt shook his head. "Have you all lost your minds?"

I chose to ignore his humorless comment. "We've got a possible lead on the Bleich killer. Tagging along?"

If we can prove it's him then he won't be an Unsub anymore. I like names. I like to know who I'm dealing with.

"Indeed," Lee replied. "Who are we after?"

"Quinn Sutherland," I replied.

The four of us trundled down the hallway to the elevator.

"Did he take anything from the jewelry store?" Lee said. "Anything worth killing over?"

"A lot of the glass cabinets were unlocked according to police – we'll know what's missing once all the stock is checked," I said. "We're waiting on the live son to confirm inventory." Despite the many times I viewed the tape I couldn't say for sure if the killer took anything. I doubted he stole from a cabinet, though he may have taken something from Bleich – other than his life.

"Would seem to be a waste of energy to kill someone for nothing," Kurt added.

"Unless robbery was to disguise the murder," I replied. "Maybe he expected police to find the body, not us?"

"Sooner or later someone would go looking for next of kin and discover the other murders," Kurt said.

"True."

"Why murder almost the whole family? That I don't understand," Kurt replied.

The elevator dinged.

Everyone nodded.

"I think we're focusing on the wrong part of the case," I said as we entered the elevator. "It started out looking like robbery and a murder ... but with no evidence of anything taken yet, there is no real point to thinking robbery."

"Yes, unless it was to disguise the murder," Sam said.

"Great disguise – jeez, no one would see through that," Lee muttered as the ground floor loomed. "He should've made it very obvious that there was a theft."

"Refocus," I said. "The mother was beaten to death, we need to know why. That could be the key."

"It doesn't fit with the other deaths," Kurt agreed.

"What we could do with - is a criminal who isn't as

smart as he thinks he is – for a change. Be nice if we could wrap this sucker up before dinner."

The three men laughed.

As I thought, no hope.

When we leveled with the front desk in the foyer the agent standing there called out to me.

"Agent Conway – I have something for you."

I veered off from the group and waited by the desk as she poked about under the counter.

"Sorry, here it is," she said, handing me a large manila envelope.

I turned the envelope over in my hands. No postmark. The return address was a post office box. Something small slid around inside it as I tipped the envelope. Interesting.

I ripped it open and peered inside. A piece of paper. I pulled it out and looked at it.

On the page was a six by four inch picture of a man leaving a building. I studied the buildings nearby and the street depicted.

"Anyone recognize this man?" I said, showing Delta the picture.

Sam and Lee shook their heads. Kurt stepped closer. "We have a name?"

"Don't think so." I turned the paper over. There was nothing there. I looked at the picture again.

"Look where he is," Lee said. "That's about a hundred yards from where we lost our man from the jewelry store."

"What a coincidence – now we need to know who he is and why he is," I replied with a wry grin. "And y'all know what I think of coincidences." I stuffed my hand back into the envelope and produced a Nano flash drive. It was tiny in comparison with the flash drives I carried and the bright yellow flash band on my wrist. "Now this is interesting." The tiny drive sat in the palm of my hand. "Wonder what's on it?" I said.

"Wouldn't hurt to know who sent it as well as what's on it," Sam said.

"True, in fact that might be rather helpful."

The agent at the desk shrugged. "Sorry, it was dropped off by a courier."

I glanced up at the ceiling. "We have this area under surveillance, yes?"

She nodded.

"Can you have the video reviewed please, find the courier for me?"

"Yes, ma'am."

"You'll forward the courier's picture and details to my cell?"

"Yes, ma'am."

I dropped the tiny flash drive into the envelope and slid the picture back inside. With the envelope tucked under my arm we carried on.

There would be time to check the flash drive out later.

Chapter Fourteen
You Got the Silver

There wasn't a lot of conversation on the drive out to Alexandria. I rode with Kurt, and Sam with Lee. I took little notice of the blossoms and tulips or that the rain stopped. The beauty of spring was lost on me. Instead of thinking about the way it would go once we reached the address I was trying to figure out what was up with Carla. There was no figuring it out; I convinced myself it would all become clear once I got home.

A quiet prayer to the big guy was in order, just to make sure I was home at a reasonable hour. God and I are speaking at the moment, so I didn't think it was too much to ask.

"Police," Kurt muttered driving past the address.

"This isn't good," I replied.

We pulled in ahead of the police car. Sam passed us and turned at the top of the street. He flashed his lights as he neared us and parked on the other side of the road.

I climbed out and ran over to meet them.

"Hey, we might have trouble," I said as Sam opened his door.

Lee was on his cell. He motioned to me.

"What's going on?" I said.

He hung up and put his phone in his jacket. "There was a car crash. Police are saying Sutherland was in a car crash. Let's get over there."

Kurt and I walked up the path first. I whispered to him, "I'm not buying the car crash. Too coincidental."

A woman in her fifties opened the door. Her expression stony and eyes red rimmed.

"Ma'am," I said showing her my ID, "is your husband home?"

She hesitated. "My ... husband is ..."

Kurt stepped forward and took the woman by the arm. "I think you should sit down." He turned her around and helped her back into the main house. Two police officers stood like cardboard cutouts in the middle of the living room, with their hats under their arms. Kurt spoke to them. "I'm SSA Henderson, FBI. Can one of you get Mrs. Sutherland a glass of water?"

The tallest officer strode away. The other stayed his ground. I flashed my badge and asked his name.

"Gregory Keenan," he replied.

"Come with me," I said, beckoning him. Gregory followed me into the hallway. Seemed smarter to get the uniforms away from the distraught woman. "Where's her husband?" I said, keeping my voice low.

"He was killed in a car crash an hour ago."

"Whereabouts?"

"Vienna."

"Do you have the details?"

He nodded and pulled his notebook out and handed it to me. I read the notes he'd made and wrote down the name of the officer at the scene in my notebook. There was a car and a truck involved. He reported Sutherland's car being rammed at an intersection, shunting it across the road and into a lamppost. The truck left the scene. Witnesses said there was no way they could get the trapped man out and that he was not responsive. An explosion forced would-be rescuers back. There was a BOLO out on the truck.

It wasn't looking good for Sutherland. I considered I might have to reevaluate my thoughts about his innocence.

I handed the notebook back to Keenan. "Thanks."

"Is this one of your cases?" he said, putting his notebook away.

"Yes. We're investigating Sutherland in connection with a murder in the city today." I heard a noise and looked up to see Mrs. Sutherland, wide-eyed and pale, staring out the window behind us. I spun around to see Quinn Sutherland walking up the path. Sam and Lee were waiting by the front door. Sutherland appeared surprised to see them.

"Dead?" I said to Keenan.

"He was identified at the scene by his driver's license and the tags of the car," Keenan said with a shrug.

Well, this just got messy.

I walked to the door. When Mr. Sutherland opened it, I introduced myself and suggested he join his wife in the living room. She hadn't moved. Then all of a sudden she said, "Who was in your car?"

"Excuse me?" he replied, turning his attention to his wife. "What's going on, are you all right?"

"Excuse me, Mr. Sutherland," I said as he hugged his wife. "Did you come home in your own car?"

"Not today. I used one of the fleet cars from work. My car is having a regular service."

Interesting.

"Where?"

He fished inside his jacket and produced his wallet. I watched as he flicked through a series of business cards then held one out to me. "Here, this is the mechanic the company uses."

"Who has access to your car?"

"No one I can think of. It's in the parking garage at work all day and in our garage all night."

"Have you had it detailed in the last few weeks?"

It wouldn't be the first time car keys were copied while the car was being valeted. I'd seen cars that looked brand new after they'd been detailed and owners so pleased with the result that they never suspected a tracking device in the wheel arch, or a bomb.

Some people aren't nice.

He looked over his wife's head; I could see his brain ticking. "About two months ago."

"Would you mind writing down the name of the company you use," I said handing him my notebook and a pen.

While he did that, I went out to Lee and Sam.

"It wasn't him. We need to know who could have produced a fake license. Also, why the hell would anyone want to make it look like Sutherland was dead?"

I leaned on the wall.

"Did you ever seriously think he was involved?" Sam asked.

"No, I thought it was possible that he was a patsy."

"Maybe he is," Sam said.

"In that case, why not kill him? Why kill someone else in a car that's been made to look like his, someone carrying his license?"

"Maybe Sutherland pissed off someone and they wanted to send a message," Lee offered. "You have to admit it was pretty clever, police arriving here to tell his wife he was dead."

"That was clever. Let's work on the Sutherland connection. I need to find out if he booked that helicopter or if it was someone else," I said. "I don't like this, there is something very hinky going on."

"I'm going back to the office," Lee said. "Going to do some research on Mr. Sutherland and see if he knows anyone who likes pretty jewelry or independent contractors."

"Good thinking." I turned to Sam. "Sam?"

"I'm going to check with the crime scene unit. They might have an inventory for us by now. Will check with Sandra too and see how close the UK is to finding the other son. Would help to know what, if anything is missing."

"Okay. See you both soon. We'll finish up talking to Sutherland here, and then join you."

I turned to go back inside when my phone buzzed.

Incoming picture. It was a photo of the courier who dropped off the photo at work and his details. I texted a thank you to the sender.

Back inside both cops were standing at parade rest. They seemed less uncomfortable. Kurt was talking to both the Sutherlands. I showed Kurt the photo. "Our courier."

He raised his eyebrows. "That's interesting but this is also interesting," he said, his voice low. "A month ago Mrs. Sutherland received an invitation to attend a jewelry exhibition in Washington, at the Ritz-Carlton."

"Did you go?" I said to the woman. She seemed a more normal color now.

"Yes, I did. The Heathcote diamonds were on display. They're stunning."

"How big are they?" The words popped out before I could stop them. I had no way of knowing how big a forty-five or forty-eight carat diamond was.

She looked surprised for a second, then answered with a smile. "About the same size as the Hope Diamond."

Good to know. The Hope diamond I'd seen on numerous occasions at the Museum of Natural History. It wasn't something a girl would want hanging around her neck without an armed escort. So what would you do with a set of diamonds that big? Assuming you weren't a King, Queen, or a Rockefeller.

"Thank you. It's interesting that you were invited. Do you often go to jewelry events?"

She shook her head. "No, not at all. I like diamonds as

much as the next girl but that was my first invite to something so swanky."

"Many people there?"

"Yes, lots, socialites and the rich and famous." She smiled. "I'm surprised you weren't there."

"I'm far from being a socialite, nor am I famous," I replied.

"Your boyfriend was there."

I removed all surprise from my voice before speaking. "Well, I hope that means I'm getting something special for my birthday."

The urge to run away grew within me but I stayed my ground. My boyfriend was there. Nice. Is there anyone on the East Coast who doesn't know I'm dating Rowan Grange? I scanned my memory trying to recall Rowan mentioning anything about a jewelry event. Nothing jumped out. He may have been performing with Gracey. The pair of them did quite a few corporate gigs together – and also fundraising events.

"Was the event in aid of anything?" I said.

She nodded. "Yes, during the evening there were auctions to raise funds for research into Autism."

"Why do you think you were invited to the event?" I said. It was possible she had an interest in autism.

"I presumed Quinn put my name down on something."

That was a possibility. It didn't matter where you went, or what you did, someone would ask you to apply for a store card or for your email address.

He shook his head.

"You're not big supporters of whatever charity was benefiting from the event?"

They shook their heads.

"Are we being targeted?" he said.

"It's possible," Kurt replied. "We'll have police keep an eye on your house."

Both cops nodded. "I can arrange that now," Gregory said and walked away talking into his radio.

Kurt and I moved to the door to converse in low whispers.

"The more we uncover, the less sense any of it makes," I said.

"You're not wrong. At least we now have a connection between the Sutherlands and Bleich."

"It's tenuous at best."

"Yes, but it's something."

A light went on in my mind.

I walked back to the confused couple. "Do you have a lawyer?"

The wife looked terrified. Mr. Sutherland nodded. "Do I need one now?"

"No, sir, just wondered who it was."

"We use Campbell, Blackcock, and Bleich."

"Is that Marika Bleich?"

He nodded again. "Do you know her?"

I shook my head. "She's the wife of the jeweler who owns the Heathcote diamonds."

I glanced at Kurt. He'd taken a sneaky photograph with his phone, of Quinn Sutherland.

Sutherland looked a little disturbed. I decided to push some more questions at him.

"Can you tell me where you were at eight this morning?"

Mrs. Sutherland answered. "He was on his way to work."

"Mr. Sutherland, where were you?"

"On my way to work."

"You didn't stop off anywhere?"

"No."

"You're quite sure?"

"Yes. What is this about?"

"I'm just trying to get my timeline in order."

"Is there anything else?"

"Not right now. Police will have a car outside your house until we tell them otherwise. I advise you to be vigilant." I handed them a business card each. "You can reach me on any of those numbers."

"Thank you, Agent," Mr. Sutherland said pushing the card into his wallet.

Kurt and I spoke with police and then left.

"This is messy," I muttered climbing into the car. It was getting late. "Can you drop me home, please?"

"Sure, you okay?"

I caught his sidelong glance.

"I'm okay. But it's close to dinnertime and something's up with Carla. I'm going to take a few hours."

"Spend the night at home. No sense rushing back to work. Until we locate the other son, nothing much is going to happen."

"I would like to find the Unsub."

"How do you know we haven't already?"

I smiled. "It's not Sutherland. That much I know."

"I'll pick you up in the morning. Your car is still at work."

"Thanks," I said as Kurt pulled up outside my home. I walked up to the gates and entered the five-digit pin. The smaller pedestrian gate clicked. I pushed it open then clicked it shut. Kurt waved then left. He was out of sight by the time I made it up the driveway to the front door. At least it wasn't raining now.

I heard footsteps and waited for Carla to open the door. It's a thing. She liked to greet me at the door. And it felt right.

The door swung open and Carla smiled at me. It wasn't her usual beaming grin, just a smile. Something was different.

"You came home."

"Is that a good thing?" I said kissing her cheek and slinging an arm around her shoulders.

"Yes," she replied, hugging me. "I didn't think you would." Her voice trailed off.

Chapter Fifteen
If I Was Your Mother

The smell of roast beef wafted down the hallway and twirled around me. My stomach grumbled like an aggravated black bear.

Carla asked, "Didn't eat lunch?"

"Not today. We were busy," I replied, linking my arm with hers. We walked down the long spacious hallway to the kitchen. "Hey, Dad."

Dad looked over and smiled. He was making gravy. The beef sat on the carving rack waiting.

"How was your day?" dad asked.

"Busy," I replied, tearing a small piece off the top edge of the roast and popping it into my mouth. I savored the deliciousness. The meat melted in my mouth. "Oh, that is good."

"You've got twenty minutes, if you'd like to go clean up."

I looked down, giving my clothes a quick once over. "Think I might."

Carla looked at my shirt sleeve and pointed to a dark brown stain. Guess I dragged my sleeve in blood at some stage during the day. Such is my life.

"What's that?"

"Not mine. Never mind. I'll be back in ten."

As I hurried away toward the stairs I heard Joey call out from the family room. "Hey, Ms. Conway."

He sounded like his usual self. Considering I was detecting something strange with Carla, that was a relief.

"I'll be back soon, Joey."

I remembered Carla wanted to talk to me about something and I had a feeling it was to do with Joey.

I hustled back to the kitchen and poked my head in. Carla was filling two drink bottles with juice. "Carla, come with me, you can choose my shirt."

She screwed the tops on the bottles. "I'll give Joey his drink," she said. There was a moment of hesitation when she reached the family room. She handed both drinks to Joey as we walked away I caught a look between her and Joey. It disturbed me. It was almost as if he shot her a warning glance.

Something was going on with them.

"You don't want your drink?" I asked as we climbed the stairs.

She shrugged. "I'll have it later."

In my room I opened the closet and set Carla the task of finding clothes for me, while I went into the bathroom and turned on the shower.

"How you doing out there?"

"This is a nice shirt," she replied, holding out a long-sleeved, pale blue button-down shirt. It wasn't black, or dark grey, or dark blue. The thin white stripes and haphazard lace down half the front panel made it feel summery.

I smiled. "Great. Thanks." I took the shirt and hung it in the bathroom. Carla passed me clean jeans. I picked out my underwear. She plopped herself on my bed and fiddled with the edge of the comforter.

"Mom?"

"Yes," I replied as I brushed the knots out of my hair. My stomach twisted, knowing she needed to tell me something.

A movement in the bedroom mirror caught my attention. I turned as my bedside lamp rocked violently then fell to the floor. Carla yelped.

Nothing else moved.

"You all right?"

Carla nodded. "Why'd it fall?"

"Not sure. That was weird," I said as I crossed the floor, lifted up the lamp and inspected it for damage. "It's not broken." I set the lamp back where it belonged.

"What made it do that?" Carla asked. Her eyes darted around the room.

"Maybe the bed knocked into the nightstand when you sat down," I offered. I was starting think there was some kind of poltergeist activity happening. Seemed best to ignore it and move on. "Did you want to ask me something?"

Her head shook a little. "It's nothing. I just wondered if you had a good day."

"Busy day, sweetheart. It got a bit crazy in the end there." Despite wanting to give her a good shake until words fell out of her mouth I kept calm. "How was your day?"

"It was all right ..."

No, it wasn't.

I took a breath.

"You do know I was a teenager once, huh? Whatever it is that's bugging you, I will try to understand."

A smile flashed across her eyes then disappeared and was replaced by a look of determination. She wasn't going to talk.

"It was an okay day. I'm glad you're home."

"All right. If you change your mind ..."

"I know ... you're right here." She muttered something under her breath that sounded like, "For now."

"I am here," I reiterated and resisted adding something about how she should make the most of it instead of wasting this time being surly and petulant.

I left her sitting on my bed and showered. Glimpses of my teenage years challenged and worried me. Surviving a mentally-defective mother by being an overachiever worked for me. My experiences overlaid on Carla's. A serial killer didn't kill my mother when I was thirteen. I wasn't sitting beside someone when they were shot to death that same night. I was never in foster care, nor was I adopted by a Fed whose husband died protecting me.

Carla fitted the profile of an at-risk teen. No matter how much I loved her and how many therapy sessions she attended, she was still at risk. More from herself than external influences.

What was with her and Joey?

Carla was gone when I finished cleaning up and dressing. I saw her in the family room with Joey as I headed for the dining room. They were watching television.

Twenty-five minutes after I first walked in the front door, we were enjoying the meal my father cooked. The dinner table conversation wasn't the usual family fare. Both kids appeared to struggle with the basics of conversation. There were far too many sidelong glances between them for my liking. Joey made a late attempt to join in. I watched without being too obvious. My mind threw up scenarios at an alarming rate. None was good. A horrible feeling that there was something up with the kids started as a seed and swelled. Something one of them was planning to do and the other didn't like it, or maybe the other was going to join in but wasn't as convinced. Of course it may not be like that at all. They may both be willing. The seed burst and a small shoot shot out. If ever there was a time for music to help me out, that was it.

"You two are hitting that orange juice like it contains vodka," I said, taking a sip of the glass of Shiraz in front of me. I let my eyes rest on Carla for a moment. "It doesn't, does it?"

"No," she snapped. "How stupid do you think I am?"

I smiled. "You've always been way smarter than you should be. I'm your mother, that's one of the questions I am obliged to ask."

I could feel my mother lurking in the shadows of my mind. Then she spoke and I almost choked on my drink. "She's hiding something. Is she having sex with that dirty

147

little boy?" I willed her to shut up but she wouldn't. "Really, Gabrielle, are you sure she's not gay or taking drugs?"

I silenced my mother by imagining Mac clamping his hand across her mouth. A silent prayer went out to the universe: please don't let me sound like my mother.

"How was school?" I asked, hoping that was a safer subject.

"It was fine," Carla said. "Wasn't it, Joey?"

Joey grunted once in affirmation.

Then Robbie the robot lurched into view flapping his claws and yelling, "Danger, Danger, Will Robinson." I bit my tongue before my mother's words could pop out of my mouth and alienate my child forever.

Carla lifted the bottle and sucked back another big swig. "Want some?" Carla offered me the bottle.

"No thanks, OJ and Shiraz are not the best possible combination."

She shrugged. "Thought you'd want to check it didn't have alcohol in it."

"Your word is all I need."

Come on mind, give me a song, and tell me what's going on here. It was not looking great.

When I did hear music, I wished it gone. Hearing Red Hot Chili Peppers' 'White Snow' was far from comforting when faced with two teenagers who were doing their damnedest not to give something away. Was it drugs? Was that what was going on? The song stopped short of the end, and when I looked at Joey, I heard something that was worse. Bon Jovi's 'Lonely at the Top'.

My fork hit my plate. Joey jumped. Carla shrank down a little in her chair.

"Whoops," I said retrieving the fork. I made eye contact with Dad. Hoping he would read my mind, hear the music, and offer an insightful nugget out of the blue.

Jon Bon Jovi's voice scared me to my core. Could it be true that one or both of the kids at my table was thinking of suicide? As horrible as it was, all I could think was, don't let it be mine. Both songs twirled making the world spin and my dinner turnover in my stomach.

Drugs and suicide.

I took a sip of the wine in front of me. Wiped my mouth on my napkin.

"Delicious meal as always, Dad," I said taking another sip of the wine. "I'll give you a hand cleaning up."

"I won't say no, kid," Dad replied.

Carla and Joey were still pushing food around their plates.

"If you're not going to eat it, take your plates to the kitchen," I said.

They both glanced at me then back at their plates.

"I'm not hungry," Carla said.

"Then you may be excused."

She stood up and took her plate to the kitchen.

"Me neither, Ms. Conway," Joey muttered.

"Go on, Joey," I said.

He disappeared into the kitchen carrying his plate. They reappeared at the doorway.

"We've got homework," Carla said. "We'll be upstairs."

"Okay, I've got some work to do later – I'll be in my little office." I had a big office downstairs past the kitchen at the back of the house. But to be closer to Carla I also built a small office between Carla's bedroom and mine. "Keep your door open."

Carla attempted a smile. They went down the hall and were gone from view by the time I stood and carried my plate to the kitchen. Movement startled me as I walked across the kitchen floor. One of the kids' plates slid across the countertop and crashed to the floor. The silverware clattered across the tiles.

"You okay?" Dad called.

"Yeah," I replied. "Dropped a plate."

I set my plate on the counter and proceeded to pick up the broken pieces from the floor.

Drugs and suicide echoed in my head.

Got evidence?

There was no evidence. Not a thing, beyond my daughter acting odd. Two teenagers behaving for all the world like two teenagers. A teenage boy who didn't eat his dinner? Now that was unheard of and disturbing as hell. The two songs were repeating in my head, overlapping and mixing lyrics until I felt dizzy. And what's with the lamp and the plate?

Dad joined me in the kitchen with the drink bottles from the table. I placed the broken plate, and mushed food on the counter and washed my hands.

"What's going on?" he asked, placing his plate and the

almost empty bottles on the counter top.

"I don't know, but I think the kids are going to do something stupid." I reached for one of the drink bottles and opened the lid. I sniffed it. There was no alcohol in it. I screwed the top back down.

I leaned against the counter and attempted to steady the surging beef within.

"Ellie?"

"How have they been today?"

Dad leaned against the counter next to me. "Carla was quieter than usual, Joey is up and down – but Joey is up and down."

I exhaled and thought for a minute, while willing Bon Jovi to shut up.

"They been secretive at all? Jumpy when you enter the room?"

Dad shook his head then changed his mind. "Maybe they have, a little more than usual. You think they're having sex?"

Well, crap, I never thought of that. "Why, what do you know?"

"Just seen them holding hands a few times, is all."

Holding hands. "I don't think this is about making out."

Dad looked at me. "Drugs?"

"Maybe."

Mac's voice resounded in the crawl space within my head, "Maybe's ass!"

Hearing him wasn't as comforting as it used to be. For

the first time ever I opted to ignore his comment. I think I'd have seen signs of drug use if this were about drugs. I searched my memory for anything that would indicate they were into drugs and came up empty.

Sex? That was a fast way to ruin a beautiful friendship.

"That could be it, Ellie. How do you want to handle this?"

"I'll talk to Carla and Joey, soon." I smiled and looked around. The kitchen was spotless. We'd done all the dishes. I sat up on the counter and remembered the times as a teenager when I used to help dad clean the kitchen and use the moment while he was busy to ask him things that I couldn't otherwise. Carla availed herself of kitchen talks in the past too, often while I was fixing dinner or breakfast. "Maybe I'll bake some cookies tonight, and she can help me."

"Good idea. I'll take Joey home when you give me the word."

"Thanks, Dad."

My phone rang. It was Lee.

"I need to take this, Dad," I said, jumping off the counter with the phone in my hand and walked down the hall. "Lee?"

"How was dinner?"

"Excellent as always," I replied. "What's up?"

"There is a woman called Maria Doyle ..."

Modern West started up. 'Maria Nay' was back with vengeance.

"And?" I tried to silence Kevin but he wasn't playing

152

nice.

"She was the one who added the Sutherland woman's name to the guest list of that autism fundraiser, late. She works for the company hired to manage the event."

"Have you spoken to her?"

"No, Sam and I took a ride over to her apartment, no one was home. I left my card in the door, with a note on the back asking her to call me about the autism event."

"Good thinking. What do we know about the company she works for and her employment history?"

"Company has been around over twenty years, she has worked for them for the last five. Doyle took a restraining order out six months ago against an ex-boyfriend but apart from that, she's never been in any trouble that required police involvement."

'Maria Nay' was starting to be tiresome. I willed the song to stop.

"Get what you can. I'm coming back in anyway."

"We can handle it."

"I know, but I do need to start working on the mystery man in the photograph the courier delivered and speak to that courier." I was standing in the living room staring at the small hole in the wall. "I'll come back in."

"Everything all right?"

"I'm not sure, she and Joey have been acting weird."

Lee bristled. "He better not be putting the moves on her, that is unacceptable and she's too young!"

"They're both too young, but I don't think it's that."

"I've seen how he looks at her, he's a guy ... she's cute,

of course it's *that*."

I hoped it was *that*. "I'll fill you in when I arrive." I hung up. It was hard not to smile. Really, for Joey's sake, he better hope he hasn't laid a hand on her. Lee and Sam might be the sweetest guys in the world to Carla, but God help anyone who messes with her. I doubt they would see any such situation as being consensual. For a split second, I already felt sorry for Joey.

I called Kurt. "You busy?"

"Nope, just eaten. What's up?"

"I need a ride back to work. Looks like Lee and Sam might have found a lead and we need to get to the bottom of this couriered photograph."

"All okay at home?"

"Two quiet and secretive teenagers ..."

"Probably having sex," he said with an offhanded dismissal. "I'll be there in twenty."

I set my phone on the counter next to me. 'Maria Nay' became Bon Jovi's 'Lonely at the Top'. If they were having sex, surely I'd be hearing a different song, like maybe 'Dirty Little Secret' or Aerosmith's 'Love in an Elevator.' Dad was making coffee. I watched him spoon the coffee grinds into the filter.

"You think the kids are covering up sex?"

He finished what he was doing and pressed the button to start the machine. "I think it's possible. You second guessing yourself?"

"You men all jumped right to sex. I'm the only one thinking drugs."

"Go talk to the kids ... you'll have time for a coffee before Kurt arrives?"

"Yeah, should do. Kurt and I will run Joey home on our way. Can you stay tonight?"

"Of course."

I kissed his prickly cheek. "What would we do without you, Dad?"

"You're resourceful, you'd manage. Go on, go sneak up the stairs, and catch them being teenagers."

I grimaced. "Think I'll make a lot of noise, the last thing I want to do is catch them doing anything!"

Dad laughed. "Welcome to parenthood."

I walked down the hallway and up the stairs. At the top of the stairs, I called out to Carla.

"Having fun with your homework?" She didn't reply. So I tried from closer to her door, "Hey kiddo, I'm going to run Joey home soon."

She didn't reply.

I knocked once on the doorframe, took a breath, and stuck my head into the room.

Joey and Carla were sitting on the floor, side by side, leaning against the bed. Notebooks rested on their knees and there were pens in their hands.

"Hey," I said. Nothing seemed untoward. No clothes awry. Not a hair out of place. No condom wrappers peeking out from under the bed. A shiver ran up my spine.

"Hey, Mom," Carla replied, smiling up at me. "We're almost done."

"Great, I'm going to drop Joey home soon." I pointed to the hallway. "You didn't hear me?"

That was when I saw the wires coming out of their ears. They were sharing the iPod. Carla dropped her ear bud. I could hear the music.

"Sorry, Mom, I thought I heard something."

"Sweetie, that is way too loud."

Carla rolled her eyes.

God, I love teenagers. I tapped Joey's foot with my boot. "Pack up, I'm dropping you home."

"Okay. Thanks, Ms. Conway."

Just as I turned to leave the room, I caught another weird look between them. I made a mental note to talk to Carla about protection. It did occur to me that I could just tell Delta that I thought they were right about the making out thing. Lee and Sam would make damn sure that Joey didn't do anything, no matter how much Carla wanted to. That was a mean but viable option if the talk didn't go well. Teenage boys have a bad rap when it comes to hormones and sex but the ugly truth is girls are often worse.

Chapter Sixteen
Long Cool Woman

I stood on the dark doorstep of a townhouse in Fairfax. My finger pressed the doorbell for the third time. This time I heard footsteps.

The porch light flickered then glowed, illuminating the porch and half the path from the road. The door opened a crack.

"Hi, I'm Special Agent Conway." I held up my badge. "Are you Kieran Smith?"

Silence.

I tried again. "Kieran Smith?"

"Yes."

"I'd like to talk to you about an envelope you delivered to the Hoover Building today."

"It's late. Can this wait until tomorrow?"

"No."

And it's not that late.

The door opened wider. He was still wearing work clothes. A company shirt with his first name embroidered on it.

"I deliver a lot of packages during my day," he said. Yet I had the feeling he remembered the one I was talking about.

"I'm sure you do. How many times did you go to the FBI building today?"

"Once."

"Where did you pick up the package?"

He shook his head. "I don't remember."

I slipped my badge back onto my belt. The movement afforded Mr. Smith a look at my gun holster. Sometimes that served as a memory trigger. From my pocket, I took a notebook and a pen. I ignored Mr. Smith while I flipped through pages and readied the notebook so I could write everything he said.

"Where was that again?"

"I ... I ... don't ..."

"You're sure? Because we can continue this conversation at my office."

"I think it was from a hotel?"

"Are you asking or telling? Come on, let's not make this any harder than it has to be. Where did you pick up the envelope?"

"The Madison."

I wrote the hotel name down. "Room number?"

"The package was waiting for me at reception."

"What time did you collect it?"

He thought for a minute. "Before nine, but I had a lot of deliveries and pick-ups so I didn't deliver it until after lunch."

"Did you see the person who wanted it delivered?"

His head shook. "No. It was at the reception desk with a note to take it to the Hoover Building."

He looked at me. I could see the wheels turning.

"And?"

"It was addressed to a special agent, Ellie Conway.

That's you, right?"

"Yes, it's me."

"I never saw the person. Try the hotel."

"I will, thanks."

I turned and hurried down the few porch steps and back to the car. Kurt started the engine before I opened the door. I jumped into the car and fastened my seatbelt.

"The Madison," I said. "Isn't that on 15th?"

"I think so."

I leaned my head back on the headrest and thought about the envelope. I needed to investigate the flash drive that came with it. It'd have to wait until we found the sender and got back to the office.

I called Lee on my cell phone. "How are you two getting on?"

"It's slow."

"Tell me about it. Kurt and I are heading to The Madison. Courier said he picked up the envelope there."

"Good luck."

"Thanks. Any word from Misha regarding the live Bleich?"

"Not yet."

"Okay, see you soon."

I hung up and pocketed my phone. Kurt turned on the radio. I hoped a song would throw magic thought seeds my way and grow some kind of an answer as to what the man and the envelope had to do with a dead family. The song that coursed through the airways and into the car took me by surprise. Kurt sang along. 'Long Cool Woman

(In a Black Dress).' The Hollies. Really?

The song flowed. I listened. I knew the lyrics by heart. The song spoke to me. It twisted the Hollies original words until I was hearing a new take on an old song. It was backwards. The woman was working for the FBI and a man did the shooting.

"Kurt."

"Ellie?"

He didn't look over; he was watching the road and tapping one hand on the steering wheel in time to the music.

"Do you think it's possible that the man in the photo was the one who shot me, or could he be the Unsub who killed Sigmund Bleich?"

"It could just be a song that your mind warped."

"It could be."

And one day I'm sure it will be, but it felt a little too coincidental.

"For safety reasons, let's approach this as if he is your shooter and the Unsub," Kurt said. "We're about three minutes out."

"Okay."

My mind ran over general procedures as I rolled my shoulders and worked some of the tension out of my muscles.

Kurt pulled over and parked. "We'll walk from here."

"The photo ..." I said, climbing out of the car, "... it had to be from a surveillance camera. Why would someone send a photo of themselves taken by a surveillance camera?"

"Do you have the photo with you?"

"Not the original, that's still in the envelope in my drawer at work. I took a picture of it with my phone though."

I handed Kurt my phone and waited while he found the image and refreshed his memory. It pays to know what people look like when you're looking for them. He handed the phone back.

"Let's go find out if this guy is here and how that photo came to be."

I fell into step with Kurt. As we walked, I shook my right arm out, and ten yards from the main entrance to the hotel I pulled my Glock, checked the magazine, and slid it back into my holster.

Kurt placed his hand in the small of my back, escorting me through the door that opened for us. I smiled at the doorman.

My eyes roamed the lobby area, looking for anyone out of place or anyone showing interest in us. Four people were in the lobby. They were all women and seemed to be together.

I approached the desk and attracted the attention of the attendant.

"Good evening, ma'am. How can I help?"

"Were you on this morning before nine?"

She smiled. "Yes. I've only just come back on." Her nametag read Duty Manager Sophia Creswell.

For once, our timing didn't suck.

I lifted my badge off my belt and showed it to her. "Can we have a quiet word, Ms. Creswell?"

"Of course. If you will follow me." She slipped out from behind the desk and motioned to the doorman. He appeared in front of us. "Watch the desk for a few minutes, please. I'll be in the office."

We followed the woman into an office.

"Have a seat," she said, sitting down behind a desk. "What can I do for you, Agent?"

"This morning an envelope was picked up from the front desk here, I'd like to know who left it."

She nodded and typed on a keyboard in front of her. "Two packages were left at the front desk for the courier this morning. Can you be more specific?"

"It was a manila envelope and addressed to the Hoover Building."

She smiled. "Sorry, of course, that was left at the desk by a guest."

I took a steadying breath. "Do you have a name and room number for that guest?"

"Yes, I do. Room 235, the guest's name is Peter Parker. He's booked here for two more nights."

I smiled and showed her the picture on my phone. "Is this Mr. Parker?"

"Yes, it is."

"Thank you. Stairs and elevator?"

A smile flickered across the woman's face. "Just outside the door here."

"Thank you, Ms. Creswell." I pocketed my phone and

passed her my card. "If you see Mr. Parker in the lobby area in the next few minutes, call my cell please."

"You might need this." She reached into a drawer and passed me a keycard. "It's a master key."

"Thank you again." I handed the key to Kurt. "We'll drop it back on our way out."

We left the room. I pushed the elevator button and leaned close to Kurt. "Peter Parker? Spiderman?"

"An alias. Unless, of course, Spiderman is real."

If that's the case, he could be scaling the exterior walls of the hotel and making his escape. That would explain how our man disappeared so quickly.

The elevator dinged.

I grinned at Kurt. "See you up there."

I opened the stairwell door, looked around, there was no sign of life. I listened for a moment. No footsteps. With one last look behind me, I ran up the stairs, two at a time. I paused at the fire doors to the floor I wanted. My heart pounded from running. I could see through a narrow slit of glass in the door. Kurt was by the elevator.

I stepped out of the stairwell, letting the door shut tight behind me before moving away.

"Direction?" I asked.

Kurt pointed down the hallway to the left. "Let's do it," he said. In his left hand was the keycard, he'd pushed his suit jacket back, revealing his holster.

Be prepared.

I wrapped my fingers around the grip but didn't draw my gun.

Standing on either side of the door to room 235, hard against the wall, Kurt leaned out and knocked. No answer.

The elevator dinged. I heard female voices, laughter, and then a male voice. The voices grew louder. Kurt crossed the distance between us. He placed his hands on the wall either side of my head. The voices grew louder.

Kurt whispered in my ear, "Takes me back to the hospital corridor in Lexington."

"We were excellent at playing the newlywed game," I whispered back.

Three people giggled as they passed us. I cast my eyes left. Three women. A door opened across the hall. I moved my head in time to see a male enter the room. Down the hall, another door opened.

Silence fell.

I pushed Kurt back.

He grinned, resumed his position by the door and knocked, this time quieter. We didn't want the guy across the hall to pop back out his door.

No answer.

Kurt shoved the key card into the lock. The light glowed green. He pressed the handle down and swung open the door.

I followed him in. Kurt went right. I went left. We cleared the room. There was no one home. No luggage. No sign anyone was ever here.

I sat on the perfectly made bed. "Damn."

"Yeah," Kurt replied, leaning over and peering into the

wastepaper basket by the small desk. He straightened up and rummaged in his pocket. He pulled on latex gloves and bent down. From the wastepaper basket, he lifted up a crumpled piece of paper. Kurt opened the paper with care, holding it by the very edges, and showed it to me.

"My name and the address for the Hoover Building."

"Now we know he was here." From another pocket, he removed a plastic evidence bag and slid the paper into it.

"But who is he? Where'd he go? Why did he have a piece of paper with my name on it? And why send me the photo with no name?"

"I see you want all the answers."

"Please."

"We might get lucky and be able to pull prints off the paper."

I didn't feel that lucky.

"Leaving prints behind would be a rookie mistake and I don't think this guy is that stupid," I said.

"The lobby. Let's go see if he had a car. There's valet parking."

We hurried back to the lobby.

Sophia Creswell was attending to a small group. We waited to one side, all the while watching for signs of a lone male. Five minutes later Sophia Creswell beckoned us over.

"How can I help, Agents?"

"Valet parking and surveillance cameras," I said. "Did Mr. Parker have a car?"

"I believe so," she replied, tapping on the keyboard.

Her long nails clicked as she typed. "Yes, he has a car. It's a white Ford Taurus, a rental."

"Can we view your surveillance tapes for the last few days?"

She frowned and considered my request. "I don't see why not. I'll take you through to the security office."

Chapter Seventeen
Who Are You?

My watch said it was four in the morning. Tuesday was upon us. The clocks on the wall of my office told me the time in various time zones - none of them made me feel less tired. For most of the night, I was with Kurt trying to find Spiderman. The later it got the less sense anything made. Lee, Sam, and Kurt were in their respective offices working on the Spiderman issue. I pulled favors and had the paper from the hotel examined for prints at the lab. Finding latent prints on paper involves chemicals. It's not something we can do in the field ourselves, yet. The results came back. A big fat zero. No prints. Which was what I expected but it was still disappointing. While I'd been out of the office yesterday, the motel in West Virginia sent a DVD copy of the surveillance footage from the motel office and a photocopy of Chad's driver's license.

I pulled the license up on the DMV screen and copied the picture into a facial recognition program. The only person who'd seen Chad was Noel. I gave him a call. He wasn't asleep either.

Twenty minutes later a quiet knock on my door snapped me out of the trance I was in. Noel entered my office without my bidding.

"Don't you sleep?" he said placing a coffee in front of me.

"Not tonight."

"I'm sure you have a good reason."

"Check this out." I beckoned him closer, without taking my eyes off the screen in front of me and the surveillance footage I watched.

"What are you looking at?"

"Him," I said bringing up the DMV photo of a man.

"The bleeder."

"Yep, the bleeder, let's call him Chad."

Anything was better than referring to him as the bleeder.

"And?"

I pulled up another photo from our internal files. "This is Mac."

Noel whistled through his teeth. "Okay."

"That's it. Okay?"

"Wow me."

I clicked my mouse pointer on an icon. A facial recognition program opened. I opened the last search I'd run and showed Noel the results.

The red words under the picture of the bleeder announced an eighty-five per cent match with Mac.

"Eighty-five per cent."

"That's why the security camera photos? What are you thinking?"

"I don't know."

"It's not him, El."

"No, it's not. But for some reason he's an eighty-five per cent replica. That's enough to fool almost anyone."

"What does that mean?"

"It means ... I dunno." I shrugged.

"And this has something to do with ...?"

"CIA. FBI. Maybe a joint task force. Throw letters at it. Could be any agency, could be all of them. Could be alphabet fuc'n soup." I leaned on my elbows. "I was never meant to come across Chad, but I did."

"Can't you ask whoever you called to help Chad, what this is all about?"

"Yeah, no, it's not how it works. I need to have something to bargain with. Until I do, I'll go looking on my own."

Well, not exactly on my own. Sean's working on it too.

"Looking for what?"

"For what he was doing and why looking like Mac helps him do whatever it is."

"You're using FBI resources to poke around in a possible joint task force?"

"Looks like it."

Noel pulled up a chair.

"Joint task force. Mac was FBI. Can you find out what he was working on prior to his death?"

"He was assigned to me in Delta."

"What about before that?"

"Cyber - as far as I know he was never in a joint task force situation," I replied.

"Before you met?"

I looked at him and started to shake my head but stopped. "He was a stock trader."

"El?"

"When we were in New Zealand I met a detective who said she knew Mac. Said he'd been in NZ as an FBI agent."

"And?"

"I thought she must've been mistaken."

Of course, it could have been Chad and not Mac.

I closed the programs and started searching our databases for anything to do with Socrates or anyone called Chad with a birthdate within five years of 1970.

"You thought, or she was?"

"If I said Mac told me he was in NZ but that Faye got the time line wrong ..."

"When did Mac tell you?"

I had to open my mouth and say Mac told me. The answer was not going to help me look sane.

A sigh escaped before I could check it.

"At the Marriott, after I got those parcels of human meat."

His eyes narrowed. "Human meat ... uh huh. That would be when women bearing the Conway surname were turning up dead all over Virginia?"

"Yeah."

"Terrorist related, El. That time you didn't share information?"

"Yeah, that time." I smiled because Noel was a champion at not sharing all he knew.

"How wrong did she get the time line?"

"Mac's ghost told me ten years - that put him in New

170

Zealand the same time I was, or thereabouts."

"It's getting complicated."

No kidding. It's Tierney. He turns things into a murky black hole of deception.

"But he wasn't supposed to be FBI then ..."

Noel rocked back in the chair. "Stock trading?"

"Cover maybe?"

"You want a hand with this?"

I shook my head. "If I find something I'll let you know."

"What about your SAC?"

"What about him?"

"He can probably find out Mac's story."

I thought about how quickly Caine issued temp credentials for Mac during the Son of Sam case. Oh yeah, he knows something.

"I want to find out for myself. Have a feeling the secrets that were kept won't be spilled by anyone involved. Short of a séance, I think I'm on my own here."

And after shooting Mac's ghost, I figured he wasn't going to be in a hurry to chat.

I pulled up another file and showed Noel.

"What is it?" he asked.

"A sound file. The security camera in the motel office records sound. I isolated a track." I opened another file, it was a sample of Mac's voice. I added both files to a voice comparison program and clicked run.

A few minutes later, we were looking at yellow words across the bottom of the screen.

"Unbelievable," Noel muttered.

"And again, a close enough match to fool people."

Noel left as light crept over the horizon and into the windows. I lay on the couch in my office and listened to the recordings of Chad and Mac. I couldn't tell them apart.

Chapter Eighteen
Maria Nay

"I don't give a fuck," I said rocking back in my chair and watching the reactions on the faces in front of me. I saw the words 'aggravated assault' and 'suspected abduction' on the computer screen. To say I wasn't enthused was perhaps an understatement.

My lack of enthusiasm came from spending the night trying to dig up leads, watching hours of security camera footage trying to find Spiderman, and not being able to understand what happened to the Bleich family. When I could have slept, I opted to ghost hunt until dawn. Tired met cranky and settled in for the long haul. The new case seemed like something best handled by police and not us. "Why us?"

Lee and Sam shrugged and shook their heads. They were also clueless.

It hadn't been the world's best week and it was only Wednesday. The week evaporated into a blur of teenage hell and I still couldn't get a song out of my head. Let's face it, songs in my head never bode well. This time I could hear Kevin Costner and Modern West singing 'Maria Nay' with such impact they could've been in front of me. It wasn't going away. Day two of the same song. Day freaking two. Okay, so the brief interlude of drug and suicide songs during the night doesn't count. No wonder I wasn't embracing a new case.

"I'm detecting a black cloud coming from around your chair," Lee said. "Anything you want to share?"

I shook my head. It occurred to me as I reached for my laptop that they didn't think I saw the sideways glances. I ignored them all for a few seconds and tried to Google the lyrics, no luck.

"Just give me a few minutes, please," I said. My hand reached for my iPod in my drawer without conscious instruction. I scrolled through until I found 'Maria Nay.' I listened using my ear buds once, then played it through my laptop twice, enabling Lee and Sam to listen. I was hoping that hearing it externally would give some clue. Yet I remained clueless. They listened with bemused patience.

Maybe I was trying too hard. I dropped my iPod back in the drawer and leaned back in my chair.

"That song mean anything to anyone?" I said.

They shook their heads. A sudden thought sprouted. The band had a website. I had a quick look and discovered the lyrics. The song had nothing at all to do with diamonds or a dead jeweler. Right, back to work then.

"Caine thinks we should look into this case," Lee stated, planting his feet flat on the ground and leaning forward.

I wasn't going let the Special Agent in Charge of Delta sway my decision this time. How often do abductions end well? Not very. Did I want to be away from home chasing an Unsub who would probably kill his victim anyway?

No, I did not.

"Our specialty is serial crime, this is one person. Delta B can do it." I scrolled through the data on my laptop screen. "They've got less than us on their case log."

"We took the jeweler case. That's not serial," Lee reminded.

"You're right, but it turned into a multiple murder." I doubted this would turn into anything but frustration and annoyance.

He smiled. "You got me." His hands went up in mock surrender.

I picked up the phone and called the SSA of Delta B.

"Claude, do you have time for another potential case?"

"Give me a run down," he said, his mid-western accent reverberating in my ear.

As I spoke, Lee spun his laptop to face me. An urgent email request flashed up on the screen.

"Never mind. Looks like this one is ours after all." I hung up.

"Eyes only?" I said, looking at the red flashing letters attached to beginning of the message.

"Delta A eyes only," Lee replied. "It's come from the Director."

I sighed. I knew who it came from.

"Fine, we're in." I considered I could still say no but if Cait O'Hare wanted us in, she wanted us in for a reason. All this for an abduction and assault. Must be a reason. "Sam?" I looked over at him. He nodded and stood. He'd sat there doing an impersonation of a stone for the entire conversation. "You okay for this?"

"I'm fit for duty," he replied.

"That's not what I said, are you okay for this?"

"Yes, Chicky Babe. I'm okay."

I smiled. That's what I wanted to hear. Sam had been on medical leave for six weeks then desk duties for another month to recover from surgery to remove bullet fragments from his chest. Hence he was not involved in our foot pursuit earlier in the week. Sometimes the body heals faster than the mind. Being shot can screw your head up and zap your confidence, I needed his head in the game and to know he was ready for anything.

Lee was on his feet. He'd already packed his laptop into a black bag. Someone knocked at my door.

"Come in," I called as I began packing up my laptop.

The door opened. From the corner of my eye I saw blonde hair. A smile crossed my lips as I stood up to greet the Director. She was holding a manila folder.

"Director."

Sam and Lee spun around.

O'Hare nodded at me. "Ellie." She smiled at Sam and Lee. "At ease, gentlemen, I thought I'd brief you myself."

I suspected that was code for 'I want to make sure you're all on board and there won't be any bullshit.'

She closed the door and dragged a chair over to my desk, motioning for us all to sit back down. "Kurt will be joining us presently," O'Hare said. "I saw him out in the bullpen."

"Saves me from calling him," I replied with a smile.

"I understand that you have a difficult case in front of you and that you are probably not thrilled about me dropping this one on you as well, Ellie," O'Hare said with a hint of apology. "But I would like Delta A on this."

"Fair enough," I replied. It's not as if the boss has to explain why or anything. Orders are orders; hers are delivered nicer than most, is all. I was glad it was her request and not Assistant Director Owen's.

"I know you've been working some long hours and things aren't great with Carla right now. If you want to take a few days I'd understand."

I shook my head. "I'm good."

Director O'Hare smiled. "I respect your wish to carry on with your case load. If anything crops up at home and you need some time, we can go on without you."

The air pressure changed in the room. Lee and Sam narrowed their eyes at me. I knew I was going to have to come clean when O'Hare left. The only other person I knew with a teenager was Cait O'Hare. I'd called her from the office last night and told her I suspected Carla and Joey were either having sex or thinking about it. I'd also mentioned that I thought it was more than that, that everyone else saw sex when I saw serious trouble, as in alcohol, drugs, or suicide, looming.

"I can do this."

At least when I head out to save the world, there's a chance I'll get it right.

"That's all I need to know." O'Hare opened the folder she held in her hand and lay it on my desk. She passed pages to us. I was reading while Cait said, "The woman in the photograph is Maria Doyle. She was taken by force from her home last night. John Brown, her boyfriend of four months was injured and raised the alarm."

And there it was. The reason for 'Maria Nay'. The song bounced into my head as if to revel in the cleverness and further drive its point home. Sam and Lee made eye contact with me and raised their eyebrows.

"Maria Doyle is a person we'd like to speak to in regard to our murder investigation," I said.

"Have you spoken to her?"

"No, Lee and Sam uncovered the lead last night ..."

Lee spoke, "We called over to her place, but she wasn't home. I left my card with a note for her to call me regarding an event."

O'Hare nodded.

"Kurt and I came in last night working another aspect of our current case, we gave Sam and Lee a hand – none of us had any luck locating the woman," I added.

"Then finding her might be beneficial for your case too."

"Police?" I said.

"Her brother called me from the emergency room," she said. "Maria is a friend."

Things whirred in my mind. Maria Doyle? I knew her name and it wasn't because she'd popped up in an investigation. I stared at the photograph and then closed my eyes – I knew her, but didn't recognize her. She looked different and I couldn't place her in context.

Sam was asking about the boyfriend and his injuries.

"He was knocked out, pistol whipped by the look of the injuries to his face and head."

"And he knows who did this?"

O'Hare nodded. "Maria's ex-boyfriend."

"The one she took out a protection order against?" I asked because that would make sense and it'd been my experience that protection orders were like spitting in the eye of the devil and incited violence from ex-partners.

"No, an earlier long term relationship."

I heard Bon Jovi. My eyes searched for the origin of the music. Nothing. Damn. It was just for me. 'Born to be my Baby.' A song I loved, but found myself struggling to find the hidden message. That was not fair, not after the whole Kevin Costner song. Too soon. Come on brain give me a break. You've been pounding me with music all week.

A sudden silence made me look up. All eyes on me. Shit. I'd missed something. There was a photograph on the desk in front of me.

"Yes?" I said, hoping no one would notice I hadn't been present.

"As I was saying," O'Hare continued and tapped the picture on my desk, "Iain Campbell is the suspect. We know he has properties in Fairfax, Herndon, and Reston. He also likes to hike."

"Northern Virginia?" I looked at the man in the picture. "We've seen him recently," I said. "I spent half the night looking for him. Only we were looking for a Mr.

Peter Parker not Iain Campbell. Hang on."

O'Hare nodded.

I opened my drawer and pulled out the manila envelope. I could feel the flash drive. I placed the photograph next to the one O'Hare gave me and palmed the flash drive. The night had disappeared and I hadn't looked at the contents of the flash drive. I hated that I hadn't got to it. Shit happens. Nothing I could do about that.

"Same guy?"

Lee leaned in. "Same guy."

"We sighted his car leaving DC. He was driving a white rental sedan, a late model Ford Taurus," O'Hare said. "Where was your photograph taken?"

"He was about a hundred yards away from where we lost a suspect in the jeweler's murder."

"When?"

"Not long after the incident yesterday," I replied. It'd been so busy it felt like two or three days ago.

"He was seen on traffic cam crossing Key Bridge into Rosslyn, at eight thirty last night."

"Key Bridge?"

"Yes, Key Bridge," O'Hare replied.

"Do we have a photograph of the injured boyfriend?" I asked.

O'Hare shook her head. "There should be photographs of his injuries taken at the hospital but they were not forwarded to us."

Now that's strange.

"We're going to follow up on the photographs," I said, making a note to get Sandra to chase the pictures. "I know he's a victim but I like to have all the puzzle pieces identified up front."

"There should be photographs somewhere, they were dating."

Facebook was a possible source.

"We're on it. You coming out into the field?"

O'Hare shook her head. "I'd love to, but it's not possible." She looked disappointed. Hell, I would be. I couldn't imagine life behind a desk.

"We'll try not to have too much fun," I said.

O'Hare smiled. "This is yours, go do what you do."

We shook hands. She indicated that I should walk her to the door. "If at any point you need to go, just go. Delta can handle this. This team of yours is more than capable."

"I know, thank you."

"Whatever is going on with Carla, I'm sure it will work out," Cait O'Hare said.

"Thank you again." I was lucky and I knew it. Most agents worked their entire careers without more than a few words from the Director. They never got to see the person behind the title or understand how hard she'd worked to get there. They also never knew how much she cared about her agents and their lives.

There was a knock at the door, it opened and Kurt entered.

"I'll be in touch," O'Hare said. "Agent Henderson, Ellie

181

will fill you in."

"Thank you, Director," he replied and held the door for her as she left.

I explained to Kurt how Peter Parker was Iain Campbell and he was the same guy the Director wanted found. Then I explained how the missing woman in the director's case was the woman we'd tried to find last night. Big fat fail on that one.

"Y'all know how I feel about coincidence."

Lee rocked back in his chair. Then sat up straight and tapped away on his laptop as frown lines deepened. "I can't find a connection between Campbell and the jeweler."

God, I loved him. We knew Doyle had a connection to the event where the jeweler's wares were on display and auctioned for charity, but there was Lee looking for a more sinister connection because Campbell turned up in a photograph, and because Kurt and I were looking for him most of the night.

I still didn't know how he'd sent a photo of himself taken from a surveillance camera or why, unless it was to prove he knew DC.

"Oh, for fuck's sake, is it possible we have a *real* coincidence?" I said. We all laughed. Yeah, right. "You can bet he's involved somehow. I know for sure Doyle is involved. Dammit, I've had that Modern West song stuck in my head from the minute we got the call about the jeweler."

Damn, I said it out loud.

Eyes watched me with amusement.

Sam spoke, "Modern West song?"

"'Maria Nay,'" I replied.

Without batting an eyelid, Sam announced that Campbell was involved in the jeweler case.

I love my team's faith.

I gave Kurt the file from O'Hare to read.

Meanwhile, I signed into Facebook and looked up Maria Doyle. I scrolled through her public profile and searched for photographs of her current boyfriend. None.

Who has no photographs of their boyfriend?

"Sam, I'm on Maria Doyle's Facebook. Found some group shots of her and her friends, lots of pictures of her and her girlfriends, not one of her and her boyfriend, John Brown."

"She posts a lot of pictures but none with him. Is he on her friends list?"

I searched. "Nope."

"Sounds like he has some issues with having his picture taken."

That's what I thought.

Kurt looked up from his reading. "What are you thinking?"

"I'm thinking Brown has something to hide."

"I'd say that was a reasonable thought to have. I'm almost done with this." He tapped the file and went back to his reading.

Just for fun I looked for photographs of Campbell on her Facebook page. None. There was one photo of her with what could've been an old boyfriend but not on her page; I found it on a friend's page. It wasn't a recent picture.

I wondered if she dated very shy men.

I let go my thoughts that centered on Brown and Campbell and considered where we could end up then checked the weather for the next few days.

I addressed Lee, "Check your go-bags. Make sure we all have survival gear, the weather forecast is for a cold snap and rain." Then turned to Sam. "GPS us. Grab three satellite phones and send out a BOLO."

Kurt slid the file onto my desk. "Something's not right about this," he muttered.

"Tell me about it," I replied.

All the men disappeared. I picked up my phone and called Dad, who'd spent the night at my place. "Hey, it's me. Got a case that might keep me out for a few days." As I spoke I turned my hand over and looked at the little flash drive. I had to find out what was on it. Couldn't quite believe I'd left it so long.

"I'll take Shrek to Aidan's and keep Carla with me at my place," Dad said.

"Thanks, Dad. Can you make sure Carla does her history assignment? There was an emailed assignment from her teacher." I paused. "Dad, can you try to enforce some Joey-free time?"

"Sure. A bit of time without Joey around might be good."

"Thanks. I hate making you the bad guy but this Joey

thing is bugging me."

"I'm old enough and ugly enough to be the bad guy every now and then," Dad said. "Anyway she's a kid, she'll get over it. Bet you get a few grumpy phone calls though."

"Yeah, bet I do." That reminded me we may end up without cell coverage. "We'll have satellite phones and Caine will have direct contact in case you need me. I can leave anytime. O'Hare has already cleared me to go if necessary."

"Ellie, relax. You survived your teenage years. Carla will find her way through hers."

"You sure?"

"Yes, go work. We'll be fine here."

I hung up and then called Rowan.

"I'm going away for a few days with this case. It's taking us out of town and cell coverage might be patchy."

"All right, you go catch the bad guys." He cleared his throat. "Hey, what's up with Carla?"

So, I wasn't alone. "I dunno. Everyone seems to think she and Joey are doing what teenagers do best, as in each other."

Rowan spluttered, it sounded like he'd almost choked. Guess he was having a drink. Never wise to drink and talk to me. "Doing *each other*. She is too young!"

"Uh huh." Yep, no argument from me. "Teenagers think they know everything."

"Joey?"

"Yeah, Joey."

"I'll kill the little fucker!" Anger tore through his voice.

"I'll rip his fucking dick off and shove it in his ear!"

"What?" Laughter erupted from me and spiraled down the phone. "Babe, chill. He's a kid too."

"He best keep it in his goddamn pants!"

I was struggling, really struggling. Men! So amazing and yet predictable and ridiculous in their responses.

"Dad has Carla, while I'm away, he's going to enforce some Joey-free time. You're more than welcome to go hang out with them." I was sending a raging bull into the arena - was I mad? "Do me a favor, chill. Be her friend but not too friendly – you're still ... an adult." It was possible that Rowan could get through to her where I couldn't. "Just listen to her, Rowan. And don't threaten to kill or maim anyone."

"I can't make those kinds of promises." He was furious. And I found it entertaining. He was behaving like a father. I'd never seen it before. But then, Carla never gave any of us cause to worry before.

I swallowed the laughter and let it play upon my lips. "We can get through this."

He took a deep breath. "I'll let you know if anything changes."

"Thank you." There was other stuff I wanted to say but not over the phone. He never mentioned the shooting incident on Friday so either didn't know or thought it was more media lies and didn't want to irritate me with it. I'd tell him when I got home, if Carla didn't first. If she did, they'd both be mad at me. Wouldn't be the first time. The messages on my machine from a private number and the tearful woman at the concert could be nothing worth worrying about but it niggled away in the background; that was something else I needed to talk to Rowan about in person.

Carla and the cat were taken care of. Focus. It was time to catch Campbell and not worry about how my beautiful daughter's life hung in the balance.

That was a bit dramatic. I pulled it back a little: And not worry about my daughter making a life-altering and stupid decision. Yeah, that nailed it.

Distractions be gone. I tapped the flash drive on the desk while I thought.

All we knew was that Campbell might have abducted Maria Doyle and taken Key Bridge out of Washington. No further sightings reported. Not much to go on. I tapped on my laptop keyboard and checked Maria's phone. It was either off or battery removed, there was no GPS signal for us to trace.

'These Days' started up in my head. So not helpful. What I needed was some miracle way of knowing where Campbell took her. I lifted my desk phone from the cradle and called comms.

"SSA Conway here, I have a query on three addresses."

"Go ahead, Agent."

I read the addresses from the file. Comms repeated them back to me. "Please send local police. Approach with caution. Notify me if either Iain Campbell or a Maria Doyle is present or have been seen at the addresses."

"Understood."

It still didn't help me to know which direction we should go.

The song in my head changed to '6345789.'

Okay, now that was just silly. The song continued getting louder and louder. I knew what it was from. Hadn't 'These Days' just played in my head? Wasn't '6345789' on the Japanese Tour limited edition bonus CD of that album? A rhetorical question; since dating Rowan I'd become a musical trivia queen. So what meant something? Was it Japanese, the phone number, or the album? I couldn't think of a Japanese garden in Northern Virginia. I took my phone and dialed the number. The first area code I tried was DC, seemed sensible.

The phone rang. I reached an answer machine. At Maria Doyle's place.

So was it also something to do with the album? Or just that it was Maria's phone number? That was going to take some figuring.

Mac's picture sat on my desk, smiling at me. I lay it down. Some days his smile just felt like a taunt.

I sighed, plugged the flash drive into my laptop and ran a virus check on the drive. What better way to infect the FBI system with a nasty virus than to send one to an agent? It came up clean. I opened the drive and found an MP3. Just the one.

I called Sandra to come to my office.

"What's up?" she said as she strode through the door.

"Someone sent me a song."

"A song?"

"Yeah, the same song I've been hearing in my head for days ... and someone sent it to me on a flash drive."

"Oh, that's freaky."

"Ya think?"

I double-clicked on the file and played the song. It sounded like the same as the version I had. "Why send me a song?" I was thinking out loud but not.

"Shift over," Sandra said, dragging a chair around to my side of the desk and planting herself in front of my laptop. "I take it you have this song already?"

"Yes. It's on one of my favorite albums."

"Where are your music files?"

I pointed to the Windows "Start" button on the screen but she'd already opened it and found my music folder. "Name of the album the song is on?"

"*Turn it On.*"

She paused before she opened the album. "Kevin Costner can sing?"

"Yeah, he can," I replied.

Sandra said, "I'll take your word for it." She looked through the album folder at the song files.

"That song is a cool nine point nine six megabytes but the one you were sent is just over ten point two megabytes."

"You think there is something else in that file?"

"Oh, yeah," she replied and scoured the properties of the new file. "Something is in it and someone wants you to find it." She pointed to the 'properties' window. Sandra checked the properties information on the original file, comparing all three screens of each file. "I think we have passwords."

I leaned closer and pointed out what I thought were possible passwords. "KevinCostnerRocks, TurnItOnOrOff, and 2010OpenSesame."

"I'd say so," Sandra replied. "Those particular phrases only appear on the version you were sent."

"OpenPuff?" I said.

"You have that on here?" she replied, already searching my programs. "Never mind. Got it."

I watched as Sandra filled in the password boxes, following the order in the properties section of the song file, then loaded the song file and clicked the 'unhide' button.

I couldn't help but hold my breath. A grey bar popped up on the screen. As I watched, a blue line skidded across the grey. Moments later a small window appeared with the report details in it.

"So there is a file," I said. "And someone wanted me to find it. Otherwise it wouldn't have been so easy."

Sandra found the file and ran a virus check before opening it. It was a document containing the lyrics to 'Maria Nay.'

Because I haven't been taunted by song this for long enough?

"This mean anything to you?" Sandra asked.

I glanced at the lyrics then rocked back in my chair, a smile crept across my face.

"Yes, maybe, I think it's a cipher. Look ..." I pointed to

the occasional letters that were italicized.

"Do you know what it says?"

I know my mind is a weird place but solving ciphers at first glance? Not my strong suit.

"Not yet," I said. "But I recognize the pattern of the italic letters."

"You know which cipher it is?"

"I think it is Francis Bacon's cipher."

Sandra found a website dedicated to ciphers and then one with the Francis Bacon cipher on it. "Then this should help."

I picked up my pen. "Print the lyrics file Campbell sent me, please. It's easier if I work on the page."

Sandra printed the cipher too.

I settled down with a highlighter pen and pieces of paper. Sandra disappeared then returned with two cups of coffee.

Ten minutes after I started, I rocked back in my chair and sipped my still-warm coffee.

"Okay, it's from Iain Campbell. He writes that Maria Doyle is caught in a bad situation and he will do what he can for her." I left out the interesting bit. The bit that said I was on Jonathon Tierney's safe list and he needed my help.

It was not the first time in recent history I'd heard I was on a safe list or that someone needed my help.

"How long have you had this?"

"A day"

"He knew what was going to happen to Maria Doyle?"

"Seems that way. He knew and tried to tell me but I was so caught up in the case I didn't look at the flash drive." I smacked the heel of my hand into my head. Dammit. She's missing because I missed something. This is on me.

"He should've been more obvious, but at least now you know he *may not* be the bad guy we thought he was," Sandra said, standing up and putting the chair back where it belonged.

"Maybe." I appreciated her words but they didn't make me feel a helluva lot better. "Thanks for your help Sandra."

"No problem. I'm still reeling from the news that Kevin Costner sings."

She waved and left the room.

Chapter Nineteen
Till The Next Goodbye

Pulling my go-bag out of the cupboard, I rifled through it. Spare warm clothes and toiletries. It's as if I've done this before. From the hanger, I took an FBI jacket and pulled it on.

I sat at my desk for a minute and went over the file again. The boyfriend puzzled me. His name was John Brown. Sure it was. Guess if he'd called himself John Smith or John Doe it would've been too suspicious. I was over anyone calling themselves John anything. It just inferred subterfuge and made me in turn want to start slapping people. I put a call through to the cell phone number he'd given the police. It went to voice mail. I left a message asking him to call me.

Campbell went to the trouble to send a cipher to me. I wished he'd told me more, like what the situation was, and why Maria was in danger. Even sketchy details would've been helpful. He went to some effort to hide a cipher that said nothing of any value. More smoke and mirrors crap.

I tried the alternate number Brown gave police. No answer and no machine.

His address was listed. I called Sandra at her desk. "Hey, can you get a uniform to check out this address. We're trying to locate John Brown."

"Sure," she said. "Standing by for the address."

"400 Michigan Avenue, North East, Washington."

"Seriously?"

"Yeah, it's in the police report. Problem?"

I could hear her tapping on her computer keys. "I'm just checking, okay." She hissed air through her teeth. "I thought I knew the address. That's the National Shrine. I'll call Monsignor Rossi. If Brown has anything to do with the shrine, he should know."

"Keep me informed."

He called himself John Brown and his address was the Basilica of the National Shrine of the Immaculate Conception. I had a feeling he was more lying scumbag than saint. Could he be the dangerous situation Campbell was trying to warn me about? This is one of those "the more information the better" circumstances. So far my information was piss-poor.

I made one more call.

It took a long time before I heard my favorite Russian's voice over the phone. "*Privet*, Ellie!"

"*Privet*, Misha! *Vy nashli propavshego syna?*" Hello, Misha. Have you found the missing son?

"*Vash Russkiye uluchshayetsya.*" Your Russian is improving.

"I try. Have you found him?"

"I have. I am convincing him to accompany me to the US."

My breath escaped in a rush and realized I'd been holding it. "Good. Thank you."

"How is Carla?"

"You will see for yourself when you get in. She is growing up fast." Too fast.

"We will be there by tomorrow morning."

"Thank you."

I hung up.

A male voice followed a knock on my door, "Hey, El, want a hand?"

Only one person ever called me El like that. And there he was leaning on my doorframe. NCIS Special Agent Noel Gerrard. He didn't look as though he'd been up all night and I hadn't expected to see him again so soon.

"Noel, what brings you over here?"

"Maria Doyle," he said.

My eyes flashed to his. "NCIS has a connection?"

"Our Directors have a connection, she's known to them both."

Interesting.

"Who the hell is she? Her name seems familiar." I've come across a lot of people over the years, she could've been one of them. Her Facebook page didn't mention family and none of her listed friends were familiar to me. She didn't have much on the page at all, no mention of the mysterious boyfriend or Campbell. I could have Googled her or even run her through our system but hadn't. O'Hare said friend. That should be good enough. Things change. It was, now it isn't.

"A Doyle."

"No fuc'n kidding." A smart ass I did not need today.

The penny dropped with a clang. "I've met her, she

looks different now."

"I believe she had her hair straightened," Noel replied.

"And darkened. She was a blonde," I replied. "Your Director, Christopher Doyle, he's her father or brother?"

"Brother."

"God, the agencies are incestuous," I muttered. Hence our case.

"I think it's Washington in general. It's not that big a place."

"So, you and your team are in?"

"Just me, I've left the team dealing with two UAs and a drug bust."

Then I noticed the bag hooked over his shoulder. My cell phone rang, sending Grange's latest single 'Agent of my Heart' out into my office, filling every available space. I checked the display. Unknown caller.

Crazy. I had no idea it was my ringtone for unknown callers. A smile crossed my lips; Carla would have done it. She was forever playing with my phone and changing my ringtones. I answered the phone and listened as a police officer told me of a new crime scene. When I hung up I looked at Noel.

"We have an address." I took a breath and gave him the address. It was not far from my new house. I hate it when shit is close to home.

"We'll take three cars," I said.

"Ride with me?" Noel said.

"Out of luck, I'm riding with Kurt."

Riding with Noel meant priorities for things like coffee

and food, which were all good, but he also thought we should be an item, and he wasn't Delta A and the Doyle abduction was in-house, meaning I wanted to be able to speak freely with my team. And Noel had an annoying habit of keeping secrets. Or not telling me all he knew. There was another reason. I needed to concentrate on the present situation and didn't want to cloud my mind with discussion about the Chad/Mac dilemma. I closed that thought down and pushed it to the back of my mind.

Working now. Doing what I'm semi-good at: chasing bad guys and attracting aberrations.

Lee, Sam, and Kurt were waiting by the elevator.

"Noel," Lee said, shaking his hand.

Sam followed suit, restraining himself to a regular handshake. Impressive. Kurt was last, and movie star cool. I was in trouble and I knew it. The trick now was to keep everyone else from guessing. Some days I could still hear him telling me how he felt about me that day in Lexington. I pretended I'd forgotten a lot of the events from that episode. It was an acceptable memory slip considering I was suffering from a form of amnesia at the time. Pretending was much safer than acknowledging feelings and other such nonsense.

"We're rolling on a crime scene at one of Campbell's properties," I explained as we headed down in the elevator. "Hope everyone has warm weatherproof clothing. The forecast is not good. We could be in for some stormy weather." Both metaphoric and real storms were a possibility. I looked at Noel as he leaned back on the elevator wall. "Noel is joining us. He'll be taking his car."

Once we were in our cars, I made a conference call. Delta A only. Another good reason to insist NCIS Special Agent Noel Gerrard took his car.

"The flash drive that came with the picture of Campbell contained a copy of 'Maria Nay' and that contained a cipher from Campbell."

I listened to the collective intake of breath. No one spoke, so I carried on, "It may be that Campbell is one of us and that his involvement in Doyle's disappearance is more to save her life than to harm her."

Another sharp intake of breath.

Sam spoke, "That's risky thinking."

"Yes, it is. But let's say, for argument's sake, that I believe him until it's proven he's not helping."

"Let's say he's a scum bag abductor until we know for sure he isn't," Lee replied.

"Fair enough," I agreed. "Nor is John Brown the most reliable witness here. His address is fake. Creative but still fake. I'm not holding out much hope for his name either."

"What is it about Campbell that makes you think you can trust him?" Lee asked. "Bearing in mind you and Kurt were looking for a Peter Parker."

Good point. Spiderman turned out to be Campbell.

I took a deep breath. "Trust might be too strong a word, Lee. I'm not distrusting of him. As for why? He mentioned a list Tierney has. A safe list. My name is on it.

He knew that."

"He's involved with the CIA?" Sam said.

"The plot just thickened," Kurt said. "This is Delta only?"

I nodded and said, "This is specific Delta *A* only information."

Forty-five minutes later we rolled in behind two police cruisers. Lee and Sam pulled in behind us and Noel behind them. I headed to the house and the officer waiting on the front steps for me.

My mood darkened with every passing second.

The weather changed for the worse. A storm front gathered momentum. A rumble of distant thunder followed a flash of lightning.

"Agent Conway, I'm Officer Dylan James," he said, shaking my hand.

"Good to meet you," I replied. I turned to Kurt. "This is SSA Kurt Henderson."

They shook and nodded at each other.

"I was first on scene," he replied to me. Good to know. It meant it was his scene.

I searched my pockets and came up empty. No gloves. It was odd that I'd forgotten to put a few pairs in my pocket before I left the office.

"Gloves," I said, holding out my hand. A pair of latex gloves landed in my palm. I pulled them on, letting the latex snap against my wrists. Blue disposable bootees were passed to me. Leaning on the wall seemed the best way to tug them over the soles of my cowboy boots.

"Let's do this," I said. "Talk me through it."

Dylan held up the crime scene tape while I ducked under, and then followed me.

"It looks like the occupant surprised an intruder in the living room," he said pointing into a room. "Mind your step."

I glanced down as I entered. Taking care, I walked down the hallway in the house. There was a trail of blood from the front door to just inside the living room. Blood soaked into the carpet in palm-sized irregular pools. Kurt and I stepped around the bloodstains as we entered the room. On the floor lay a battered disfigured body.

The walls and furnishing bore splatter. Streaks of blood ran down the windowpanes. It was one very vicious attack that took place.

"The blood-soaked carpet near the living room door and the trail down the hall, what caused that?" I said. The body was about eight feet from the doorway and there was no blood leading up to it or away from it.

Dylan shook his head. "I don't know. If you look at the blood spurt and the pooling near and under the body, it looks like she bled out where she lies."

"Kurt? Another victim, maybe?"

He nodded. "It's possible."

I scanned the room, taking in the scenario. It was my feeling that there was another victim. I could feel myself drifting, watching the attack on the woman play out like a movie.

Senseless, brutal, terrifying.

I pulled myself back to the scene in front of me.

"Murder weapon?" Kurt said.

Dylan pointed to a lamp and a large kitchen knife.

"The lamp appears to belong here and the knife is from a block on the kitchen counter."

"There is either another victim or the assailant was injured," Kurt said.

I crouched next to the body, looking for signs that she'd fought back. There were none.

"Who are you?" I whispered to the battered body.

"Ma'am?"

"Name, please."

"Mary Southey."

"We will find the person who did this to you, Mary," I said patting her shoulder with my gloved hand before I stood up.

"Mary Southey, Sixty-seven, widow living with her friend, moved here five months ago," the police officer said.

"Where is her friend?"

He shook his head. "No sign of him."

"Him?"

"Yes, ma'am, George Foster, aged seventy-two."

"You think maybe he could be the other victim?" I tried hard to keep the condescension from my voice; up until I figured there was another person involved, he'd done well being in charge of the crime scene.

"I wouldn't like to say, ma'am."

I bet you wouldn't.

"Did you conduct a perimeter and house search when you arrived?"

"I checked the house, ma'am."

"And? Any sign of Mr. Foster?"

He appeared flustered. "Not that I could see, ma'am. I was on my own."

"Is this your first homicide?"

"Yes, ma'am."

I sighed. "You and I will talk about this but right now I need to try and locate Mr. Foster." I pulled my phone off my belt and called comms to request paramedics at the scene. For all I knew Foster could be alive.

Dylan paled and hurried away. Kurt and I split up and searched the house. Foster wasn't hiding inside.

"Storm cellar?" I said with a nod of my head toward the back of the house.

"If he went around the house there should be some kind of trail," Kurt replied.

We went out the front door, watching for signs that a wounded man had left the house. "Transfer," I said pointing to a dark mark on the grass where blood had transferred from shoes or clothing, rather than having dripped from a moving person.

Kurt and I hustled around to the right of the front door, following the occasional dark stain leading to the storm cellar. It was at the back of the house. Smears of blood trailed across the door.

I stood aside.

"On three," Kurt said. "One, two, three."

He flung open the cellar door, letting light flood the dankness below. I could see a shape, face down on the ground.

"FBI!" I called. The shape didn't move.

Kurt holstered his weapon and ran down the stairs. I followed him

"Looks like he fell after shutting the door," Kurt said. "No one's head should be at that angle. He felt for the man's pulse. He looked up at me and shook his head.

Damn.

Kurt and I rolled the man over onto his back. Cloudy dead eyes stared at nothing. His blood- soaked clothes told of his encounter with horror. Unlike the lady of the house, George had defensive wounds on his arms and scraped knuckles. He'd put up a fight.

Kurt went through the man's pockets, found his wallet, and passed me his driver's license. Confirmation that he was George Foster. I crouched beside George.

"Don't suppose you can tell us what happened, George?" I waited, just in case he could tell me. Because stranger things have happened. That was when I saw something in his hand. "Kurt, is that a cell phone?"

I pointed at his right hand. Kurt pried the object from the dead fingers that encased it and threw it to me.

"His phone."

"Oh, George, did you take pictures?" I whispered, unlocking the phone and scrolling through the image files. "You did. Good man." There was more joy than I expected in my voice as I found pictures of the assailant and a vehicle.

"Look," I said to Kurt handing him the phone. "They're not great but I don't think that's Campbell. What do you think?"

"I don't know, doesn't look like the man in the photo we have, but then, it's blurry." He scrolled to another photograph. "What about the car?"

I looked at the picture of the car. It wasn't in front of the house. It was up the driveway, not far from where we were in the cellar. A dark red sedan. I could just make out the very edge of what could be another vehicle in front of the house, that vehicle was blue and looked like a much bigger vehicle.

"What do you think?" I said.

"Okay, there were two vehicles. Campbell may or may not have killed the couple."

"Reasonable doubt?"

"Yes."

I climbed out of the cellar and went to find Dylan. Sirens wailed in the distance reminding me I'd called for paramedics. I called comms and said they were unnecessary and they should send a medical examiner instead. As I hung up, the siren stopped.

Dylan was pacing up and down in front of the house. "Where'd you go?" he asked.

"We found George. He's dead."

"Oh, man, I'm sorry." Dylan stepped backward and made to remove his hat but knocked it from his head. "I'm sorry. I should have looked for him ..."

I picked up the hat and handed it to Dylan. He took it and seemed to be struggling with whether or not to put it back on his head.

"It wouldn't have made a difference if you'd looked for him or not, he broke his neck falling down the cellar steps."

"But I should have—"

I held my hand up to stop him. "And next time you will," I said with a small smile. "We learn and we apply that knowledge, that's how this works. You will never fuck up like this again."

He nodded. I knew it'd take him a few weeks to see it my way. I knew that, because he was good and he cared. His fingers worried the rim of his hat.

"I'm sorry." Dylan said.

"Another point, when you arrive at a scene like this, call for paramedics. Just in case you get a live victim."

"Yes, ma'am. What now?" Dylan asked.

"Put that hat on your head, officer, you're working this scene."

"Yes, ma'am."

"An FBI crime scene unit will be here soon. Until we know otherwise, let's consider this as part of my case."

He nodded. "We canvassed the neighbors. A man and woman were seen entering the property. A neighbor identified them as Iain and Maria Campbell." He flipped through notebook pages. "Next door neighbor, Mrs. Gillian Jessup, eighty-two, says she thought our victim, Mary Southey, knew the visitors."

"She identified them as Iain and Maria Campbell?"

"Yes, ma'am."

Well, that makes him more than just an ex-boyfriend and yet we found nothing to indicate a marriage in any of our searches.

"Which house?"

He pointed to the house on the right.

Mrs. Jessup had a good view of the front of Mary Southey's house. She might also be able to tell me why she described Iain and Maria as married. I pulled off the gloves and bootees, rolled them inside out and handed them to Dylan.

"I'll be right back," I called over my shoulder. "Kurt, can you carry on here?"

"I got it," he called.

Mrs. Jessup's front door opened before I knocked.

"Mrs. Jessup?" I said showing my badge.

"Yes, dear."

"I'm Special Agent Ellie Conway. Can I ask you some questions about your neighbors, Mrs. Southey and Mr. Foster?"

"Come in, dear, we'll talk in the parlor."

I followed her and her Zimmer frame along the hallway and into a cozy room filled with well-polished dark furniture and thick, deep green velvet drapes. A faint smell of lemon Pledge held an undertone of lavender. The room smelled like an elderly woman. It wasn't unpleasant and it wasn't hiding a death. It was comfortable, warm, and inviting. I opened my notebook and was ready with my pen poised.

"Did you see the visitors to your neighbor's home today?"

"Yes, I did. I was out getting the mail when a car pulled up out front."

Even better.

"Do you know what type of car?"

She shook her head. "No, dear. It was big and blue that's all I know."

"Sedan or four-wheel drive big?"

"Yes, one of those big truck things that people get about in these days. Not a pick-up, no. More fancy than that."

"Was it clean?" Rentals are always clean.

"Now that I think about it, no, it wasn't. There was dirt up the sides and on the front."

"Was it raining when they arrived?"

"No. We're not expecting rain until late today."

"Have you seen the woman before?"

"Of course, dear. Iain and Maria lived next door for a year or so before they moved away. They rent the house out, you know?"

"They were married?"

"I assumed so, Iain introduced Maria to me as Mrs. Campbell."

I wrote that down.

"Did Mrs. Southey know the couple?"

"Yes, she seemed to, although I don't remember them ever visiting before. A property manager looks after the house for Mr. Campbell. He doesn't come out here as general rule."

"Any idea why they came out today?"

"No, dear. They didn't stay long. Iain called out when he left and said Mrs. Southey wasn't home."

"Was she home?"

"I didn't see her go out."

I sensed that Mrs. Jessup was the unofficial neighborhood watch. "Did you see any other cars this morning?"

Mrs. Jessup looked thoughtful for a few moments. "I saw the yellow car that Mrs. Fendalton down the street drives, go by my place. It's her market day." She stopped talking. I figured I was out of luck. "Come to think of it, I did see another car. A dark red car. I don't know who was driving but I thought it pulled out of Mrs. Southey's driveway." She smiled. "I must've been seeing things. Two visitors at once are unheard of next door. She has never been very social, bless her heart."

"Do you know when that would've been?"

"It was before I saw Iain and Maria arrive. I think the red car left as they were just going inside."

Interesting.

"Who was out in the street this morning when Iain Campbell came?"

She rattled off the names of four neighbors and their addresses.

"Were the Campbell's carrying anything when they left?"

"Yes, Mr. Campbell carried a big bag. A pack. He used to go hiking when they lived here. I thought maybe he'd left something in the attic."

"Thank you very much, Mrs. Jessup. I wish my neighbors were as vigilant as you." I shook the woman's hand. "I'll let myself out. You stay in the warmth."

I walked with decorum from the house and back over to her neighbors, fighting the urge to run back with my findings. Kurt was waiting in the hallway.

"Anything?"

"She thinks Campbell left with a pack or a bag. Even commented that it may have been left in the attic when they moved out."

"Let's find out what else is in the attic," Kurt replied. We walked down the hallway looking up, trying to locate the trapdoor. It was out in the laundry room. "What else did she say?" Kurt pulled a ladder down from the ceiling. I passed him the flashlight from my belt.

"A dark red car may have left not long after Campbell arrived."

"Before someone killed the occupants or after?"

"I don't know. That's what we need to find out. Campbell is in a big blue car, maybe a four by four and it was dirty. So he's ditched the white rental," I said.

"The blue four by four could be his personal vehicle rather than another rental. He could've been off-road recently."

"That's what I thought, I'll get Sandra to search for vehicles registered to Campbell. We might get lucky.

What I don't get is why Maria went with him. Although the neighbor told me Iain introduced Maria as his wife when they used to live out here."

"That's interesting. I take it you mean you don't know why Maria didn't or hasn't contacted her brother and called off the hounds, if Campbell is the good guy in this scenario?"

"Yep."

Kurt climbed the ladder and peered inside the ceiling. "Roomy. Proper floor. Looks like a store room." He climbed inside. I followed him. As I reached the top, lights flickered on. "Power."

"Yay," I replied. I didn't have to stoop and nor did Kurt, the ceiling above him was a good six inches away. This room was functional. I wondered why it didn't have proper stairs. Would've made an excellent upstairs bedroom or office.

Boxes were stacked along one wall. Kurt moved. Dust puffed in small clouds where he stepped.

"If Campbell was the bad guy then he would have sent her up here, otherwise she could have used the time to escape or make a phone call," I said and began looking for a note or something to indicate what was going on and corroborate my thoughts on Campbell's involvement.

"And if they'd arrived to find a dead body he may have sent Doyle up here to keep her away from the scene downstairs," Kurt said. It sounded as if he was with me on the Campbell being a good guy scenario.

My eyes scoured the walls; she could've written

something anywhere. Nothing that looked like a note caught my eye. Furniture was piled at one end of the room; a desk with chairs stacked on it, several empty bookcases, and an old rocking horse.

The desk seemed a likely place. I pulled out the top desk drawer. Empty. The second drawer was jammed. But the third contained a notepad and a small well-used pencil.

I patted my pockets looking for new latex gloves. Kurt threw me a pair and I pulled them on then lifted the notebook out of the drawer and flipped through it. The inner pages revealed a scrawled note.

"Kurt, it was her. She writes 'I am Maria Campbell née Doyle. Iain's taking me to his cabin in the woods – he said I'm in danger. Someone killed the couple who are renting our house. Help me.'"

"Someone killed ... not Campbell killed them. That's interesting. Makes the other car's presence more intriguing," Kurt said. He looked at the note. "That was written in a hurry."

"Née Doyle? She is referring to herself as married and to this as their house. Why were we not given this information up front?"

"Good question. This case is full of questions."

"Would've been nice if she'd said where the cabin is," I said. The pad felt odd in my hand. I flicked through it again. "Pages missing, but nothing else written anywhere. She could have taken some."

"You think she'll try leaving notes?"

"I hope so."

There was nothing else of interest in the attic. We took the pad with us. Lee and Sam were waiting at the bottom of the ladder with a plate of cookies.

"Cookies?" I said.

Sam grinned. "Nice neighborhood."

I took one. "These are good," I declared between bites. "I love coconut."

Sam was right. This was a nice neighborhood full of older people. Retired. Cooking, baking, neighborly folk. When they found out what happened to Mrs. Southey and her friend Mr. Foster it was going to hit them hard.

"Where's Dylan, the cop?" Kurt said looking around.

"Outside the front door," Lee replied.

We followed Kurt back down the hall to the front doorway and listened as he spoke to Dylan. "I think we should get support services in here before the coroner turns up to take the body. This is a close, neighborly place. I can get FBI victim assistance here, is that all right with you?"

Dylan nodded. He was chewing a mouthful of cookie. He swallowed fast. "Yes, sir."

Kurt walked away and made a phone call.

Chapter Twenty
Fear

We stayed in the area canvassing neighbors, hoping to get more information for almost two hours. During which time I'd asked Sandra to look for vehicles titled and registered to Campbell.

My phone rang. It was a call back from Sandra.

"Hey, got anything?"

"There are no vehicles registered to Iain Campbell," Sandra said.

"Crap."

"That doesn't mean he doesn't have vehicles. Could be that he uses a third party, a company for example."

"He's not making this easy."

"No, he's not."

I hung up.

There were no reported sightings of the dark red car or the blue truck. We did know the truck was not the same car in which Campbell and Maria left Washington. A BOLO was out to locate his white rental car, which might hold some clues.

Instead of going back to DC, we decided to set up a base in a motel. All we knew was that Campbell was headed to a cabin, it could be anywhere, or nowhere. Sandra was searching public records looking for his cabin. Meanwhile, we needed a direction.

Without knowing why, 'west' popped into my head.

West.

Not a song, just a word. Nice to have something simple for a change.

"Hey, anyone seen Noel?" I called across the front lawn to Sam and Lee who were climbing into their car.

"Nope," Sam replied. Lee looked back to where his car should've been. "He didn't say anything."

"Great, now we have a runaway NCIS agent," I muttered. Only Kurt could hear me. "Can we go save this woman *now*, please?"

"After you," Kurt said with a smile. He held the passenger door open for me. I looked around for Noel, one last time. He was in the wind.

I climbed in. Kurt pressed the door shut. Impatient, I found myself tapping on the armrest and muttering, "T-t-t-today people, today."

Kurt eased into the driver's seat, glanced at me, and then pulled his seat belt across his body. Everything seemed to take so fuc'n long. I watched with pent-up annoyance as he clicked the locking mechanism into place. Adjusted the rearview mirror. Fiddled with the wing mirrors. Moved the seat back. Good grief! He was the last person to drive the car so surely nothing had changed. My fingers tapped.

Now's good. I glared at the road in front of us. T-t-today, people.

"You all right?" Kurt said, pulling away from the curb. I caught his eye in the edge of the rearview mirror and looked away.

"I'm okay."

"You seem agitated."

I didn't reply. His simple observation made me want to scream. Scream. Of course I was agitated. There was a dead old lady and a dead old man; a man claiming to be helping keep a missing woman safe; and a dark red car indicating that someone else was at the scene of the deaths, as did the note left by Maria who is married to Campbell. Also Brown isn't Brown. There are four dead people in one family and I have no answers. None.

What the hell was I going to tell the one surviving member of the Bleich family when Misha brought him home? Sorry? We did our best but the Unsub who killed your family was just too clever? I'm sure we'll catch him sometime? Meanwhile we were chasing an abducted woman all over northern Virginia instead of investigating the deaths of your entire family.

Where the hell is the justice?

God sucks.

And just like that he and I were back to not speaking.

I settled into the seat. Best to keep my borderline rage to myself. Kurt may not view it as helpful to the case. Dark clouds rolled across the grey sky. Lightning shot from the center of the blackest cloud bank, filling the sky with an eerie white glow. The storm erupted.

Thinking time was what I needed. And where the hell did Noel disappear to? Who does that? Who begs in on an investigation then just leaves? That's not right. Sure he's kept things from me in the past, but not while working with us on something. Odd behavior. Odd indeed.

I leaned my head on the window and thought. My eyes closed. All distractions floated off into the blurry distance. The one face I saw made zero sense. It wasn't Mac. There was no butterfly. I was looking straight into the eyes of Christopher Chance and recalling what Lee told me about the actor behind the character. As irrelevant as it seemed, I knew the twisted way my subconscious worked. I went with it. Hell, if Christopher Chance is all I have, then he'd best be good enough.

Blue eyes stared back into mine. The expression I saw was interest, not confusion, or concern.

Interest. He knew something and I needed to know what he knew. Somewhere beyond the scene that immersed me, I could just detect reality. Like a half-open door you catch sight of in your peripheral vision. I kicked it shut. The world disappeared with a bang. Chance stood his ground.

"Who are you?" I said.

"Christopher Chance," he replied.

"Really?"

A grin blasted across his face then disappeared. "Nah, I'm an actor."

I swallowed. "And you're here because?"

"Because you have a warped imagination and you think I know something about one of the men involved in this case."

"Do you?"

"I might."

"Do you?" I repeated.

"What do you think?"

My thoughts needed to stay within the confines of my skull because I thought he was shaping up to be an infuriating sonofabitch and that wasn't helpful.

"Are we going to do this all day, or are you going to tell me?"

He smiled. It was boyish. I liked it and that annoyed me on a whole new level. But his charm was not going to sway me from my course, after all this was *my* fantasy.

"Tell me, please."

"Campbell is military. Or I should say he was on active military service."

Searching my memory banks I struggled with the military aspect. Why does everything that turns ugly always have a military connection?

"Was?"

"He's not active military now."

"You were army, was he?"

"Yes, he served in Desert Storm."

"And you know him?"

He shook his head. "I know he was army and I know he served about the time I did."

"Thanks."

"Don't mention it. Now, you have to find out why he's involved and who is after them."

"I will." I thought of something else as his blue eyes began to fade. "One more thing ... why am I talking to you and not my dead husband?"

Chance took one step forward. He was an inch from my face and he melted. His hair dripped blonde streaks, beneath the blond I saw familiar black. His eyes darkened, leaving the light blue behind, as flecks of gold and brown swam in hazel eyes. His height and body shape remained the same. Mac's hazel eyes smiled and his lips touched mine. "I thought you didn't want me around anymore," he whispered. "But I didn't want to go yet."

There was no bullet hole in his forehead. Maybe Sean was right and I aimed high or you can't shoot ghosts after all.

"But Chance?"

"Every girl deserves a Christopher Chance rescue ..."

I smiled. He quoted me from another time and another place.

"Not me, dude. As Lee once said, I am a human target."

Mac faded to nothing before my eyes. Moments later, I was pulling my cell phone free of my belt and calling Sandra.

"Hey, it's me. The ex-boyfriend, Iain Campbell. He might be Maria's estranged husband, not an ex-boyfriend. Also, check out his service record. Army. He was Army. I want to know why he left and everything else about him,"

"Sure, on it now."

I loved that she didn't ask how I knew. I heard her

218

nails tapping on the computer keys and waited. Sandra was good and she was quick.

She sighed. "We have an interesting situation. His service record is incomplete."

"Incomplete?"

"He was army. He served in Desert Storm. He was stationed in Germany. We even have a posting back to Virginia. But after nineteen-ninety-three there is nothing."

"Discharge paperwork?"

"Nothing. The rest of his file is confidential."

"He never left the army." A cold river of blackened foreboding stormed through me searching for a culvert to take it straight to hell. Not active military service. Another joint task force or did he jump right over from the army to CIA? "See if Caine can work his magic on the file. We need to know what he was involved in and why his record is confidential."

Sandra hung up after assuring me she'd call me back as soon as she found something. She rocked. She was the best Delta support person ever.

I'd have to be dead to not feel Kurt's brewing questions. I smiled at him. "Go ahead, ask."

"I get you can see things ... but you appeared to be sleeping and now you know our man was army and where he saw action. How?"

His question was valid but didn't make it any easier for me to answer. It was Kurt. The man who saved my life and helped me recover my memory. I could tell him even though I didn't want to hear my words once they escaped the safety of my skull. They sounded a little insane.

"Christopher Chance told me." I watched the words sparkle and glow as they floated in the air just above the dashboard.

"Who the hell is he?" The words fell from his mouth right before a sudden dawning. "Oh, that canceled TV show you liked. *Human Target*." He paused for a second. I could imagine the hamsters running on the wheels in his head trying to keep that light going. "You've moved on from talking to the dead?"

"Not quite. He turned into Mac at the end of our conversation."

"And none of this bothers you?"

Of course it bothers me. "Nope."

"I saw that show a few times. If Guerrero turns up and wants to tell you something - we could be in a power of trouble, and you better listen," Kurt said.

Jackie Earle Haley played the perfect Guerrero. "If Guerrero shows up, we're way past listening."

My phone rang. I answered it. Any interruption was welcome.

"Caine has gone to O'Hare, we need the Director to wield some weight to open the file," Sandra said.

"Thanks." I hung up and muttered to Kurt. "Who does this guy think he is? Jack Reacher?"

Kurt laughed. "That's all we need, to be tracking a Jack Reacher wannabe gone to the dark side."

"It scares me that you think Reacher is the light side."

"Scares me that you might end up talking to him."

All conversation stopped while I considered his comment.

It was legitimate.

Kurt was watching me with a thoughtful expression. I waited, expecting his next comment to be interesting.

"You don't know the meaning of fear do you?" Kurt continued. I frowned and shook my head. I've been plenty scared on and off during my life and more so since becoming a parent, but for me fear was something that told me I was alive.

A grin spread across his face. "Fuck everything and run."

I smiled back. "Seems about right."

I understood what he meant. I just couldn't seem to translate it into something that would deter me. It's not as if I hadn't wanted to run many, many times.

In fact, so often it became a too-many-to-count situation.

Yet here I am.

Recently I'd experienced such a moment - a powerful urge to run - and it stuck with me. I felt it climbing around the walls in my mind, the partitioned walls that stopped the thought from becoming action. I had to stop it because of the shit storm that would ensue if I acted upon it. I'd be running forever. And I know I can't outrun myself.

"You okay?" Kurt said, his hand brushed my shoulder.

"Sure."

"Nuh uh, not buying. Something you want to share?"

"Nope."

"Conway?" His voice softened. "Ellie?"

"No." I gave my best impersonation of a smile. "Leave it."

That indiscriminate thought climbed higher. I watched as its long fingers clung to the top of the wall, nails visible on the other side. If it climbed much further it would find daylight. I took a deep breath and willed it back down. But it stayed, clinging to the wall. Determined. Impulsive. Terrifying. But it wasn't terrifying, not really. Because I knew I could do it. I could run. I could run away from it all. I looked out the window.

Trees, concrete, traffic, and overlaid over the landscape was Kurt's reflection. He wasn't helping. I reached forward and pressed the power button for the radio. Music would help.

Grasping at straws is what I do best.

Kevin Costner and Modern West filled the car with 'Maria Nay.'

Oh, for God's sake, not again! I gritted my teeth so hard my jaw ached.

"Can you hear that?" I said. Knowing full well how it sounded.

"The song? Sure. Am I not supposed to?"

"I've been hearing it for days. It's the song that Campbell sent me."

"Conway, you're special," he replied. "So what does it mean, now that we can both hear it?"

"It's got something to do with the case. With Maria. It can't just be the vehicle Campbell chose to hide that cipher in, that's way beyond weird."

"That is stranger than I'd expect from you. What do you think the relevance of the song is?"

"It's possible that Maria Doyle has something to do with the situation. We think we know that she's not the captive we thought she was. But what if Campbell is being played. What if ..."

"Something altogether different is going on and she is involved on some level?"

"That could be it ... it has something to do with whoever killed that couple but how it all links to our original case, I do not know. I just know it does. Proving it may well provide extra entertainment, but I do think there is a strong link."

The song ended. I waited for my mind to mirror the song and replay it. Nothing happened. Did figuring out that Maria and the mystery man were involved with the Bleich case mean I wouldn't be subjected to Maria Nay again? I didn't dare hope.

"If she's involved then why the note?" Kurt said.

"Because she doesn't want anyone knowing. Chances of getting caught?"

"Quite high, she's related to some weighty folk."

"But if you're the victim and you're caught ..."

"Nothing will happen."

We both thought about that for a bit.

Then Kurt said, "So it could be that she's involved with

Bleich in more than her job indicates. What I don't get is why Campbell abducted her, or at least let it look as though he did. How stupid is this guy?"

"I have some concerns about the way he took her from her home. I could understand it if the threat against her was from someone she trusted and she wouldn't believe it, perhaps."

"Is this an abduction at all?"

I smiled. "She's not free to leave. For whatever reason. He took her with force from her home and knocked out the boyfriend in the process."

"That's looking like abduction."

"If I didn't know who to trust and I knew someone was in danger and they wouldn't believe me ... I would do what Campbell did."

Kurt pulled over and stared at me. I think it was horror etched into his face.

"Your mind is a dark place," he said.

I shrugged. "It makes sense. The danger has to be from someone close to her. He left me a message which I was too slow in picking up. Lee knocked on her door and left a card which may have been the tipping point for the Unsub. I would imagine Campbell was watching, hoping that Lee was the cavalry but then discovered he wasn't. His options must've been limited. He took her to keep her alive." Postulating, speculating, and running with the crazy thoughts in my head.

As soon as I said it, I knew that couldn't be right. He knew Maria. He knew who her brother was. Why didn't

224

he go straight to Director Doyle? Why didn't he contact me again in a more direct manner? Why don't we have any pictures of the mysterious John Brown?

"You seem very sure of Campbell," Kurt said.

"It worries me that I think this man is some kind of knight in shining armor and that I can see his possible reasoning," I confessed.

"Got evidence?"

"Nope, you?"

We smiled at each other. It was going to be fun finding out the truth.

To me it still felt like Maria was involved somehow and that Campbell was trying to protect her and maybe even knew of her involvement. It had to be more than just working for the company that organized the fundraising event. That wasn't anything I considered dangerous.

"You want to put money on whether or not Campbell is the good guy in all this?" I asked Kurt as he turned the key in the ignition.

"I'm not stupid enough to bet against you," he replied, checking the traffic then pulling out.

"Fair enough." And true. He wasn't stupid at all.

Chapter Twenty One
What About You?

My phone rang, or more accurately, a song blared from my phone. I answered.

"It's Sandra. I found something."

"Go ..."

"Iain Campbell was having an affair with Marika Bleich."

"Whoa, Nellie, that's a big something. You're certain of this?"

That's three connections to the Bleich family. Maria worked for the event company. Campbell was banging the wife. Marika was Quinn Sutherland's lawyer. I dismissed the Sutherland issue for the moment. Campbell and Maria were front and center.

"It seems that way. I'm still working, will have more soon. Oh, and Misha called with the

flight number. I'll have Caine meet him and Zachary."

"Freaking fantastic. Thanks Sandra."

Kurt looked at me and smiled. "Share?"

"Sandra thinks Campbell was banging Marika Bleich."

"Now that's a corn starch moment," Kurt said.

One of my eyebrows rose. "Say what?"

"Corn starch, it's a thickening agent," he said with a grin.

"I know what it is and what it does. Smartass."

Smartass he maybe but he was right about the latest

news regarding Campbell. "Which makes me wonder ... did he kill her?"

"That would explain why her death was so different from the other three."

"Campbell is forty-four, Marika was fifty-nine," I said.

That was a decent age gap but not ridiculous. My mind spun as it tried to understand why a man like him wanted an older married woman.

"Does that make her a cougar?"

"He's not young enough to make her a cougar. I think it makes her an adulteress," I replied. "But this puts a new spin on things. You think it was love or lust or something more sinister?"

We looked at each other and grinned. Sinister.

I made a quantum leap and called Cheryl. "Hey, it's Ellie. Bit of a weird question for you."

"Go ahead," she said with a smile in her voice.

"Are Ephram and Jonah and Zachary brothers?"

There was a pause, before she answered, "It was assumed so ..."

"But you had doubts about the twins' parentage?" So do I.

"If someone asked me for an explanation I'd be hard pushed to come up with one, but I have doubts."

"You've already done DNA, haven't you?" My fingers crossed. I hoped so, then we'd be that much closer to an answer.

"I have and I'll have the results soon. We will know for certain if the twins are Sigmund and Marika's offspring.

I'd like to run a DNA test on the surviving brother as well."

"If he refuses have Sandra get a warrant."

"Will do."

"So why the DNA?" Curiosity got the best of me. "You must have seen something that made you suspicious."

"Maybe I'm starting to think like you."

"Now that's scary." A voice in my head laughed. You can't be like me, so don't even try.

"You're telling me."

"And the real reason?"

"I had both parents on tables and when I brought the boys in it felt like I was playing a game on Sesame Street. All of a sudden I'm Mr. Hooper and three of these things are kinda the same."

I laughed. "You are becoming me. That's spooky."

"You find it spooky and I'm just scared," she said with a chuckle. "Anyway, Sigmund Bleich doesn't seem to fit. I thought it was worth investigating."

"Let me know."

"You take care out there."

I hung up.

So, Marika may have played the adulteress game before.

And without any sort of encouragement whatsoever, a new song started up. 'Carrie Anne.' I was hearing The Hollies.

I groaned.

"You all right?" Kurt asked, glancing at me. I noticed

he was checking mirrors too, preparing to pull over if necessary.

I sighed. "Sure. I'm just fine and dandy." The song continued.

"Share?"

"I can hear The Hollies singing 'Carrie Anne', and I don't know why. Hell, I don't even like that song."

"They're doing what now?"

"Singing 'Carrie Anne.'"

"No doubt this will get interesting later."

I choose to ignore him. I don't know how but I knew I was off base thinking Maria was involved in this Bleich situation. I couldn't explain why I'd changed my mind apart from ... it was my right as a woman. Mac grumbled inside my head as my mother applauded.

"I don't think Maria is involved in this, apart from stumbling across information and calling in the tip-off."

"Okay, expound on that ..."

I couldn't. I had nothing. My mind changed without rhyme or reason and I went along with it. All because the damn song wouldn't shut up. I hoped I'd find something within the lyrics but there was nothing but an annoying song.

"All I have is a song that won't quit and a gut feeling it was her who tipped us off."

"Can't wait to see how that theory pans out."

Me too. Time to distract myself.

I pulled out my phone and signed into Twitter. I wasn't looking for magical answers; I was checking up on the

Foundation kids and creating some static in my mind. There were a zillion @ replies to me and they all seemed to be from Butterfly Foundation kids. I'd been slack at tweeting all day. Some of the questions were funny, some disturbing. I sent replies to the disturbing tweets first, asking that the tweeters sign into the Foundation site and talk to a counselor.

I tweeted that I was on a case, that it was difficult and I mentioned that I hated being away from my daughter. Twitter hummed with replies. As I replied to a few of the kids, I saw an unrelated Twitter post. It made so much sense. I checked the name on the post twice because I didn't quite believe it the first time.

It was Thaao Penghlis. There was no holding back a smile. My life became very *Days of our Lives* and he was Tony DiMera and here to prove it. I read the post several times.

It is in the darkest hour that the soul is replenished and given strength to continue and endure. And it is at that time that we finally see.

I tried searching the internet from my phone; the quote seemed to be from H.W. Chosa. I read it again. So much sense in one hundred and forty characters. I replied to Thaao Penghlis and thanked him for sharing. Twitter can be a good thing. If ever I needed to hear something that made sense, it was that moment.

Then I hit upon an idea. Why not harness the power of Twitter? I took my notebook from my bag and tweeted that I was looking for a car and included a description.

My next tweet was that I was looking for Maria Doyle and I gave her description and last known location. I asked that the messages be retweeted and said it was urgent. I signed out of the Twitter application. I set Twitter to send any replies from people I followed to my phone via text message. For half an hour my phone went nuts with messages from followers who were re-tweeting for me.

"You're smiling," Kurt said. "What are you up to?"

"Eyes on the road, buddy. Mind your own business," I said as a flurry of incoming tweets landed in my inbox. And to think I'd wanted to ditch Twitter after the Mailbox killer started sending chopped up bodies to some of the people, including me, who were using the #wheresmymail hash tag. An involuntary shudder rocked my body. If it walks like a duck and quacks like a duck, it might be a psycho mail carrier.

Yeah, my mind is a twisted place. Anyone looking in would be confused by my thoughts. Hell, my thoughts confuse me and I live in there.

"You all right?" Kurt asked.

"Yes. I. Am."

"What's going on in that head of yours, Conway?"

"If it walks like a duck and quacks like a duck … it's probably a duck."

That did it. Kurt pulled off the road.

"We're talking about ducks now?"

"No, Campbell."

"Campbell is a duck?"

Well, better a duck than a psycho mail carrier.

I could imagine Kurt making a call to a secure psych facility on my behalf.

"No, Campbell is a soldier who works with Tierney, he's got a plan. This is all part of it. He's leading us somewhere. He's planning on keeping Maria Doyle safe from whatever is threatening her life, and he's going somewhere where he hopes he'll have a tactical advantage."

Tuesday, like Monday, was shaping up to be another day that wouldn't end. Lack of sleep wasn't making anything any easier.

Chapter Twenty Two
Dear Doctor

A call came in as we were settling into a hotel room in Winchester. Why Winchester? I had no idea, but my gut said head west and that's where we ended up.

Sandra was still at her desk, running down information about Maria and Iain Campbell, and working on the Bleich leads.

"He could be heading out to Harper's Ferry," Sandra said.

I put her on speaker.

"Say again ..." I said. "... Kurt is here listening."

"Harper's Ferry. I found mention of a cabin there. No address. Nothing showing in property tax records. I called local police and they've never heard of Iain Campbell."

Which could just mean he'd never garnered any police attention and didn't stand out.

"Could have bought the property using an intermediary like a trust," I said. "He could also be using another name."

"That's what I thought," Sandra replied. "Needle in a haystack."

Kurt stopped making coffee and joined me on the sofa. "Does he hunt?"

"He owns several hunting rifles and two hand guns," Sandra said.

"Great, thanks," I replied. "Go home and get some sleep." I hung up.

We sat looking at each other for a few seconds.

"They're just the weapons we know about," Kurt said. "He could have anything stashed in a cabin in the woods."

It wasn't easy to ignore the song that burst from around the imaginary campfire, 'In a cabin in the woods.'

"Harper's Ferry," I said. "Wouldn't be the first time someone on the run ended up in Harper's Ferry."

Kurt smiled. "Nope, wouldn't be the first time."

"I don't think he's going to shoot at us or view us as a threat to Doyle. But he will try to keep Doyle safe from whatever threat is after her."

"Which makes it just as dangerous for us," Kurt said. "Bullets don't stop mid-flight to ascertain if they've been fired at the wrong people or not."

True. At least this time if I take a bullet I'll be expecting it.

The Hollies started up again; I was pleased it wasn't a scout troop singing by a campfire but not that pleased. I let the song play and this time I listened to the lyrics with care.

On the second run through, I fished around for a pen and my notebook and started writing the lines I heard repeated. Kurt moseyed out of sight. I felt him leave, and then heard the door shut.

My notebook page was filled with circled words. They must mean something. First up I needed to know who the hell Carrie Anne was.

I called Lee. "Hey, have you come across anyone called Carrie Anne while investigating either of these cases?"

"I'm almost afraid to ask why you want to know."

"Me too, don't worry about it." I'm not ready to try to explain this just yet. "But have you?"

"As it happens, I have, and so have you ... Maria Carrie Anne Doyle."

"You're fuc'n kidding!"

"Problem, O Genie of Pop?"

"Maybe."

I hung up as Mac's voice resounded in my head and spilled into the hotel room. "Maybe's ass." Another voice in my head replied to his comment, "Shut up or get shot again. Your choice." Took a minute for me to realize it was my voice.

I turned on my laptop and pulled up photos of Maria. "So, Maria Carrie Anne, what game, if any, are you playing?"

She stared back at me from the screen. It wasn't her game. It was his game. She was always something special to him. This wasn't just Iain Campbell going rogue. He was intent on keeping her safe. I just wished I knew from what. Why couldn't he go to her brother? Why not go to the police? Was it Campbell's idea for Maria to add Sutherland to that invitation list? I doubt she would have added Sutherland to the list for him, the estranged spouse – but she might for a new boyfriend.

John Brown. What the hell did we know about John

Brown? Very little and we still hadn't seen a photo of the man.

Director Doyle seemed to have liked him. Maria was dating him. Did Campbell know him? What if John Brown was the threat? And Campbell knew that.

Lee's card. I ran a new scenario based on Lee's card. He wrote a note on the back of his card saying he wanted to talk to her regarding the autism function and stuck it between her front door and the doorframe. Anyone could have read that card.

Brown could have thought we were on to something.

We were, we just didn't know it.

Holy crapdoodle.

A cold sinking feeling told me Brown was the one Campbell was protecting Maria from, and that Brown had seen the card, which triggered a response Campbell did not like.

It was dark and cold. Rain pelted against the hotel windows. We weren't moving on tonight. The search for Maria would have to wait until morning. I hoped she'd be okay and that I was right about Campbell being a good guy. No one was able to find Brown since he reported Maria missing. Was he the one who killed the couple? If so, why not hang around and take out Maria and Campbell?

Where were the hospital photographs of Brown's injuries?

I made another call to Sandra knowing she'd still be at work. "Thought I told you to go home?"

"You did. I didn't."

"Did those photos from the hospital, of Brown, ever show up?"

"No, I chased them three times today. They have no record of photographs. The only thing saying he was treated is the open file on their computer system. The paper file started in the ED is gone."

"How long was he in the hospital?"

"He discharged himself within an hour, against medical advice."

"No photos, no current address, no idea where the man is?"

"Correct."

"Thanks." I hung up.

Nothing made much sense. I left my laptop on the coffee table and flopped down onto one of the beds.

The door opened. I turned my head and watched Kurt come back into the room.

"All right over there?"

"Yep," I replied.

"I'm ordering pizza, anything special you want?"

"Nope."

I stared at the ceiling and listened to Kurt as he ordered pizza and let Sam and Lee know dinner was in our room. The ceiling offered no intuitive insight about why Iain Campbell took Maria or why Brown, if it was Brown at the house, didn't kill them both. Apart from both men wanting to bring down a special kind of hell onto themselves, there didn't seem to be a logical reason.

"Kurt?"

"Yes."

"What do we know about the boyfriend, John Brown?"

"Not much. He doesn't seem to have existed prior to a year ago."

"Legend? Could he be a spook?"

He shook his head. "I doubt it, more like an independent contractor."

Independent contractor put a different spin on things. Why would someone want Maria killed? I let my mind mull that over.

My phone was going nuts every few seconds. I rolled over on the bed and picked up the phone to silence it. Incoming tweets were causing the noise. Sightings of a car that could be the one. People who thought they'd seen a woman matching the description of Maria. I waded through them all. One caught my eye. Just one.

I jumped up and went back to my laptop. I needed to find the person who'd tweeted it. It was the only sighting anywhere near Harper's Ferry. So it could be Maria.

The person behind the tweet was not one of my followers but one of mine re-tweeted my request and she'd answered. I found the origin.

One tweet later I'd added the person and asked that she add me. Then I could send her a private message. She did. Always nice when people want to help. I direct messaged her with my phone number and asking for more information.

"You got something?" Kurt said.

"I hope so."

My phone announced an unknown caller.

"Special Agent Conway speaking."

"It's Carmel from Twitter." She sounded nervous.

"Thanks for calling," I replied injecting bounce and happiness into my words. "I appreciate your help. What can you tell me about the woman you saw?"

She hesitated then cleared her throat. Words spilled forth. "I was at work in Harper's Ferry. First, I saw her getting out of a pickup truck with a man. I was outside having a cigarette, and the truck pulled up just down the street. I finished my smoke and I went back inside. They came in not long after me. He was wearing like, army clothes, or something."

I got a description of the clothes and of him, then of the woman. The woman on the phone served them in the store. He'd bought coffee and grilled cheese sandwiches for them both. They sat in a booth to eat.

I grasped at straws when I asked my next question. "Any chance the table where they sat hasn't been cleared?"

"They came in right before closing. I was going to do it soon as I cashed up."

Maybe God does exist.

"Can you do something very important for me?" I said, stressing the importance with careful enunciation.

"I guess."

"Don't touch the table or anything on it until I get there."

"I dunno. I need to go home ..."

"I'm half an hour away, three quarters tops."

I signaled to Kurt to grab our gear. Someone knocked on the door. I smelled pizza. Hunger rumbled.

"Can I get someone else to wait for you, I need to go home."

Not really.

"Gimme your number, lock up, go home. I'll call when I arrive."

"Okay." She read out her cell phone number which I added to my phone's directory.

"Thank you, Carmel," I said. "Just remember not to touch anything they used at the table, okay?"

"Okay."

The smell of meat lover's pizza filled the room as I hung up. Kurt was eating. I took a slice. Sam and Lee walked into the room. Drawn by pizza.

I chewed and swallowed then filled them all in.

"So much for spending a quiet night here," Sam replied, taking another slice of pizza. Cheese dripped from the cut edges.

"We could, but that would mean the woman wouldn't be able to open her store until we've dusted for prints in the morning."

Sam nodded. "It's good of her to help."

"Goes some way to restoring my faith in human nature," Lee said, opening the second pizza box and surveying the contents before choosing his piece. "How'd you come by this information?"

"Twitter," I said, taking a slice with lots of ham and little pineapple. Everyone stopped chewing and stared at me. "Swallow before the pizza falls out of your mouths."

"Twitter?" Lee said, shaking a limp piece of pizza at me. "Twitter?"

"Yes."

"Tell me you're not using hash tags again."

"I'm not using hash tags." For this anyway. "I sent out a request, saying we were looking for a woman and gave a description. I said she was traveling with a man and they may have been heading to Harper's Ferry. That fitted with what Sandra told us about Campbell having a cabin there."

"Good use of social networking, O Genie of the Twitterverse," Lee said right before he took a huge bite of his pizza slice.

"I thought so." I finished eating. Pizza almost made up for the sleep deprivation. "When we're done here we'll pack up our gear and head out to Harper's Ferry."

"We're moving on?" Lee said. "Already?"

"I believe they have hotels and such in Harper's Ferry."

Chapter Twenty Three
To The Fire

Rain pelted the car. Visibility shrank to a few feet.

It'd be a crying shame if we didn't bring Maria out of this unscathed. I hoped she was safe. Rain poured from the sky rendering the window wipers damn near useless.

It was a slower drive than I'd envisaged. Traffic was minimal. Not surprising. If we hadn't needed to be on the road we wouldn't be. Driving in this sort of rain was not my choice, but a warm trail made it a duty.

Sam and Lee were behind us. Every now and then the headlights from their car broke through the rain to illuminate the interior of ours. I found the sudden light comforting. The good thing about the night was the lack of wind. At least we weren't being blown all over Route 340.

Lightning flashed. Thunder rumbled. Hail followed.

Kurt and I looked at each other for a second.

"This is not fun," Kurt said.

"This is ..." The road almost disappeared under a curtain of hail. "... is ridiculous," I said.

Kurt swore. His hands moved on the steering wheel. The car swerved, skidded, and came to a halt over a mile marker.

"I think it's dead," I muttered as both our phones rang.

"There was something on the road," Kurt said. Behind the hail pounding the car roof and the phones, I heard voices yelling.

My door was wrenched open. Lee's face peered in at me. Hail became rain.

"Chicky?"

"Uh huh," I replied.

"Okay?"

"Uh huh."

Sam opened Kurt's door. I looked over. Kurt gritted his teeth and smiled at me. Scary.

Water ran off Sam's bald head and onto Kurt.

"What the hell happened?" Sam said.

"There was something on the road. Didn't you see it?" Kurt replied.

"No," Sam pulled back out the car, leaving a puddle on Kurt's pants. He shone his flashlight onto the road behind us, sweeping the beam of light across the shiny road surface as he walked away. "Found it."

He ran, almost disappearing into the murky wet night.

We jumped out of the car and followed.

Sam was kneeling next to something dark on the side of the road. Rain ran in rivers around the shape. "Kurt!" Sam yelled.

Kurt slid to a stop by Sam's legs.

"Crap," Kurt said. "Conway, get paramedics out here. She's hurt."

The shape lay face down on the gravel and moaned.

"Did we hit her?" I was sure we didn't.

"Nope. She's been shot." Kurt was checking for other injuries. Sam held a flashlight steady on the woman. Kurt turned her with care and carried on with the examination. "Left shoulder and lower right abdomen."

I unzipped my jacket and used it to shelter my phone. I called 9-1-1 after checking on our GPS to find our location. We were about a third of a mile back from the Union Street intersection. Lee disappeared while I was talking. He arrived back carrying Kurt's medical bag and a large umbrella. Lee held the umbrella over the woman and Kurt. Sam held the flashlight. I went for road flares and set up a perimeter to help guide emergency services and keep traffic away from us. The rain persisted but diminished in volume.

I dropped to one knee next to Kurt.

"Do you know who she is?"

"No, nothing in her pockets. See if you can find anything on the road. She came from somewhere."

I used her position to track backwards. "Rain will have washed away any blood trail."

Lucky for whoever did this.

I scoured the wet road. Rain ran down inside my collar. Pretty soon, I was as wet as if I hadn't worn a jacket at all. Nothing on the saturated ground stood out.

Kurt called me back. I hurried over and crouched down. "Check out her shirt, she's wearing a work shirt, uniform."

"Where does she work?"

Kurt pointed to a ripped piece of shirt and a partial name. I could make out the last two letters. E and L.

"At a diner by the look of it."

My heart sank. Melting into the rain puddles on the side of the road. "Carmel?"

The woman whimpered. Her eyes opened then closed.

"You know her?" Kurt said. He ripped open a package with his teeth. I took out the contents for him. "Put that here." He lifted his hand from the woman's shoulder. I placed the wound pad and he put his hand back, pressing hard. "Can you hold this?"

He moved his hand and I took over.

"Sure. I think she is the woman who called me."

While I kept pressure on the shoulder wound, he turned his attention and free hands to her abdomen, and I tested out my theory. "Carmel, I am Special Agent Conway."

She blinked and said, "I called you."

"What happened?"

"I was robbed, on my way home from work."

"You were walking?" In this rain, that didn't seem right.

"I live over there," she said trying to point then became confused. "I don't know where I am."

"Just down the road from Union Street."

"By home," she replied. Her face contorted with pain.

"Sorry," Kurt replied. "I need to press hard."

"Carmel, where do you live?"

"Across the road from the hotel."

Sirens sounded.

"Where did this happen?"

"I was almost home. Two men took my bag."

"And shot you," I added.

"They said no one would get hurt." Her breathing was ragged. Tears rolled from her eyes and trickled into her wet hair. "If I didn't give them the bag they'd shoot me."

You can't trust criminals.

The sirens screamed closer. The wail drifting as they approached.

"Do you recognize them?" I said, flipping through photos on my phone for ones of Iain Campbell and the Unsub from the jewelers. I was beginning to think our Unsub was John Brown. No one had been able to provide us with a clear photograph of the man who was supposed to be Maria's boyfriend. I showed her the first of the pictures on my phone, the Unsub from the jeweler store.

"He was the one with the woman this evening," she replied.

"You're sure?" My heart thumped. Now we just needed to identify the man.

"Yes. Him."

I swiped my finger over the screen revealing the next photo. "Seen him before?"

"No."

"Did either of them attack you?"

"No."

Everyone knows how I feel about coincidence and yet here we were face to face with one. The attack on Carmel seemed unrelated to the appearance of Maria in the diner, and not related to Carmel calling me. I was surprised that Carmel didn't identify Iain Campbell as the man with Maria. She identified our Unsub, the mysterious John Brown.

So where was Campbell?

An ambulance cruised to a stop close by. Doors opened. I was running out of time.

"Carmel, did Maria say anything to you?"

"She said …" She turned her head to look at me. "She said something to the man. She said he'd saved her."

"Do you think they knew each other well?"

"Yes."

"Thank you."

Paramedics crowded in under the umbrella. I hurried away to our car, grateful to be warm and out of the rain.

Maria thinks the Unsub saved her? The developing intrigue was full of brain scrambling potential.

An odd thought crossed my mind. Sometimes your knight in shining armor is just an idiot wrapped in tinfoil. In this case, a killer wrapped in tinfoil. She wasn't safe. Where was Campbell?

Kurt opened the driver's door.

"Let's check into the Holiday Inn over there and get dry," he said, pulling the seat belt across his body. "We can't do much to find Maria in this weather."

He was right. We had no idea where she was. Knowing where she'd been was helpful in determining we were on the right track.

"Let's give the local park ranger a call once we've checked in." He may know something useful. It was certainly better than twiddling our thumbs.

We opted for one double room. All we needed was a base. Somewhere dry to make calls and plans. I pushed Doc toward the bathroom. "Shower."

He looked at his clothes.

"I won't be long."

"Good because there's a queue for that shower."

I shrugged out of my wet jacket and hung it over a chair. Doc was right, he wasn't long. I jumped into the shower right after him. The bathroom felt like a sauna. My eyes glanced at the large mirrors; I didn't want to look too long in case Mac appeared. Tonight I just wanted to get clean, warm, and dry, and get to the diner where Carmel worked before the evidence disappeared and find that cabin.

Hold that thought.

I showered fast, dressed faster and hurried out into the main room while towel drying my hair.

"We need to get to the diner," I said.

Lee headed into the bathroom.

"She identified our Unsub and Maria," Doc replied, suggesting there was no rush.

"I know, but it was the Unsub not Campbell. I want his prints. We know squat about that guy."

My gut told me the Unsub was Brown. But I had no proof. Brown, the guy who gave his address as the Basilica of the National Shrine of the Immaculate Conception. Top marks for creativity. Brown, the man who wasn't in any photographs, not even cozy ones with his girlfriend.

"How are we going to get in?"

"Pretty sure I can pick a lock," I replied.

Doc smiled. "I'm sure you can too. And how are we going to get in?"

"Thought I'd try enlisting local police help."

He nodded his approval. "I bet they'll be thrilled to know we think there is a killer in their quaint little town."

"Wouldn't be the first time." Harper's Ferry was no stranger to killers or police chases.

Once we were all showered, dry and clean we found the local cop with the help of the hotel front desk and explained our situation. He was obliging and took us to the diner where Carmel worked. Nice thing about a small town is everyone knows everyone else, and where they work. We gave him the run down on Carmel's injuries and suggested he get himself to the hospital as soon as he could to interview her regarding the shooting. To be shot twice after handing over the cash was way over the top.

One table hadn't been cleared. There was a note sitting on top of the salt and pepper shakers, asking that no one touch anything. We gathered evidence from the table, bagging, tagging, hoping for some clear prints. Intel and the need for answers, sooner rather than later, kicked in. Back at the hotel, I watched as Lee uncovered latent prints on both coffee cups. He photographed them with his phone then added the photos to the FBI fingerprint database application. Yes, there is an app for that. Technology is our friend. He also emailed the photos to Sandra. She'd run them against all the databases when she arrived at work in the morning. Meanwhile Lee's phone application did what it does.

I put a call into the local park ranger and ended up leaving a message on his answer machine to call me back.

We ate a late dinner in the hotel dining room, despite the pizza we'd all consumed earlier. This time we weren't in a hurry. Dinner was pleasant, yet unremarkable. It was food. The coffee was good.

Back in the room, Lee had zero hits from the fingerprints.

"How is that possible?"

"He's not on any of the databases attached to the application," Lee stated.

"Sandra should be able to get a hit though?"

"Yeah, she has the full power of our system at her disposal."

I flopped onto my bed. "You know how we considered Brown was a spook?"

Lee's head shook. "Don't go there yet. It makes no sense for him to be a spook and be killing a jeweler's family."

"It makes screw all sense him being an independent contractor and killing the family," I replied.

Doc sat on the edge of the bed. "There is not much sense to be made here at all. Misha might be able to shed some light when he brings the remaining Bleich boy back."

Zachary. Yeah.

"Did we ever look into that Heathcote Diamond?" Sam

said, fishing his laptop from his satchel.

"Don't think so. We have no confirmation of anything missing, so no reason to."

"Maybe I'll just do some poking around."

"Good thinking."

Better to do something productive than sit there twiddling his thumbs.

There was a knock at the door. Kurt opened it.

"Sorry to interrupt," said the server who waited on our table downstairs. "I thought you might need the tea and coffee replenished."

"Sure, come in," Kurt said.

Our conversation paused as the woman did whatever she did by the coffee pot and electric kettle.

"I left some hot chocolate sachets, they're quite good ones," she said then left the room. The door shut behind her.

Hot chocolate sounded good. Kurt must've picked up on my thoughts, because he decided to make drinks for everyone. He opted for tea; Lee and Sam wanted coffee and I chose chocolate. This met with approval from Kurt; he'd been trying for weeks to wean me off coffee at night.

While Kurt delivered our drinks, I carried on with my thoughts about the current situation. "When was Misha due to arrive?"

Everyone knew it was rhetoric. I knew when he was arriving. Women all over the world heralded his arrival by turning the next page in their current Mills and Boon novel and swooning as he stormed across the field to rescue them from a life of drudgery. I was in bad shape. First Kurt and the Kevin Costner thing and now Misha was back to being someone from a trashy romance novel. I was seconds away from seeing him as Doctor Luka Kovač from ER and it wouldn't be the first time Misha became Luka to me.

I had to do something to stop the insanity. I was in a room full of larger than life men with no privacy to speak of, so no hope of a quick and dirty phone call to Rowan. I glanced around the room. Guess I could always take my phone to the bathroom. A smile wandered around in my consciousness. I heard mom's voice, "Behave, Ellie."

It seemed smart to try to concentrate on something else.

I took a sip of the hot chocolate that Kurt gave me. It was good. Half the cup later it was time to give the relationship between Iain Campbell and John Brown some thought. What I needed was confirmation that Brown was our Unsub. That thought was set aside while I considered the relationships. We knew Iain was army with a classified record and Brown didn't exist. I didn't for one second think their only connection was through Maria Doyle. So where did they meet? Where would someone like Campbell meet a non-existent potential killer like Brown? And Noel disappearing like he did pissed me off. Unacceptable rudeness.

I drained the cup and set it back on the counter.

Flopping back onto the bed, I carried on trying to make sense of the Campbell/Brown meeting. What did their meeting have to do with the Bleich family? And the Sutherlands? And Maria Doyle was what to whom? And who was related to whom? I was starting to appreciate the *Days of our Lives* aspect of the case. All that was missing was someone lying comatose at the bottom of a set of stairs with another person buried in an avalanche and we'd have the makings of about five new episodes. The tangents spun on and on, the darkness climbing higher. Mac leaned over a thick concrete wall covered in graffiti. His voice echoed into a brick alleyway, "Come on, Babe. You can do this."

I blocked out the soap opera aspect of my earlier thoughts and focused on one fact. One thing I did know. Four members of one family were dead. That, I knew was truth. Clawing fingers reached for that last solid thought, trying to drag it into the abyss. I watched as the Bleich parents contorted in agony as they spiraled downward into a fiery pit.

"Earth to Ellie."

Flames leapt and the whole room smelled like a barbeque.

"Damn, I'm hungry," I said wiping my mouth with the back of my hand.

"Conway? Hungry again?"

So, that was out loud then. "Smelled barbeque, made me hungry."

"I'm not even going to ask how that was possible or where you think you were."

"What'd I miss?"

"Sam found something about that diamond," Doc replied. He was lying propped up on one elbow, facing me. His expression bordered on concern. I detected a smidge of amusement and that tempered the unease drifting across his face.

"What'd you get, Sam?" I rolled over and sat up. My head spun. Should've done that slower. I swallowed and let the spinning stop.

Doc's hand closed around my arm. "Hold on there, tiger, you okay"

"Yeah, why wouldn't I be?"

"Because all the color just drained from your face and you swayed." He was off the bed and crouching in front of me. "Look at me."

Look at him? I wanted to smack him. There he was doing his doctor impersonation, except he was one, and doctors should not be as cool or sexy as he was. It's just wrong.

Atta girl, go *there* again.

"I'm okay. Sat up too fast, that's all."

"That's it? Nothing else going on? No headache?"

Fair enough, I let him have his moment. It's not like I haven't flipped out on the team before while suffering from a massive migraine.

"I'm good. I swear."

He was still right there scrutinizing me. "Show me your hands."

I held my hands up and sighed. "See, fingers not crossed. Now can I talk to Sam about sparkly things?"

There might've been something going on, but I didn't think it was anything important. Tiredness, maybe. "Yeah, go ahead, I'm making more tea."

I left that alone. Tea. Don't even go there.

"Chicky Babe?"

"Wow me, Sam ..."

"The Heathcote diamond was cursed or magical or something. To control the power contained within the original stone, a person must own all the pieces," Sam said.

Awesome. That's just what we needed, because the case wasn't interesting enough so far, we needed magical curses to muddle things up some more.

"Bleich cut it into five, yeah?" I said.

"Yes, but not just those five stones. Everything from the original diamond pre-cut," Sam said, he appeared to be paraphrasing from information on his laptop screen.

"That wouldn't be possible, would it?"

"I don't know how much is sliced off when they cut diamonds?" Sam replied. "Let me get some stats here, so we have a ball park idea on the loss." He typed on the laptop keyboard. "A lot, depending on the diamond. The Centenary Diamond was five hundred and ninety nine carats uncut weight and a mere two hundred and seventy-three carats cut."

"Okay, so, the diamond is cut into five but to activate the curse all the dust and whatever from the cutting *and* the five stones must be owned by a single person?"

"That's how I understand it," Sam said.

"Why did Bleich buy it originally?"

Why buy a cursed stone?

"The story on his website is that he bought the rough diamond with the intention of keeping it whole. Then strange things began happening. He found out about its history and the curse," Sam grinned. "Are all diamonds cursed?"

"Seems that way," I replied. "You never hear of happy stories about big diamonds. What happened next?"

"Bleich was told that cutting the stone would destroy the curse as long as the pieces were kept in different places and anything cut from the stone was buried."

"He brought all the stones together for that charity affair." I felt it was my duty to point that out.

Lee hummed the *Twilight Zone* theme. "He did, but one would assume the filings or dust or whatever were buried and not dug up again for this occasion and therefore the curse wasn't reactivated."

I leveled my eyes at him. I was too sleepy for curses.

"We all know my views on assuming anything."

Sam piped up, "Never assume, it makes an ass out of u and me."

I grinned. "Exactly."

"What would be gained by digging up the dust and activating the curse?" Lee interjected.

"Oh, I don't know, maybe the deaths of everyone involved in the separation of the stones." Yeah, I pulled that out of thin air. But it was pretty good.

"The stone is killing?" Doc said. He couldn't hide the

skepticism in his voice and I didn't expect him to. This was way into *Twilight Zone* territory. Deep, deep into the realms of improbability.

"I've never yet come across a stone of any description with opposable thumbs," I replied. "People kill." They also create curses and torment each other for fun. "This isn't about a curse, but it could be about greed."

Fighting a feeling of major space between my ears, I palmed my phone and made a call to Misha. If he answered, he was on the ground. If not, he'd get my message when he was able to turn on his phone again.

"*Privet*, Ellie."

"*Privet*, Misha. Good flight?"

"*Da*. I am taking Mr. Bleich to a hotel."

"Keep him close, Misha. I have a feeling …"

"A feeling?" I knew by the way he spoke that he knew what I was thinking but couldn't talk. Not with the man seated next to him.

"He could be involved."

"Good enough for me. I will be in touch."

I hung up. All the eyes in the room were on me. Lee spoke first, "We've gone from talking about diamonds to thinking the remaining son is involved somehow?"

"Yep."

"If we could bottle your gut instincts we'd make a fortune," Doc said.

"I might be wrong." The room erupted into peals of laughter. "Seriously, I did think Maria was involved and then I thought she wasn't – so I could be wrong."

Their faith in me was comforting. I lived fearing the possibility that one day the music wouldn't be there for me and I'd be lost, fumbling in the dark unable to do what I do now. Mac chuckled inside my head. His warm voice reminded me of all I'd lost. Didn't see that coming. Proof that I was fallible like anyone else.

"Where do you stand on the Maria situation now?" Doc said.

"I think she's been used, and I think Campbell is right about her being in danger." Tiredness was taking over. To be honest, it was kicking down the door with steel-capped boots and demanding I give in.

They all nodded.

"We need to find Maria and the Unsub," Sam said.

"We need to find Campbell too," I added. "Although finding him alive might be beyond our abilities."

I yawned. Rain battered the windows. I needed to sleep.

"Sam, you and Lee see if you can find a park ranger. I'm done waiting."

"On it."

The door opened and closed. I left another message for the park ranger asking someone to call urgently. My eyes didn't want to stay open much longer. I tried walking around the room and sitting by an open window but nothing was working.

"Get some sleep, Ellie," Kurt said. "If they find him and can get an address then we'll wake you."

"We need to find her."

"We will. Patience, grasshopper."

Chapter Twenty Four
Shine A Light

On Wednesday morning, I woke to Kurt announcing the rain had stopped and my phone going nuts. Waking in the morning meant no one found the park ranger. That wasn't ideal. I checked the phone display hoping it was the park ranger. Carla.

"Carla?"

"Mom ..." She sounded mad. It was too early for mad. What happened to the kid I took to a Grange concert in the weekend? Where was my happy, excited, joyful teenager who couldn't wait to tell her friends she was on stage with Grange? *OMG it was sooo cool.*

"What are you doing awake at this hour?" I said, wriggling up in the bed until I was sitting.

"It's seven o'clock, it's not that early," she snapped.

"Too early for your tone, young lady." I rubbed my eyes and cautioned her, "You might want to rethink your approach."

A long sigh preceded her next sentence. "Why can't Joey hang with me today? It's not fair. He's my best friend."

How to answer that without sounding like the Wicked Witch of the East was tricky. "It won't hurt you two to spend a day apart. Anyway, you'll see him at school."

"We hardly have any classes together." Every word grew in volume until she was yelling, "It's not the same!"

That's no way to change my mind or negotiate. "He's not coming over after school or tonight. That's all there is to it."

"You're mean!"

"It's part of my job description. I love you. Have a good day."

"But ... but ... it's not fair!"

Click. She hung up on me.

When I looked up Kurt was holding a cup out to me.

"Thanks," I replied. I took the cup, peered at it, sniffed it, and took a sip. Coffee. I dropped the phone on my bed.

"How is she?"

"Mad as hell at me." I took a sip of the hot black liquid. Bliss. "She'll get over it." Sunlight crept across the floor as clouds parted. "Thought we were starting at dawn?"

"I think we all needed a little sleep," he replied.

I looked around the room. "Where are Lee and Sam?"

"Having breakfast."

My phone rang it was Cheryl.

"Morning, have some results for you. Sorry it took so long, it's busy over here."

"Shoot."

"The twins are not Sigmund's sons, they are Marika's."

"Don't suppose your magic machines could tell you if Sigmund knew that?"

"Science can only do so much," Cheryl replied with a small chuckle and hung up.

"The twins weren't Sigmund's," I said to Kurt. "That means Marika has played the adulteress card before but

I'm not sure what it means for the case, yet."

Kurt sat in the chair by the window.

"Interesting," Kurt said. "Breakfast in the dining room when you're ready. You okay?"

"Yeah." Breakfast in the dining room. I'd sooner skip it and just get moving. It felt like we were trapped in a quagmire of nothingness. "Still no word from the ranger."

"We'll track him down," Kurt replied. "Breakfast first."

He was right. We had to sleep and we had to eat. We'd do no one any good if we didn't look after ourselves.

"Gimme ten minutes." I drained the last of the coffee in my cup and hit the shower.

I stood under the streaming water for a few minutes. Letting the hot water wash away the feelings of guilt associated with Carla. How is it kids do that? I know that enforcing some Joey-free time won't hurt her, so how does she make me feel guilty about it? Not cool.

Showering, dressing, and packing took a little over ten minutes. It was quick without incorporeal interruptions or musical interludes.

The quiet in my head defied logic and normality.

Breakfast was entertaining but fast. There was no mention of how the day would go until Sandra rang me while we were finishing up.

"I got a hit back on the prints from the diner," she said. "Interpol databases, not ours."

"He's not American?" No one mentioned an accent; okay, so only one person we'd spoken to had heard him speak and she'd been shot. Might not be the best witness considering the circumstances.

"Nope, he's British. From Northern Ireland to be more exact."

"And he's our Unsub?"

"Yes. He's also known as John Brown."

"Now that's interesting. The hospital staff never mentioned he wasn't an American. No one seems to have known he wasn't American. You'd think someone, maybe Director Doyle, might have mentioned the man was Irish."

"Until we investigated him he was just John Brown, Maria Doyle's boyfriend and an innocuous one at that." I heard her fingers tapping on the keyboard in front of her. "Interpol says he is Pearce Maguire, wanted for questioning regarding several assassinations in Europe."

"Assassinations? This guy is a hit man?"

Independent contractor sounded nicer than hit man.

"Looks that way."

"And he's a Brit national?"

"Yes, holds a British passport."

"How much time has he spent in the USA?"

"It's hard to tell. Interpol told me he uses aliases and false passports. They have him entering the USA in 2004 and leaving three months later. No record of him being in the USA at the moment."

"So our Unsub has a name. I suspected Brown was the Unsub. Good to know my instincts still work. We're looking for Pearce Maguire not John Brown." And then the penny dropped. "John Brown and Harper's Ferry.

Guess he thought that was funny."

John Brown made an unsuccessful raid on the armory at Harper's Ferry in 1859. Later that same year, he was tried for treason against the state of Virginia, the murder of five pro-slavery Southerners, and inciting a slave insurrection. He was subsequently hanged.

Great. A killer who is throwing our history in our faces. He's not as funny as he thinks he is. In fact, he's funny's cousin. Joke's on him. I'm not above a good ol' fashioned lynching.

"Did you find out any more about Iain Campbell? Any luck getting into his records?"

"We've hit a wall, but haven't yet been told to back off."

I could feel it coming. The military were sensitive about us snooping into their people.

"Keep trying. Will you ask Caine to interview Zachary Bleich? Misha said he was checking into a hotel with him last night." I didn't want to influence Caine's questions so said nothing about my feeling that Zachary could have something to do with the deaths of his family. If Caine came back saying he thought the man was withholding information, then I'd tell him. If not, then I was wrong.

"I'll get Caine onto it. He's got a few hours between meetings this morning."

"Thank you."

"Anything else?"

"I don't think so." I held my phone out to the table. "Anyone want to ask Sandra anything?"

A chorus of good mornings resounded but no

questions.

Then Kurt changed his mind. He took the phone and asked Sandra about Carmel and if she could find out from local police what happened. When he hung up, he placed the phone next to my plate.

"All right?" I said.

"Yeah, just seems a little too coincidental that Carmel was shot over the day's till money, right when we were going to meet her."

We all agreed.

It was time to see the local park ranger and ask him if he'd seen Maria, Campbell, or Maguire. None of my calls had been returned so an 'in person' visit it was.

The sign on the ranger station said they were open and a bell above the door jangled as we entered the foyer, lined with historic maps and old pictures. There was a long desk and beyond that a closed door. No one came to answer the bell.

There was a name on the door, Raymond Harris.

I knocked on his office door then opened it and walked in.

"Raymond Harris?" I said, holding my badge up for him to see. "I'm SSA Conway. I left a number of urgent messages overnight." My eyes roamed the room and spotted the flashing message light on his phone.

"Ma'am?"

"I think you'll find you have messages from me on your phone," I said, pointing. "You don't check messages?"

"There was no one on last night. It's just me and a few volunteers in the office this week, we have a lot of guided tours happening." Harris moved papers across his desk and picked up a pencil. "How can I help?"

"I'm looking for two men and a woman. We have reason to believe this man has a cabin somewhere here." I passed him my phone with a photo of Campbell on it. "Police said you'd probably know where."

"That's John Fredericks. He's a weekend fisherman. Keeps to himself. I spoke to him for a few minutes yesterday, he was planning on doing some fishing."

"We know him as Iain Campbell. Ever heard that name?"

He shook his head.

I leaned over and flicked the screen of my phone, revealing a photo of Maria.

"She was with him," he said.

"Thank you."

"She was quiet, didn't make eye contact. I thought she was ill and offered to call the local doctor but Fredericks said she was motion sick."

"Ever seen her before?"

"No."

"Is Fredericks married?"

"Not that I know of. He only comes out for weekends and I haven't seen him in a good while," he said.

I flicked my finger across the screen again. "Seen this man?"

"No."

"Thanks." I took my phone back. "Where's Fredericks' cabin?"

"Three miles upriver. The road stops about a mile back, you'll have to hike the rest of the way."

"Thanks."

I left his office.

Outside the ranger station, we conferred for a few minutes. Our cell reception was still good, given the huge number of tweets and text messages that arrived over the morning. Carla had text messaged me at least twenty times. Every message said she just wanted to hang with Joey. I considered calling her teacher and having her phone confiscated.

The majority of the tweets were from Foundation kids, with a few from others saying they'd seen a woman matching Maria's description in various places around the State. No more sightings in Harper's Ferry. I discounted the other supposed sightings.

"All right, we'll drive as far as we can, then hike in," I said, looking over at the fork in the river.

"If she's with Maguire, they may not be at the cabin," Sam said.

"That's true, but that's all we have. And Campbell is somewhere."

Sam followed my gaze. "Wonder how deep that river gets ..." A sudden breeze carried his voice away.

"I think we should find out ..." I replied. "Might have to call in divers."

Lee shuffled from foot to foot. "Divers?"

"Uh huh. Problem?"

"No. Not at all," he replied, his skin flushed a little pinker than usual and his eyes crinkled as he smiled.

"Is there a particular diver we should call?" I said, feigning innocence. Did he think we didn't know about Tara? Tight team, spies everywhere. She was the world's worst kept secret. Tara was a member of the FBI Underwater Search and Evidence Response Team, stationed in Washington.

He rocked from foot to foot, plunging his hands into his jacket pockets. "Nah. Yeah. Maybe."

"Man, I hope USERT aren't busy when our call comes in," I said walking to the car. I looked back over my shoulder. "She is in USERT working out of DC, isn't she?"

Sam slapped Lee on the back and laughed. "We *all* know."

Lee grinned, his eyes danced. "I shoulda known better."

"Yeah, you should," Kurt replied as he eased into the driver's seat of our car.

Sam and Lee tossed a coin to see who would drive theirs. For us, it was easy. Kurt drove and I zoned out and let my mind go mad trying to figure things out.

Chapter Twenty Five
Two Story Town

The heavens opened, sending a deluge to earth. Kurt pulled off the road, unable to see anything out the windscreen. A few minutes later the rain stopped. Clouds parted and the sun broke free. A good omen? Time would tell.

My phone rang. Grange blared. I turned down the volume on the ringer before I answered the call. I read the name on the display. Noel Gerrard.

"Noel, I'm putting you on speaker. Kurt's here with me. Where the hell did you go?"

"Hey, Kurt. I was called into the office," he said. "The Director decided you could handle this without NCIS input."

Noel sounded too perky for someone called off a case. Kurt and I both frowned at the phone sitting between us.

"What's going on?"

"SEALs confirmed a kill. Take Bin Laden off the most wanted list."

"Seriously? Good job!" Kurt said.

"Guess there will be some celebrating tonight?" I said.

"Low key, but you can bet on it."

"And the real reason you called right now?" I knew him. This wasn't about explaining his absence or giving us the news about Bin Laden. He had information.

"Campbell. No one seems to be able to access his

military file. Be very careful."

"Will do. And why can't anyone open it?"

"He's still on active service, which may mean he's under cover."

"Don't suppose you have anything else?" Kurt said.

"Afraid not. He's involved in abducting Doyle and if he is as dangerous as her boyfriend has led us to believe, then tracking him could bring down a world of hurt on you and her. I think his cover is well established and that he's been using it for years."

Or that he shelved the cover intact and pulled it out again to help Maria. But why? Why come back into her life at that exact moment? How did he know what was going to happen?

"Thanks. I've got a bit to think about," I said. "See you when we get back, Noel."

I hung up and looked at Kurt. "I need a minute to think."

He nodded. Sam climbed into the back of our car, followed by Lee. The three men talked about the conversation with Noel.

I fished my iPod from my pocket and stuffed in the ear buds. Music. I needed to hear something other than their talking. Something that would help my mind sift through the information so far and make some kind of order from it.

I remembered everything from the file O'Hare gave me on the abduction of Doyle. He wasn't using a disposable cover. Backstopping popped into my thought process.

Backstopping was a CIA term for providing appropriate verification and support for an alias used by an agent. He and Doyle lived in the house where the elderly couple was killed and the neighbors knew them as Iain and Maria Campbell. What confused me was the appearance of Brown or Maguire or whoever he was at that house. What was he doing there? How did he know about the house?

As if this case wasn't messy enough, with the CIA involved it almost guaranteed this would get even messier. I was the only one who believed for sure that Campbell was working for the CIA. They had a long history of working with the military.

I removed the ear buds and turned off my iPod.

"We need to know why Campbell is involved," I said. "He's using an established cover but I doubt knowing that will help us."

"You are convinced he is who you think he is?" Sam said.

"I have no doubt in my mind," I replied. "I also am thin on proof, which is often the way when the CIA are involved in anything."

"Which begs the questions, what the hell does a spook have to do with a hit man and why were the Bleich family killed? And why abduct Maria Doyle and how come no one else mentioned they were married? Why not try harder to get hold of us, or go to her brother, the Director?" Sam said.

"All good questions," I said.

"I think he has trust issues," Sam said. "There is

something big going on here and we're just scratching the tip of it."

I twisted around in my seat and leaned on the door. "Very good points, Sam." It could be that he doesn't trust anyone. If that's the case, then we need to know why. "What if Campbell is lost, or maybe he's been set free by whatever agency. Maybe he has no backup? If he did a few things to put us on his trail ..." Sending me a flash drive telling me Maria was in danger was sure to get my attention.

"You think whatever he was involved in has turned bad?"

"I have no idea, I'm simply conjecturing."

We all considered the conjectural developments as more rain pelted from the sky, drowning out any hope of conversation for several minutes.

"This can't be about diamonds, no matter how cursed, surely?" Lee said.

"Diamonds are currency," I said. "You can buy a lot of weapons with diamonds that big."

"We have nothing to suggest weapons trade," Kurt replied.

"No, you're right, we don't," I said. "We have someone with a secret military file and an Irish contractor."

Sam tipped his head back and chuckled. "You're right, Chicky Babe, this could be about arms."

That's why nothing made sense. We didn't know what it was about. We were lacking a motive.

"I have a suspicion that Zachary thinks this is all about

something else."

"Chicky Babe?" Sam said. "How so?"

"I think for him this is about greed. I'm still waiting on DNA confirmation but if Zachary suspected or knew his brothers were half-brothers, and his mother was an adulteress, that could be a tipping point. I don't think the father knew. Or if he did, he'd only just found out." I was pulling things from the air and sliding them into position on an electronic board in my mind. I was playing Tetris with someone else's life. "Zachary made contact with either Maguire or Campbell first. He wanted someone to get rid of the competition – his family – and get him the stones."

They sat open-mouthed as I reeled off my speculative and unsubstantiated ideas.

"He doesn't want to trade the diamonds for weapons. He wants to utilize the curse, to harness the power."

Lee sat forward. "Why?"

"Because power is control. He wants power."

"And, maybe Maguire came on board for the whole purpose of taking the stones for other reasons?"

"I'd say so."

"Campbell was banging Mrs. Bleich. Coincidence? Or is he somehow involved in the deaths of the family? Maybe that wasn't enough, maybe he couldn't get close enough to the family that way, or get the diamonds - perhaps he is a greedy bastard and just wanted the pretty stones."

"Maybe," Lee replied. "Or maybe he just likes older

273

broads and that part of the equation is coincidence?"

Mac piped up in my head, "Maybe's ass, Babe."

My internal voice responded, "You need to learn to shut up."

You'd think a double tap would silence a ghost for longer than it has.

"Let's go, this rain is going to be on and off all morning. We need to get Doyle, no matter what Campbell is into."

I had a feeling that Maria Doyle didn't believe Campbell when he said she was in danger and that her beloved boyfriend was a cold, calculating killer. She may have even told Maguire/Brown that and where they were going. That could explain why it was Maguire at the diner with Doyle but it didn't explain why Doyle was still alive. He could kill her and frame Campbell and be gone before anyone figured it out. I knew he was supposed to be Doyle's boyfriend but I didn't for one second think he had any feelings for the woman – my gut twinged again. To me the relationship with Maria Doyle seemed more like a convenience but I didn't know why. I climbed out of the car. Sam and Lee grabbed their gear from their car.

I pulled on an FBI jacket then took my backpack from the trunk and hooked my arms through it. We stood in a huddle on the side of the road. The rain was now nothing more than a misty annoyance.

"We ready?" Kurt said. He was going to lead the team. There was a collective nod. Kurt held his right hand out. I put mine on top of his. Sam and Lee followed suit. "Alert and safe."

"Alert and safe," we echoed. The circle broke away into a single file unit. Led by Kurt we left the roadside and wound into the woods.

We'd walked almost a hundred yards before I was sure I could feel eyes. Not animal eyes. Electronic eyes. I fell back two paces to Lee.

"You got your toy?"

He nodded. "Got a new RF signal detector last week."

"Is it good?"

"It's fifteen thousand dollars' worth of awesome. You think we're under surveillance?"

"Yes."

"Why?"

"Because if I were either of them, I'd have the woods rigged with wireless cameras."

Hell, I have the entire perimeter of my property under constant video and audio surveillance. I don't advertise it. Sean O'Hare's security company handles my security needs. It's no happenstance that he shares the same last name as our esteemed Director. They're twins. Sean has a deep dark past and a few years ago made personal security his specialty. I suspect the reason he is so good at safeguarding others is because he was excellent at circumventing security systems and personal security to get his target. Whatever. It worked for me and my family, right up until Mac's ghost came to call and drank my tequila.

Lee shucked his backpack from his shoulders,

unzipped it and dug out a hard case. Moments later, he held a smallish object in his hand. But then everything looks small in Lee's hands.

I caught up to Kurt and tapped his shoulder. "Wait up."

Kurt turned to face us. Sam stepped up until we were back in a small circle.

"Chicky thinks we have eyes and ears on us," Lee said. "Turn off all the cell phones and the GPS unit."

We did as Lee asked before he turned on his new toy.

A few minutes passed and then Lee grinned at me. "Check this out," he said, walking over to a tree about five yards from our position. I followed.

Lee touched something on the unit in his hand and a constant beep sounded. He'd turned it from vibrate to audio. He parted the leaves on a branch about head height and revealed a very small black object, about the size of a matchbox.

"Smile pretty for the camera, folks," Lee said before picking it up, He handed me the box. I opened the casing and removed the tiny batteries. I shoved the batteries in one pocket and the camera in another. The machine in Lee's hand continued to beep. He followed the sound to another camera on the other side of the track, about fifteen yards forward.

Kurt took the camera this time, removed the batteries, and shoved the whole lot in his pocket.

The RF detector fell silent.

"Think I'll keep this on vibrate mode while we

continue," Lee said. "Whoever is here doesn't want surprise visitors."

"We're not surprises anymore," I replied, racking the slide and then holstering my Glock. One by one, the men all chambered a round. I walked two yards behind Lee, who now had point. We were staggered, in even increments. Going slow, watching for traps. Lee, me, Kurt, Sam, walking in silence as adrenaline surged.

I checked my compass. Sometimes old tech is the way to go, undetectable old tech. I signaled to Kurt and Sam that I wanted them to break away to the right. I caught up to Lee and tapped twice on his left shoulder. He and I continued left. Now none of us was on the faint path we'd been following. The cabin was ahead on the path. I wasn't happy about walking into an ambush. We didn't know how much of our approach had been transmitted via the cameras. Safer to imagine Maguire knew there were four of us and act accordingly.

We were going old school. No cell phones, no electronics, no way of communicating except through visual signals. My body conducted its own fight trying to control the escalating adrenaline and calm my breathing. Coming around the other side of the cabin was half my team, making the danger of shooting and death by friendly fire ever present. I stopped thinking.

No one was going to die today.

Lee and I separated as soon as we saw the side of the cabin through the trees. We took up covered positions. Beyond the cabin I saw movement - I recognized Sam for a spilt second before he disappeared again into the undergrowth. I took off my backpack and slid it to the ground. From the gun bag attached to the pack, I removed my rifle and attached the holographic sight. I moved a little, found the highest spot that gave me the best view into the single grime-covered window. Lying prone on the wet ground between a tree stump and a boulder, I used the sight and looked for movement.

"Lee," I whispered. "What you got?"

"Nothing."

I kept looking. No movement. No sign of life.

"He may not be in there," Lee whispered. He commando crawled forward, making good use of the undergrowth.

A twig snapped.

I scanned the other side of the clearing in front of the cabin. I saw something move toward where I knew Sam and Kurt were. Using the sight I watched for more movement, hoping it was an animal and not Maguire. I glimpsed faded blue jeans through the scrubby plants under the trees. Not an animal. I hoped Sam and Kurt could deal with it.

I swung my rifle back to the cabin. Something glinted beyond the grime. Someone was in there. Looking through the sight on my rifle, I found a relatively clear patch in the window.

The window shattered from the inside. Lee crawled backwards, taking cover behind a rock. We knew there was the possibility of a hunting rifle in the cabin, but we didn't know what other weapons Maguire or Campbell had. But something fired through the window.

I watched. My finger played on and off the trigger. My elbows dug into the stony ground. Another shot. I thumped the ground with the toe of my boot. Lee heard and reacted.

From cover he called out. "FBI! Put down the weapons and come out the front door!"

An answering shot followed.

Lee tried again. "FBI! Put. Down. The. Gun. Exit. With. Your. Hands. Above. Your. Head."

I waited.

Another shot erupted from the cabin. I couldn't see much beyond the jagged glass in the window. Best guess. I fired.

More gunfire followed.

I missed.

A shaft of light reflected from broken glass and hit my eyes as I adjusted my position on the ground. With a slow deep breath, I focused on what was beyond the smashed window.

I could see the barrel of the gun as whoever it was raised it to fire again. Using the position of the barrel as a guide, I took the shot. There was a clatter and a thump followed by silence.

From beyond the cabin, I heard Kurt's voice. "We have Doyle."

Lee and I moved on the cabin.

Inside we found Maguire with a hole in his forehead.

Lee high-fived me. "Impressive."

I shrugged. "Would sooner have taken the prick alive." I toed his body, no reaction. I didn't expect one. His brains were all over the far wall.

No reanimation worries here.

I yelled to Kurt. "Don't bring her in here."

He called back, "We'll wait outside."

Lee and I searched the cabin. We had no real idea what we were looking for: diamonds, signs that Campbell was there, a clue as to what the hell was going on. We just needed something to start making sense. How did I kill him so easily? I could hear the question rolling around my head and then the answer that followed. Just because he's a hit man doesn't mean he's good under fire. I thought about it for a second. Maybe he just sucked at his job.

I pulled out a drawer and flicked through the contents. It contained letters, random rubber bands, a few pens, and a key.

"Lee, this look familiar?" I held the key up so he could see it.

He nodded. "It does. Looks like a key to a locker."

"Do they still have lockers at any of the Metro stops?"

He shook his head. "Don't know about Union, but I doubt they have them at the others."

"It's got a number on it."

"If we can figure out where the locker is, we should be able to find it," he said with a smile.

I looked at the pieces of paper and brochures in the

drawer, hoping something would jump out. And it did.

"He likes museums." I held up brochures for a recent exhibit at both the Freer Gallery of Art and the Natural History Museum. I turned on my phone and called Sandra.

No signal.

Crap.

I pocketed the key and the brochures. They seemed important. With no sign of Campbell, we went outside. Kurt was crouched beside Maria Doyle, sitting on the ground.

Sam stepped beside me. "She's clean, wasn't armed," he whispered.

I smiled a little. Good to know.

"Maria, I am Ellie Conway, we met a while ago," I said introducing myself. I handed my rifle to Lee, who shouldered it and went back into the woods for our backpacks.

"What happened to John?"

My mind flipped over the name. John. Who was John? John Brown. Pearce Maguire.

"He's dead."

A bit blunt but there aren't too many ways to say it.

Tears welled in her eyes.

"What are you doing out here?"

Lee came across the clearing carrying the backpacks. I showed him my phone. He nodded and walked back down the track to try for cell reception.

Maria was struggling with words.

"Iain said I'd be safer with him than in the city because whoever wanted to hurt me wouldn't know where I was ..."

"Where is Iain?"

She shook her head. "I don't know, he went out yesterday afternoon with John and never came back. John said he'd gone for supplies and not to worry."

"Did you leave the cabin with John yesterday evening?"

She nodded. "We ate at a diner in Harper's Ferry."

"You didn't wait for Iain to come back with supplies then?"

"No, I thought he'd be back by the time we returned."

"Maria, do you know who Iain is?"

"Of course, he is my husband. We've been separated for a number of years." Confusion clouded her eyes. "Why?"

"Where does he work?"

She tilted her head as if the question didn't make sense. "Work? He works for an insurance company."

I guess you could put it that way.

"Which one?"

"An international company, that's all I can remember."

Well, it ain't State Farm.

"Did he ever talk about coworkers, his boss?"

"He mentioned a boss a few times when we were together, I'm not sure, Jerry or Jeremy or Joe. It was a J name. I think." She paused. "John. Jonathon something. Yes, that was it. He used to blame him every time he disappeared for a week or so, on business."

Jonathon Tierney. I'd put money on it. And that was good for me, I needed corroboration that Campbell did indeed know Tierney as he mentioned in his cipher.

"Jonathon Tierney?"

Her eyes lit up. "You know him?"

Yup.

Now I was more willing to contact Tierney and ask for the information I needed on Campbell's operations.

"Maria, did Iain say anything to you about John Brown?"

"He didn't like him."

"He said that?"

She shook her head. "He didn't say anything to me about him. I overheard them talking outside."

"And what were they talking about?"

"John wanted to know why Iain and I left the city and who Iain was working for."

Oh, now we're getting somewhere.

"What did Iain say?"

"He said we were taking a break, a fishing trip. He said we had to make a decision about some of our properties."

"How did Brown know about the house Mrs. Southey rented and that you'd go there?"

Tears rolled down her face. "I told him. A long time ago, I told him about the houses Iain and I still own together."

"Okay, let me get this straight... Iain showed up at your apartment at night and suggested a fishing trip so you can discuss what to do with properties you jointly own."

"Yes, he said that. But that wasn't the real reason he wanted me to leave with him."

I nodded. "John Brown was already there at your apartment?"

"No. John showed up before we left."

"So, how and why did you leave DC with Iain?"

"Iain was trying to convince me to leave the city. He wanted me to go to the FBI and tell them I was in danger and it was something to do with the Heathcote diamonds. Before I could, John turned up. He saw the card your people left. It was sitting on the hall table. Iain and John fought. Iain knocked him out and grabbed me."

Things began to slide into place. Iain Campbell was after the same person we were, but Maria's presence compromised his ability to take out Brown.

"Why the FBI and not your brother?"

"I don't know. When I said I'd just tell my brother, Chris, and let him deal with it, Iain said no, it had to be the FBI."

"Did you call my office and leave an anonymous tip?"

"Yes."

"We need to get you out of here. Are you hurt?"

She shook her head. "I'm fine."

"And you were outside because?"

Her face flushed a little. "There is no bathroom in the cabin."

And he let her go without him, knowing we were coming? That didn't make sense.

284

"Why didn't you go back in the cabin? Why were you walking in the woods on the other side?"

She shrugged. "I was scared. You arrived before I could go back in."

"Why not keep walking and escape?"

"Because Iain said he'd come back for me."

"Let's get you out of here. I bet your brother will be pleased to see you."

Sam took some crime scene tape from his backpack. He tied it to the door and wound it across the front of the cabin.

It bothered me that there was no sign of Campbell. I moved faster than I intended, forcing myself to slow down and stay with the group. We caught up to Lee. He called Sandra and alerted local police to the crime scene. He'd asked that they secure the scene and guard the body until our forensic people could get out there. At the car I waited until everyone but Kurt was in the vehicle. Lee occupied my usual spot as navigator/front seat passenger. Sam and Maria were in the back. Kurt was going to drive. I'd sit in the back with Maria and Sam. Thank God we don't drive sedans.

I made the first of three calls that I needed to make while Kurt and I leaned against the hood.

"It's SSA Conway, Delta A, I'm out at Harper's Ferry, and we need divers."

"What's the situation Agent Conway?"

"Possible body recovery."

"We're on our way."

285

"Is Tara Sutherland on today?"

"Yes, she is."

"Awesome. I hear she's very good." I grinned to myself as I hung up.

The second call was to Misha.

"We will be on our way back to DC later today. How's it going with Zachary?"

"I don't see an involvement. I have been talking to Zachary about his family and his friends," Misha said, his Russian accent was quiet, yet dripping with bodice-ripping sex appeal. "He asked that I call his friend, John Brown. I am unable to locate Mr. Brown."

"His *friend*, John Brown?" I repeated.

"That is what he said. You know this man?"

I put a bullet in his head half an hour ago.

"You could say that. Find out as much as you can about the relationship between Brown and Zachary. Let's see how much of his story measures up with what we think we know."

"You are confusing me ..." Misha laughed. "Always one step ahead, my beautiful friend."

"I'll see you soon."

I hung up and made another call.

Déjà vu.

"Shangri la special services."

"Just put me through to Tierney."

"Yes ma'am," she replied.

"Thanks."

There was a click and then silence. Two breaths and

then another voice.

"Agent Conway?"

"Yes."

"Another problem?"

"Perhaps. Who is Iain Campbell?" I asked.

"We need to meet."

"I'm in Harper's Ferry. I'll be in the city later tonight."

"The usual place at the usual time?"

"I don't know yet. I'll call you when I'm in town. Be available."

I hung up.

Kurt coughed. "Everything all right?"

"Sure. Campbell is CIA. Tierney wouldn't want to meet me if he wasn't. Misha said Zachary referred to Brown as his friend and asked that he be called. He doesn't think he hired him to take out the family."

"The subversion is coagulating," Kurt said, tapping his fingers on the hood.

"Think it was easier when the plot was thickening," I said with a grin.

Kurt smiled. "Probably was."

"There is something fucked up about this whole thing." It was just the extent of the fucking and the upping that I wasn't sure of. "I am wondering if Campbell was after Brown/Maguire the whole time."

"You think we crossed inadvertently into a CIA operation?"

"It feels like that."

"Hotel?"

"Yeah, we need coffee while we wait for everyone to congregate here."

We got into the car, Maria between Sam and me, and my thoughts wandered as Kurt drove us back to the hotel.

A funny feeling writhed around and suggested that Maria's call to tip us off jeopardized Campbell's operation, and I didn't know if that was intentional. There were still things about Maria that bothered me.

I wanted to smack my head into the passenger window as a new and unexpected song pulsated through my head. Nuns singing 'Maria.' *The Sound of Music* came to life right there inside my head. I had no idea how to solve a problem like Maria.

Chapter Twenty Six
Hot Stuff

I saw the black sedans pulling into the parking lot from our window and knew the dive team had arrived. I nudged Lee.

"Divers."

He ran his fingers through his hair. "How do I look?"

"Not like you were crawling through the woods two hours ago, if that's what you're asking."

"That'll do."

"You still look like a rock star," Kurt said then ducked the open hand that flew at his head.

"Smart ass. You've been around Chicky too long," Lee muttered. He tucked in his shirt and attempted to rub dirt off his shoes.

"She's not going to be looking at your shoes," I commented.

Sam laughed from the other side of the room.

Maria looked on, confusion clouding her face. Not surprising.

"Want to meet the USERT team?" I said to Kurt. We both faced Lee and watched his mouth flap open and shut. "Oh, did you want to brief the team?" I asked Lee with utmost innocence.

His hand was already on the doorknob. "I'll take this."

Kurt grinned. "I'll go with you."

They left Sam and me chuckling.

"He seems nervous ..." Maria said.

"His girlfriend just arrived, she's a USERT diver," I replied.

"What's USERT?"

"Underwater search and evidence response team."

"Oh, I see." She must've given the diver comment some thought because a few minutes later she asked, "What are the divers for?"

"We're looking for Campbell."

"In the river?"

"Yes."

"But John said he'd gone for supplies—"

"Maria, John is not who you thought he was." Or was he? "And Iain didn't go for supplies."

"What do you mean?"

"Did either of them have a package with them?"

She shook her head.

"You're sure? You didn't see any diamonds?"

"Diamonds? No." Her head shook, then stopped. She looked at me. "You wanted to talk to me about the autism fundraiser, why?"

"The guest list. You made a late addition, a Mrs. Sutherland." No relation to the USERT diver that Lee fancied.

She nodded.

"Why?"

"I was asked to by Mr. Bleich."

"Bleich senior?"

"Yes."

Well, that changed things again. Sigmund Bleich must've known the Sutherland woman. We were still missing a huge piece of the puzzle. Damn.

I left Maria to drink her coffee and took my phone outside the room. I called Sandra.

"This might sound like it's coming from left field ... but look into the Sutherlands, in particular Mrs. Sutherland. Insurance policies she may have on her husband and links to Bleich, compare her phone records with Sigmund Bleich's and it wouldn't hurt to compare them to Marika's as well."

"I'm on it. Everything okay out there?"

"It's one twisted nest of lies so far. Par for the course."

I couldn't expect anything less from something that involved the CIA, an Irish hit man, and diamonds that may or may not be missing. I'd thought this was maybe about diamonds but we didn't know if they were missing or not, yet. That was a situation I could remedy.

"When are you planning on returning to DC?"

"As soon as possible. USERT are on scene now, I'll wait a few hours and see if they find a body." I paused for a moment. "Did anyone open the safe in the twin's apartment?"

"I believe so. You want the report forwarded?"

"Yes, please. Find out if the Heathcote diamonds are missing."

"Do you know where they were stored?"

"I think they were split between the twins, Zachary, Marika, and Sigmund. So I imagine in safes

291

corresponding to the owners."

Sandra said goodbye.

I flopped down on my back on the bed and closed my eyes. I could sense Maria watching me. I knew Sam was sitting in an armchair by the window, also watching me.

I needed to create white noise in my head, to cancel out everything I thought I knew about this case and view the facts all over again.

As I concentrated on creating a thinking space, I could hear Sam and Maria.

"Is she all right?" Maria said.

"Yeah," Sam replied. "She's thinking."

"Does she always think like that?"

"Nope." Sam then directed a question to me. "Okay, Chicky Babe?"

I lifted my right hand and made the okay sign with my fingers. From then on in, it was just me and my thoughts.

They wound through the woods and circled the cabin. A trail of words that when I put them all together said, "Catching Maguire was too easy." I could see him on the cabin floor, a pool of sticky blood spilling all around his head. Splatter across the wall behind him. His rifle on the ground. Why didn't Maria go back into the cabin? Where was the computer that Maguire used to monitor the cameras?

That's what I'd missed. No computer. Surveillance cameras were feeding to something, but whatever it was, it wasn't in the cabin. I started to doubt that Maguire did know we were coming. Perhaps they weren't his cameras.

So who did he think was out there? Maria? Campbell?

We walked into something that wasn't meant for us. So why shoot when we identified ourselves? An internal laugh bubbled up. People do dumb shit when confronted by us.

Never seems to occur to anyone to just do what we ask and live.

I opened my eyes and blinked at the ceiling. Someone monitored those cameras and somewhere there was a laptop or something that received the signal.

"Sam," I said without moving.

"Chicky?"

"The cameras, there was no laptop in the cabin."

I rolled over. He was already on his feet in front of Maria.

"Who set up the cameras?"

She frowned. "What cameras?"

"The ones that told you we were coming?" I said. "Where's your phone?"

"Iain took it from me when we left DC," she said.

"Did he give it back?"

Her eyes darted to the window and back as she lied to my face.

"No."

"Where did you leave it?"

"I don't have it."

That was truthful. She had nothing on her. But she did have it before we arrived. That's how she knew we were coming. That's why she was outside at that moment.

"Where did you hide it?" I said again with growing impatience.

She swallowed hard.

"Tell us," Sam said. He can be quite persuasive with his controlled voice and LL Cool J meets Mr. T exterior.

"It's in the woods," she stammered.

"Where?"

"Behind the cabin, not far from where you were."

"You want to tell me why you lied, why you had the phone, and why you didn't call your brother?" I said.

"Iain gave it to me right before he went for supplies. He told me to hide it, that there were cameras in the woods and an application on the phone to view the images." She leaned forward. "He said someone would come and that Brown couldn't know when that happened."

I looked at her. "He told you to write the note in the attic?"

"Yes. But I couldn't remember where the cabin was."

"Did Brown know who your brother is?"

"No, he'd met him as my brother, not as anything official."

"You're certain?"

"Yes, why?"

"Because there's a chance that your brother is a target and this whole god-awful mess was to make him more accessible."

She paled. "How?"

"They may have thought that NCIS would come after

294

you and maybe he'd join the hunt. I don't know, but so far nothing makes sense."

And Noel was pulled back in a big fat hurry. Sure, a SEAL team took out Bin Laden but that wasn't here, and it wasn't anything that would involve NCIS.

Sam stepped back and turned to face me, surprise etched across his face. His phone was in his hand and he was pressing buttons.

"This isn't about my brother ..." Maria said. "This is insane."

No more than everything so far has been.

The sun broke through the grey. It streamed in the window creating dancing sparkly dust particles. The glittering spiraled and twisted until a butterfly emerged with diamond wings and sprinkled the room with glitter. I turned, following its path; walking toward me from the door was a familiar figure.

"You again ... what this time?" I said.

Chance grinned, his eyes shone. "Campbell was never the bad guy. You're right about the CIA. You're getting warmer with the Director thing."

"Warmer?"

"Where was the bomb?"

"Crap!"

"Where are the Directors today?"

I shrugged. "I don't know."

"They're together. This is a twofold situation."

"Be nice if you were real. I could do with someone to flush out the bastards, Maguire sure as hell wasn't working alone."

"You can do it, Babe."

"Babe? Little informal don't you think?" I watched as his blond hair and blue eyes melted away, replaced by dark hair and hazel eyes. "Mac. What's with the whole Christopher Chance thing?"

"It amuses me," he replied then melded with the wallpaper and disappeared.

My phone was in my hand and I was scrolling through the directory for Cait O'Hare's number. She didn't answer at any of her numbers. I left messages and called Sean. There was a chance he'd know where his sister was.

"It's Ellie Conway. I'm looking for Director O'Hare. Do you know where she is?"

"No, what's up?"

"A gut feeling and a set of weird events." I lowered my voice, but was unable to keep the urgency from it. "Cait could be in danger."

"She's never anywhere without security, you know that," Sean replied.

Nothing fazed him. His voice remained devoid of emotion. I knew mine was revealing my apprehension.

"Doesn't matter what I know about her security. She could still be in danger. Can you find her?"

"Yeah," he said. There was a beat of heavy air. "I can tell this is really worrying you. What the hell is going on, Ellie?"

"I wish I knew. I'm in Harper's Ferry. I'll be in DC tonight. Find Cait, please."

"What are you doing in Harper's Ferry?"

"Cait asked Delta A to take an abduction case involving the NCIS Director's sister. We found her out here."

"Good chance Cait is with him then. I'll find her. Do you have a precise threat?"

"No, just my gut. Could be a bomb or a sniper." Either or maybe both.

"I'm on it."

I hung up and called Sandra again.

"What did we find out about visitors capable of leaving the Berretta in the bullpen?"

"I have a list, six names."

And I had a thought. "Whoever did it fucked up. I think it was supposed to be there when O'Hare was in my office, but the timing was screwed up. The gun was left a day early. This means Maria was supposed to be abducted a day earlier than she was."

"That Maria is quite the problem, isn't she?"

"I'm beginning to think so." How do you solve a problem like Maria? Find out what the root cause of the problem is. "Run the names, see what you turn up."

"Will do," she said, her fingers already tapping on her keyboard.

If anyone could find a connection between Maria, Brown, Campbell, Sutherland, Bleich, O'Hare, Director Doyle, and the Berretta – Sandra could.

Sam was on his feet pacing, his phone at his ear. He was alternating between talking fast and listening.

I waited.

Maria curled into the chair by the window. Reading her was difficult. It was almost like a thick blanket of snow covered her and obscured her real thoughts. People with nothing to hide don't pull a blanket over themselves like that. It was reminiscent of the meeting with the Sutherlands; the same obstructive feel.

Sam's arm dropped to his side, his phone still in his hand.

"What's up?" I said as I detected more weight in the air.

"Noel Gerrard is missing," he stated.

"Nothing unusual there, he's always missing or wandering off." I might have been more dismissive than I intended to be, Sam's brow creased.

"That's true, Chicky, but no one knows where he is. None of his team knows where he is."

That was a problem. I'd always thought that Noel could look after himself and most others around him right up until a thug disarmed him while we were on a recent case. If his team can't locate him, then we have a problem.

"Last known whereabouts?"

"On his way to meet Director Doyle."

"Pack," I said.

Sam left the room and I all but ignored Maria while I packed Kurt's stuff and mine as fast as I could. When I was done I suggested she use the bathroom, as we wouldn't be stopping at all on our way back into DC.

Sam and I hauled our gear to the cars, taking Maria

with us. Kurt and Lee were nowhere to be seen.

"River?" Sam said.

"Yeah, I'll call them."

Kurt answered his cell phone on the second ring.

"Hey, Conway."

"We're heading back to DC, you coming?"

"Yes."

"Lee?"

"He'll come," Kurt said.

"How's it going?"

"Divers are out, found nothing so far."

"I doubt he's in the river."

I hung up. Sam was waiting.

"I think Campbell was in the river but I don't think he is now."

"Chicky?"

"Nothing I can explain to anyone or provide any evidence to verify. Just the gut thing going on."

Sam smiled.

There was notable absence of music in my head. The jury was out as to whether that was comforting or not. It kind of felt lonely.

Chapter Twenty Seven
Brokenpromiseland

The emptiness continued all the way back into DC. Emptiness and a distinct lack of conversation. My mind was trying to fathom the twists and turns of the case. Maria attempted conversation on occasion but I just couldn't go there. Too much was happening in my head for external things.

I willed Wednesday to give me something useful.

No phone calls telling me O'Hare was safe somewhere. No phone calls telling me if the diamonds were missing. Nothing from Noel. I checked my phone several times thinking that maybe the battery was flat. But no, it wasn't flat. There just weren't any calls. No news in this case wasn't good news.

Kurt pulled into a space under the Hoover building and parked. Lee pulled in next to us. By the looks on their faces they all felt like I did. A mix of cold dread and adrenaline.

It's not as much fun as it sounds.

Sam took Maria to an interview room while Kurt, Lee, and I went to find Sandra. She wasn't at her desk. The bullpen was buzzing like a hive. Delta B was working on something. Lee and Kurt hung back with Delta B. When it came down to it, we were Delta and we stick together. Delta B needed to be brought up to speed. Information has a way of popping up from odd sources, but it's only useful if you know what to do with it.

I opened the door to my office and found Sandra at my desk.

"Hey, wondered where you were," I said, dropping my shoulder bag next to the desk.

"Do you mind?" she said, indicating to the computers in front of her. There were two laptops running plus my desktop.

"Not at all."

"Too noisy out there with Delta B in," she said with a nod toward the bullpen.

"You find anything?"

"Four diamonds are missing."

"Only four of five ..." I muttered. "Which ones?"

"The twins, Sigmund's, and Marika's."

"Do you know where the fifth diamond is?"

"Yes," she replied and opened my drawer. Sandra lifted a large jeweler's case from my drawer and set it on the desk. She opened the lid. "Here."

"Wow. Where was it?"

"In the store. Zachary told us there was a hidden safe under a counter out back. That's where his was. He expected his father's to be in the safe with his and doesn't know why he would have moved it or why a thief would leave this stone behind."

Interesting. I remembered every second of the video surveillance footage from the jewelry store. No one went behind the counter.

"Zachary is quite sure that his father diamond was in

the same safe as his?"

"Yes."

"But it wasn't there, was it?"

"No. The only stone in that safe was Zachary's."

"So, was the missing forty-eight carat diamond stolen like the others or moved somewhere else," I said.

"Maybe Mr. Bleich lent it to a museum or something …"

Sandra put the stone back in the drawer.

My eyebrows rose at her museum comment.

"Is there anything to suggest he may have lent out the diamond? And wouldn't he be more likely to lend the set, much more impressive that way?"

Sandra was reading the screen in front of her.

"Nothing I've come across, but that doesn't mean he hasn't got records somewhere other than on his computer," she replied. "I'll look into it."

"Something feels hinky," I said.

"You're right. You'll want to see this," she said and turned a laptop to face me. "Phone records from the Sutherland woman, with Sigmund's phone number highlighted. These calls were all made and received over the last four months."

I scrolled through the call logs. There were over a hundred calls to and fro.

"No denying they knew each other then."

"No."

"The calls end the day he died, there's nothing to Sigmund from nine that morning," I said studying the records. "She doesn't try to contact him again at all."

It's as if she knew he was dead. Was she crying because she thought her husband was dead, when we arrived at her home, or was she already crying because she knew Sigmund was? And how would she know that? How?

"Someone told her Sigmund was dead, or she knew he was going to die," I said. "Latest calls?"

Sandra turned the laptop back toward her and typed. I rolled a spare chair around to her side of the desk. We sat elbow to elbow, peering at the screen in front of us.

"She's made a lot of calls to several unknown numbers over the last five days."

And there was no overlap. Same person changing phones? A call from the unknown preceded all calls to the unknown. Someone was letting her know which number to call.

"When did the calls start?"

"Within an hour of Sigmund's death," Sandra said.

While we were looking for his killer.

"What do we know about the phones?"

"Burn phones. We traced the phone numbers to the manufacturers and they told us where they shipped those phones. The first one was bought at Best Buy in Fair Lakes. The second one was bought at Radio Shack on 12th Street NW."

"You've been busy," I said.

"No more than usual," she replied.

"Store surveillance?"

"We may get lucky, the Best Buy manager is searching

sales records to find when the phone was sold, and they keep their surveillance tapes for four months. The manager from Radio Shack is looking for sales records, she says the video is monitored and stored off site – she'll request the data once she knows what day the phone was sold."

"Good. Most obliging of them."

Some people like to help without making a fuss.

"They both have warrants requesting the data."

I nodded. The covering of everyone's ass was necessary. I didn't want to get this mess to court to find some smarmy defender could have everything thrown out because someone made a mistake.

"I'm heading out to see Mrs. Sutherland." I had a feeling she had Sigmund's diamond. I didn't know why, but my gut was twanging up a storm over the diamond going missing prior to the killings. Given away maybe? Given to her to shut her up for some reason? And then she got greedy and wanted them all?

"Who are you taking?"

"Kurt. Sam and Lee have two interviews to do."

She smiled. "Maria and Zachary."

"Yep. Where's Misha?"

A light knock sounded on the doorframe. I looked up and there was Misha Praskovya, looking every bit as if he'd stepped off the cover of a Mills and Boon novel. He strode into my office, his long strides covered the distance from the door to me as a smile played upon his lips.

"Ellie," he said.

"Privet, Misha. Are you well?" I indicated a chair. "Have a seat."

"*Ya khorosho.Vy vyglyadite ustalymyou. Mozhet byt', segodnya na uzhin?*" I am well. You look tired. Perhaps dinner tonight?

"*Mozhet byt'*!" Perhaps!

"Zachary is in interview room four," he said. "Your Russian is improving."

"You give me plenty of practice," I replied. "Lee and Sam will do the interview."

My chair rolled. The desk wobbled. The room swayed. Sandra jumped to her feet. Misha was on his feet; his hand reached out and took mine.

"Come," he said.

Unbalanced by the moving floor I missed a step and almost fell on him. His arm encircled my waist. The fire alarm sounded. I looked at Sandra clutching the moving desk. "Go."

She hurried past us.

"What the hell?" I said. I'd heard no explosions or crashing noises. Didn't seem like an act of terrorism. What was left? Earthquake? What were the odds? Fire alarms sounded. At the door to my office I saw the bullpen empty as everyone filed down the corridor and the stairs. "Carla!"

I shrugged Misha's arm away and hurried back to my desk. I picked up my phone and called Carla.

It took her a while to answer.

"Mom!"

"Honey, everything okay there?"

"What was it?"

"An earthquake, I think it was an earthquake." There were no columns of smoke visible from my window, so I doubted it was a terrorist attack although part of me couldn't quite grasp that it wasn't. I flicked up a browser on my computer and looked at the USGS website. "It was an earthquake. It's showing on the USGS website. Centered in Virginia, about forty miles North West of Richmond. It was a five point nine." Maybe I should've kept that to myself but it was too late, the words were out there and already hitting home.

"Will there be any more?"

I willed my words to evaporate before they flowed, but they wouldn't. "We might get some aftershocks," I said then added, "they're smaller, Carla." My fingers crossed. "You probably won't even notice them." Just shut up.

She dissolved into tears. Sobbing accusations down the phone. "I told you it would happen. The house would fall down and you wouldn't be here."

"The house fell down?"

"No," she sobbed. "But it ..."

Sometimes being a parent sucks. I silenced her. "Shush now. I'm on my way." Another sob let loose. "Carla, I'm coming home."

I was puzzled, unable to figure out when or why my stoic child became a drama queen of such enormous proportions. Misha held my bag and waited by the door.

"Mommy, I'm scared."

"I know. I'm coming. Stay with Grandpa."

I hung up, pocketed my phone, and looked at Misha.

"Go to her, I will come. Delta, they can take care of this case," Misha said.

So much to do. No answers. No closer to solving the riddles. And now an earthquake. *Days of Our Lives* would *kill* for a script like this. I nodded at Misha.

"Let's go."

On the way out of the building I saw Kurt and told him that I needed to go home for a little while. Lee was nowhere to be seen.

"You want to relocate the whole thing into Virginia?"

Could I do that? Would bringing Delta home make her feel safer? Maybe.

"Good plan. Deal with Zachary and Maria first. I don't want potential suspects in this whatever-the-fuck-it-is in my home."

"I'll take Maria to the Navy Yard. NCIS can handle her debrief."

"Good. Make sure they know I'm not happy with her level of involvement." I was not even sure what her precise level of involvement was, but there was something there.

My phone rang. It was Carla.

"Please, mom, hurry."

My heart thumped harder than ever. "I'm on my way."

Kurt raised an eyebrow and reached for my phone. "Carla, we're all coming with your mom. Warn your

Grandpa, we'll need coffee."

He handed me the phone and shook his head.

I said goodbye to Carla.

"It's not like her to be so emotional," he said. "Wonder what else is going on."

I smiled. "See? Not my imagination."

"Meet you at home," Kurt said with a grin. "For the record, I *never* thought it was your imagination. I just thought it was a teenage hormonal thing to do with Joey."

"And now?"

"I'm not so sure." His hand rested on my forearm. "I'll find Lee and Sam, you go home."

"And Cait? Where the fuck is Cait O'Hare? I haven't heard from Sean." This doesn't bode well.

"We'll find her. Have faith."

Misha and I continued down to the garage and my car.

My phone rang again before we were out of the parking garage. It was Rowan. He'd felt the earth move and was checking in. It must've been shallow and strong for it to be felt in New York.

Getting out of Washington wasn't the easiest of tasks. Buildings were evacuated while engineers checked for damage. People were everywhere. The energy was familiar. I'd felt it before, this time it was subsiding into a shaky normality as everyone realized it wasn't a terror attack. A random act of violence from mother earth. There is no way to fight that.

I started to see why it upset Carla so much.

Chapter Twenty Eight
Sweet Virginia

Carla met me at the door. Her tear-stained face and bloodshot eyes told me all I needed to know about how she felt. I hugged her hard. "It's going to be okay. It's just the earth having a tantrum."

Mother Nature needs to lay off the caffeine and take a little blue pill of instant calm.

"Can you stay home now?"

"Yes." I regretted my firm reply. Yes, as long as I don't need to interview anyone. Yes, as long as I can direct the investigation from here without having to do the leg work myself. Aware that Misha was trapped in the front doorway and unable to pass, I stepped aside, taking Carla with me. "Welcome to our new home," I said.

My father appeared from the other end of the hallway. "Misha!" he called. "Come, we have fresh coffee."

I eased my phone from my pocket while still hugging Carla.

"I'm home, but I need to work, okay?" I whispered.

"Okay." She wasn't letting go. Together we walked into the living room. I shrugged my shoulder bag to the floor by the sofa. Carla and I sat down. I conference-called Delta B and C's agents in charge.

"It's Ellie Conway. Have either of you seen or spoken to Director O'Hare today?"

"No," Claude replied.

"No," replied Tina.

"I am having trouble locating her and Director Doyle from NCIS." Never mind that Noel went to meet Doyle and his team lost contact with him.

"What do you need?" Tina said.

"Help. I need your teams to run down recent contacts. There is a visitor log, ask Sandra for it. Our inability to locate the directors may have something to do with the IED in the bullpen earlier this week."

My request met with silence as they digested the information.

I waited. Carla curled up on the sofa and leaned on me. Claude spoke first, "We'll divide the list."

"Thank you. You can reach me on my cell or call my home number. I've relocated Delta A for the time being."

"Understood." They said at once.

I hung up, and leaned my head back on the sofa.

"Mom, if Ms. O'Hare is missing, where is her son?"

"I hope he's with his father," I replied, opening my phone again and making another call. "Sean, any news?"

"Nothing. Cait arrived at her office at seven this morning. The building records show her leaving at seven forty-five with her briefcase. She took her car, no driver."

"Direction?"

"I got her on a red light camera. She was heading toward the Navy Yard."

"Doyle?"

"He left his office at five to eight carrying a briefcase. Took his car, no driver."

"Let me guess, he headed toward the Hoover Building?"

"Uh huh."

"So they met somewhere?"

"I'm going to need help with all the traffic camera footage, Ellie, if we want a shot at finding them before whatever it is that's going to happen happens."

"I'm at home. I have Misha and Dad here, I'm volunteering them."

"Computers?"

"We can cope. Send me links. I'll get them set up."

"Great. Usual email address?"

"Yes."

"To be honest, I'm a little concerned that Cait would disappear without telling her aides," Sean said. "Not surprised – because she's always been headstrong, ornery, a pain in the ass, she's always been Cait - but concerned."

I laughed. "I'd hate to hear what you say about me if that's how you describe your twin."

"You two at times are like peas in a pod."

Well, that answered my question.

"Send everything you have."

Sean and I hung up.

Maybe I could conduct this investigation from home after all.

"You didn't ask him where Sam was," Carla said, her quiet voice rimmed with sadness.

"You're right. I'll call him back."

I redialed. "Sean, Carla would like to know where your nephew is."

"He's with his father. I spoke to him after the earthquake."

"Thank you."

I hung up again and told Carla. It seemed to satisfy her.

"Right, kiddo, I have to go open my main office and fire up those computers."

"Here?"

"Yep, coming?"

Like she was going to stay behind when I left the room. I had myself a fifteen-year-old shadow.

My office was down the other end of the house, past the kitchen, down a short hallway and off to the right. I poked my head into the kitchen.

"I'm going to need you two to check through some traffic cam footage, is that okay?"

Misha and Dad nodded. "I'll come get you when I'm ready."

Three people could unlock my office door via a retinal scanner. Me, my father, and Carla.

"You want to?" I said to Carla as we stood in front of the door.

She nodded, and stretched her neck a fraction to look into the scanner. The door unlocked. I swung it wide open. The room was warm, light, and spacious. There were two doors on the left, one for the library and the other led to a bathroom. To the right was a large leather sofa with a coffee table in front of it. Under the window was a huge desk, which ran the width of the room. On it sat two desktop computers. There were also three desk chairs and enough space for a laptop. When I decided to build, I worked with an architect to design the house, and made sure my office was big enough to accommodate Delta A. The architect also included a panic room, which was accessible from the library. It was underneath the house but not reachable from the basement. My little concrete bunker. It wasn't so little as to be claustrophobic. The room had its own water supply, power supply, air filtration, and purifying system. No point having a safe room if someone can gas you when you're in it, or shut off your water or power.

I turned on the computers.

Damn, my laptop was in the living room.

"Carla, can you grab my laptop for me?"

She frowned. "It's down the other end of the house," she said.

"I know. Will you get it please?"

Carla shook her head.

"I'm right here," I said, as the first of the computers displayed the start screen. She shook her head. "Fine, I'll go. You stay here."

She shadowed me as I left and hurried down the hall. I've always wanted a shadow behind me that cries. My life is complete. Dad called out to Carla but she ignored him. I even heard the word cookie.

There was a train-like rumble.

The floor under us vibrated and jolted. The painting on the wall next to me tipped, I saw it move from the corner of my eye.

Carla squealed and grabbed me. "Another earthquake!"

I hugged her back. "Aftershock, Carla, that's all."

Dad called out, "You girls all right?"

"Yep," I hollered back. "We're good."

Carla sobbed. "I'm not good."

Maybe I needed to call Joey and get him over here. I decided to talk to Dad about it, if I could get two minutes without the shadow child.

On my way back to the office with my laptop, my cell phone rang. I checked the display and showed Carla. Rowan. She just shrugged.

"Can I take this?" I said to her. "Which means I want some privacy, Miss. Go into my office, I'll be out here in the hall."

She did as I said with evident reluctance.

"Hey, did you feel the latest shake?" I said as I answered Rowan's call.

"Yeah, made for an exciting few seconds. I called your place and spoke to Carla right after the first quake."

"Me too, you must've called right after me."

"Yep, she said I had. Is there something I don't know?"

"You mean something else as well as the Joey sex scandal?"

He spluttered into the phone, "Have you confirmed that's what is going on?"

"Calm down. I was kidding." Maybe.

"Then why is Carla so upset?"

"I think this is on me. I sort of promised her earlier this week that we wouldn't have an earthquake here in Virginia and we not only had a decent quake but we just had an aftershock."

"Damn."

"Yep."

"And that conversation came about why?"

"Because she was freaking out about another earthquake in New Zealand, and was super mad at me for not being home, or hating me for not letting her see Joey. I dunno. I think I have myself a teenager."

"Good luck."

I could hear him laughing. "Laugh it up, Chuckles, I'll send her to stay with you again."

"Threats now?"

"Empty ones ... she's not like this with you."

He was still laughing when I hung up. So glad I could amuse someone today.

Carla sat at one of the computers playing solitaire. She looked over at me as I set up my laptop on the coffee table. "Is Rowan okay?"

"Yes, he is. Think he quite enjoyed the shaking."

She shrugged. I could see in her expression that she wanted to ask me to let Joey come over but didn't want to hear me say no again.

The power of texting came into play. I sent a message to my father in the kitchen. Oh, how I have scoffed in the past at people who text each other when they're in the same house. But now I could see a benefit: private conversations you don't want a kid to overhear.

Should I let Joey come over?

Dad replied, *It's up to you.*

Fat lot of help you are.

Dad replied, *She hasn't seen him for the last few days. We're all here. It's not like they're unsupervised.*

I thought about it for a minute. He was right.

Okay, I will invite him over, or have Carla do it.

I pushed my phone into my pocket and sat down next to Carla.

"Do you want Joey to come over?"

She reacted with suspicion, as if it were a trick question, then said, "Yes."

"Okay, call him and invite him." I picked up the phone from my desk and handed it to her. "Land line."

The phone on my desk was the only one in the house that wasn't mobile. She was tied to the room by the cord. Therefore I could hear her conversation. I didn't listen. I busied myself. I dropped the email from Sean containing the links into Dropbox, and then retrieved it on both computers. Now, Misha and Dad could get to work, watching screeds of traffic camera footage to find either Doyle or O'Hare's car.

"Mom, he can come," Carla said with a smile. "His parents aren't home anyway."

"Does he need a ride?"

"No, he said he'll get the bus."

"Okay."

She didn't ask if she could go meet him at the bus stop. I guess she still wasn't feeling that brave after today's events.

I called out to Dad and Misha. When they appeared, I said, "Pick a computer, the links are in an email in Dropbox, just open Sean's email and away you go. He also included detailed descriptions of the vehicles and tag numbers. In the drawers on the left of the computers you'll find pencils and pads."

Carla's face exploded into a huge grin.

"Problem?" I said to her.

"You sounded like one of my teachers."

"Good or bad?"

"Bad."

"Good to know."

Misha chuckled and nudged Dad. "We will have to be careful, my friend. Ellie may smack us with ruler if we misbehave."

"*Vy umnyy zadnitsy* , Misha." You are a smart ass, Misha.

"*Ya ne tak khorosho kak vy.*" I am not as good at it as you.

"*Ochen' smeshno.*" Very funny.

"That's really rude, Mom," Carla said, glaring at me.

"What is?"

"Speaking Russian, Grandpa and I don't know what you are saying."

I glanced at my father. He smiled. Carla was wrong.

She was the only one who didn't know what we were talking about. My father spoke five languages and Russian was one of them. He didn't let on.

"*Raz, kogda vy nauchilis' govorit' na russkom,*" I replied. Time you learned to speak Russian.

"*Ya nauchu yeye,* Ellie," Misha replied with a nod at my father. "*Simon pomozhet, da?*" I shall teach her, Ellie. Simon will help, yes?

Dad smiled, his head inclined in agreement.

"Rude!" Carla squawked.

"Misha just said he will teach you Russian," I replied, it was best not to say that her Grandpa would help, not just yet.

She smiled. "Okay then."

"Now, relax a bit, kiddo. Joey will be here soon, and I have to work."

Panic scrawled across her face like someone had taken a sharpie to it.

"Work where?"

"Here. Chill."

She exhaled. "Okay."

A buzzing sound emanated from the wall behind us. I walked over and pressed the button on the intercom.

"Yep?"

"It's Kurt, Lee, and Sam," Kurt said.

I pressed a series of seven numbers into the keypad on the wall.

"Gates open," I replied.

"Thanks."

My shadow and I went out to meet them and Bon Jovi launched into 'We weren't born to follow.' A quick look behind me told me the band wasn't singing at the end of my hallway. They were so loud I was sure I'd see them there. I have to confess to a bit of disappointment at not seeing Bon Jovi behind me. How cool would that be?

"What is it, Mom?" Carla said, grabbing my hand.

"Nothing, thought I could hear Bon Jovi, that's all."

She twisted her head around and looked too. How could I be the only one who could hear the song? Because I'm the one who needs to hear it. I shrugged and opened the front door for Delta A.

Kurt was standing on the porch facing the driveway. Lee and Sam were collecting gear from the car.

"Hey," I said. Kurt's head turned to me.

"Didn't hear the door open," he muttered. "I liked the door at your old house better, you couldn't sneak up on anyone then."

That was true. It was not an easy door to open. Sometimes I forgot that this door was easy and applied the same force, only to have the door get away from me, and crash into the doorstop on the wall behind or worse, smash into me. That was pretty embarrassing.

"Come in," I said, stepping aside.

Sam and Lee crossed the distance from the car to the porch and front door.

"Chicky Babe, just like old times but in a fancier house," Sam said, handing his laptop bag to Carla. "Thanks, Carla, lead the way."

With everyone in the house, I paused at the open door and looked for Joey. No sign of him. I closed the door and caught up.

Sam, Lee, and Kurt took a few minutes to say hello to Misha and my dad, then settled into setting up their laptops and getting comfortable. Kurt handed me a file.

I flipped through it and read parts of the interview with Zachary.

"He had no idea, did he?" I said, as I read the statement he'd made on the last page.

Kurt shook his head. "No, he's just a nice guy who was on a buying trip for his father. He knows diamonds. He's very good and well respected in the circles he moves in, but none of those circles intersect with killers and terrorists."

"Then how?" Kurt knew what I was asking.

"Brown – Maguire – made first contact or the first approach if you like, while Zachary was in Antwerp on a buying trip. They met in a bar."

"Accidental or on purpose on Brown's part?" Yes, it was rhetorical. There was no way all this hell was unleashed on the Bleich family and the initial meeting was accidental.

"When did they meet?"

"Two years ago."

"Two years. That means over two years of planning."

I pulled my phone from my belt and indicated to Kurt to keep Carla with him as I left the room.

I made what was becoming a familiar call. I waited for

Tierney to answer.

"How can I help, Demelza?"

"Let's start with you using my actual name. Could you do that, please?"

"Old habit, Ellie. Old habit."

"One we need to have broken. Now, my issue ... Campbell was working an operation?"

"Yes, you know he was."

"Have you heard from him?"

There was a pause. Damn, he'd heard.

"No," Tierney replied.

He failed to convince me.

"Yes, you have, he isn't dead. Can I pull the divers out of the freaking Potomac now?"

"I would. They might find things you don't want to do the paper work for."

"Related to this?"

"Not necessarily."

"Jonathon, I need to know more about Campbell and the operation. There maybe two directors' lives at stake."

"Shall we schedule that meeting?"

"Where and when?"

"Woodrow Wilson Plaza."

The usual place wouldn't work this time.

I took a breath. "I can't get back into the city. I'm out in Fairfax."

"Fair Oaks mall, by CVS there is a—"

"I know ... there is a sunken seating area between CVS and the escalator."

"Be there in forty minutes."

I hung up. Now how to get away without Carla freaking out and who was I going to take? Lee. Kurt could handle Carla. Sam could supervise Dad and Misha. Lee with me. That worked.

I went back into my office.

"Lee, call the dive team. Campbell isn't in the river. Let's get them home."

He nodded and made the call.

Kurt cocked his head somewhat as he surveyed me. "What's up?"

His question caused Carla to spin around. The intercom buzzed. Saved by the bell. I reached out and depressed the button. "Hello."

"Hey, Ms. Conway, it's Joey."

"Buzzing you in the gate now."

I entered the seven-digit code.

Carla smiled and took off toward the front door.

Finally.

"Kurt, can you and Sam stay here with Carla and supervise what's happening here?" I waggled my finger at Misha and my father. "If they find the cars, let me know Asap."

"Sure," Kurt said. "What are you up to?"

"Lee and I are going to meet Tierney. He knows what this is all about. He knows where Campbell is. Time we got to the bottom of it."

"Be alert and safe," Kurt cautioned.

"Of course," I replied. Lee was on his feet and ready to

go.

Chapter Twenty Nine
Fingerprint File

We parked outside Sears and headed for the closest entrance. Together we walked into the mall. I paused between Gold Links and the Cold Stone Creamery. I could see the entrance to CVS in front of us and to the right, I couldn't see if anyone was sitting in the sunken area in front of it.

Lee smiled. "Ice-cream on the way out?"

"I reckon so," I replied and led the way. "What day is it?" There didn't seem to be many people out shopping and I was fast losing track of days. They blended to become one big blur.

"Still Wednesday," Lee replied.

A gentleman sat alone on the couches. I saw him as he saw me. His tight lips attempted a smile. Scary. Lee and I descended the steps. I sat on Tierney's right, Lee on his left.

"Jonathon Tierney, this is Lee Davenport." I introduced them. Fast firm handshakes followed.

"I know of you, Agent Davenport. Tim Cosgrove spoke well of your abilities."

Lee nodded and said nothing. A few months ago, Tim Cosgrove rode in with a rendition team and removed a terrorist who wanted me dead. It wasn't the best of circumstances but Lee and Tim worked well together.

I leaned into Tierney and hissed, "You're not here

headhunting, Jonathon. I need Campbell. This situation has to be resolved now."

"I'm afraid I can't give you Campbell," he said, smoothing an imaginary crease from his suit pants.

"Yes, you can. He's the one who knows what is going on and who the actual players are."

"He's an asset. I cannot give him to you. He is still working on this situation."

"Then I need to talk to him and compare notes."

"Are you suggesting a joint operation?"

"I don't know because I don't know if your operation will work within the constraints provided by the rules that govern me." There was a quiet internal joy at the way I was maintaining my cool by not letting any of Tierney's stalling tactics annoy me.

"Let's say it won't. Then what?"

"Then I want to know why the CIA is running another operation within the US. That'd be the second in a week that I've come across. Doesn't look good. I hear select committees get snippy over such things. Also why we were not notified of a direct threat to my Director? I believe you know something about that situation." I leaned back. "I also want to know how many other operations are in play right now, here inside the US. I'm going to ask questions. I'm going to demand answers and when I don't get them, I'm going to leak like a fuc'n sieve all over the nearest journalist."

A smile meandered across my lips.

"We miss you in the unit," Tierney replied. "You've

improved with age."

And he was more bird-like and creepy.

"Campbell," I said. "Now."

"I can't jeopardize the operation."

Lee coughed once. I looked right and saw a familiar man looking at sunglasses in the front of CVS. He made eye contact with me. I knew him all right. I'd seen his photograph enough times to recognize Campbell.

"You can't, but he can," I replied, indicating with my head to the man. As I watched, the man approached us; he walked down the steps and sat about a foot from me.

"Did you all enjoy the earthquakes?" he said with a welcoming smile.

"They were interesting," I replied. "You're Campbell."

"Asking or telling?"

"Telling. We need to talk. Or more importantly, You. Need. To. Talk. To. Me. As it stands now Maria Doyle will be arrested for things we know she didn't do, but the circumstantial evidence is compelling." I threw a nice juicy lie right in there for effect. She wasn't in any genuine danger of being arrested but I still didn't know if she had any real involvement in the case.

"Not here," he replied picking up a newspaper from the seat next to him and opening it up. "Here, I want to read the newspaper."

"Great. I'm sure she'll be thrilled."

I saw a warning glance from Tierney directed at Campbell. It was met with a defiant glare. Campbell was not a happy camper and he was going to talk. There wasn't a damn thing Tierney could do about it.

"Is there somewhere we can talk without being overheard?"

Crap.

Somewhere safe for both of us.

My house.

It was the safest location I could think of. No one could get in without being buzzed in; the entire exterior is under constant surveillance. Plus I could use the internal audio recording system to capture everything he said. Even so, the thought of inviting him into my home made me groan. I hoped it wasn't audible.

"My home."

Lee coughed twice. That was his protest at my decision. For what it was worth, I agreed. Bringing Campbell into my home didn't seem that clever but with more thought, all of Delta A would be present, plus Misha Praskovya and my father and that ameliorated the idea. I also considered it was the only way to find out how this all tied into the Directors of NCIS and the FBI, the deaths of the Bleich family, the bomb, and the diamonds as well as help us figure out how the Sutherlands worked into it and who else Brown/Maguire was working with.

"All right. Give me the address."

I pulled one of my cards from my pocket. Tierney took a pen from his inside jacket pocket and handed it to me. I'm not suspicious at all. I twisted the end of the pen until the nib slid out. Pens that have twisty ends could conceal all manner of things in the barrel. Like a USB drive. I rolled the pen over in my hand and saw it. A pinprick of a hole above the gold clip. I unscrewed the barrel while Tierney watched, took it apart, and revealed the USB stick; I also saw the tiny switch that turned the pen from video and audio to still photos.

I screwed the pen back together, wrote the address on the back of my card, and gave it to Campbell.

Tierney held his hand out for the pen.

"I don't think so," I replied, reaching past him to Lee's outstretched hand. "Lee, can you download the contents then wipe it?"

"Sure," he replied and pulled his laptop from the bag he carried. Within a few minutes the USB contents were on Lee's laptop and he'd reformatted the USB drive leaving no trace of the information it once recorded. He passed the clean pen back to Tierney.

"Old trick, Jonathon. Did you think I wouldn't know?"

He smiled. "Just for a minute I forgot who I was dealing with."

"I haven't. Turn out your pockets."

Campbell leaned toward me. "I like you."

It's not a popularity contest. It's my life.

Bang. Bon Jovi was back, this time singing 'It's my life'. They were right about some things though. I'm not going to live forever and I don't back down.

Tierney took his time emptying his pockets. Lee watched for mall security. Mall cops had a habit of being nosy and nosy was something I didn't want right now. I removed everything Tierney carried. I gave him back his keys, but after I'd taken the plastic case for the beeper apart and checked it for foreign objects. Nothing. I handed Lee two more pens, his phone, and a packet of mints.

The mints were a recording device.

Nice.

With all recordings dealt with, Tierney's possessions were returned and Bon Jovi faded into the background of my mind.

Lee spoke, "Security. Mall cop on a Segway heading toward us."

Nosy on wheels. That we did not need. Tierney stood up, brushed off his clothes, straightened his tie, and nodded to me.

"Always a pleasure, Ellie."

"Likewise, Jonathon. No hard feelings. I'm just doing my job."

"None at all."

With that, he turned, climbed the steps toward Sears, and vanished into the department store.

Campbell folded the newspaper and placed it back on the seat.

"Where's your car?" he said. The mall cop buzzed by us on his Segway, rounded the seating area, and buzzed away.

"Sears car park. Yours?"

"Outside Champps. I'll get my car and come to you. What am I looking for?"

"A black Escalade," Lee replied.

Campbell grinned. "Of course."

We went our separate ways. Lee and I stopped in at the Cold Stone Creamery for ice cream to go. Coming home with Oreo ice cream would redeem me in Carla's eyes. What teenager didn't love ice cream? None that I knew.

By the time we reached our car there was a nondescript grey sedan parked beside it. Campbell was behind the wheel.

"Lee, let's get him into our car. If he's being tracked. I don't want him tracked home."

"Good thinking. I have my toy. I'll scan him too."

We approached his car like old friends who'd just seen someone they knew. A patrol car cruised past just as Campbell opened the driver's door. Mall cops were everywhere. His smile was wide, making sure the cop could see we were friends.

"As soon as he is out of the way, we're going to run an RF signal detector over you. Nothing personal. I just don't want the type of people you hang out with near my house."

"All right. What do you want me to do?"

"Turn off your cell phone."

The cop drove into the covered car park area. Campbell climbed out of the car.

"You want to search me for weapons?"

"Nope," I replied. "I'd be worried if you weren't carrying." Anyway, I still considered that he was one of the good guys. Associating the CIA with good guys made me smile, just a little. Not everyone would make that connection.

Lee took his toy from his laptop bag and turned it on.

"No video, audio, or cameras here," he said a few minutes later.

"GPS?"

"There is nothing transmitting from him right now. GPS doesn't transmit all the time, so I'll monitor him for the next forty minutes."

There goes our ice cream.

"Okay. We're swapping cars here. You're coming with us."

Campbell nodded. "I'll get my stuff from the back. The last thing I need is some opportunistic thief smashing into my car and stealing my bag while the car is unattended."

He reached in and took a bag from the back seat. Lee scanned it. Nothing.

"Let's go. We're going to drive around for a bit, while we make sure you're not carrying any GPS units. Don't turn your phone back on. Leave it off until Lee gives you the all clear."

"All right."

I drove. Campbell sat next to me. Lee in the middle of the back seat.

I headed over to the Fair Lakes. The ice cream needed eating – I parked under a tree near Target and turned to Lee.

"May as well eat the ice-cream. I can hop into Target

and get Carla some Ben and Jerry's before we go home."

"Cherry Garcia?"

"Uh huh," I replied.

"Good call."

The three of us shared ice cream. Lee and I shared a spoon. We let Campbell have his own spoon. No telling what diseases he harbored.

With the ice cream gone, I decided to ask Campbell some of my most burning questions.

"Why is your marriage to Maria Doyle such a secret?"

"Her brother is not a fan of mine. We married in Vegas without his knowledge. When he found out, he refused to accept us as a married couple. He made life difficult for Maria. He was happy when we separated and assumed we divorced."

"But you didn't?"

"No, we didn't."

"Where is my director?"

"With Doyle."

"Okay, where is Doyle?"

"I don't know."

"Is this how it's going to be?"

"If I don't know, I can't tell you."

"Don't know or you're waiting for something before you'll tell me?"

"I'm not sure the threat is nullified and I honestly don't know exactly where they are."

"I put a bullet in Maguire. He is no longer a threat."

"And the others?"

Oh, good, there are others. "The Sutherland woman?"

"Her and her posse from hell."

I wasn't surprised. I suspected something hinky with Mrs. Sutherland.

"Why don't we go pick her up right now and then you can tell me where my director is and everyone will live happily ever after."

Seemed reasonable, straightforward, and not even that difficult. Drive over, pick up Sutherland and take her into DC. Oh, okay, therein lay the problem. How long could I leave Carla? I've already pushed the outer limits as far as she's concerned. Pretty sure she would've seen through my letting Joey come over move by now. Of course, it could be more of an actual logistics problem. DC was in chaos because of the earthquake. The thought of the madness that ensued made me want to scream 'suck it up princesses, it wasn't a big deal' from the Capitol building, presuming one could get into the freaking building after the whole evacuation panic. Anyone still in DC, was trapped in DC until the streets were cleared.

"Three of us, we're all carrying handguns. What else do you have in the car?" Campbell said.

"Two rifles," Lee replied. "Four bulletproof vests, four high visibility vests, a flare gun, and the best damn first-aid kit you've ever seen."

Before I realized it, I'd crossed myself and mentally thanked Kurt for our first-aid kit.

"Can you prove the Sutherland woman has culpability in this case?" I looked at Lee in the rearview mirror.

"Right now, all I have is phone calls from her to several burn phones – no proof that Maguire owned the phones, and phone calls to and from Sigmund Bleich. We know there was some sort of a relationship."

Lee's eyes met mine in the mirror. I could see his thoughts. He was running the inventory of weapons through his mind again, checking, rechecking.

Campbell said, "I have proof that she was blackmailing Sigmund Bleich."

"He paid her off with the largest Heathcote Diamond before the robbery/murder ...," I said. "You'd think a diamond that size would make a woman happy."

"I can also prove that she arranged for Maguire to kill her husband. He contracted out to an idiot who screwed it up."

"We can bring her in on conspiracy to commit murder," Lee said.

Proof will cover our asses and make legal happy.

"I'm going to need your proof on my desk as soon as possible," I said to Campbell.

"And you'll have it."

"I need to make a phone call, and then we're going. I have a feeling she'll be in the wind if we don't act today," I said. The phone call was quick. I spoke to Kurt, he checked on Carla and Joey. They were drinking juice and playing video games in the living room. All was well. He mentioned there was a little attitude regarding my leaving, but that it was minimal. With Joey around she seemed more like her usual self. Good to know. He also said he'd watch to make sure there was no funny business.

There'd be no underage sex on his watch.

Despite knowing it shouldn't amuse me, it did. It was okay having Delta offer support and walk beside me on this terrifying ride that is parenthood. Made me feel a little sorry for Carla: not much balance in her life. Most of the influential people around her were male. Apart from me, Gracey from Grange, and Cait O'Hare, she was surrounded by men.

I turned the key in the ignition. "Let's do this thing," I said.

"Are we going to need backup?" Lee said to Campbell.

"I doubt it. She's playing it cool. As far as she's concerned, no one has put this together. She probably doesn't even know Maguire is dead yet. Did the media report my death?"

I turned out of the parking lot. Not much traffic.

"Let's find out," I replied.

That was Lee's cue to make some calls. He started with Sandra. She'd opted to stay in DC, her computers were more powerful than any at my house, and she needed her equipment to continue working. Plus, Sandra worked with all three Delta teams, not just us, as I kept being reminded by the other SSAs. We needed to clone Sandra.

A few minutes later Lee obtained a full report from USERT and all media releases regarding their deployment to Harper's Ferry.

"They reported a missing person. No names. Just that

it was feared a missing man, a hunter, drowned in the Potomac by Harper's Ferry."

"Good," I replied. "For once they haven't gone nuts with details."

Campbell leaned back in his seat. I heard the leather creak.

"How did you survive?" I said, as I indicated and changed lanes.

"I almost didn't," he said there was a hint of strain in his voice.

My eyes flicked to his face. He was losing color.

"You all right?"

"Sure," he replied.

"You don't look like you took a beating. Maguire went back to Maria." I was thinking aloud. "He shot you or stabbed you?"

"For a contract killer, he's crap with a pistol and a moving target," Campbell replied.

"Through and through?"

He nodded. "I dove into the water when I saw the gun. He's also crap at moving targets in water."

"I can have a doctor meet us." Kurt wouldn't hesitate to come if I made the call.

"I'll be okay. It's a flesh wound."

I lifted the two-way radio from its cradle and held the squawk button. "SSA Conway to comms, over."

"Go for Conway, over."

"Request police backup at the following address, over." I gave the address and listened while comms read it back to me. "Silent approach. Over."

"Four cars responding, Agent Conway, over."

"Thanks. Have paramedics join them. Over."

For about three minutes, we traveled in total silence. Campbell was hurt and would need medical attention as soon as we could get it, flesh wound or not. I didn't want to lose him. He was all we had to make sense of the mess in front of us.

"Campbell," I said, tapping his forearm with my right hand. "You still with us?"

"Yes," he replied. "I'm okay."

Lee laughed. "Know someone else who says that."

"So what is this all about?" I said. "It's not diamonds for the sake of diamonds. It has to be diamonds as currency. There's more to it though, and it isn't anything to do with the curse of the Heathcote diamonds and the remaining Bleich, Zachary, wanting all the power. I don't think the family was killed over diamonds. The fact that Bleich was a jeweler seems incidental as far as the deaths go. What was Sutherland blackmailing him with?"

"You're pretty smart," Campbell said. "I've been tracking Maguire for three years. I thought I knew everything there was to know about him and his connections, which by the way are vast and not people anyone in their right mind wants to be involved with." He took a breath and adjusted his position. "I thought he'd met Zachary by accident. He looked like the perfect guy to get diamonds for Maguire. I kept a close eye on them, but there was never anything that changed hands. They seemed to be friends."

"That's what Zachary says, he wanted Maguire notified of his family's deaths, but he calls him Brown," I said.

"He would, Maguire has been using that cover for many years, on and off," Campbell said.

"So the connection was friendship?"

"No, it wasn't. They're half-brothers," Campbell replied.

A fitting Sir Walter Scott quote popped into my mind. 'Oh what a tangled web we weave, when first we practice to deceive!'

"You're going to have to explain that connection. I know the twins are not Sigmund's children but that Zachary is," I said.

Campbell smiled. "You remember that prime time soap from the eighties, *Dallas*?"

"As in who shot JR?"

"That's the one ... the story surrounding the Bleich family could rival any soap opera, even the Ewing's."

I wasn't far wrong with my *Days of Our Lives* imaginings then.

"Zachary doesn't know any of it, does he?" I said.

"Not as far as I am aware."

"Sutherland?"

"She married that name."

"So who is she?" I said.

"She's Maguire's mother."

"And Zachary is Maguire's half-brother? So Fiona Sutherland blackmailed Sigmund Bleich by threatening to tell all ... obviously one diamond wasn't enough and she wanted to do some serious damage. Guess it's true what they say about a woman scorned."

"Yes. Told you this was a soap opera."

I saw two Fairfax Police Department cars just ahead of us. "We'll follow these guys in."

A few seconds later we were parked and exiting the car. Lee handed out bulletproof vests.

"You should fit Sam's," he said to Campbell handing him a vest. "You need a hand?"

Campbell nodded. "Thanks." He struggled out of his jacket. A bloodstain spread across the right side of his shirt above the waistband of his jeans.

"That doesn't look too good," I commented. "I think we need to get someone to look at that."

"I'm fine. No need."

"As soon as paramedics arrive you're out of here," I said. "You sure you're okay to come in?"

"I'm okay."

My turn to laugh. It's exactly what I would say. I wasn't about to argue with him. "Let's go."

Four police officers stood near a marked car, five feet from us. I watched as a police car angled across the street about a hundred yards up the road. Behind me, I knew the same thing just happened. The police officers in front of me were wearing vests. Good to know they were ready.

I stopped by them. "We'll take the front door. Two of you take the back – go right. The other two take the back – go left."

They all nodded.

The police officers split up. They ran in front of us then disappeared from view. I slipped my Glock from my holster and racked the slide. The telltale clicks from next to me confirmed Lee and Campbell had chambered rounds as well.

"We good?" I said.

Lee nodded, his open palm slid across mine catching my fingers in his. "Alert and safe, Chicky."

I led the way to the front door of the single story home and knocked.

The waiting was a killer. Adrenaline pumped.

I knocked again and reminded myself to slow down my breathing, to steady my pounding heart, and adrenaline-fueled jittery nerves.

The last knock was followed by footsteps walking toward the solid door. I heard a click. Lee tapped my arm and pulled me sideways as a blast hit the door blowing a fair-sized hole right through it, spraying where I'd been standing with splintered wood. I glanced at Campbell. He winked. He was fine.

Police called into the house from the back. Lee hollered from the front, "FBI! Drop the gun! Come out with your hands in the air!"

How many times do we have to be in this position? Why can't people just play nice?

Another shot followed, blowing more of the door outward.

"What's her first name again?" I whispered to

Campbell.

"Fiona."

I turned my attention to the person with the shotgun.

"Fiona, please. We need to talk to you about your son."

No answer.

"You don't want to talk about Pearce? Then how about your husband. Is Quinn there? Can we speak to him?"

"No one speaks to Quinn," said a female voice. "No one, am I clear?"

"Very. Is that you, Fiona?"

"Yes."

"I'd like to talk to you about your son."

"I don't have a son."

I signaled to Lee and held up three fingers, he backed away holding his phone. Keeping out of the line of fire, he made the call to SWAT 3.

I whispered to Iain Campbell, "Looks like I might need my rifle, it's in the back of my car." I slipped the keys into his hand.

He nodded and moved away. I saw his hand seek his injured side as he walked. He wasn't okay. He was stubborn but he wasn't okay.

"Fiona, where is Quinn?"

"He's here."

"Is he hurt?"

"No." A little indignant twinge sounded in her voice. Maybe she'd decided to play innocent when it came to wanting him dead or maybe the moment passed and she now needed him alive.

"Can you send him out here to me?"

"I can't do that."

"Don't make this a hostage situation, Fiona. Just send out Quinn then you and I can have a chat about your son."

"I don't have a son!"

"Okay, then just send out Quinn."

"No."

I changed my approach. "Do you know our policy on hostages?"

"No."

Shoot the hostage if necessary. Once they're out of the equation it's much easier to deal with the hostage taker. Level that playing field.

"I have no qualms about shooting a hostage to remove him from the equation. Negotiating with terrorists is not my thing."

Silence.

In the background, I heard a man's voice. Pleading.

Sucked to be him today.

"I'm not a terrorist! This is a domestic situation. Nothing that needs police or FBI," Fiona hollered from deep within the house.

A cop appeared across the porch from me. I beckoned him to come closer and we stepped away onto the driveway and out of sight of the door and any overlooking windows.

"SWAT is on the way. What's it like around the back?" I said.

"Lots of windows, someone pulled all the shades."

"Did you see the male occupant?"

"I got a look in before the shades were pulled. I saw a male tied to a chair in the middle of a room. Looks like a living room. Back of the house, between the kitchen and bedrooms."

"Thanks." I gave him my cell number. We were going to be a while and they needed to be able to keep me apprised of any developing situations. "Keep your heads down. Stay alert. Be prepared to return fire if necessary. We're counting on you."

"Yes, ma'am."

I smiled at him. He was fresh, young, and wide-eyed. He made me feel old.

"You know the way it works when you guys help out Delta A?"

"No, ma'am."

I was tempted to grumble at the 'ma'am' but in his eyes I was a 'ma'am'. His eyes and my mirror. Funny how I don't feel any older than eighteen. Damn that mirror and that ma'am.

"When we're done and the case is closed, I run a bar tab for all LEOs who helped us. Murphy's bar." And a good time is had by all. A legacy left over from Mac. He started the bar tab thing as a way of thanking police and it enabled us to get to know the officers who stepped up to help. We've made some good friends that way. Making friends and influencing people. I preferred to think of it as undoing years of bad feelings and building good policing relationships. We're all in this together.

I caught my thoughts. They made me smile. I sounded like something from a recruitment pamphlet.

The cop I'd been speaking to grinned and hurried away, keeping his head low.

I moved back up to the porch but remained out of the way of the destroyed front door.

"Fiona, it would be better if you sent Quinn out. You and I can resolve this much easier without distractions."

"I can't do that. He's just as involved as I am."

I doubted that. I whispered to Lee, "Find out what she means by Quinn Sutherland being just as involved as she is."

"Enough now! Put down the shotgun. Let's get this over with." Places to go, a kid to supervise, no time for idiots.

I saw Campbell coming back carrying my rifle. My eyes scanned the area looking for a vantage point. Garage roof of the house next door was a possibility.

Campbell and I walked down the driveway to the very end; there were some big trees in the back yard. I waved to the two cops who watched us. With the blinds closed on all the windows, we were hard pushed to acquire a target anyway, so a vantage point wasn't vital yet. What I needed was eyes inside. SWAT and their clever little fiber optic cameras would be awesome.

My cell phone rang. When I checked the screen, I saw Andrews' smiling face.

SWAT was on site.

"I'll come to you, wait for me," I said and hit the end button. I took the rifle from Campbell. "Let's go meet Andrews and his team."

We hurried, giving a wide berth to the gaping hole that was once a nice front door. A boom made me jump. Shot pounded the side of the garage next door.

The temptation to yell, "You missed!" was strong.

If Fiona Sutherland was determined to end her life in a messy blood splatter there wasn't much I could do to stop her, but I didn't want her taking her husband along for the final ride. That was my preference, whether I could do anything to help him remained to be seen.

On our way to the roadside I asked Campbell if Quinn Sutherland figured in anything he'd found. He said he hadn't. As far as he could tell, Quinn was a good man who loved his wife and had no idea she was a mother. I doubt he expected her to have a child who was a contract killer. The Sutherlands were not blessed with children of their own. They met later in life and they'd been married six years.

They were in their fifties Why the hell is a sensible loving wife holding her husband hostage and shooting at us with a shotgun? Of course, she was the same woman who allegedly hired someone to kill her husband in an accident. I wondered what it was all about. Money? Maybe she didn't want to share that big fat diamond.

I leaned on the black SWAT truck parked behind our car.

"You all right?" Andrews said.

"Yeah, this doesn't make sense."

"Since when do nut jobs with guns ever make sense?"

"Good point." I cradled my rifle in my arms. "I need eyes in that house."

"I'm on it. Two of the boys are running in the cable now. They found a way under the house. Those cops you have with you are on to it."

Campbell cleared his throat. "Conway, do you mind if I ..." He fell toward me. I threw my gun at Andrews and caught Iain, breaking his fall with my body, and taking him to the ground with as much control as his dead weight would allow.

"Paramedics?" I said, as Andrews crouched next to me.

"There is an ambulance across the road. I'll get them," Andrews said.

This was not the best thing that could've happened. I needed more information and now Campbell was out of commission. If plan A doesn't work, stay cool, there are twenty-five more letters.

We needed to end the standoff. It was time to go see if we had eyes in the house, take Fiona out, and rescue Quinn. There was a good chance he now knew what was going on. That meant he was valuable to us.

I wasn't sure if Fiona intended to kill him or not. She'd tried once but that was by proxy. Doing the deed in person, now that's a whole other skill set. I didn't know enough about her to know if she possessed such talent.

Campbell was crushing me under his weight. My legs were losing feeling. He was still breathing. That was good.

Two paramedics arrived with a gurney. They lifted him off me. I gave the paramedics a run down, told them he was shot, a through and through, that his current condition could be because of the wound and that I had no idea where or if he received medical attention.

The bigger paramedic held a clipboard and a pen. He asked for Campbell's name. The Bonanza theme came from nowhere and damn near floored me.

I rallied and without thinking, I replied, "Joseph Cartwright."

I apologized for not knowing his birthdate or any other personal information and put Delta A down as emergency contact. They took off his vest. Underneath the vest was a deep red wet stain. Blood ran around his waistband coloring the top of his trousers a brownish red.

A cop appeared. "Can I help?

"Yes," I replied. "Escort this ambulance to Inova Fairfax and stay with the patient. He is Mr. Cartwright."

"Yes, ma'am."

They were all so young.

"Officer?"

"Ted Konstram."

Now that was a familiar surname name. "Josh's brother?"

He beamed. "Yes, ma'am."

"It's a family business, I see."

Ted nodded. "I'll stay with Mr. Cartwright."

"Thanks."

Ted followed the paramedics. Andrews helped me up.
"You all right?"

"Yes, of course," I replied. "Let's do this thing."

Lee was at my elbow with a concerned expression. "Chicky?"

"I'm okay. Campbell, not so much."

Fifteen minutes and seven shotgun blasts later we had a good view into the living room via the sneaky little fiber optic camera doo-dad that SWAT threaded into the house via some devious hole drilling. I sat in the SWAT truck watching the screen.

I could see Quinn tied to a chair while Fiona paced up and down the room talking on the phone.

"Can we jam that phone call?" I said. I didn't want to yet, but would be nice if we could.

"It's not cellular."

"Are we tracing it and recording it?"

"We are."

"When we're done letting her talk, can we break into the call?"

"Sure can. We can also prevent her from calling out and anyone but us calling in."

Now, that sounds like a fun way to shit with someone.

"And she's talking to whom?"

The agent manning the monitors and wearing a headset replied, "A male. She hasn't mentioned his name."

"Conversation is about?"

"It's incongruous. In one stream, she says she wants

348

this over, in the next she is vowing to fight to the end. She says Quinn is going to die and then that he isn't."

"Sounds conflicted."

"I think it's more than that." He was writing fast on a legal pad on the desk. "Here, they seem to be talking about mythology amidst the to-ing and fro-ing. What do you see?"

I took the pad and read the conversation.

"I'll be back," I said ripping off the page and jumping out the truck. "Lee!"

A voice called back followed by running feet on the sidewalk.

"Chicky?"

"Check this out, it's a code."

We hurried to our car. Conducting a conversation in code is not easy. Conversation has to flow. She wasn't reading it from anything. She's not an ex-lover-blackmailer turned crazy bitch. She's practiced talking like that.

Damn - would be easier with Campbell here. I think he likes codes and ciphers.

"Can you crack it?" Lee asked. "Hang on, look ..." He pointed to the second line. "She's giving a location."

"We need to work on this. We need her not dead." A shotgun blast punctuated my words. "That might not be as easy as it sounds."

"Tell me about it."

"Do you think that means New York?" I said pointing at the part we thought was a location.

Lee shook his head. "No, but it's a reference to apples."

"The Garden of Hesperides. Golden Apples. Greece?"

"Could be," Lee said but sounded unconvinced.

"Nah. Greece is wrong."

"Who produces apples?"

"We do. Laptop?"

Lee pulled his laptop from the case by his feet and handed it to me. The waiting for it to fire up involved more patience than I possessed. I opened Wikipedia as soon the browser was running.

Good old Wikipedia.

"Okay. Big apple producers of the world in order, China, us, Iran, Turkey, Russia, Italy, India ..."

"I'd say it's between Iran and Turkey."

"My money is on Iran." I slid the laptop onto Lee's knees and jumped out the car.

I scouted around for Andrews. He wasn't far away and watching me. I beckoned. He came over. "Problem?"

"You mean besides Fiona and her hostage?"

"Yeah, besides them."

"She's been talking to someone, using code. I need to crack the code – and I need her alive, for now."

"We're not shooting back here, in case you haven't noticed."

"Excellent. You want to start negotiating and try keeping the husband alive while buying me some time?"

"Yeah, why not." He shrugged. "Got nothing better to do today."

"I appreciate it."

Lee and I hunkered down in our car and worked on the code until we thought it started to make sense.

"She's making plans to leave the country. She's going to Iran to meet someone," I said. "She's meeting whoever is on the other side of this conversation."

"Fiona is a real sweetheart," Lee growled.

"I'm thinking this isn't just about money or diamonds or anything we've considered so far. I think this is revenge."

Lee nodded.

"Revenge is starting to make sense."

"Hang on. What did Chance say? A twofold situation. Twofold." And then I realized I'd said it aloud. Lee held his phone in his hand. "There's no need to make that call," I said. "No need at all. Nothing is going on here." I waved my hand in front of my face. "I'm all good. I promise."

"Chance?"

"I misspoke, can we leave it there?"

"Twofold, you just said Chance said it was twofold ... if I let this go, promise it won't come back and bite me on the ass."

My fingers crossed. "Of course." I chewed on my lip. "There is no need to mention this to Kurt, ever."

"So, tell me, what else did Chance say?"

"I'll tell you but, you have to stop looking at me like that!"

"Like?"

"Like my head's about to spin and green vomit is going

351

to spray across the inside of the car."

"You can see my point though, right?"

I wished I could just shut up. "Would it help to know it wasn't Chance but Mac being a dick?"

"Yeah. No. Not really."

His frown deepened. He was going to need Botox if he kept up that level of creasing.

"How about you forget I said it and I try to forget I saw him." Crap! I did it again. Spat out a big ol' reminder of my lurking insanity.

"You've moved on from seeing Mac in Messenger windows, receiving text messages from him and seeing him in a hotel bathroom. In the last week you shot him while he drank tequila in your living room. Now you're seeing him as an actor. Any of this bother you?"

"A little bit."

The spark left his eyes. "When was your last MRI?"

"That's a mighty serious question." I stalled because I couldn't remember. As I drifted back over the last year or so to find the answers I was conscious of Lee talking and I knew it wasn't to me. Every now and then, I heard shotgun blasts. Nothing much bothered me though. They seemed too far away to be of much concern.

Light shimmered then folded. The world I saw was a storyboard complete with thick black lines surrounding each frame.

My office was right in front of me but the colors were all wrong. They were too simple and flat. I knew it wasn't right but what was the point fighting my mind now? I walked into the room and closed the door behind me, blocking out all sounds of weapon fire and all the noises associated with the situation outside Sutherland's house.

His voice surprised me. How I didn't see him sitting at my desk when I walked in was a mystery. But there he was, Christopher Chance, smiling at me over my computer screen.

"I'm in enough trouble because of you," I said perching on the edge of my desk and watching my words form within a speech bubble. "You shouldn't be here."

"I know. They're going to send you for another MRI. Lee thinks you have a brain tumor." His speech bubble flattened against the background of the frame we occupied.

I looked behind me and saw we'd moved into another frame. The speech bubbles and outline sketches of us remained in the previous frame like a ghostly imprint. I leaned forward but couldn't see the next frame.

"Great." I didn't mean it.

"You needed Campbell ... fake name for him at the hospital was a nice touch. Seems like the code is causing issues?"

"Seems like you are a cartoon character."

"You want my help or not?"

"Sure, what the hell. I'm already in the crapper here." I watched him with interest. "I think Sutherland is planning to leave the country and go to Iran."

"Sounds about right. Sutherland, Fiona – whatever you want to call her – wants the diamonds but you are correct in thinking this isn't just about diamonds. She also wants revenge. She's not working alone. She's part of a wider organization. For the last twenty years she's been involved in fundraising," he said with a half a smile.

"Charities?"

"As it would seem on the outside but in fact funding militant groups, buying arms." He was a mine of information. Maybe I didn't need Campbell at all. Maybe I just needed to rely on the freaky workings of my imagination and whoever was drawing these scenes.

"Any in particular?"

"Any and all that worked with the Irish Republican Army," he said.

The frame jumped as my new speech bubble grew. "I thought they'd signed a treaty, hung up their bombs?" I said.

"Yeah, because a twenty-five-year civil war, with the ultimate goal to reunite Ireland, is just going to stop?"

Boy, my imagination can give me attitude. "Wasn't there something signed in 1994, a cease fire? Didn't the players decide to play like good friends?" My bubble burst, words flew through the air like shrapnel.

He ducked as a word spun by him and lodged in the wall.

"Look closer, Ellie. It never stopped. It's just been muted. This year there has been a sizeable upswing in violence."

"So what are you telling me? You need to be clear," I said.

"Fiona is working with others – worldwide, they are raising funds for terrorist groups. Her husband has no clue."

"How the fuck do I prove that?"

"Fast, before you end up in hospital."

Who knew that Christopher Chance was such a smartass? "Not helping."

A double-decker bubble filled the top of the frame. "I'll tell you where to look. You need to get into her financials. She has secret accounts. Some are offshore," Chance said.

"Swiss?"

"Yes."

"I'm going to need a damn good reason to get a warrant for her financial records." I thought for a minute. "Great, I already have grounds. She's shooting at us, holding her husband hostage, and we know she has ties to Maguire, a man that Interpol said has terrorist connections, and she was blackmailing Bleich prior to the killings."

"There you go. Now do it before Lee freaks out and has Kurt meet you here."

"Well, no one would be freaking out if you didn't start popping up and talking to me–"

"It's what I do, I help people." A cheeky lopsided smile broke free.

"You're helping me right into a secure psychiatric facility."

"Not if you work fast."

"Yeah, thanks for that. Hope you can break me out

once I'm locked up."

"I'm multi-talented, you'll be fine. Trust me."

I stood up and walked back out the door. The bubbles behind me all flattened onto their frames. The colors faded until there was nothing there but black line drawings. It seemed like a good time to use the Synergy in my pocket - just in case the cartoon thing was some new type of migraine.

Lee was still talking to Kurt.

"Hang up," I said.

Instead, he passed me the phone.

Kurt's calm voice tickled my ear, "I need you to tell me that you're okay."

"Never better."

"Lee's worried."

"I know. I got this. I'm okay."

"Do you need me out there?"

If I said yes, he'd come. He'd come. Am I okay? I just had a conversation with a fictitious character in comic book format. How okay is that?

"It'll make Lee feel better if you're here. Make sure Sam can stay with Carla and help with the car search."

"Now you're worrying me."

"Don't. I'm okay."

And I knew he'd be coming under lights and with his siren too. Way to freak everyone out, Ellie. I was surprised that my thoughts didn't appear in a bubble.

I hung up and called Sandra while I reached for the laptop on Lee's knee.

"Sandra I need a warrant, I need it fast. I want you to get me access to Fiona Sutherland's financials, can you do that?"

"Of course. Say the special words ..."

"Patriot Act. We suspect Fiona Sutherland has ties to terrorism."

"Done, I'll have an electronic version of the warrant sent to your phone within the next five minutes. Meanwhile, I'm sending you everything I have been able to access while we've been talking."

"I owe you," I said and checked my email for one from Sandra.

"Buy me a bottle of wine and help me drink it," Sandra replied. "Warrant is on its way."

I have no idea how she gets things done so fast. Best if I don't ask. I dropped Lee's phone into his outstretched hand. "All yours, thanks."

I started searching through the links that Sandra sent, typing in possible passwords and I didn't stop or look up until I accessed the financial records Chance told me about. Weird that he didn't fade to Mac at the end of our conversation. Weird that I didn't notice it right away. I scoured the records looking for deposits and withdrawals; after about five minutes I saw something.

"Okay, Lee, she's treasurer for several charities. Large charities. Money is being syphoned from charities to several bank accounts, in small increments. It's then shifted in larger amounts to various accounts offshore."

"Good work."

"Tell that to Chance."

Shut up, Ellie.

"Jesus, Chicky, Chance again?"

I ignored him. "The diamonds would mean she wouldn't have to carry on syphoning from charities. They would provide enough funds for whatever terrorist groups she's been working with for years. More than that though, she could leave with her son and the unknown male she spoke to on the phone and start a whole new life."

"So why didn't they? Why not just take the diamonds and run, why all this mess?" Lee said tapping his phone on his leg.

"Because she wanted revenge." Revenge is a vicious bitch that screws up everything.

"She's a vengeful ex-lover? Wiping out the family, that's a special kind of overkill don't you think?" Lee said.

"Hell, yes. But she is a very vengeful ex-lover who has ties to scarier people."

"Okay, we established she's a bitch, but what does this have to do with Director Doyle and Director O'Hare?"

As soon as their names left Lee's mouth, I knew the connection was Ireland.

"Who planted the bomb in the bullpen?" Lee said, taking his laptop back and tapping on the keys. "Sandra had six names?"

"Yes, that's what she said. She was running backgrounds." She was, and yet we had nothing. We were sitting in the dark.

No, really, we were sitting in the dark. When the hell did night fall?

Another gunshot echoed.

"I'll look into it," Lee said.

"I'm going to see Andrews. See what you can find. Call me."

I climbed out the car and walked toward the SWAT truck. Lighting plants were set up, floodlights pointed at the house. The brilliance would blind anyone looking out the windows. It was okay for anyone outside where we were though. Down the street I saw a support truck. The cops who were there from the beginning were having hot drinks and something to eat. They'd rotated with fresh cops. Good to know people were thinking.

I knocked on the SWAT truck door and pulled it open.

Andrews waved me in. He was talking to Sutherland. She was on speaker. I waited in silence, listening to her demands. She wanted to leave the country.

I could arrange that. A smile crept up on me. Damn, I could. I tapped Andrews on the shoulder and mouthed he should accept her demand to leave the country.

He frowned.

I smiled.

He nodded and spoke to Sutherland. It was a short phone call after that. She seemed happy to be able to leave.

When the call went quiet, I sat down next to Andrews.

"I can arrange for her to leave the country ... it won't be quite what she expects once she's airborne but she'll be leaving."

"You sure about this?"

"Oh, yeah. She's a terrorist. Let me deal with her in time-honored fashion, okay?"

"If you say so, Conway." He leaned on his elbows. "What about the hostage?"

"He might not make it," I replied. "Collateral damage."

You win some, you lose some.

"You're talking like one of us." He grinned. "Have you given any thought to joining SWAT three?"

"Lots of thought, and I'm happy at Delta." I pulled my phone from my pocket and stood up. "I'll just call and arrange that ... flight."

Extradition.

I stepped down from the truck onto the grass verge and walked away from the police, support personnel, and bystanders. As I walked, it grew darker. The call went well. Tierney wasn't surprised to hear from me again, nor was he surprised by my solution to the issue of Fiona Sutherland. He asked after Iain Campbell and I lied. The last thing I wanted was Tierney to make Campbell disappear before I had everything he knew. I said he was helping us. We were helping each other.

Tierney put everything in motion. I ran back to my car and asked Lee to pull up the names of everyone in the charities who could access the financial records. He found two people. Within a few minutes, we'd narrowed that to just one - the one Fiona Sutherland called while we were here. The one who spoke to her in code. We got the address.

New York.

I called Caine. Sometimes you need the help of the SAC. I told him we were going after someone from New York and that the arrest must coincide with Sutherland's extraction. I would call when everything was in position. The crew of the plane Fiona Sutherland was traveling on was a rendition team. I figured I'd be crossing paths with Tim Cosgrove again. My favorite CIA relocation expert.

Before I made my next call, I opened the trunk of the car and found the burn phone I knew was in the first aid kit. We kept burn phone for emergencies. I used that phone to call the hospital just in case Tierney was monitoring my cell phone. If I was him, I would. I wanted to know Campbell's condition. It wasn't great. He was in surgery.

From the darkness in front of me, I heard familiar footsteps. I finished my call and threw the burn phone back into the kit as Kurt stepped under the street lamp.

"You okay?" he said.

"Yes."

"How's it going here?"

"Pretty good now. Did you find O'Hare?"

"We think so. Sam sent Noel's team to bring them back."

"Them?"

"Director Doyle and Noel Gerrard are with O'Hare."

"Where were they?"

"We think they're at an embassy."

Embassy. Sanctuary. "No, they're not. They're in a church."

"Conway? Their cars were at the British embassy."

I shook my head. "They aren't. They're at the National Shrine. Go to the Basilica."

"Based on what?"

"Sanctuary."

I turned in time to see Chance running toward me from an open page of a comic book. He ran out of the page and thrust a piece of paper in my hand which read, "Doyle is working with Sutherland."

"Kurt, I need you to act without argument. Doyle is working with Sutherland." I looked to Chance for confirmation as I said, "Not Maria Doyle, but Chris Doyle. Director of NCIS, Chris Doyle."

Chance's lopsided grin came back. "Now you got it."

"Ellie, what are you looking at?" Kurt eyes traveled from my face to my hand. I looked down. I thought I was holding a piece of paper but there was nothing there.

"Nothing. Just find Director Doyle."

That was the connection I couldn't find and that was why none of it would slot into place. Campbell couldn't go to Doyle. He knew. Maguire knew Doyle. He'd been in on it with Doyle. And all too ready to lay all the blame for everything on Campbell. Delta's task was to catch Campbell. I was sure Doyle hoped we'd shoot him, and that would be the end of that. I suppose he didn't expect his little sister to toss a fuc'n great big wrench in the works by tipping us off to a murder.

Sam was able to get a lot of information from Maria during his interview with her. It was unfortunate for Director Doyle that his sister overheard a phone conversation. Maria heard Brown/Maguire's side of the conversation and recognized the jeweler's name. She thought someone was planning a jewel heist but had no idea Maguire was on the phone to her beloved older brother or that the jeweler and his family would be killed. She called anonymously. If police had received the tip off, we'd never have become involved, and the rest of it would've melted away.

Twofold.

So, Doyle asking O'Hare to help was to throw us off. She must've started to figure it out, that's why he kept her out of the way. And Noel? Doyle's his director. What the fuck?

Kurt was on the phone when I pulled myself out of my head.

I could only hope it was to mobilize the troops and not the men in white coats.

Chance stood next to me. I could feel the heat from his body yet I knew he wasn't there. He slung his left arm across my shoulders and whispered in my ear, "You got it. I can go now."

A hint of mint hung in the cool night air. I watched it twist with the faintest waft of cologne in the pool of light.

It occurred to me as Chance walked away that I might miss him.

I wanted to call out, to stop him, but thought better of

it. The MRI was guaranteed at this point but the men in white coats were still rooted in the realm of fantasy, I'd like to keep them that way. He stepped back into the comic book. The page turned and he was gone.

"Come on," I said to Kurt. "Let's get Lee to trace the connections and get us hard evidence."

"Police are converging on the Basilica now. We'll know in the next ten minutes if you were right. Sean is with them."

"I am right," I replied. "Have a little faith, Doc."

Chapter Thirty
Hand of Fate

"Conway!" Andrews hollered from his truck.

"Coming," I yelled back, running toward him.

"How we doing on the airplane situation?"

"We're a go, there is a Learjet standing by, fully crewed at Manassas Regional Airport."

"She wanted international travel," he replied.

"And she'll get it. Tell her we can't take off from Dulles on a commercial airline, that's not feasible. She has a private plane and can go wherever she wants."

"I hope she goes for it."

"Oh, she will, she wants out. The other way is a body bag."

"You're very sure," he replied.

"Have a little faith, Andrews."

Moments later, he came back to the door. "She agreed."

"Of course."

The opportunity to get away with millions of dollars' worth of diamonds? Of course she agreed.

"Get the cars ready, escort her to the airport."

"What makes her think we won't double cross her now?" he said as he radioed for his teams to ready two cars for the trip.

"She thinks she got away with it. She's got four enormous diamonds with her and she doesn't care about anything else now."

"You're shitting me ..."

"Nope. She believes someone is holding our director hostage and that we'll do whatever she wants to get O'Hare back unharmed."

"How do you know that?"

"The code, the person she spoke with had been in touch with the other party involved. The person who is holding O'Hare, until everyone escapes American soil."

Doyle, you son of a bitch. I wouldn't mind if there was an accidental discharge of Sean's weapon when he and the NCIS team find you.

A flash of panic crossed Andrews face. "Where is O'Hare?"

"Safe," said a relieved voice from behind me. Andrews looked over my shoulder. I knew it was Kurt.

"Get her and her husband out of the house," I said. "She won't kill him until she gets on the plane. Just in case one of your boys gets trigger happy."

I took a deep breath and let the last crazy few hours wash over me.

"We'll tag along," Kurt said.

Lee thundered up behind us. "Chicky, you won't believe who planted the IED in our bullpen ..."

Bet I would. Bet it was Doyle himself. No one would suspect a director.

"Doyle." I laughed.

"What's so funny? The Director of NCIS tried to take out our Director, and you think that's funny?"

"No, it's just something that someone said to me. This whole case could've been a season of *Dallas*." I preferred *Days of Our Lives*.

That shut them up. There are some lessons to be learned here. Valuable lessons. Wish I could think what those lessons were.

"I have a feeling that it's going to be days before I get the paperwork finished for this mess," I said with a smile.

Kurt grinned. "And I have a feeling that half the paperwork is going to disappear."

"Who's bringing out the delightful Sutherland woman?" Lee said.

"SWAT," I replied, giving Andrews a nudge. "I never got to fire my rifle. I feel kinda cheated."

"I doubt this will be the last time you call us out, so there's always next time."

"We'll follow you," I said. Kurt, Lee, and I walked back to where our cars were.

Lee paused by the driver's door of my car, turned to Kurt and said, "You drive, I'll take your car."

I held up the keys and jangled them. "You will need these then."

Kurt gave Lee his keys and then took mine.

"Any reason why you opted for Kurt's car?" I said before Lee left.

The smile plastered across his face gave much away. He wanted to talk to Tara.

"I need to call someone."

"Uh huh, tell her I said hi."

We sat there for five minutes, waiting for SWAT to bring out Fiona and her husband. I watched in silence as they bundled them both into a black Explorer and pulled out. One car in front, one behind, and then our car bringing up the rear.

Lights but no sirens. It was after midnight before we reached the airport. Security was briefed. Our convoy drove straight onto the tarmac and up to a waiting Learjet.

I stepped out the car and saw a familiar person standing at the top of the airplane's steps. Tim. He didn't acknowledge me.

Andrews took the Sutherlands from the car. They were taken on board. Two minutes after boarding, Andrews returned to his car. Tim ran down the steps carrying a package.

"Nice to see you, Conway," he said placing the package in my hands. "Did you want Quinn Sutherland back?"

"If you don't mind, I think he'd like to remain on American soil."

"I'll have him brought out."

"Be safe up there," I said pointing to the star-filled sky.

"Always."

With that, he was gone. Quinn Sutherland walked down the steps unaided. He crossed the tarmac to our car.

"Thank you, Agent Conway."

Not necessary, I *was* prepared to shoot him if the need arose.

"You're welcome. Lee will take you back to our office in DC, and debrief you. Then you're free to go."

"Can I ask?"

"Ask what?"

"What's in the package?"

"Four fifths of the Heathcote Diamonds." Really, really big diamonds. Diamonds are a girl's best friend. "Worth a rather large fortune and they were intended to fund terrorist operations."

"I had no idea."

"I know." He was a genuine decent guy. I felt a compulsion to offer him some life advice. "If someone offers you a lifetime supply of candy, and it's only one piece. Don't take it, it's probably poison."

"What does that even mean?"

"If you ever need that advice, you'll know what it means."

Damn, I was cryptic and mysterious. The cloak and dagger shit was rubbing off on me. Or I'd lost my mind.

Chapter Thirty One
The More Things Change

We met Sean and Cait O'Hare in a safe house outside Washington, after taking Quinn Sutherland into our office for a debrief.

He knew nothing. Poor bastard. He thought he'd married a woman who devoted her life to charity work and was doing good deeds all over the Eastern Sea Board. The harsh reality was that she was ripping off orphans and the sick with no regard for anyone but those involved in causing terror.

Cait greeted me with a smile.

"I knew I could count on you," she said, shaking my hand. I didn't want to refute her statement by telling her it wasn't me who figured it out. I had a feeling if I mentioned Chance again I'd be wearing a jacket with long sleeves and hugging myself.

"What happened?" I said.

"Doyle thought he could use us to do his dirty work for him. By dropping Iain Campbell on our radar and twisting some facts, he thought we'd go after him, guns blazing. It didn't bother him that his sister might end up in the firing line," she said.

"Charming." Not.

"Yeah, that's always been his problem. A silver tongue. He could get anyone to do anything for him by being charming. This time he screwed up."

"Where's Noel?"

Cait sat down, and suggested I do the same.

A sinking feeling hit me. "Noel?" I said again.

"He's fine. In light of the situation, he has resigned from NCIS," Cait replied.

No more Noel Gerrard. That was a shock.

"Why would he resign?" I'm sure I sounded confused. Noel was NCIS. Noel resigning didn't make sense.

"He arrested his director. That's not an easy thing to do," she said.

"That's b-s and you know it."

"That's the reason he gave," Cait said.

Things I knew flopped about inside my head and I kept them there. It was what happened in West Virginia. It was Nicky escaping from the cuffs and taking that cop's gun. It was his comment about getting too old for this shit. Maybe he was right.

"What was Doyle's involvement with Fiona Sutherland?"

"You'll love it, they were lovers," Cait said with a smile.

And the *Days of Our Lives* aspect continued. I'd grown to expect nothing less from this case.

How many men was the woman sleeping with?

"Lovers? I thought she was banging Bleich for old time's sake."

"Yeah, she was. Because Doyle told her to," she said.

"He told her to?"

"He's the biggest player in this game. Campbell was so close to tipping it all upside down and exposing the truth because of Sutherland and her inability to let go of the past. She wanted revenge and screwed up their plans," Cait explained. "Doyle has all the contacts. He can even access weaponry. Christ, he spoke to the SECNAV on a weekly basis."

Secretary of the Navy. No, that wasn't an actual secretarial position. He was the head of the Department of the Navy.

"SECNAV's clean?" I said.

Don't let this go any higher than Doyle.

"Yes. There is no doubt."

"Why did Doyle do it?" I said.

"Misguided loyalty, a belief that what he was doing was for the greater good."

"And how did this become our problem, Cait?"

"It became an FBI problem the minute he asked us to help find Maria. Police should have handled it. She was abducted."

"I'm not following ..." My brain was tired and complaining.

"He wanted her and Campbell dead."

"How did you know?"

"I wasn't sure, just a feeling, but I did some snooping after the IED. He was in the bullpen that morning and when I asked why he'd been in the Delta bullpen, he said he got lost trying to find me," Cait said.

"That was a mistake, they got the timing wrong. He was a day early with the IED. He wanted to hit you with that."

Cait's eyes widened. "Doesn't surprise me as much as it should after being forced to spend time with him."

I thought about Doyle getting "lost." "Visitors are supposed to be escorted," I said.

"Yes, but when Owen signed him in she was called away."

"Owen, signed him in. That's priceless."

"Thought it would amuse you."

"And you arranged to meet him even though you suspected the IED was his doing?" I said.

"Yes. I wanted to know for sure. I wanted to hear it from him," she replied.

"You should've told Sean, or me, or hell, any of the other agents working for you." That's right. I'm dressing down the director. "You didn't even have your driver with you and you took your own car." All our cars carried GPS units, meaning we could track them in an emergency. Private cars did not. "Putting yourself in danger like that is unacceptable."

"Have a little faith, Conway," she replied, smiling. "I did. In you."

Misguided faith. It almost went to hell in a hand basket.

Sean knocked on the doorframe.

"Come in," I said. "Everything all right?"

He nodded. "We are clear. Doyle is being held by the Department of Justice until his arraignment in the morning." He sat on the sofa. "How goes it in here?"

"Agent Conway was expressing her opinion on the

current events," Cait replied.

"Bet she used nicer words than I did."

Cait smiled at her brother. "Bet I find a GPS tracking device attached to my car tomorrow morning."

"It's already there, and it better stay there," Sean warned. "I can still kick your ass."

Guess it didn't matter how old brothers and sisters were, they were still siblings.

I liked the O'Hares. A lot.

"I'm outta here, unless you still need me?" I stood up.

"Go home, say hello to Carla."

I looked at my watch. It was morning. Going on for eight o'clock.

"I think I'll head into the office and get some of this documentation for this case out of the way. Then I'm going to take a few days and hang out with Carla."

"You do that."

I left the room. A yawn crept up on me. I couldn't remember when I'd last slept. Kurt was talking to a police officer while he waited for me.

"I'm driving," he said taking the keys out of my hand. "Home?"

"No, if I get the paper work out of the way first then I'll take a few days off."

"Office it is then." He shepherded me to the car. As usual, Kurt's chivalry knew no bounds, he opened the passenger door for me. He paused until I was comfortable and pressed the door shut.

My eyes wanted to close. Daylight was bright and hurt.

Part of me was afraid of what I'd see if I closed my eyes. It was all so much worse when sleep came. Dreaming was dangerous.

"You are okay, right?" Kurt said, pulling out of the driveway and onto the quiet street.

"I am okay," I replied. They were the words he wanted to hear. They were the words I said. Were they truthful? Maybe.

"So what's eating you?"

Oh, such big choices. It was hard to know where to start. Not by telling him that he was. Bad move.

"Nothing."

He indicated and turned onto Lee Highway. We found the traffic.

"Conway ... I know you. It's never nothing."

"I know you too," I replied and before I could silence them, the words came out. "That's part of the problem."

"Knowing me, or me knowing you?"

Abba. My worst nightmare. I was hearing Abba. "You suck!"

"What?"

"I can hear Abba in my head and it's all your fault." I leaned forward and flicked on the radio, trying my best to kill the unwelcome earworm. 'Knowing me, knowing you' was killing me.

No matter what song blared from the radio I was stuck with Abba in my head.

Abba. Dear God, why do you hate me?

"Okay, that's it!" Kurt said. He took the next left and

found a quiet place to park. "Talk to me."

"Why? So you can implant another Abba song in my head?"

He grinned. It confused me.

"Conway. Ellie. Chicky." I could hear amusement in his tone. "You're breaking up with me?"

"I'm what?"

"That song ... it's about a break-up." He laughed. "They know each other so well that they know it's over."

"Then why is it in my head?"

"You tell me and we'll both know."

And I did know. It made sense when he explained the song. "I can't ..." I swallowed hard. Tiredness mixed with a peculiar sensation of loss swamped me. "I can't."

Two men.

One me.

I blocked out Misha and Noel. They didn't count. Misha was a hopeless flirt. My father trained Noel – as far as I was concerned that took him out of the running. Plus, Noel was gone to parts unknown.

Kurt unclipped his seat belt and swiveled to face me, his left arm dangling over the steering wheel. His smile drove daggers into my chest.

"You think I don't know?"

"No, I always knew you knew." Stupid song was back.

"You want me to make this easier for you?"

I shook my head. "No, I do not. What I want ... is to know is that I'm right."

"No guarantees."

"I don't think I can do this."

"Life is too short not to follow your heart," he countered.

He never faltered. Not once. Kurt was always so sure. It was unfair of me to turn this around and put it on him but I did.

"Could we even work as a couple?"

His damn smile was rock solid. "Yes."

"That's it, no hesitation?"

"None."

"What makes you so sure?"

"You're all I've ever wanted."

"But I'm impossible. I drive you nuts. I eat crackers in bed. I talk to dead people. I hear songs that aren't playing. I see things. I shoot ghosts." My head may explode at any minute. "And for the longest time I saw you as Kevin Costner."

There was a high level of exasperation as Kurt replied, "You're mentally hilarious. You drive me nuts. You scare me with the things you see and hear." He grinned. "Kevin Costner?"

"Yeah."

"Do you still?"

"No." It was true. The conversation turned him from Kevin Costner to Noah Wylie. The sky was falling and I was in no fit state to be entertaining relationship thoughts.

"As I was trying to say, you make everyone else seem flat. People lack in depth and dimension when you're around."

"You'll grow to hate me."

"I'd like the opportunity." His right hand brushed thick strands of hair off my face. "Life with you is never boring."

"I need time."

The nice thing about Kurt was he got it, there was no pressure, and nothing felt awkward. He turned the key in the ignition, checked his mirrors and we continued the journey into the office.

My phone rang as we walked up the stairs from the parking garage.

"Morning, Carla, everything all right?"

"When will you be home?"

She didn't sound mad at me for leaving yesterday. I guessed that was because Joey was there with her.

"Soon. I am at the office. Have some paperwork to finish then I'm coming home."

She sighed. I knew that sigh. She knew how long paperwork could take.

"Mom ... don't freak out, but I have a question."

Don't freak out is not the best way to start a conversation with a parent.

I took a breath and stopped walking. Kurt turned when he noticed I wasn't beside him and waited.

"Okay, I won't freak out. Ask."

"If you found a way to take away all the bad memories, would you?"

"No. I wouldn't be me anymore."

"When you lost your memory, or some of your memories, you were still you."

"That was different. I had no control over that and I was me with chunks missing."

"Did you ever wish you could forget everything not just some things?"

"I never wished to forget anything." Yes I did. I wished to forget Mac dying and my childhood and some of the things I'd seen as an agent but memory loss is not the answer. "Everything we experience and do makes us who we are today. Where are we going with this?"

Red flags were waving in all directions.

"Nowhere," she said. "It's an assignment for school. We are supposed to write about a different reality."

And from that she decided to erase her life? "What would you erase, Carla, if you could?"

"Mom's death and Mac's death. Maybe life would be easier without those memories."

"Maybe."

"Oh, I don't really want to erase them," she said quickly. "It's just an assignment."

"We'll talk when I get home. I won't be long. I'm almost done here then I can help you with that assignment."

"It's okay. I think I know now."

"See you soon."

I hung up. Kurt waited.

"All right?"

"I don't know," I said.

Chapter Thirty Two
Dress Rehearsal Rag

It was midafternoon when I opened the front door. Tiredness caught up to me. I wanted to spend the rest of Thursday hanging with the kid and not thinking. A melancholic drone emanated from the living room.

"Dad?" I called closing the door.

"Laundry room," he called back. "Just washing up. I've been trimming the trees out back."

I peered into the living room on my way past. No one in there.

"What is the album you're playing? Music to slit your wrists by?"

"Thought you liked Leonard Cohen. I found this album in among your CDs."

"These days I prefer something a little happier." I sipped the coffee. "You couldn't have played *Various Positions* and let them hear 'Hallelujah'?"

"The kids wanted to hear *Songs of Love and Hate.*" Dad smiled. "Wouldn't hurt to widen their musical knowledge base."

I could see how the title would appeal to melodramatic teenagers.

"You know they're not in the living room?"

He nodded. "I didn't expect them to hang around for the whole album a second time. Surprised they stuck around for the first play. Didn't think it was screamy enough for those two."

Screamy is not an adjective that I'd ever put anywhere near Leonard Cohen. I laughed. I figured that was pretty accurate.

They liked metal and stuff that gave me a headache. Carla also liked Grange but not when Joey was around. Guess it's cool to like metal around boys. I finished my coffee and listened to dad's rendition of the day. Sounded normal apart from the music selection.

'Dress Rehearsal Rag' started.

"Tell me there aren't any razor blades in the house," I said as I handed Dad a towel for his hands.

"You want me to change the record?"

"It's a CD, Dad, it's a CD. And yeah, try something happy, will ya?"

A bang from the dining room startled me.

"Probably the kids," Dad said.

I crossed strode down the hallway and into the dining room. No kids. One of the dining chairs was tipped back against the wall.

Maybe the cat. I ducked down and checked on the chairs that were pushed in around the table. No sign of Shrek.

Back in the laundry I told dad there was no one there. I caught sight of Shrek stalking across the grass beyond the laundry room window. Not the cat then.

I walked up the stairs and along the hallway to my room. The flashing light on the phone beside my bed indicated more messages. Great. I listened to them all.

The same crazy woman left me another ten messages about how she and Rowan were in love and I was standing in their way. This time I caught her name. Julia. No surname. Shame. I could've run some checks with a surname.

I wiped the messages.

I dropped my belt and holster on my bed. It felt good to be home. The music downstairs came to an abrupt stop. When it started up again it was Grange. I smiled. Grange was a good choice.

Dad said Joey and Carla were doing homework. I figured I would surprise Carla with a trip away; just the two of us to make up for me being gone both figuratively and physically while we waded through the craziness that was the Heathcote Diamond case. And at the same time take her to her second ever Grange concert. I patted my pocket, reassuring myself that the tickets were still there. Even Rowan didn't know we were going to be at his spring concert at Madison Square Garden. I'd scored front row tickets.

Surprises all around.

Carla and I were taking the train to New York City. Spring break in New York. Pure awesome. I wanted a weekend just with Carla. I wasn't planning on spending much time with Rowan. My plan was that once spring break was over, I'd make the time to talk to Rowan. We had a lot to talk about and the potential was there to make his bitch publicist very happy if we decided to call it quits. As much as I liked Rowan, I'd always doubted we were a long haul thing, our lives were just too different. It surprised me he was still around.

Part of me hoped that this trip with Carla would end the weird behavior that'd been ongoing for a week now. Carla was surly and secretive while I was away. I knew that already. She was demanding and clingy when I was around. The phone calls during the last week alone were enough to drive me to distraction. The way she lost the plot after the earthquake was disconcerting to say the least. A peculiar rhyme came from nowhere and lodged in my brain, *Round and round the marijuana bush the druggie chased his dealer; he lost his stash and didn't have cash, Pop! goes the Glock.*

Where the hell did that come from? Dad hadn't mentioned anything untoward today. They had weird taste in music and were listening to Leonard Cohen. Okay, that was peculiar. Dad said that both kids were cagey and so forth while I was off working. Carla was clinging to Joey more than usual. Fair enough, I suppose, I promised that I'd work from home after the earthquake but shit happens. And I'm the one who has to clean it up.

Dad was of the opinion that they were either already having sex or on the verge of. Good luck to them doing anything like that with Sam, Misha, *and* Dad in the house. The weird rhyme suggested I might be right about drugs and Leonard Cohen suggested razor blades. It was anyone's guess.

I made my way to Carla's room and slowed when I noticed her bedroom door standing ajar.

"How's that homework coming?" I called out.

There was no reply.

Carla wanted to get her assignments finished so she could enjoy spring break. The phone call she'd made to me before I left work circled in my head.

I knocked on the doorframe, just in case. I don't want to have to scrub my brain because of something I saw teenagers doing. Huge ick factor involved.

There was no answering, "Come in." Or worse, answering, "No, wait!"

I sauntered through the door giving the appearance of way more confidence than I had. Don't let teenagers see your fear.

Joey was lying on the bed. Carla was semi-lying, propped up with pillows. Neither moved. As I approached Joey, Carla said, "Hi, Mom."

She sounded half-asleep.

"You guys were supposed to be doing homework, not napping," I said, giving Joey's shoulder a shake.

He didn't respond.

I gave him another shake. "Come on, Joey, I'm going to drop you home."

No response.

"Carla, what's wrong with Joey?"

She yawned, her voice sounded lazy. "He's tired."

He was more than tired. Something about him looked wrong.

"Joey!" I shook his shoulder.

No response.

I rubbed his sternum and called his name again. Nothing.

"Joey! Come on wake up. I thought you guys were up here messing around, not napping." Joey would've laughed; this kid was a pit of nothingness.

I looked at Carla. She seemed to be struggling to keep her eyes open.

"Joey! This isn't funny, wake up!" I pulled my phone off my belt as Bon Jovi's 'Lonely at the Top' filled all available space in my mind.

I yelled for Dad and reached over and touched Carla's shoulder. "Look at me."

Her head lifted but her eyes died.

Fuck!

"What did you take?"

She smiled with a creepy serenity.

It's not even close to being an okay thing. How did this even get to be my afternoon? The plan for the afternoon was to help Carla with an assignment and tell her we would go away for the weekend. I felt for Joey's pulse. It wasn't easy to find but he still had one.

Dad ran into the room.

"They've taken something," I said to dad. "We need to get him on the floor." Dad and I lifted Joey to the floor. Dad knelt down next to him and attempted to wake him up.

Carla shuffled to the edge of the bed and watched. She appeared amused. What the hell? She should've been at his side, trying to wake him up.

"Carla! What did he take?" I said, flipping my phone in my hand and pressing several buttons.

She shrugged and for the first time I felt a sense of frustration at my daughter's deplorable lack of reaction. She sometimes used what I called her "place saver expression," a blank look she adopted when she didn't know how she was supposed to feel. But this, a shrug? When faced with such a dire situation? Not even I expected that.

The drama over the earthquake and now, nothing.

I spoke to the 911 operator and told her I needed an ambulance. As soon as I knew they were on their way I turned my attention to Carla again.

"Carla? What did he take?"

She shook her head as if she didn't know, but I knew better than that.

"Is this something to do with the phone call, with the erasing memories thing?"

She didn't reply.

Joey lay unconscious on the bedroom room floor. His breathing was shallow and slow. I'd rolled him into the recovery position and called Kurt.

Carla sat on the edge of the bed and said nothing.

Nothing.

"Kurt, How far away are you?"

"Close, why?"

"Joey and Carla have taken something, and I don't know what. Joey is unconscious."

He hung up. I dropped my phone into my pocket.

"Carla. Did you see him take pills?"

I detected an almost imperceptible   m o t i o n ;   s h e shook her head, her smile secretive.

"Did he take pills?"

The blank stare returned. Large black pupils filled her blank stare. "Look at me," I insisted. "What did you take?"

She struggled to hold her head up. It could be any drug, illegal or otherwise. Dilated pupils. Spaced out. I ran through my limited knowledge of drugs. Maybe not an opiate, unless she took Demerol. Would they have done that? Yes. I have Demerol in the house.

Demerol acts like heroin and depresses the respiratory system. They were still breathing. My brain kicked in, Demerol overdose is fixable. Narcan or Naloxone reverses the effects like magic.

"Baby, what was it?"

I reached my hand out to touch her and she toppled off the bed and into my arms.

Jesus mother Mary.

I looked from Carla to Joey to Dad. "Is he breathing?" I said.

"Just."

"His lips are going bluish," I said. I struggled to find the terms I was looking for. Cyanosis caused by hypoxia. That wasn't good. I picked up his hand and checked his nail beds. Blue tinged.

I reached for my phone and called Kurt again. Kurt answered within seconds.

"Carla's unconscious, I think they both took the same drugs," I spouted down the line.

A siren replied before Kurt did. "Hang on, I'm almost with you. Get the gates?"

The gates.

I shifted Carla from my lap and lay her next to Joey.

"Dad?"

"Go, I have them."

The closest control panel was the kitchen. I tore down the stairs and pressed the button to open the gates and then a second button to lock the gates preventing them from closing, then swung the front door wide open, and ran back to the kids.

Joey's pulse was hard to find. I couldn't tell if it was because my hands were shaking or because it was so slow and weak. Carla's was a little easier but not much stronger.

While I waited for Kurt and the ambulance, I turned out Carla's pockets and called Sam and Lee – three-way calling was an awesome invention. There was not even residue in a baggie in their pockets that indicated they'd taken drugs. There had to be something somewhere that would help us.

Sam and Lee answered their phones. "It's me. I have a situation at home with Carla and Joey. We'll be heading to Inova Fairfax Hospital soon."

"What the hell happened?" Sam said.

"I don't really know. They've taken something and neither of them are responding."

Lee spoke, "I'll get Joey's folks."

"Good luck." He'd need it. To my knowledge they'd never shown the slightest parental concern over anything to do with Joey.

I dropped my phone and checked Carla's pulse and breathing. Her pulse was slow and her breathing irregular. Her nail beds were still pink.

A car pulled up fast outside the front of the house. Now if I could just get my heart to stop pounding so hard and my mind to focus on what we needed more than what was happening.

"Dad, I have to check their bags. We need to know what they took. You okay?"

Dad nodded. "Is that Kurt?"

"Think so." I scrambled out into the hallway and hollered down the stairs. "Carla's room!"

Footsteps pounded up the stairs as I went back into the bedroom.

"Ellie, Carla has a box in the bottom of her closet – her diary is in it," Dad said.

Kurt stepped into the room.

I swallowed hard and dragged the box out of the closet. Her diary was a red leather journal. I snatched it up and flipped through her thoughts and dreams until I found the last week. Skimming. Pages turning.

There it was.

Four days ago: Joey's parents are taking him away. He wants to stay with me forever. I want to be with him. Then an entry that said Mom won't let Joey come over for a while. That's so unfair.

Two days ago: I have a plan. I told Joey we should talk to Mom. She can help him stay. He thinks his parents won't listen. Maybe he's right. It's too risky. Mom is always at work. If she doesn't get home in time they'll take him away. We need a better plan. We will be together forever.

One day ago: Stupid earthquakes here now, not just in New Zealand. A sign of things to come. The world is falling apart, now it's our turn. Am I doing the right thing? What will Mom and Grandpa do when I'm gone? It's too late now. We have everything we need. Mom is gone again. Why can't she see what a mess this is? The world is ending.

My hands shook as I turned the page and read more.

Today: Why doesn't she see that there is only one way to stop the pain and the memories? It's not wrong to want to forget. No more pain, ever.

My breath came in short sharp bursts. Kurt's voice broke through the words I read. "Find anything?"

"No." I closed the diary and searched through the papers and treasures in the box. I found an empty prescription bottle with my name on it. Vomit rose.

"Heads up." I threw the bottle at him.

"Empty Demerol prescription bottle," Kurt said, setting the bottle aside. Joey twitched. "How long have they been down?"

"I don't know, I found Joey like that, ten maybe fifteen minutes ago, Carla was sort of talking then."

Joey started convulsing. "This is not good," Kurt muttered, motioning for his bag. I moved it closer. He pulled out his stethoscope and listened to Carla's respirations.

"Do you think they took Demerol? It's the only empty drug bottle in here and her diary says they had everything they needed. Plus—"

"Dilated pupils," he said. Kurt reached into the black bag next to him and looked for something.

My legs buckled, I sank to my knees next to my pale daughter. The front door sucked in an ambulance siren and let it scream up the hallway. Dad stood up and went to meet the paramedics.

"Stay with me, Carla," Kurt whispered as he administered Narcan. "If she took anything in the opioid family this will reverse the effects."

Magic.

"What about Joey, did you give him some?"

He shook his head. "He's convulsing, barely breathing, and hypoxic. I don't know how long he's been down. It only works while the patient is still breathing."

"He's breathing."

"He's hypoxic."

Maybe I was looking blankly at him.

Kurt rephrased his answer, "Conway, not enough oxygen to his brain."

Two paramedics hurried in and joined Kurt. One took Joey, the other Carla. Kurt spoke to them about the possibility of a Demerol overdose. I'd seen him administer the Narcan and I knew how fast it worked, but Carla wasn't waking up. Was I wrong? Was it not Demerol?

"She should be better ... why isn't she awake?"

Kurt shook his head. "She took something else, she must've."

A paramedic talked about Benzodiazepine.

"Valium?" I said, watching everyone working to keep the kids alive. A paramedic was bagging Joey, trying to force life-preserving oxygen into his blood stream. IV lines, bags of fluid, paramedics, Kurt. Organized chaos.

"Yes, anything in that family. Lorazepam, Xanax, anything like that ..." he replied. "They're common sedatives or anti-anxiety medication ... a lot of people have them."

"Medicine cabinet in my bathroom. Maybe there is something there," I said.

"Go look," Kurt replied. "Also, could be Roofies - they're not hard to get on the street."

A paramedic went down the stairs. As I ran to my room I heard him come back in with a gurney.

I opened my medicine cabinet and searched through the contents. Demerol, Tylenol, Advil, Triazolam. I shook the Demerol bottle and checked the label. It was current. I hadn't taken any. I pulled off the top and tipped the little white pills into my hand. A quick count revealed ten pills missing. I did the same for the Triazolam. The bottle was dated the day after we'd returned from New Zealand and labeled for jetlag and insomnia. The prescription was for thirty tablets. I'd taken two, but there were just four left.

I took the bottles downstairs.

Gurneys carrying the kids were wheeled to the door. Kurt was with Carla. Dad was with Joey. Joey was in a bad way. I knew there wasn't enough room in the ambulance for all of us. I gave the pill bottles to Kurt and told him how many I thought were unaccounted for.

"Triazolam, that's a benzodiazepine?"

"Yes. And you found an empty Demerol bottle plus these?"

I nodded. "I noted the date on the bottle. It was one I'd lost about four months ago."

I lost it. It was a full prescription. Thirty 100-milligram tablets.

Four months ago.

Ah, crap, she'd planned this longer than just the last three days or she'd come across it. I lost it when we moved to the new house. I assumed the bottle was thrown out by accident. I broke my rule, never assume.

"Go with her," I said to Kurt. "I'll follow."

He didn't argue. They disappeared out the door. Dad helped load the gurneys then jumped down from the back of the ambulance.

"You want to drive?" he asked as the ambulance pulled away. I nodded. I can't be a passenger with my kid's life hanging in the balance.

Passive versus active.

I was driving a federal car, following an ambulance.

The siren from the ambulance broke through the clear spaces within my siren. Blue and red flashing lights pulsed from my grill, the corner of my windscreen and from the back window.

Red and white from the ambulance.

Mac's voice was trying to break through the noise. I was trying to block him. I didn't want to hear him tell me it was my fault. I didn't want him to tell me Carla was with him.

My phone rang and rang. I ignored it. Dad's phone rang. From the corner of my eye I saw him switch it off. There was nothing to tell anyone, and no sense saying anything.

We didn't know.

"She rang me this morning and was asking about erasing memories." I flexed my fingers and adjusted my grip on the steering wheel.

"Wanting to forget something is not the same as taking your life," he said. "I've been trying to figure out when they did it."

"While listening to Leonard Cohen would be my guess."

"Jesus ..."

I shouldn't have said anything. My eyes flicked to his drawn face and breath caught in my throat as I tried to speak.

There were no words.

Chapter Thirty Three
Holding Out for a Hero

I parked behind two Fairfax police cars just in front of the ambulance bay. I walked into the ambulance bay, my stomach twisted into knots of pure terror. The gurneys were already out. I couldn't tell who was who anymore. Kurt was standing on the edge of a gurney performing chest compressions; a paramedic was using an Ambu bag.

All I could hear was Queen, 'Another one bites the dust'. For a second it felt like a sick joke on the part of my brain then I realized the song and Kurt were keeping perfect time. A distant foggy memory told me I'd heard it before while someone was doing CPR.

It was Kurt. He was humming the song. That's how he got the timing right.

People in scrubs rushed from the emergency room door.

I stopped.

Both gurneys disappeared beyond the glass doors.

Dad kept walking. I saw him follow a gurney. The doors closed and all I could see was my reflection. There was no way my feet were walking through those doors. Not yet. Staring at the closed doors, willing everything from the last hour to be a nightmare, and wishing I could wake up, were all I had left. Another ambulance arrived, full noise. Busy Thursday night at the Inova Fairfax emergency room. I shrank into the shadows of the bay, away from prying eyes and away from those saving lives.

From the shadows next to me, a dark figure stepped into a lesser shadow allowing me to see his eyes.

"If you're going to say I told you so, you're too fucking late," I said.

His hazel eyes shone. "Did you hand Carla the pills and tell her to take them?"

"No." Then I thought about what happened. If they took what I thought they'd taken, that's a lot of pills to swallow. "How did they take the pills, we're talking a handful each or maybe more?"

"Took them with juice," Mac replied, running his hand through his hair and pushing it off his face, it fell back over his forehead. There was no bullet hole in his forehead.

"They were drinking something. I saw their drink bottles with them in the bedroom. Crushing that many pills into juice ... it would be disgusting. They probably swallowed them a few at a time."

God, I remembered the night at dinner when I suggested they were sneaking vodka. I wondered if that was the dry run. Maybe they'd crushed a few tablets to see what it was like. What would she have done if I'd taken the offered sip of her juice? Let me, or come clean? Maybe it was her way of trying to get me to stop them. I failed. I missed the point.

The warm spice of his cologne wafted over me. I remembered how the heat from his skin used to draw me in and how it felt when his fingers entwined mine.

"This is not your fault and there is a plus side – at least everyone has an idea what they took," he whispered. "That's half the battle won, right there."

"I should've trusted my instincts. I failed them."

"Go to Carla," he said. Mac leaned close and kissed me, I felt butterfly wings on my face.

"How does this end?"

"I can't tell you that."

He stepped back, turned around, pulled up his hoodie, and walked into the darkening night beyond the ambulance bay. I watched him fade into a shadow.

Moments later I saw Sam and Lee coming toward me.

I waited until they were level. "Did anyone pass you?"

Sam shook his head. "No."

"Why?" Lee said.

I smiled and shook my head. "No reason."

"Ellie, who did you see?" Lee's voice was low and steady.

"No one."

"How are the kids?" Sam said.

"I don't know," I replied. "Joey's parents?"

"Packing to leave town. I stressed how serious this is but they didn't seem concerned," Lee snarled. "For Joey's sake I hope they pick now to care."

"You should be in there," Sam said, his voice was soft, gentle, encouraging. At that moment I hated him just a little bit.

I shook my head. "You two go, I'll be along soon. I

need to make a call."

Sam threw an arm around my shoulders and hugged me fast. "She needs you," he whispered. "I'll tell her you're coming."

"See you inside in a few," Lee said. They walked away to the automatic doors and the unknown.

Time to make the call. I dialed and waited. The waiting required pacing. As I neared the point of giving up I heard a click, a pause, and then his voice.

"Ellie?" he said, his speech filled with a smile.

"Yeah ..." My ability to speak was failing me. I tried again but the real words stuck in my throat and all I managed was, "It's me."

"What's wrong?"

I failed.

"Something ..." I faltered. It was harder than I thought, and I thought it would be hard. "Something happened ..."

"Honey, where are you?"

Great, I'd transferred my fear into his panic. "Fairfax Hospital."

"Are you okay?" His voice showed great restraint.

"It's not me." If it was me, someone else would be making the hard call. "It's Carla ... she overdosed." My words sounded hollow as they trailed down the phone.

"I'm on my way."

"Thank you."

"Don't thank me. I was already on my way. Did Carla tell you I was in town?"

"No," I replied. "No, she didn't." She told me nothing

except she wanted to erase her memories. I bit my tongue to stop me adding my thoughts on what she did do. She just swallowed a bunch of pills with her juice and tried to die.

"I spoke to her earlier, mid-afternoon ... Surprise."

I could tell he was moving by the noises from the phone.

"Where are you?"

"Crossing Key Street Bridge. I was heading over to see you."

"Go east on George Washington Memorial Parkway, then take the I-66 East, US-50 exit toward Rosslyn."

"Okay, how long will it take me?"

"Twenty minutes from Key Bridge to me." I knew he would have GPS in a rental. "Put Inova Fairfax Hospital, gray entrance, into your GPS. I'll be in emergency. You'll see us or ask for me if you don't."

"I'll be there soon."

"What are you driving? Gimme the tag number."

He rattled off his license tag and car make and model.

"You drove down, that's your car," I replied.

"Yeah."

"Were you at a fundraiser here a few weeks ago? For autism?" Because now is the very best possible time to be thinking about the case we just finished the paperwork for.

"How'd you know about that?" There was a hint of surprise or maybe suspicion in his voice.

I got the feeling I wasn't supposed to know about it. "I

didn't know it was a secret."

"It's not ..."

"But you didn't tell me you were in town."

Atta girl! Start something now.

"You were out of town at the time," he replied.

Traffic noises in the background reminded me he was driving. Rowan always used a Bluetooth headset when he drove so I knew it was okay to talk to him.

"Where was I?" I couldn't think why I was out of town and hoped Rowan knew.

"San Francisco on a case."

"Oh, that week. Yeah, I was." Let the lunacy go, fool. "Anyway, the jeweler who owns the Heathcote diamonds was murdered. I've been working that case for the last week and a half."

"I met him."

Rowan being at that autism fundraiser bugged me because he hadn't told me about it. Focusing on that was so much easier than thinking about what was going on beyond the doors in the emergency room.

"Watch for an escort, Rowan."

I hung up before he could ask what I meant.

The emergency bay doors opened. Kurt appeared. I didn't want to look at him. I made another call.

"Josh, its Ellie. I need a favor."

"Sure, what is it?"

"Escort this car to Inova Fairfax emergency department." I shared the tag number and car description. "He's on his way now, taking the US-50 from

Key Bridge."

"I'll have someone provide escort."

"Thank you."

"You okay?"

"Yes. Carla isn't." I hung up.

Kurt was by my elbow.

"Conway ..."

I swallowed, pocketed my phone, and turned to face him.

"Yes."

"You need to come in and be with her," Kurt said.

I blinked hard and fought a lump in my throat. "Not yet ..."

"Ellie, she needs you," he replied. "Now."

"Rowan is on his way," I replied, looking toward Gallows Road, hoping to see a police car leading him in. "Rowan is coming."

"It's okay, he'll find his way to us," he said. "Come in."

He hadn't touched me, and for that I was grateful. The struggle to remain composed felt like a losing battle. Beyond Kurt the doors slid open again, a nurse hurried out waving her arms. Kurt spun on his heels and ran toward her. The walls of the ambulance bay moved and the sliding glass door loomed.

I was walking.

My feet took over and I was running.

I followed Kurt through the door; the nurse was talking to him as they hurried down a hallway and through another set of glass doors.

Right behind them.

The doors closed after me. I watched them shut. My reflection stared back at me. When I turned, Kurt was gone.

I walked on, peering into each room I passed but not wanting to see.

Doctors, nurses, equipment, patients, blood, crying, coughing, and the worst rooms where there was no noise but machines pinging and the soft hiss of a ventilator.

There was nothing comforting about the noises.

Struggle for life noises.

End of life noises.

They all sounded the same.

"Kurt!" I whispered into the illness and pain-filled sterility.

An arm waved through a gap in a curtain, inside one of the glass-fronted rooms.

"Here," he replied. The curtain parted more. "In here."

I stepped inside the curtained area. My daughter lay still, her eyes open but unblinking. A ventilator next to her forced air into her lungs via a tube in her mouth. A machine recorded her heartbeat and another brain activity. Tubing ran into both her arms. I noticed condensation on the bags of saline that hung from poles at the head of her bed.

"Carla ..."

"Sit with her," Kurt said, motioning to a nurse to move and get chair. A chair appeared. Kurt pressed me into it.

"Why doesn't she blink?" I said, lifting her hand and

holding it. It was like holding a rag doll's hand. It just lay cool and heavy in mine. I watched her face for signs of the kid I knew. Her right eye twitched once, and then she blinked. Her eyes closed. "She feels cool. Can we get a blanket?" I said.

Kurt pulled a sheet up to her shoulders, lifting her arms clear and placing them on top of the thick white sheet. "It's better for her to be cool right now," he said.

"Okay."

It wasn't just Carla that felt cold. The room was cold and drafty. That was when I noticed fans blowing air over us. Guess he was serious about cold being better for her.

"She's in a coma," Kurt replied. "Talk to her, she might be able to hear you."

Might?

So, I did. I told her about my day. Then a long involved story about The Heathcote Diamonds and how beautiful they were. She loved sparkly things.

Her hand lay in mine like a dead fish.

I told her about how Kurt got soaked earlier in the week when an awning ripped and how funny it was. The whole time I talked, Kurt watched the reaction on the machines.

"Tell her something you know would elicit a strong response," he said.

From my pocket I took the tickets. "Wake up, baby. I got us front row tickets to Grange in New York next weekend. It's a surprise. Even Rowan doesn't know."

Nothing. Not a glimmer, not anything. Maybe she

didn't hear me. I leaned close and pressed her fingers around the tickets. "We're going to see Grange. You and me in New York for a whole weekend." This time I watched the screen for brain activity. I asked her to squeeze my hand. I told her Rowan was on his way.

She lay there like a rag doll. An empty rag doll. The ticket's I'd closed her fingers around lay on the white sheet. A question I wanted to ask kept sticking in my throat. It took a few attempts before it crackled forth.

"Can she breathe by herself?"

Kurt's blue eyes rested upon Carla's face.

"She was breathing by herself."

"She was or she can?"

He gave the merest shake of his head. "Her heart is still beating. At this point, I don't know if she can breathe without help."

"Now what?"

"Intensive care."

"For how long?"

"Until we know if she is going to recover."

If.

I looked at the shell that was my kid. "How long?"

"We have to wait until all the drugs are out of her system. Then I can begin the brain function tests."

Then he can begin the process of declaring her brain dead that was what he meant.

"Where's Dad?"

"With Joey, for the moment."

"How's Joey?"

He shook his head. "Joey is not going to make it."

Joey's not going to make it.

I heard a noise outside the room. A female voice, then Rowan's. I stood up and left.

"He's with me," I said to the nurse who was trying to stop him entering Carla's room.

"Sorry, ma'am," she apologized and shrank away.

Rowan's arms circled me and I pulled back. I couldn't let him do that. My mind screamed. Don't touch me. I can't do this if you touch me.

"Ellie?"

I held up my hands and stepped back. The confusion on his face softened as he got it. He knew me well enough to know that it wasn't the right time, yet.

"She's in here," I said but my voice faded so I didn't think he'd heard me. I tried again. "She's in here."

Kurt was standing next to the bed, talking on the phone. He motioned me to sit back down. Rowan grabbed another chair and moved next to me. The ventilator hissed.

Kurt finished his call. "Rowan," he said. "We've got no news at this point. We're waiting. All we can do is flush out her system and wait."

"How long?"

"Million dollar question. As long as it takes."

"Can she hear us?"

"If she can she's not responding. But, that doesn't mean she doesn't hear," Kurt replied.

"When is she going to Intensive Care?" I asked,

touching her hand and willing a response. If she were anything like me, she'd do it just to spite Kurt.

"In a few minutes. You can both go with her. It's a good idea if you do. Settle her, talk to the staff."

"Who is the neurologist up there?"

"Who do you want?" Kurt asked. Picking up his phone again.

"Leon Kapowski," I replied. "At least get him to consult with whoever they have in ICU."

Kurt made the call. I swapped places with Rowan, so he could talk to Carla and hold her hand. I fought tears listening to him tell her about his day, and how he was supposed to be surprising us, not the other way around. He pulled out his phone and played her a song. I hadn't heard it before. As it played, he told her it was hers, the one they'd written last time she stayed at his place. It was going on the new album.

Waves of anger rolled over me. There was so much good in her life. So much love. I watched Rowan stroke her hair and I wanted to slap her. Slap her hard. Wake her the fuck up and yell at her. How fuc'n dare you be so goddamn selfish? How dare you!

Kurt's hand landed on my shoulder. "They're taking her up in a minute."

I nodded. "Why did she do this ...?"

His fingers squeezed my shoulder. "I don't know."

I doubted we'd ever know, or ever understand.

"I'm in the middle of wrapping up a case. I need to get back to work." I tried to stand but couldn't. Kurt's hand pressed me down into the chair.

"No one's working the case tonight. We are done with the case. The only thing you wanted was Campbell's take on the situation." Kurt's voice was firm. "Not tonight. You need to be here."

"No, I don't. I need to work. Dad is here, Rowan is here."

Panic rose. I couldn't say what I wanted to say. I couldn't let those words out.

I can't be here.

I can't watch her die.

Kurt checked his phone. I heard it buzz, a text. "Sam and Lee are waiting outside asking if they can come back in," he said. "Do you want them in here with you?"

I nodded.

His phone buzzed again. He smiled and showed me the text. I read it out. "'Kurt, please tell Ellie that I am here. Caine.'"

Another buzz.

"The Director is here ..." Kurt said taking his phone back and reading the next text.

"Great. It's a regular FBI party," I replied.

"News travels fast."

Bad news travels fast. Good news takes its own sweet time.

Sam and Lee entered the room. It felt crowded, claustrophobic. They looked from me to Rowan to Carla.

"Chicky Babe, we'll be outside," Sam whispered in my ear. "We'll wait out there for you."

"Thanks. Caine is here somewhere."

"Hang tough, Chicky Babe."

My words left me.

Lee moved around the other side of the bed to get close to Carla on the other side of the bed. "Carla. It's Uncle Lee and Uncool Sam. You need to fight, kid." Lee's voice cracked like I'd never heard before. He looked at me as he left. A tear ran down his face. I looked away.

It was too close, too much, and too soon.

Their footsteps faded.

I blew out a long breath.

Seconds later, two women in scrubs appeared in the room. Kurt introduced himself, then me and Rowan.

The blonde was Maria and the brunette Daria. I waited to see if 'Maria Nay' would start up again in my head. Nothing happened. I was thankful the songs had paused.

Kurt and the intensive care nurse and doctor – turned out Daria was a specialist in intensive care – began the process of moving Carla. They attached her to a portable ventilator for the journey down corridors and up the lift.

As I walked behind the gurney and the people charged with keeping my child alive, it occurred to me I hadn't asked if she was going to be okay. If she did survive, would she be the kid I know and love or would she be brain damaged? I just assumed we were fighting a battle that we would lose. I heard footsteps behind me. I didn't look. I knew who they belonged to. Caine, Cait O'Hare, Misha, Sam, and Lee.

Running feet.

The running feet that joined then passed them, the panic I felt coming up behind me. That was Aidan. My brother. The hand that grabbed my arm to slow me down, the one I didn't shake off, but that dropped off as soon as I looked at him. My brother.

"Where's Dad?" I said.

"With Joey. His parents aren't here yet, and Dad won't leave him. He told me to tell you, he'll meet you and Carla upstairs."

"Okay, thanks Aid."

"It's quite the parade behind you, or hadn't you noticed?" He smiled. I knew he was trying to get me to react. It's what he did.

Procession not parade. Funeral procession. That's what it was.

"Aid..." I looked at him for a second. "If only she knew."

I stopped walking and leaned on the wall. Rowan carried on, because I made him. Sam said, "You want us to stay?"

I shook my head. "Go with her."

Go with her and make her fight! She's not trying. She's not trying to live.

First I was walking, and then I was running, back through the hospital, out through the glass doors and into the ambulance bay.

Cool night air. Away from everyone. She didn't need me.

Not now.

I couldn't think what she did need but it sure as hell wasn't me watching her fade away. Or maybe it was me that didn't need that. At the end of the ambulance bay, I stood and watched traffic on Gallows Road. Across Gallows was a wooded area that bordered the entrance to ExxonMobil and a flood of memories. My eyes scanned the night, and hearing a trail bike somewhere bought a host of feelings to the surface. Mac was there once with me.

I waited by the traffic lights. The lights were taking too long and traffic was sparse. I ducked across the road. The entrance to ExxonMobil was almost hidden by the night. I stayed on the left hand side of the road that led to the complex within the woods. It was hard to see my way. There were no lights and the woods cast creepy shadows every time the clouds parted and the moon shone. I was okay with creepy shadows. My hand reached for the Glock I wore on my hip and came up empty. That was confusing. I felt for my holster. Nothing.

I hurried along the edge of the road looking for the path I knew that led off the road in and into the woods. During the day, it was a beautiful meandering trail through to the other end of the entrance; at night, it was dark, marked by occasional trail markers that glowed in the moonlight. To my left I could hear traffic on Gallows Road. It wasn't loud, but I could still hear the cars as they slowed for the lights. I walked along until I came to a seat secluded in the woods. I sat down for a while. My arm bumped my side, a reminder that I wasn't armed. The events leading up to me being in the woods without my gun played out on the movie screen in my head. I saw my Glock on my dressing table. I was home and safe.

Home and safe.

No one could get to us at home – yet I couldn't protect her from the enemy within.

I didn't do a very good job of keeping my kid safe at home. How is it I could build a panic room, install state of the art surveillance and security to protect her from threats but couldn't protect her from herself?

Time sank into the darkness taking me with it.

I was startled back to the present when a voice rang out from the road behind me. "Ellie!"

The voice called out again. It wasn't any closer. I figured he didn't know where I'd gone. Time to move. Hell, I didn't know where I was going. Just back, back to a place I knew once. I doubted I could find my way to the underground parking garage in the dark, not that I wanted too. I didn't want to follow the old tunnel all the way into DC.

A smile crossed my lips. If I did, no one would find me.

No one would find me. Then what?

Disturbing thoughts echoed in the caverns of my mind. Could I disappear? Run away? Even I knew I couldn't run from this, or me. My phone rang. The noise disturbed wildlife. Things skittered in the undergrowth. I pulled the phone from my pocket and checked the display. Kurt.

I pressed the end button. The call stopped. The phone rang again while I held it. Kurt.

"I'm here," I said.

"Conway, where'd you go?"

Behind me somewhere on the trail I heard footsteps.

"For a walk," I replied. "I need air."

"Stop, let me catch up."

"That's not a good idea."

"Conway. Stop."

His voice was in my ear. His voice was behind me. My feet stopped walking but I didn't turn around. I ended the call and shoved my phone back in my pocket. No sense talking on a phone, he was about to catch up with me anyway.

The waiting afforded me more opportunity to listen to the rustling in the woods next to me. It took a lot of energy to remind myself that clowns weren't evil and there wasn't one in the woods. Maybe it wasn't a clown. Maybe it was Christopher Chance. Kurt's footsteps were soft but unmistakable on the asphalt path.

"Ellie?" he called. "Ellie, wait." The sound of his words tore into my brain. They twisted, contorted, and became a child's cry. My child's cry. I spun on my heels my eyes searching for her as she cried out again. "Mommy!"

My heart pounded along with a sudden surge of adrenaline.

"Ellie ... where are you?" Kurt again.

"Ahead of you, fifty yards maybe," I replied. "I'm waiting." As the words left my mouth, they flew, like butterflies. Dipping and soaring, silvery words on diaphanous wings.

Circling Kurt's head as he came into view were silver butterflies. He didn't seem to notice.

"Hey ..." he said.

What else do you say to someone who has run away from a hospital and into the woods? Carla cried out, "Mommy!"

"Hey," I replied.

"You want to come back with me?"

I shook my head. "I don't, but I can hear her crying and I have to."

Kurt's blue eyes locked on mine, the color faded by the night.

"You hear her?"

"Yeah."

Mommy!

I expected to see a raccoon carrying a balloon in the woods beside me. Little feet scrabbled in the leaf litter and twigs. Instead I heard Bryan Adams singing, 'Everything I do I do it for you'. My breath caught in my throat as I waited to see if Robin Hood would emerge from the thickets, or at the very least an arrow whiz past my head and the Sheriff's men scatter under a hail of arrows and rocks.

No arrows. Not even a glimpse of Alan Rickman. Yet, Bryan Adams was still doing everything for me. The song wound around my heart and squeezed. It is worth trying for. And whatever was wrong, it was not worth dying for. It squeezed tighter.

"Kurt ..."

"Right here."

"Suicide pact. It's a Romeo and Juliet situation."

"You're sure?"

"I read her diary. She said they don't want to be apart and that they have everything they need now." I kicked at a branch. "Joey's parents were taking him away."

"That sounds like a pact or at least a plan to stay together forever." His eyes burrowed into mine. "What else is going on?"

"I can hear Bryan Adams singing—"

"Conway, I didn't know Adams sang a suicide song."

"Everything I do I do it for you, apparently it was worth dying for ..."

"Could that be about something else, I always thought that was a love song?"

I shook my head. "Yeah, me too, but what else could it be about and why am I hearing it?"

I know I wasn't thinking straight but Kurt was right in front of me telling me it was a love song. Duh!

"The reason Rowan is in town?" he suggested without making it about himself, even though I thought it was about him and how he felt.

Rowan called Carla today. He had a surprise. She knew about it and she still did this? I clapped my hands over my ears but the song wouldn't stop. I heard myself talking to Fiona Sutherland and saying I hoped I was getting something special. It was nowhere near my birthday. He'd been at an event with diamonds. Diamonds are a girl's best friend.

Kurt took my hands from ears. "You still think you can stop the noise in your head by covering your ears ... jeez, Conway."

"Did he say something to you?"

"No, he showed Carla something that was in his jacket pocket."

"Did she react?"

"No."

"He carries his cell phone in his pocket ..."

Kurt shook his head. "He didn't show her his cell phone. It's a love song and for what it's worth, I think it's about Rowan. But I think you're right about the suicide pact anyway."

"I know I'm right, and Rowan is probably here for a gig, and wanted to surprise me."

He could've been here for a concert, but he wasn't. I knew that much. His next concert wasn't until the event in New York. I gave Carla the tickets.

Kurt's phone rang. Skittery noises followed. I glanced around expecting to see evil red eyes watching me from nearby. Hell, between Mac, Costner, Pennywise, Chance, and the world turning into a comic book in front of my eyes, I was just glad I could still walk and talk without drooling.

To be honest, I wasn't sure I could.

Kurt may have been talking but the words scrambled between his mouth and my ears. Damn, a speech bubble would be handy for moments like those. He reached out and grabbed my hand. "I'll help you out with this one, okay?"

I nodded. "Go on then."

"Rowan was going to propose." His hand tightened around mine. "We have to go now."

Chapter Thirty Four
Everything I Do I Do It For You

Kurt let my hand go as we approached the nurses' station in the intensive care unit. He glanced at me. "Don't go anywhere. Stay with me."

I didn't know what he meant.

Carla cried, "Mommy!"

When I turned toward her voice, she was standing in the doorway. "Carla!"

Everything jumbled.

She stood in a hospital gown. Crying.

"Carla!" The closer I got the farther away she appeared. She turned and followed Kurt into a room.

Dad reached out to me as I entered. "Ellie, come here."

From above Carla's bed, I detected movement, my eyes focused on a shadow figure melting into the wall. Joey.

"No, I can't. Carla wants me," I said, shrugging his hand off my arm and hurrying to the bed. "Carla ..." There was a chair by the bed. I perched on it and took her hand. It was cold.

Confusion crowded in. She didn't react as I squeezed her hand. Her eyes were closed.

Leon walked in. "Ellie," he said, moving close to me and offering his hand. I swapped hands, holding Carla's with my left, and shaking Leon's hand.

"Thank you for being here."

"Has Doctor Henderson told you anything?"

I shook my head. "No. I heard Carla call me."

The doctors looked at each other.

"We're trying something. Kurt started the process by giving her a cold IV in the ambulance. We've been decreasing her core temperature since she arrived in the emergency room. It may protect her brain from oxygen deprivation for longer."

"She's on a ventilator, won't that protect her brain?"

She was so cold. I wanted to rub her hands and warm her up.

"The hope is that we can hold her core temperature low enough to allow her body to begin to recover from the effects of the drugs, while protecting her brain. The ventilator is necessary because she is so heavily sedated she cannot breath for herself."

"She was breathing when Kurt gave her Narcan?"

Kurt nodded. "She was. We hope we started treatment early enough. But she didn't respond as well as she should have to the Narcan. Could be that she didn't take much Demerol but took more of another drug, that we suspect was Triazolam."

That made sense: The Triazolam in my bathroom cabinet.

"How long will you keeping her cold?"

"Twenty-four hours then we'll start warming her up and then we'll start running some tests."

"She was talking, she was walking." My stomach back flipped to what Dad told me about lunchtime, she was walking and talking. Focus Ellie. "What are the tests for?"

"Brain function."

"You have to wait?"

Leon nodded. "Yes, until we're quite certain the drugs are no longer causing this."

"It hasn't been long enough?"

Kurt shook his head. "We're giving her every chance, Ellie. She's young and right now we're hoping that's enough."

"Can she hear us?" I said Leon.

"We don't know. It would be best to assume she can," he replied. "I didn't think you were going to show. Kurt says you were gone half an hour."

That didn't make sense. Half an hour? I'd only just left for a walk. More like ten minutes. Half an hour, my ass.

"Where was I for that long?" I didn't mean to say that aloud and judging by the looks my question received I should've tried harder to check my thoughts.

Both Leon and Kurt opted to ignore the question. I knew it would bite me on the ass at some point in the not too distant future.

Whatever was happening in front of me was not registering the way it should. I knew that. But it didn't help. Seeing Joey fade into the wall above her bed. Seeing Carla turn her head and try to smile. Didn't help.

"Dad, where's Joey?"

I knew by the pause where Joey was. I needed to hear it. I needed him to say the words.

"Joey died while you were gone. I called Kurt and told him."

That was what the last phone call was. "Did his parents get here in time?"

"They arrived about five minutes after they called time of death. He was already gone. They failed him for the last time."

Dad said those words. They failed him for the last time.

He echoed what I felt about Carla. I failed her. I failed Joey too. I never saw this coming. I should've been able to save them.

"Where's Rowan?" I looked around the room expecting to see him emerge from the white walls.

He didn't.

Of course he didn't. He wasn't dead.

Grab reality with both hands. It occurred to me at that moment that I was going to need to hold on to reality a lot tighter than ever before. Processing information was becoming a nightmare.

"He went out to call the band," Dad said. "He'll be back in a few minutes. You know, Ellie, he sat here while you were getting some air." He wiped his hands over his tired face. "I've given you a bit of flack over dating a rock star, but kid, I'm seeing another side of him tonight." Dad touched my hand, his warm hand enveloping mine. "I think I now see what you have always seen. The real Rowan Grange." He squeezed my hand. "He has a lot of love to give."

An uncomfortable feeling loomed that my father was about to admit he was wrong. Wrong? Unbelievable.

He was still talking. "Good thing you didn't listen to me and ditch him for Noel."

I smiled. Dad was trying to lighten my mood a little, best if he thought he'd succeeded. I wasn't about to leave Rowan for Noel. Not because the idea was repulsive or anything. I liked Noel. He is a friend, a colleague, a lot older than me, and trained by my father. Four strikes.

Ever since Lexington, things haven't been great between me and Rowan. I never got over how I forgot who he was. Sure Rowan's fun and he's easy to be with. But when it came down to it, a lot of what happened with Arbab and Lexington was because of my involvement with Rowan. His management treated me like the devil but he was the one putting my life and Carla's in danger, because he was Rowan Grange, rock star, who attracted a lot of attention and a good deal of it was bad. I needed someone who understood my life and who didn't get freaky over the Glock on my hip. He was getting there. He was at least trying.

It's my life. Time I owned it.

"I want to check my messages, I'll be right outside the door," I said. I felt this overwhelming compulsion to check my voice mail. It made no sense. I could tell by the looks I received when I said I was leaving the room that no one thought it made sense. At least no one demanded an explanation.

I leaned on the glass doors just outside her room. Using my cell phone, I accessed the home phone voice mail system. Seven new voice mail messages on my private line and four on the house phone.

I listened to the private ones first from newest to oldest, they'd all arrived since I got home from work. I remembered clearing my messages before finding Carla.

Six of the messages were from Julia, all telling me how much Rowan loved her and how they were getting married in six months. I deleted them. This was not the time to deal with one of Rowan's overzealous fans. The seventh message was from Sean O'Hare.

"Ellie, call me. I have the DNA results you wanted."

I banged the back of my head against the wall. He was here at the hospital with everyone else. I wanted those results. Could I deal with the hell that could rain down with the results right now?

The house phone line had four waiting messages.

First two were from Joey's parents. First, they weren't coming to see their son and then they were. And they arrived too late. They were ass-hats.

The next one was from Noel Gerrard. He'd been trying to reach me, wanted to know if I'd go to dinner with him. He pointed out he was no longer a LEO, if that helped to get me to the dinner table.

Nope.

A new message arrived while I was listening. I skipped to it. Iain Campbell announced himself.

"Before I go, I have the proof you wanted – I doubt you still need it, but it's on its way to you at the hospital. Tierney told me about your daughter." He paused. There was hollow air as if he didn't want to say what he couldn't avoid. "I've sent two envelopes, the second is personal. Your choice if you view the contents. All the best, Agent Conway."

He knew I was at the hospital.

Yeah, that was my take-away from that message.

I pressed the button to retrieve the last message and that was when I heard Carla's voice.

I listened. "Mommy, I'm so sorry. I love you."

I slid down the wall. My fingers pressed the button and I heard her voice all over again. Again. Again. Again.

On the fifth replay, I listened to the time stamp. She'd called the home phone just after I got home from work. I searched my mind. Where was Dad when I arrived home? In the laundry room, scrubbing his hands after trimming trees out back. I didn't go into the kitchen where the main phone sits on the counter. I went right up to my room to take off my gun and checked messages on my private line. I never went to check for messages on the main phone in the kitchen.

A shadow fell over me, and a hand reached down. I took it. He helped me up. I gave Rowan my phone and pressed replay.

He wrapped an arm around me and pulled me close while he listened. I could hear the faint murmur of her voice. It stopped. The mechanical robotic voice of the message service kicked in. Rowan listened to the instructions. He looked at me while he pressed the appropriate number to save the message.

He handed my phone back.

Both his arms wound around me and held tight.

A few minutes later he said, "Come on, we're going back in. While we wait, let's get the people waiting out there to come and sit with her."

I nodded.

People needed a chance to say goodbye to her.

"She's already gone," I whispered. "Her body hasn't figured it out yet."

"We don't know that Ellie, not yet."

We sat next to her lifeless body willing her to fight, to breathe, to remember how it felt to be treasured.

Cold crept over me. I shivered. Rowan snaked an arm around my shoulders and hugged me close.

"You're freezing." He slid off his leather jacket and wrapped it around my shoulders.

"Thank you."

He smiled.

His jacket smelled like his cologne. Warm, musky, with just a little hint of promise. I figured it was wrong to think like that considering the circumstances. He was right there next to me in his shirtsleeves. Leaning forward with his elbows resting almost on his knees. His expression was hard to read. I knew Rowan well enough to know he didn't worry about things that were out of his control but I still couldn't read his expression. Sitting wrapped in Rowan Grange's jacket was a movie-worthy moment. If this were a movie, there'd be the possibility of a happy ending.

I bumped my shoulder into his. He put his arm around

me.

"Someone once told me he'd lay down his life for me but he didn't think I'd let him," I said. "He was right. That's unnecessary macho bullshit." A tiny bit of incensed annoyance crept into my voice. "Like I can't shoot straight."

"What happened to him?"

"He's dead."

He never flinched. "Did you?"

A little smile dabbled in the edges of my voice. "No, it wasn't me." Unless you can kill someone twice. "All that shit means is he couldn't live with his decisions and the ramifications of whatever situation he was in. Dying for someone, that puts it all on them. No one wants to carry that."

Rowan's breath brushed my hair. "Are you trying to say something here?"

"If you're a LEO or a soldier, laying down your life for anyone else is par for the course, serve and protect and all that jazz. It's noble. I have no hesitation in stepping in front of a bullet for the President or anyone in my team. But the fallout is a real bitch. Being the one left behind sucks."

And I am so sick of being the one left behind.

"Ellie." His arm tightened around me, pulling me closer. "I'm so fucking sorry that you've lived with that for so long."

It didn't matter how hard I swallowed or blinked, tears slipped down my face. "Why did she do it? Why did *they* do it?"

"I don't know."

"I want to understand but I just don't." A sob escaped. "I thought she was doing so well, until recently. But you know, I thought she was happy and knew how much we loved her."

"She knows how much you love her, how much we all love her."

"Tell me she is going to wake up and that everything will be like it was."

I felt his lips on my forehead. "I wish I could."

Lee came in and bent down to me.

"Chicky, okay if I hang for a bit with the kid?"

Pushing away tears and hoping my voice was steady, I replied, "Of course."

I watched for a few minutes as Lee did his best at remaining positive for Carla, and for me too. It was a whole new kind of hell. I didn't much care for it.

Kurt came back into the room. He checked Carla and spoke briefly to Lee then crouched down in front of me. "You holding up okay?"

"Yeah."

There were manila envelopes in his hand. "You're not going through this alone, remember that."

I wiped my eyes and smiled at him.

"I'm okay."

"A courier just gave these envelopes to the nurse outside. I thought I'd bring them in for you." He handed me two manila envelopes.

"Thanks."

Rowan's arm gave me shoulder a squeeze then slipped away.

I looked at the writing on the envelopes. One said it was information for Delta A, the other said it was for my eyes only.

I untwisted the string on the envelope for Delta and pulled out the papers. After a quick scan, I showed Kurt. He nodded.

"We didn't really need it in the end," he said.

"Nope, but it's good to have. Backs up everything we found."

Kurt stood up and walked over to where Lee was by Carla's bed.

I pushed the papers back into the envelope and opened the second one. I peered into the yellow envelope and saw photographs. My hand delved in and pulled up the first photo. I didn't take it all the way out there was no need. I could see it. I nudged Rowan. He looked into the envelope.

I sucked in air through my closed teeth. I didn't need this shit now.

All kinds of rage grew, pushing everything else I felt away. I swallowed it all and went in for another picture. They grew worse. Rowan was at the autism function and he wasn't alone. The woman seemed familiar. I could feel my mind whirring, images flashed past at an alarming rate. One image froze. The woman I'd seen at the Grange concert, the one in the front, in hysterical tears.

It was her.

I bet her name was Julia.

"Who is this?"

"Julia. She works for the Autism Foundation that asked me to play at the fundraiser. Who sent you the pictures?" Rowan didn't sound troubled.

"A friend," I said. "This woman is probably the one who has been leaving me messages at home."

"Messages?"

"Uh huh. Messages telling me to leave you alone and how you and she are going to get married."

"Jesus, she seemed so normal." He slumped back his chair. "She seemed normal, professional, nice. She asked me out for coffee. I declined."

"You look pretty cozy in these pictures." I pulled one out and handed it to him. "You look attentive."

There was a voice in my head telling me that's how he looked no matter who he was talking to. This is Rowan working. This is him being him. I couldn't explain the anger I felt.

"Don't Ellie, not here, not now."

"She left *me* messages," I said.

In front of me I saw Kurt and Lee's backs. They were talking in low conversational tones. No speech bubbles hanging in the air to tell me what they were talking about. I turned to look at Rowan. He leaned forward, his feet flat on the floor, and his elbows resting on his knees. He lifted his head and looked at me. All I saw was pain.

"Tell me you didn't lead her on."

"I didn't. I never would."

"Have you got a pen?" I said to Rowan as I stood up. "I need space and to write."

"Yes, and a notebook."

"Can I borrow both?"

"Yes. Check the inside pocket of my jacket you're wearing." I did and found the notebook and pen.

"Do you want me to come with you?" Rowan said.

"No."

I walked over to Kurt and whispered in his ear, "I want to be alone."

Kurt nodded.

The words in my mind pulsated on a pale blue canvas.

My haste to get out the door didn't get me far. I needed to write the words that dripped off the blue. Leaning on the wall, I dropped the envelope on the floor and started writing in Rowan's notebook. Words I'd seen a long time ago but which now felt a desperate need to see daylight.

In the Dark of the Night.

The moon is rising in the sky -
darkness swallows me. I wonder why.
There's nothing left for me to say
the wind has carried my words away.
A shimmering star lights a far off land
and somewhere someone writes names in the sand.
Blackness flows in the deep of night.
Magnified violence comes to light:

All has gone and all that has been
comes back to haunt me in a dream.
Promises broken and lives are shattered –
how I wish tonight that none of it mattered.
Mist from the river rolls down the street,
and in the still of the night, I hear my heart beat.
Streetlights put out an eerie glow,
illuminating fog.
It's a horror show.
Somewhere someone learns to live again
and I wish tonight that this wasn't my pain.

I read the words I'd written. They stood still on the white notebook pages. Cold, blue, motionless. I closed the notebook, trapping them forever in a white paper prison. Maybe they didn't need daylight after all.

I shoved the notebook and pen into the pocket of Rowan's jacket. I gathered the envelope from the floor and went to the waiting room.

Caine was drinking coffee. He looked up as I walked into the room.

"Don't mind me," I said. "I just need … a miracle."

He said nothing.

I dropped the envelope on the coffee table. Caine stood, walked to the coffee pot on a counter that ran the length of the room. He handed me a coffee.

"It's not great, but it's wet, hot, and may have caffeine."

"Thanks." I took the cup.

"Any change?"

"No."

"You want to talk?"

"I don't think so. I just had to get out of the room before I did something or said something stupid." I pushed the envelope on the table at him. "Take a look."

He did.

"And? Come on Ellie, this isn't about your rock star boyfriend chatting up a pretty girl."

"Her name is Julia. I had a lot of phone messages from someone called Julia who warned me off Rowan and said they were getting married."

"What did Rowan say?"

"That she seemed normal when he met her at a fundraiser."

"They always do, don't they?"

"Yeah."

I finished my coffee and set the cup on the table.

"Where's Simon?"

I went blank. I didn't know where my Dad was.

"I dunno."

Caine sighed, his lower lip twitched. "I think I heard him and Aidan talking about going to the chapel."

That sounded right.

"Do you want me to walk you down there?"

"No."

"You sure?"

"Yes. Praying for her soul is not going to help."

"Might help you."

I choose not to respond to that. There was this thought that I'd been trying to hide from, a horrible twisted hangover from my Catholic upbringing. Suicide is a sin.

"Caine, can I have a few minutes alone?" I said.

"Yes." He nodded at me as he eased himself out of the armchair he'd been sitting in. "I'll be in the chapel."

He pulled the door shut on his way out.

I spent a few minutes trying to block out everything I felt, but I knew I'd failed when I saw those photos in my hands again.

Coffee. The crazy woman asked him out for coffee and that led to threats left on my home phone? I get that people can be stupid but that made no sense. How did she make the quantum leap from him turning down a coffee date, to her saying she was marrying Rowan?

Something else must've been going on. The more I thought about it the angrier I became. There was a chance my anger wasn't anything to do with coffee or Rowan but even knowing that didn't help. I shoved the photographs back in the envelope.

I opened the door to find Sam waiting.

"What's going on, Chicky?"

"I'll tell you later."

Sam went into the room.

Carla was still lying in the bed, beeping, hissing, and not responding.

"Rowan, can we talk?"

I dropped the envelope on a chair and waited for Rowan to follow me out.

Steam was pouring from my ears. All control was ebbing away. I made him follow me to the elevators before I spoke because I needed to count to twenty and regain control.

"Why didn't you tell me?" I said, mustering as much calm as I could. I didn't want to raise my voice. Not here, not now.

"Tell you what?"

"Tell me about Julia," I said, my voice harsh and low.

His eyes widened. "There's nothing to tell. It was nothing."

"I don't think she sees it that way. She asked you out for coffee … and now she thinks you're getting married. What the fuck?"

"She seemed normal."

"Really?"

"I didn't have coffee with her."

"So she decided you two are a thing, all by herself?"

Rowan took my hand.

"Ellie, I didn't do anything. I am not that stupid."

I didn't think he was stupid but damn, now another crazy person had entered our lives because of him. The dumbest thing was I knew he didn't do anything wrong. I knew he didn't.

"The crazy people you meet impact on me, and Carla too. A heads up would be good."

I walked away. I walked back to the ICU and to Carla's room with Rowan following me. He caught up to me, grabbed my arm, and spun me around.

433

"Are you angry with me?"

"No."

"Are you angry because you got messages from this Julia woman?"

"No."

"This is about Carla?"

I clenched and unclenched my jaw. "Why the hell did she do this? What the fuck was she thinking? I get that teenagers are selfish creatures but this is the fucking ultimate in selfish bullshit."

"Lower your voice," Rowan said.

"Why, because she'll hear me?"

"El ..."

I leveled a stare at him. "She did this on purpose!"

"If you are going to stand here yelling, you may as well get it all out ..."

My right hand balled into a fist. As I swung at Rowan, someone intercepted the punch. My eyes darted right. Kurt held my fist in his hand.

"You are not mad at Rowan," he said. Each word was calm and measured. "Don't take this out on him."

My body angled toward Kurt, my left hand swung. He blocked.

His hands held mine.

"We've danced this dance before," Kurt whispered. "Don't make me sedate you."

For a split second that seemed like a good idea. Sedation. Feel nothing. Remember nothing. I shook my head. The crazy thoughts about sedation slipped

434

sideways and fell to the floor. Encased in a shimmering bubble they rose and floated just below the ceiling.

"Ellie?" Rowan was behind me.

Kurt's eyes never left mine. "If I let you go, can you control yourself?"

I nodded. The anger melted into the floor under my feet. Kurt let go my hands and slipped back into Carla's room.

Rowan tapped me on the shoulder. "All right?"

"I think so."

"Let's go back in."

We entered Carla's room. The envelope of photos was where I'd left it on the chair, I saw the other envelope underneath it. I picked them up and sat down.

"Any change?" I asked Kurt, who was leaning over Carla's bed checking one of the drips.

"No."

No worse, no better. Status quo. I couldn't decide if that meant she was holding her own or couldn't get any worse. I leaned forward and dropped the manila envelopes onto Lee's knee.

"Can you look after these?"

He nodded. "Sure, anything important?"

"Confirmation of everything we discovered regarding Bleich and photos of Rowan with some audio files. The woman in the pictures has been leaving me threatening phone messages. We'll deal with her sometime."

Rowan's notebook was in my pocket. I pulled it out along with his pen.

I handed the notebook to Rowan. If he wanted to, he could read it and make of it whatever he desired. He opened the notebook and flipped to my poem.

Moments later, he closed the notebook. "Dark," he said.

It's a dark day.

I rested my head on Rowan's shoulder and closed my eyes. Listening to the hum of machinery and the rhythm of voices. Dozing. Drifting in and out of the present but never wandering too far.

A sudden sharp beeping made me jump. My heart pounded.

"It's okay," Rowan said. "They're changing the fluids, it's just the IV pump."

My eyes focused on the room, my heart rate slowed to normal.

"I need some air."

"You want company?" Rowan said.

"No, stay with Carla, please."

"Of course."

Outside the door, I saw Caine, Sam, Cait, Sean, hell, almost everyone I cared about and who cared about us. Us. Oh the irony.

The one person I wanted to see wasn't there.

The one person I wanted to see died in this very hospital. And then last Thursday night I thought I shot him in the head.

Yep, I'm about as normal as it gets.

I nodded to everyone as I walked by. Then walked back

to Sean. "Got a minute?"

He nodded. We stepped away from everyone else.

"I heard your message," I said.

"You want to do this now?"

"Yes." What the hell. How much worse could this day get?

"DNA came back as Mac."

I felt a wave of holy hell wash over me. "Excuse me, what?"

"Tell me again how you got the blood sample?"

"From the man who called himself Chad. Direct contact. His body to my hands." My head spun. Grey fog rolled around the edges of my brain.

"No chance of contamination?"

"Zero."

"Walk with me, you don't look so hot," Sean said, indicating we should walk to some chairs. "Sit. You okay?"

"Not really. One second." I fumbled for the Synergy bottle in my jeans pocket, unscrewed the top, and breathed in the vapors. No migraine, not now.

"All right?"

"Yep." I screwed the top on the bottle and dropped it into the pocket of the jacket I was wearing.

"What is that?"

"It's an essential oil blend for prevention and early treatment of migraines," I said.

"Where were we?"

"You were telling me Mac's alive?"

"You know that's not possible," Sean replied.

"His DNA ..."

"I have a theory. My people are working on it. It's not Mac, Ellie."

"DNA says otherwise. I told you when Tierney is involved things get screwy."

"Concentrate on Carla. I will figure this out."

I stood up and headed for the exit. The last place I saw Mac was the ambulance bay. Maybe he'd come back and I could ask him. Kurt blocked my way. I thought he was still with Carla.

"I got this, Kurt."

"You're sure?"

"Uh huh, I just need air. I'll be in the ambulance bay."

See? I even told him where I'd be.

"Are you all right?"

The unguarded truth slipped out. "No, not at all."

"I'll come with you."

My eyes searched his for hope. I didn't find it. "No. I just need some air."

I got this. It's familiar territory, however much I don't want it to be, it is. Cold tendrils of grief curled through the air like smoke. I moved so the smoky grief couldn't suffocate me.

"Don't be long."

I thrust my hands into the jacket pockets as I walked down the brightly lit corridor. The fingers on my left hand hit something hard. It seemed safest to stop walking and investigate. I closed my fingers around the square object and took it from my pocket. A jeweler's box. I recognized the emblem on the top. It came from Bleich's shop.

I held the box in my hand unsure if I should open it or not. I decided not and pushed it deep into the pocket it came from.

People passed me as I carried on walking. I wasn't sure how I felt about a jewelry case being in Rowan's jacket but I wasn't surprised, not after Kurt told me what he thought Rowan was planning.

I wished I hadn't asked Sean about the DNA.

Life as I knew it was over. I was looking for a miracle. I plunged my right hand into the other pocket and pulled out the migraine Synergy. I took several deep breaths drawing the aroma of the oil blend deep into my lungs.

Yeah, there's the miracle ... it's a miracle I'm not a drooling wreck.

When I turned back to the hospital, Kurt was standing five feet from me.

"You ready to come back in?" Kurt didn't wait for my answer. He placed his hand in the small of my back and steered me back into the hospital.

Rowan was sitting next to Carla, writing and humming. A few times he sang a few lines, then went back to humming and writing.

People came and went, and nothing changed.

One day someone would write a short film and Grange would do the sound track. Or maybe what Rowan was now writing would be the foundation for the short film.

Welcome to my version of Jon Bon Jovi's 'Destination Anywhere.'

Dark, ain't it?

I just hoped Whoopi Goldberg would be my cabby and dispense sage advice that made this all make sense before I ended up like Demi Moore.

Although I didn't see me stealing a baby from a neonatal unit anytime soon.

Down the hall from Carla's room was a family room. Somewhere relatives could rest. I wandered in through the open door and found a couch that looked comfortable.

My head fell back as soon as I sat down. Eyelids heavy, mind full of fog. If I closed my eyes, I could pretend I was at home.

Home in my bullet-holed living room, not here.

Not here.

The smell of coffee hung in the air. A thick blanket of institutional coffee floated just above the sterility. No blossoms sprinkled like pink snow on the grass. No tulips nodding in the warm breeze. Institutional coffee and disinfectant were the new smells of my life. Death toyed with the living. Taunting, reminding. One day it gets us all. One peaceful day this will all end.

One day death will come for me.

But not today. Today death sidestepped me and latched onto the young, vulnerable, and undeserving. There was no sense in it. Or at least none that I could see.

I opened my eyes and stared at the ceiling before

growling, "Hey, God — looks like you fucked up again. The kid wants to die and Mac's DNA came from a live person, clearly you have fucked up."

My eyes closed. There was no answer. Not even a well-placed lightning bolt. God wasn't feeling chatty.

Footsteps approached the room. They paused before entering.

"You awake?"

My eyes flickered open. "Yes."

Kurt loosened his collar and dropped into a chair. He looked beat. He looked like I imagine I looked.

Absolutely fucked and not in a good way.

"Mind if I join you?"

"You already have."

A smile flicked across his lips. "There's no change ..."

I didn't expect much change. "You should go home," I said.

"I'll leave when you do." He closed his eyes. "I'll leave when Delta leaves."

"I'll leave when her lights go out."

Silence blew over us as the finality of my words hit the wall above Kurt and dripped down.

"At least get some sleep."

"I will, if you will," I replied.

When my eyes agreed to open again there was daylight streaming in on me from the windows. A blanket covered me. Kurt was asleep under a blanket.

Coffee.

Fresh coffee. Not institutional cooked-to-death coffee.

"Hey," Lee said, holding a Styrofoam cup out to me.

"Thanks," I replied taking the coffee. "Don't wake him."

"Too late," Kurt mumbled. "Got more coffee?"

Lee pressed a cup into his outstretched hand.

"Any news?" I asked Lee.

"No. Your dad is still with her."

Sam poked his head into the room.

"Mornin', Chicky. I added the information from Campbell to our case files."

"Thanks. Was there anything we'd missed?"

"He did have the proof that Sutherland hired Maguire to kill her husband. He hammered that nail right on in for us."

"Excellent."

I sipped the coffee. It was good.

Sam waited. I sensed there was something else he wanted to say but he waited until my coffee was half-gone.

"Rowan left about an hour ago. He said he'll be back and that he has his cell if you need to reach him."

I nodded. "Did Grange show?"

Sam grinned.

"Yeah. They've all gone with Rowan. Your father is asleep in Carla's room. Your brother and his wife went home for a few hours. They'll be back later. Tierney came by and said Campbell was readmitted. He'd like to see you."

"Let's go talk to Campbell. You know what room he's

in?" I stood up and stretched.

"Yes, I do."

"Okay. Time to say good morning to Carla, and then I'll talk to Campbell and see what he wants."

Dad was still asleep when I crept into Carla's room. The ventilator hissed. She remained as she was last night. Comatose. No change. Neither good nor bad.

I kissed her cool head. Kurt read the chart hanging in the end of her bed.

"Anything good in there?" I said.

"Nothing's changed."

That's what I thought as soon as I saw her. "Will anything change?"

"I don't know." He hung the chart back on the hook and joined me next to Carla. "Come on kid, don't keep us in suspense. Wake up."

Nothing happened.

"Let's go see Campbell," I said. I bent down to Carla's ear, "I'll be back soon and then you have to wake up. You *have* to, Carla."

Dad opened an eye. "Bring the old man coffee when you come back, will you?"

"Sure, Dad."

Something jostled around in my brain, something I'd seen on television or read in the newspaper. Something about a sleeping pill. I sat down on some chairs not far from Carla's intensive care room and Googled from my phone. Sam sat down next to me.

"What are you doing?"

"Google. You got a laptop, might be faster."

"Yeah, come on."

We headed back to the family room. Sam turned on his laptop and watched as I surfed, trying to find the information I once heard and hoped it wasn't a dream.

"This!" I showed him the screen. "Zolpidem. It wakes up people in comas. Look."

"Ellie, it's not even a clinical trial, it's a few isolated cases across the world."

"Yeah, but one of the people they tried it on, had tried to commit suicide and it worked on her."

"Grabbing at straws, Chicky Babe. It's dangerous."

Kurt walked in. "What's dangerous?"

"This ..." I spun the laptop on my knee. "She has nothing to lose."

He read in silence, then took the laptop and left. We followed.

We followed Kurt to Leon's office. He knocked once and walked in, he started to shut the door, but I held it open.

"Ellie, I'm doing this," he said. "Doctor to doctor."

I dropped my hand.

"We'll be with Campbell."

Sam and I walked away as the door closed.

Chapter Thirty Five
Blinded by Rainbows

I knocked on the door to the room the nurse on the ward sent us to, and then opened the door.

"Iain, you feeling better?" I said, pulling up a chair next to his hospital bed. I noted a drain running from him to a bag.

"Just a little hiccup. I'll be fine. You got the information?"

"Yes, thank you."

"I'm sorry about the photographs, but it looked like he was getting himself in trouble."

I shrugged.

"He kinda was. You did me a favor, now I know why I was the target of a crazy woman who has been leaving me messages."

He nodded. "At least he's smart enough to know not to encourage the nuts too much." Iain moved a little. He didn't look comfortable.

"You sure you're all right?"

"Yes."

"Explain to me why you were having an affair with Marika Bleich?"

He smiled but it faded fast. "I needed to be close. Maguire was making like Zachary's best friend and I wanted to be close." He paused. "I liked Marika. She was a nice person. We never did anything. We were taking it slow. Her marriage was almost over and I was okay with waiting."

He was settling in for the long haul. I could tell by his tone and his manner that he really did like Marika Bleich.

"You didn't kill her?"

"No. I suspected the Sutherland woman of that, could've also been Maguire," Iain said.

"There was a lot of rage."

"Sutherland then." There were reports of a man in a suit hanging around. Wouldn't be the first time a woman dressed like a man to throw everyone off.

"I'm picking."

"Why did you never divorce Maria Doyle?"

"Just one of those things, we never got around to it. I still love her. The usual reasons."

"You going to give another go?"

"I'd like to, but this time I need to tell her the truth. The whole truth."

"Good idea."

"How's your daughter?"

I shook my head. "Not good. We might try an experimental drug, maybe …"

"Hope it works."

"Me too."

I stood up and said goodbye to Iain Campbell. Then remembered the locker key we found in the cabin in the woods. I patted my jean pockets until I felt the outline of the key. I stuffed my hand into my left jeans pocket and pulled the key out.

"This is yours. I imagine you'd like it back." I dropped it into his hand.

"Thank you. Did you?"

"No, turned out we never needed to locate your locker."

"Okay."

Once I was sure who he was, the locker was of zero interest to me. I knew it would contain money, passports, other assorted identity papers and maybe a weapon. Everything needed to start a new life. I understood his life and it paid to be ready.

"Did you ever come across a guy called Chad or Socrates?" I pulled out my phone and showed him a picture of Mac.

"No. New case?"

"Old case. I came across him a week or so ago, works for Tierney." The whole thought of Chad being my dead husband wiggled around in my head poking holes in my brain. It made zero sense and wasn't something I wanted to say aloud now.

"I'll snoop around if you like, when I'm out of here."

I nodded. Another thought occurred. We never found the shooter from F Street. Whoever it was didn't want to kill me, just get my attention.

Thoughts rolled and gathered on my tongue, before long they were hitting air and free. "You ... you shot me?"

A small smile settled on Campbell's lips. "I winged you. You can hardly call it being *shot*."

"Fuck. Why didn't you just knock on my door and say,

'Hey, Conway, I need your help?'"

His smile widened. "I didn't do my homework well enough. I thought winging you would make you mad and you'd follow me, then I could lead you to a safe place and tell you what was about to happen." A small laugh echoed in the room. "I did not know how serious you are about coffee."

We shook hands.

I walked back through the corridors and smacked straight into Sean O'Hare.

"Ellie, can we talk?"

"Sure, make it fast. I need to get back to Carla."

He looked around and then pointed out a bench type seat. "Over there."

We sat.

"What is it? Is this something to do with the DNA?"

"I found him."

"Who?"

"Chad. He's very real. He's also identical to Mac."

"I'm not nuts?"

"Not in this instance."

"How?"

"How much do you know about Mac, really, know about his family and early years?"

I didn't like the sound of that.

"I thought I knew a lot."

Sean nodded. "But how much does anyone really know, right?"

"I guess."

"My people worked on this all night. We've opened sealed files and now have a massive can of worms to deal with, but that's our problem. You just need to know the answer to the DNA question."

I took a deep breath and prepared myself.

"Mac was an identical triplet."

Holy crap!

"How the fuck did that get to be hidden knowledge?"

"Beatrice Connelly and her weakened mental state. The babies were delivered by caesarian. Two of the babies were given up at birth. The decision was made by doctors and Bob Connelly. Beatrice never knew there were three babies. She was told she was having twins and that only one child lived."

I chewed my lip and thought about it for a minute. Nope, never heard that before. Mac or anyone else in my presence had never spoken of a multiple birth.

"Why not take all three?"

"Far as I can tell it was a medical decision agreed with by Bob Connelly. I found a comment from a doctor saying taking all the babies would be too traumatic. She was deemed capable enough to take care of one baby but not three."

"How is this the first time I've heard of it?"

"I don't know. Maybe Mac didn't know. They fed the Connelly woman a line about how the *other* child was terribly deformed and died at birth. Meanwhile the babies were adopted by a family in Manassas."

"Manassas," I repeated. "Mac hated Manassas, really,

did not like that town." I rubbed my temples with my fingers. So dumbass Eddie really did think he saw Mac in Manassas. But it was Chad or the other brother?

"You all right?"

"Sure, what the hell. This thing with Mac being a triplet, par for the course really. I told you things got fucky when Tierney was involved."

"They really do. Chad was recruited two years after Mac."

And there it was. The first confirmation that Mac was agency well before he met me and supposedly went through Quantico to become an FBI agent. The secrets we bury always come to light eventually.

"So what's with the scar on Chad's arm?"

"He's working the same case Mac was on before he was killed."

I held up my hand to stop Sean.

"Mac was working with me when he died."

"He was working for the CIA too on a long running case."

I didn't know him at all.

"Go on."

"They, the CIA, needed Chad to be Mac."

"Did they replicate the scar for real or used some amazing latex movie-type scarring?"

"For real."

That's dedication to the job.

"Can I meet him?"

"That would not be a good idea."

"And the other brother?"

"His name is Jay, he's a contractor ... owns his own building renovation company and lives in Manassas."

So it was probably Jay that Eddie saw in Manassas and not Chad. My head spun with the new knowledge and the secrets kept.

I wanted Sean to hurry up so I could get back to Carla but I had questions.

"The fingerprints on the glass?" I snapped.

"Mac's not Chad's. I checked out the rest of those glasses, they were Mac's, yes?"

"Yes."

"There were prints on most of them, both yours and Mac's. Some smudged but some okay. Did you ever use them?"

"No, not since his death."

"Where have they been?"

"They were packed away with other pieces of crystal and stored in Dad's garage before Carla and I moved into the new house."

"There's your explanation."

Very few things were packed and stored, and they became the only things left after the explosion.

"What about how the glass full of tequila got to the table? What about the sofa being tipped over?"

"I have no explanation for how the glass arrived on the table or how tequila got in it. Could you have poured the drink and taken it into the living room?"

"No. I know I didn't."

"It wasn't your Dad, the only prints on the glass were yours and Mac's." Sean frowned. "What happened to the sofa?"

"Kurt and I found it up ended, about half an hour or so after you left."

"You got me. I have no answer for that."

"Guess you can't answer how my bedside lamp rocked off the nightstand or how a plate slid off the kitchen counter or how a dining chair tipped into the wall."

"All on the same night?"

"No, the lamp and plate were Monday night and the chair was not long before I found Carla and Joey."

"Hate to say it, Ellie, but maybe you do need a ghost buster."

"It's starting to look that way."

My fingers rubbed my temple again. I felt time ebbing away. Or was it life. I stood up and took the small bottle from my jeans pocket. I unscrewed the top and inhaled the vapor.

"You're hitting that stuff pretty hard."

"I haven't had the best few days." I took another long inhalation then screwed the top back on and put it back in my pocket. My mind whirled through the information from Sean. Jesus, what a mess. "I need to get to my kid."

Panic surged. I needed to get to Carla.

"You want me to come?"

"No, I just need to go. We'll talk when I can ... when I can process everything."

Might be a long time.

"I'll check in on you and Carla later."

I pushed the elevator button and waited. Looking around I saw the door to the stairs. I needed to be moving. Change of plans. I flung the door open and ran up the stairs two at a time. At the ICU floor, I shoved the heavy doors open and ran to Carla's room.

Drawing in a ragged breath, I rushed into the room and heard the monotone beep of an alarm. All the organs in my body froze at once.

Leon and two nurses were working on Carla. Dad was leaning on the wall trying to keep out of the way. His expression carried more pain than I could cope with. Kurt rushed into the room behind me.

"Kurt." My voice croaked.

"How long as she been down?" he asked.

A nurse glanced up at the clock on the wall and replied, "Six minutes."

Kurt looked at me his eyes glistened. He shook his head.

Leon said, "What do you want to do?"

"Let her go," I said. "Let her go."

She doesn't want to be here.

The beep ran on and on until Leon turned off the machine.

Everyone backed away. I climbed onto the bed and pulled her lifeless body into my arms. As I hugged her, my tears fell upon her face.

I closed my eyes, trying to stem the flow of stinging salty tears and imagined her laughter. The sound that always filled my heart with joy. When I opened my eyes, one last lilting laugh spiraled down from the ceiling and covered us both. The sound became a string of silver dragonflies that disappeared out the door.

"...Life's but a walking shadow, a poor player
That struts and frets his hour upon the stage
And then is heard no more: it is a tale
Told by an idiot, full of sound and fury,
Signifying nothing."
Macbeth Act V Scene V

About the author:

Cat Connor is a prolific crime thriller author hailing from New Zealand. Her expertise in the genre is reflected in her engaging and suspenseful narratives, which have garnered a loyal following. Her work is known for its intricate plots, dynamic characters, and relentless pace, keeping readers on the edge of their seats until the very end. She has authored multiple books, including the popular "Byte" series, which follows the exploits of an FBI unit that investigates serial crime.

Cat's passion for crime and espionage is evident in her writing, as she strives to create a world that is both authentic and thrilling. Her meticulous attention to detail and extensive research have won her critical acclaim and accolades from readers and peers alike. In addition to writing, Cat enjoys speaking on topics related to writing and publishing. Her talks are known for their candidness, humour, and practical advice. With her unique blend of talent, expertise, and passion, Cat Connor has established herself as one of the most exciting and accomplished authors in the crime thriller genre.

Her other passions include music, reading, tequila, red wine, coffee, and chocolate. When she's not writing she can be found binge watching TV shows and spending time with her much adored animals; Diesel the mastador, Patrick the tuxedo cat, Dallas the tortie Birman, and Jimmy the thug.

You can follow and contact Cat at the following places:

Website: www.catconnor.com
Twitter: @catconnor
Facebook: @cat.connor
Instagram: @catconnorauthor
Bluesky: @catconnor.bsky.social
Threads: @catconnorauthor

Also by Cat Connor:

The Kiwi set Veronica Tracey Spy/PI series:
[Nothing happens here] -2020
[Lure the lie] - 2021
[Leave a message] - 2022
[Whiskey Tango Foxtrot] - 2023
[Foxtrot Mike Lima] - 2024

The FBI based Byte Series:
Killerbyte - 2009
Terrorbyte - 2010
Exacerbyte - 2011
Flashbyte - 2012
Soundbyte - 2013
Snakebyte - 2013 (novella)
Databyte - 2014
Eraserbyte - 2015
Psychobyte - 2016
Metabyte - 2017
Qubyte - 2018
Cryptobyte - 2019
Vaporbyte - 2020 (red)
Vaporbyte -2020 (purple)
Raidbyte - 2021 (collection of short bytes)

Whispers in the water - the poetry of SSA Conway and SA Connelly
Torrent - a collection of short bytes

If I were a carpenter - SSA Kurt Henderson's story
(novella)

Array - a collection of short bytes